D0366977

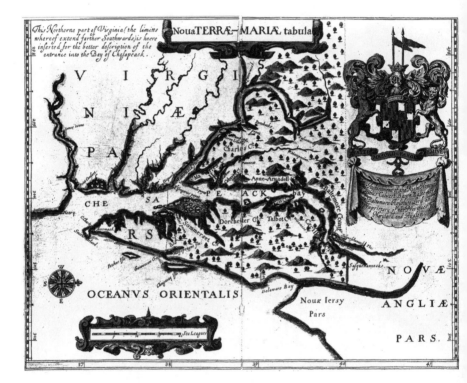

The
Wished-for
Country

a novel by
Wayne Karlin

FIRST EDITION, 2002
Copyright © 2002 by Wayne Karlin
All Rights Reserved

Printed on acid-free paper by Transcontinental Printing/Best Book

Cover design: Les Kanturek

cover image: Theodore de Bry, after John White. "The Town of Secota" from "America" Pt. 1. Colored engraving, Frankfurt, 1590. Rare Books Division. *Courtesy of The New York Public Library/Art Resource, NY.*

All characters, with the exception of the historical figures noted at the end of the novel, are fictional. Journal, diary, letters, and other entries in italics were written by the attributed authors: sources for these entries are listed in the acknowledgements at the back of this book.

This book was published with the support of the Connecticut Commission on the Arts and donations from many individuals. We are very grateful for this support.

Library of Congress Cataloging-in-Publication Data

Karlin, Wayne.
  The wished for country / by Wayne Karlin.— 1st ed.
    p. cm.
  ISBN 1-880684-89-6 (pbk. : acid-free paper)
  1. Maryland—History—Colonial period, ca. 1600-1775—Fiction.
  2. African American men—Fiction. 3. Indentured servants—Fiction.
  4. Piscataway Indians—Fiction. 5. Slaves—Fiction. I. Title.
  PS3561.A625 W57 2002
  813'.54—dc21
                                2002008775

Published by
CURBSTONE PRESS • 321 Jackson St. • Willimantic, CT 06226
info@curbstone.org • www.curbstone.org

For Ohnmar

Having now arrived at the wished-for country, we alloted names according to circumstances.

Father Andrew White, S.J: Narrative of a Voyage to Maryland

From the Introduction to the Letters of George Alsop, Indentured Servant:
The author had in some way acquired a quantity of ill-assorted information, and also an extensive vocabulary, but was without sufficient education to enable him to make proper use of either. His style is therefore extravagant, inflated and grandiloquent. It is also coarse and vulgar, even for the seventeenth century. Certain passages which add nothing to the narrative, but were apparently inserted merely for the sake of their impropriety, have [not] been omitted from the following text.

Wesort's Song

I am Wesort, Werowance of the Wesorts
As I take the Name of my People
I must sing their songs
I must sing them to the East
I must sing them to the West
I must sing them to the North
I must sing them to the South
I must sing them to the Living
and to the Dead
and to those waiting to be Born
I must sing their songs
I must sing in their voices
so they will live.
And I must sing the songs
of those whose voices
my tongue will not shape
For they name us also
As Night names Day
As Hole names Thread
As Knife names Blood
As the Waking World is
a Dream of the True World

Prologue:

A Meeting in Barbados

January, 1634

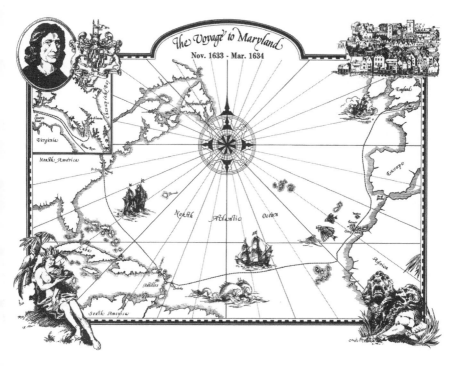

From the Narrative of Father Andrew White, S.J.

When we had sailed beyond the Fortunate Islands, Lord Leonard Calvert, the commander of the enterprise, began to consider where he could get any merchandise to load the ship with, on its return, in order to defray the expenses of his brother, the Baron of Baltimore. For he, having originated the whole expedition, had to bear all the expense. No profit was expected from our countrymen in Virginia: for they are hostile to this new settlement; accordingly we were directing our course to the Island of St. Christopher, when...we turned our prows to the south to go to Bonavista. This island, situated near Angola on the African coast, 14 degrees from the equator, is a post of the Hollanders, where they collect salt, which they afterwards carry home, or take to cure fish with in Greenland. The abundance of salt, and also the number of goats which are found on the island, were inducements for us to go there, for it has no other inhabitants. Only a few Portugese, transported for crime, drag out their lives the best way they can. We had gone barely 200 miles, when changing our plans a second time, at the suggestion of some among us, lest the provisions should fail us, in going so far out of our way, we turned aside into Barbadoes....

The watchful care of Divine Providence consoled us for the bitter harshness of men. For we understoond that a Spanish fleet was stationed off the island of Bonavista, to keep all foreigners from engaging in the salt trade. If, keeping to our appointed route, we had gone on thither, we should have fallen into the net, and become the prey of our enemies. In the meantime, we were delivered from a greater danger at Barbadoes: the servants throughout the whole island had conspired to kill their masters; then, indeed, after having gained their liberty, it was their intention to possess themselves of the first ship which should touch there, and venture to sea. The conspiracy was disclosed by one who was deterred by the atrocious cruelty of the enterprise; and the punishment of one of the leaders was sufficient for the security of the island and our own safety. For our ship, as being the first to touch there, had been marked for their prey.

3

To the right of the quay was a tree unlike any tree I had ever seen before, though I had shaped wood for much of my life, boy and man. A cabbage, it seemed, spiked by a slender, swaying stalk that must have risen two hundred feet into the air, standing against the sun. I laughed at the absurdity of it. The ship rose and fell and I spread my feet to steady myself. The bright white sand, the shattered turquoise sea, needles of sun dancing off it, penetrated and tore aside a gray veil I hadn't known had been hanging before my eyes all of my days until now.

On the other side of that same dock, growing from a square platform, was a more familiar tree. Its fruit twisted in the air, stretching taut the rope from which it hung, the creak and groan rising against an echo in my memory, traveling as clearly across time as the sound that came over the water between myself and the shore of Barbados. A pink tongue protruded between the negro's lips. The tongues of the white men I'd hung in the Spain would turn black. I wondered at the balance. The negro's hands and feet had been hacked off, a warning to others against rebellion and running, the slave's mortal sins.

Another black was standing below and just in front of the hanging man, all his appendages intact, as if he were demonstrating what the complete form should be. He was looking at me.

The white blaze of light under the gallows sparked a bright dissolution: the black transmuting into my Meg lifting her skirt and smiling at me, like a soldier's dream of homecoming or forgiveness, until I drew closer and saw the red rash she was showing me, the pustular swellings on the flesh of her thighs, what I had thought a flash of welcoming lust only the gleam of the disease burning behind her eyes. I remembered how, at the end, when the weak gray London light had leaked in through the crude shutter I had made to fasten over the window, she screamed as if someone had stuck flaming brands into those already scorched eyes.

The light in this place would have turned her to ashes.

Ezekiel's Song

A white man is standing on the deck of the ship Ezekiel would have seized, staring at me as the sun awakens a path of dazzle on the water. A useless arrow pointing to that ship. Pointing beyond it. Pointing nowhere. The day before Ezekiel had pointed and the overseer Trent had grabbed his right hand and strapped it, and the axe rose and fell and the hand lay in yellow dust, its sixth finger still twitching, describing small circles in the air. Writing his name on the skin of my heart.

Once I had been a name my lips won't form around now, and once I had been Lucius and now I will be Ezekiel. The white men name carelessly, without thought, as I have seen them reach into a pot and throw scraps of meat to dogs. But names and words call things to themselves, the way my hands called forms from wood, and I know that when the old words are no longer shaped by my mouth or heard in my brain, what they call will have died in my heart. I hope that time will come soon. Ezekiel was the last with whom I could speak in the old words, and now I have taken his name, and it is only when I am near sleep and when I dream that I feel those Dahomey words soften and hatch in my mouth, where they lay in a hard egg under my tongue.

I look back now at what had been Ezekiel, husked and dangling in the air. *You are their hands, Lucius,* he had whispered to me in the old words, as I'd helped fasten him to the chopping block, next to the gallows my hands had built. *Your hands cast their dreams for them, Lucius, and I am only bones now, but I will be released by their axes to travel back over the water.*

You'll only travel as far as your swing in the air, I had said to him, *and I'll breathe the air tomorrow, Ezekiel, and so will the others I've saved by giving you to them.*

You'll breathe my dreams and I give you my name with them, the name of a white man who saw bones rise and dance the way you'll see bones rise and dance, Ezekiel said, Ezekiel falling and Ezekiel rising, cursing me with a third and final name, another birth that was the same time another death. *You'll breathe me in every wind tickles your nostrils tomorrow; you'll breathe my dreams into your bones; your fingers, visible and invisible, will pull me into you from time,* he said, blowing his final breath, his name, into my mouth.

Come along then, James, they called to me that night, come taste the rum and warm your liver before the dark forests and the savages take all of us, and a pox on all Calverts and their American wilderness. I sat in a damp pinewood box of a tavern, off a mud lane stewing with rotting coconut husks, and drank with Jeremiah Barnes, Richard Harvey, Cedric Raley and Oliver Standrop, indentured all, sold their years and hands, as I had, to the promise of an eventual unfettering. The uneven pine boards, streaked and beaded with moisture, pressed a wet heat in on me, hot as fevered flesh against my flesh. There was a packed dirt floor and the roof was thatched palm fronds, yellowed and brittle, and when I put my head back I could see the stars through them. A line of blacks: five whores and two crippled beggars and one gap-toothed smiling man whose nose and ears had been cropped off, stood against the opposite wall, staring. We drank, and not one of us said a word about the blacks, as if we were unsure these existed outside of our own rum-stoked, sea-shook perception.

"Drink t'Fairyland, James," Barnes said. "T'the fairy kingdom of new Avalon." He hunched over the table and drained his goblet, bony shoulder blades poking up his shirt in the back, his nose sharp-pointed, his peaked ears tufted with clumps of the same black coarse hair that furred his cheeks. A little bat perched in my brain.

The others laughed uneasily. Avalon was George Calvert's New Foundland colony, a land, his captains had assured him, never brushed by the breath of winter. A name, a failure, we had been forbidden to even whisper. I pushed a finger along the wood. It left a snail trail of sweat.

"Sure, and Leonard Calvert is a wiser man than his father, and his brother Cecil more clever yet," Barnes said suddenly, loudly, as if speaking to an invisible spy. I watched the others around the table nod, solemn as monkeys under that thatch. As if they owned Cecil Calvert's wisdom because he'd bought their bodies. Bats and monkeys, scratching themselves, picking each other's pelts for squirmy lice, each reassuring the other that the master to whom they had sold their lives was shrewd because unlike his father, he had deigned to look at a map before sending us across the seas.

"Ce-cil-i-us," Oliver Standrop drawled out, and cackled madly.

Barnes glared at him.

"Guard your tongues," I cautioned both of them. I didn't care what they said, but I had no desire to be hung for sitting next to fools.

Barnes wagged a finger at me. "Tis my tongue I brought out t' air and water and speak my dreams tonight. Just as you, James my James. Before the great awake."

The line of blacks suddenly, in unison, groaned, as at some private but shared pain.

I put my hand on the table, flattening my palm against the rough, unfinished plank, looking at the veins netted under my skin, the blood pulsing through them. "I dream nothing," I said to Barnes. "I'm a bit of scrap in Calvert's dreams."

"Nay, you dream the same fifty acres I do."

I looked up at him, a bat trying to little me to fit its own caveish vision.

"My dreams, Barnes," I said, "would burn out your eyes."

Hurt crossed his face. "Why I meant nothing by it."

Standrop was staring at my hand. He raised his own, both hands, suddenly, as if to show us where dreams led. They were warped out of their natural bent, the fingers twisted and frozen to claws from his years tending thousands of tobacco plants, the same sotweed that had rooted in Barnes' fervid brain, in the fifty acres on which he saw himself as a little American lord of the manor. Begun anew. He, Raley and Harvey. Bats and monkeys dreaming of being gentry.

Standrop cackled again, turned and spat on the dirt floor. Spat on their monkey dreams. They stirred nervously. Standrop had been one of the Virginia colonists, had once had what they had come to get now, only to see his wife burnt alive in their cabin, his children brained like cattle during Opechancanough's uprising twelve years before. I suddenly saw Pattern in this, the plague that rotted and burnt up Meg and my children in London twisting into the painted face of the Powhatan who'd fried Standrop's wife and tomahawked his young ones. Standrop and I both here now with our children laid like offerings on the altar of the New World, on this table of rotting cypress planks.

"Standrop, y'sour pot 'a piss," Barnes said. He reached into a stained wooden bowl that cupped greasy, peppered rice on top of a banana leaf, rolled a ball of rice, then threw it back in, glumly, without eating. Took another long swig of rum. "Sour-me Standrop, Sour-me Standrop," he chanted. "Perched there, cawin' at us like a bleedin' bird 'a bad omen. Why in bloody 'ell have you come back, then?"

Standrop winked, lowered his hands. "Why, 'cause I dreams fur now, y'daft twist. Beaver pelt." He made a stroking motion with his crooked fingers, peering at us with insane shrewdness. "Tobac gluttin' the market now in London... three or four pence a pound. But beaver—nine shillings a pound last year, ten already this year, before we sailed. Beaver, that's what the toffs are mad for now. That's what I come back for."

"Tis no comfort to me. I can scratch the land, good as any man," Harvey said gloomily. "What d'I know about bleedin' beaver?"

Standrop grinned like a skull. "No need t'learn beaver, lad. Only t'learn savages. Their tongue, what they wants. Trade, that's all. Trucke for fur. Fur for love. Only need make 'em love you. Such as what they loves Claiborne. Claiborne knows. Makes the savages love him and they make him rich."

I kept my face expressionless. It was another name

forbidden to us. Claiborne. Claiborne and Avalon. But if the one had drawn Calvert's dreams across the water, it was the other, it was the Virginian William Claiborne and what I knew of him and his enterprises, that had scratched a path on my mind. A Kent man like me. A hollowed man who had filled and named himself in the tug and twist between fear and greed. In the unformed place we were going.

"What in the hairy bleedin' 'ell is a Claiborne?" Barnes looked around nervously, spat on the floor, glared at Standrop. "And what the bleedin' 'ell are you, Sour-Me Standrop? How can y'speak all this learnin' and lovin' savages after they skewered your fambly, your wife and wee 'uns?"

"Nay, may as well hate the winter as hate the savages." Standrop looked slyly at me, as if there were some secret bond between us. "The plague took your young, in't it? Do you hate the plague, Hallam? Is there any use to such a hatin'?"

"Plague had a neck, Standrop, I'd throttle it," I told him. "As I'll throttle you, you keep your tack at this heading."

Standrop flinched and looked stricken. Men such as he and Barnes have always clustered around me. Like mice trying to befriend the cat, Meg would say. But it was their need, not mine. I felt nothing. Only a cat-need to torment. To display the difference between cats and mice.

"There's a good dream now," Barnes nodded to me. "That throttling. Throttle Sour-me, pisspot Standrop. Did them savages cut out your heart then?"

Standrop laughed wildly. "You thinks I don't dream my Will and Jen, Jeremiah Barnes? I'll spill 'em right into your skull, y'poxed bastid." He reached down to the rope he used for a belt, loosened a leather bag, reached in and then slammed what he had extracted onto the table. As if throwing dice. A row of broken, blackened teeth grinned up from the little pile of small, splintered bones, like a reflection or extension of Standrop's gaped smile. Standrop stirred the pile with his finger. "Y'want I should tell you how I dream them, Barnes? How you will too?"

"Nay, y'll shut yer gob now, or I'll split yer brainpan," Hervey said, his fat face as sullen as the Africans, his drunkenness pursing his lips into the pout of the woman sitting behind him. I could see the others were all uneasy too, vaguely angry around Standrop, as if he held the bitter bones of their own futures in his hand.

"We need more rum, Standrop," long thin Oliver Raley said finally. "More rum an' less shite. Stow your gab and your bones, both. We're to Maryland for tobacco. For tobacco and land. Not for your damned rodents nor for your damned savages."

Standrop laughed again. He raised his cracked and twisted hands again, turned them in the candlelight, then flapped them towards the back of the rude wooden hut where the beggars and the whores stood, their faces sullen and shadowed in the candle light, a wall of gleaming eyes and black flesh, their misting sweat mingling with the sweat of the whites, rising in a wet haze that filled the small hot room. The smile left his face, like something draining away.

"Starin' at us like they starin' from a forest," he said, almost in a whisper. "Makes no matter they loves you or not, these."

Something roiled through and opened in me now like the shifting water over which I had stared that afternoon from the deck of the Ark, sharded with glare and dreams and bathed in a light clear and bright as Hunger, and a hung man marking the edge of it.

I rose.

"Where are you off to then, James?" Barnes said.

"Away from bats and monkeys and mice," I said.

Ezekiel's Song

And this is my naming song. The first time I was born I had six fingers on each hand; twelve fingers and twelve children born so to each generation in the village whose name I have lost. In Dahomey. In Africa. Two names I remember. The boys marked for carvers of gods and weapons, the girls for musicians and poets: our Gifts, our sixth and twelfth fingers, scratching out shapes hidden in wood and in words and in stones and in time, and all of us cursed with skill and difference. So that we were both valuable and feared, all at once. Half marked to be given so the village might live, half sold and half kept. And the Six of us to be given knew who we were when the sixth fingers on our left hands were taken for burnt offerings after the hair had sprouted on our bodies, and what was cut off us was given to the gods, along with our foreskins and menstrual flow and our birth names.

For that cutting was my second birth and it mirrored how I would be cut from the body of the people. *The child that is given. The child that is given.* The old language, mother-tongue, mother's tongue licking my cheeks, rolling my tears under its tip. *You're the child that must be given that the village will live*, my father said, tears rolling down his cheeks, hands trembling, in a language older than memory. The six-fingered hands in my brain parting a mist to a blaze of African sunlight, the feel of the itching dust on my privates, sharp grains grating in the flower of my anus, the scratchy orange cloth draping the adults; Ezekiel and I with different names then, names buried so deep now even Ezekiel's bloody fingers couldn't reach and pull them out. Ezekiel and I led out from the village, whose name I have drowned in my brain, with the other six children, three boys, three girls, torn from mothers' arms and fathers' howls: the children that must be

13

given clinging to each other's naked flesh in a circle in the white sand as the horsemen came, white hawkskull faces laughing, long fingers pinching, and that was my third birth.

And my fourth? Easily conjured. I look over the dark water now and my nostrils remember, coaxed back by a whiff from the gallows to the stench in the belly of the ship, shit and piss and the rot of death and even spilt seed, the rot of life fermenting in that black and fetid womb, the belly of the *Jesus and Marie* from which I was pulled and spanked bare-arsed alive with a bull pizzle and named Lucius on an auction block here in Barbados town.

And born again yesterday into the name I will carry into my death, shaped and named again by fingers that had once learned the shapes and roughs and smoothes of wood as my own had.

Come out to the water, Ezekiel had whispered to me, two days and a night before that, and we rose and went from the naked bodies packed between the coconut-palm walls in the fetid darkness of the slave pen, packed like fish steaming in a pan. Like slaves in the belly of a ship. Like slaves in a slave pen, their uneasy dreams leaking in moans and hisses from between their compressed lips, as if they'd learned to conceal themselves even in their sleep, these sleepers, my village now. *Come out to the water, Lucius,* Ezekiel whispered then, and I followed him into the moonlight, and Peter Trent the overseer, an indentured white, his face bumpy with oozing boils, looked at us for a moment, then nodded indulgently for we were Borten's favorites, his master carpenters, and allowed to come outside at night, as I am allowed to sit here now, in the moonlight.

And it was moonlight I followed Ezekiel into, on that night, and we sat at the edge of the dock, in this very place I sit now, and the water slapped against the pilings, as it is doing now. A bird cried as if it had carried a dream from the slave pen to release it here. Our legs dangled and shook over the water as Ezekiel's body would dangle and shake from the gallows. That I can see now in the light of moon, if I wish to turn and look.

The ships come in, the ships go out, Ezekiel had said to me then.

And I had laughed. *But we stay moored.*

The ships come in, the ships go out.

I'd felt a shiver in my blood then. I knew what I'd hear Ezekiel say next. We didn't need words. We were the last two of the Six and we had been twins in a womb in the belly of *Jesus and Marie.*

The next ship will come in three days. I heard Borten speak of it. Four hundred tons.

That ship is a dream. Keep it in your skull.

You remember how Borten planted diffenbachia in the mouth of every child in the row when he got drunk, said their cries annoyed him? They died with their jaws locked, their eyes wild. And I stood like I was in a dream and did nothing.

To do something now will kill us all.

Dreams give me slit white throats now. Dreams give me machetes. But machetes are no dream, Lucius. They lay in that shed behind us, no don't look. They lay behind a door with hinges that can be torn by even one of us. Lay like dreams. Like knives dreaming of blood. Dreams give me a ship, come in three days.

Dreams tell you how to point that ship? Dreams take us back to the World? No markings on the water, and we crossed it in the blackness. You think that ship knows the way in its dreams?

We'll go where the ship's dream takes us. Finish its voyage.

You dream that also?

You learn to mock the truth in dreams, Lucius?

Yes. I'm a slave.

Then listen to the dreams of another. You remember Nestor, from Matthews' Fields? Nestor talked to a Nevis slave who talked to other slaves who had run away, gone to the Red Ghosts up north.

Is that your dream, man? There are no more Red Ghosts —they all jumped in the sea.

Nestor said the Red Ghosts have villages like ours in Dahomey. Have eyes that see like our eyes. Take our people in. Say we're their dream children, dead children lost across the water, come back. I dream that, Lucius. I see us free in a village of Red Ghosts. In the forest. In the dream land. In the north. Nestor says that, says that's what the Nevis man saw. We're ready, Lucius. Ready to rise and go.

Ready to die.

I'd said to Ezekiel sitting next to me, alive then, legs dangling over the edge of this dock, mouth talking his dream. I'd said to Ezekiel before I became Ezekiel.

The village that gave us lives because we were given, I had said. *We are here because we were born to be here. When we carve, we carve the shape already in the wood. We were given. They live and we live.*

You think a village still sits in Dahomey, sun and yellow dust, saved because of us? Ezekiel asked. *Empty houses, maybe. Echoes of songs in the wind maybe. Our village is an empty skin by now. So are we.*

I had reached down and squeezed myself. *I'm not dead, me. Dead is what you're going to make us all if we rise against guns. Dead is fist against gun and sword. Machete against cannon. Our village is in that shed now too, those people sleeping behind us. Dead is what you'll make them.*

No, slave. We're dead already. Need to be born again, the other side of the water. Every day now, what we do? Build bigger pens, more pens, more blocks. How long have we been here, Lucius? How many villages we seen coming off the ships, off Jesus and Mary? We were only Six. Not enough to feed Sugar. The whites are emptying the World of us, Lucius.

A flame had flared in the blackness then. I saw Peter

Trent, looking at us, his face bent over the white clay stem of a pipe.

In my dreams that night the gallows groaned and hissed. A forest of gallows, four hundred, one for every slave in the pens. Swaying back and forth heavily in my skull. Creaking. Ezekiel's dripping fingers kneading the clay of my brain into Borten's red face, broad under a mane of silver curls. His devil-green eyes staring at me on the next morning.

A word, Lucius.

Yes sah.

Borten nodding and smiling as I climbed down and stood in front of him, as if the two of us shared a joke. As soon as I saw that smile and even before Borten's first words, before his caress, I knew that the white man knew; I knew that Ezekiel's plans were as transparent to him as clear water.

I knew who had to be given.

Borten reaching down, picking up my hand, holding it flat as a fish in his palm, stroking it with his fingers.

Are you fed well, Lucius? he said.

His fingers caressing gently.

Have I treated you badly?

Have I bent you in the sugar cane?

Have I kept you from women so your part shrivels?

Have I not given you a roof, sleep, food, the sound of strange and intricate music, the sight of lights and color and soft laughter leaking from the veranda of a white house on a hill?

Have I not given you Christ?

Have I not withheld terrible pain?

Caressing. Stroking.

Have I not withheld the bull pizzle lash?

The iron collar

The iron tongue

The diffenbachia

The burial alive

The flayed alive

The burial to the neck in the sand and the face covered
with dead meat to bring the crabs
The fingers torn from the sockets
Caressing
The hand bones broken to powder
Caressing.
Have I not given you all you deserve?
Have I not saved you from all you deserve?

Have I not saved a village, yellow straw, an old man
squatting in the dust, a mother's tears, from the Arab, by
bringing you to me in Jesus and Marie?

Will I not spare four hundred if you only give me one?
Only a name
Only one so that the Village will live.
Only one, not twelve. Not four hundred.

I saw a ship molded into my dreams by a dead man's
hands. I saw Red Ghosts, waiting for me, a lost child. But
even though I knew then the course they would fly in the air,
my words still surprised me when they flew from my mouth:

What will you give me, sah?

You impertinent bastard, I'll have your tongue torn out
by the roots.

But then he'd smiled. As I knew he would. When they
think we echo their hunger.

What is it you'd have, Lucius?

I'd have Ezekiel's name.

If I stay afterwards, sah, they kill me. I'd be no good to
you. No value, dead niggah.

Damn you, will you have me free you?

Nah, suh. I'd have you sell me.

I look again at the ship waiting for me in the harbor.

I'd have Ezekiel's dream.

Outside, the moist breeze brought a peculiar smell to my nostrils, a hot, fecund breath heavy with spices and lemons and rot. Stars swarmed around me, over my head and reflected in the black whispering mirror of the water, so it was as if I were walking among them, anchorless at the edge of infinite choices. At the end of the quay the corpse was still swinging, fly blown and bloated, a thing that had moved out of my heart into this dark oozing mass over my head, swaying in its dance against the stars. I stopped and put my hand on the curved, segmented trunk of a palm near the gallows, looked up at it silhouetted against the moon, and laughed aloud. There was no true difference here, not in trees nor in men. Only in my own unmooring from their hypocrisies. In my inner vision, I saw something red-fleshed and hot, a heart inside my heart, opening finally into myself.

I heard a creak of boards that echoed the creak of the stretched gallows rope. I turned. The priest, black-robed Father White, glided towards me, smudged across the dazzle of moon- and star-light. White. For a black stain against a radiance.

"*Et iter praebuit populo terrae ut enarrent mirabilia Dei,*" the priest said.

I didn't know what to reply.

"*Mirabilia Dei*—the wondrous things of God." White pointed the rosary towards the hanging man. "The African servants planned to rise and kill their masters, then take possession of the first innocent ship to enter the harbor," he said. "But Providence softened the heart of one of them, and he told his master; the leader of the planned insurrection was arrested yesterday. That is he. And we were that marked ship, carpenter. Who can doubt we are blessed?"

On the Ark, the square spritsail under the bow—it should have been furled—caught a breath of wind, filled and collapsed with a flapping noise. The noise made both of us start. I wondered if White thought those sailors who had been on the Dove were blessed also. That pinnace, the smaller of the two vessels on the Maryland expedition, had been lost with all hands to a hurricane off the coast of Ireland. When the storm began, I had told Jeremiah Barnes to lash me to the Ark's mainmast. You need not push hot wax in my ears, I'd yelled to him, over the scream of the wind. Nay, your brains have already leaked out them, Barnes had screamed back. Fastened, the mast pressing my back like gallows wood, I'd watched the two signal lights that hung from the Dove's mast head draw peaks and valleys against the black sky in jagged lines of fire while the four hundred tons of the Ark, beneath my feet, bucked and slid like a bit of bark down the slopes of mountainous gray waves and barrels of salt pork and snarls of rope and loose tools flew past my head and the deck dipped and rushed headlong into a trough of darkness, no Sirens but the wind screaming into my ears and my dead wife and sons and every man I'd hung in Spain dancing spastically from the spars, their eyes flaming with Saint Elmo's fire. Swallowing water, sputtering I had wiped my eyes and saw two burning circles haloed against a blurring living mass of cloud and water, the malevolent eyes of God.

"I pray for the souls of those on the Dove," White said, as if he had read my thoughts. "As well as for the soul of this wretched black before us." He waved at the feet of the hanging man. "Yet we are here. And you were on the Ark, not the Dove, by the grace of God, now on your way to a land without churches, by the grace of your skills as a carpenter and as a soldier. And as a Catholic. I understood you are that, James Hallam. Am I mistaken?"

"I have been both carpenter and soldier, and sometimes the two together," I said. "And, aye, I have been Catholic also."

"How mean you that 'have been,' James Hallam?" The priest worried the corner of his eye with a finger that was trembling slightly, with rage or nervousness or weariness. I wanted to answer. Years of bitten-down words pushing at my lips, the edge of some flood tide drawn out as if by the looming weight of that continent I sensed close by now. But I held my tongue. I knew priests like White too well, priests and officers and gentlemen-adventurers who feigned a bright interest when all they truly wished was a nod and beam; if you gave them the truth they asked for, they would find some way of fashioning it into a knife with which to stab you. Jesuits like White. I knew them. Once I might have been one of them. When I was a child they had taken me in as if I were the relic of a martyr, some saint's finger bone or lock of hair. They had given me words to say the world and eyes to see it as it was, and for that I would never forgive them.

"Why, only that I had to hide my faith when I was in the King's service," I said, turning the innocent eyes of a seeker to White. "If my men had known that all my life I had been a Catholic, come from a home that contained a hidden altar, they would have torn me to pieces."

"What concerns God is that we have a faith to hide."

"Tis well said, father." Nod and beam.

"And a place to worship as brethren in that faith." The priest placed a smile on his lips, like an afterthought, and I knew why he had come to stand next to me. White and the other Jesuits had been pressing to lend me to the building of a church in the colony: I was indentured to Leonard Calvert, the governor himself, and not the Society of Jesus. It mattered not a wit to me; I'd build what they wished, church or gallows, all the wondrous things of God; for five years I was their unbrained hands.

"Tis my pleasure to serve your worship," I said. White, I had heard, had lived for a time in a Spanish monastery, gone to flee the English persecutions. A choice my own father had never had. Had the priest been in Spain when I was there? I thought of how it would have been to meet him in that place, how I would have served him then.

"It isn't me you'll serve or worship," White said, cracking into my thoughts once again. Smiling, pleased, at his own word play. "Why else do think we have come here, carpenter, but to build the house of God?"

I wondered how far I could take his question, in the light of this place.

"I have been carpenter and soldier, as you say, father. And when I soldiered in Spain I killed Catholics, in battle and at the torture and on gallows I built with these hands. Priests like yourself, father." I held my hands up, turned them in the moonlight. "Do you think them worthy to build your church?"

The moored ship groaned. A rope flapped against the side, like someone beating a drum. White didn't even blink.

"Our Lord suffered tax collectors and whores and centurions to come unto him; I am certain he will not disallow a fellow carpenter. Even one who has built crosses to crucify his flesh."

I looked at the sea. I said nothing.

White followed my gaze. "We all begin anew on this side of the water," he said. He nodded and glided away into the dark.

AND I BACK TO the gallows. Examined them, admiring the craft of the builder. Sturdy and solid, the notch of the cross bar fitted exactly to the main beam, the wood smoothed, even though the structure must have been erected quickly, in answer to the planned rebellion. I felt a drunken sense of fellowship with the unknown carpenter. I looked more closely at the corpse. A cloud of flies, buzzing like the last panicked thoughts of the hanged man, had settled on the face and tongue and made black shifting lips in the moonlight. Father Black. Father White meet Father Black. I reached up and grasped the legs, above the ankle stumps and pulled the flesh to my forehead, breathing in its rot. *Bless me father, for I have sinned. Hear my confession, Father Black. Suffer me to come unto you. Now and in the hour of your death.* A buzzing started in my head, as if the flies had gone inside my brain. I grasped the legs tighter. As if to keep myself from shivering out of myself. The way we would shiver out of ourselves in Spain, out of father, husband, lover, child, like animals shaking water off their hides. Out of ourselves and into ourselves, into Mankind, made in His image, our rutting shadows dancing their human dance on the white stone wall of the monastery. The wall that was His Skin. *Help us*, the priest mouthed to me silently. Hooking out my rage, for what hidden altar did he think he saw in me that he didn't see in the others? *For whom do you do this, soldier?* he whispered. As if such sights were uncommon. As if he's not dangling from this rope now, again, forever; his member risen and poking the air, black to black, bird-torn, like a mocking echo of my own lust. Like all the hanged men I'd ever seen. Like all the men I've ever hung. Black face now. Pale white moon of a face then. Father Black and Father White. *King and country and custom, priest*, I answer and the words leave me as emptied and free of these as my sacks are of seed and my heart of God. The thick black commas of your eyebrows, your pale cheeks over your black robe in the light of the flames. Saying nothing, but your lips twitching finally into a beatific, forgiving smile. Into flies. *Forgive me, father, for I have sinned, but I will never forgive you for your forgiveness. I will never forgive your forgiveness on the morning when I built my first gallows. Now and in the hour of your death. Now and in the hour of my birth.*

Out of the corner of my eye, I caught a movement, a shadow. I released the legs and turned, my heart pounding, and watched the shadow grow into a tall black man. Or perhaps not too tall: he grew only to my own height as we stood eye to eye now, though some effect of the slave's shadow, his silent rise, had at first made him seem gigantic. I took a deep breath, then another, until the scramble of panic in my chest subsided. Foolishness. The black had been squatting near the base of the gallows, on the other side. I saw the tools hanging from a rope belt around his waist: a hammer, an adze, a chisel: as if, in this milky foreign night that smelled of lemons and death, I had finally come face to face with my own black soul. The slave ran his hand over the wood of the gallows trunk and I knew from that brief, proprietary touch, if I wasn't sure before, whom this was. Then I looked again at his hands, seeing clearly now what had snagged my eye at first. There were six fingers on his right hand; the extra a smaller appendage growing out from the side of the hand opposite to his thumb. Grown for a carpenter's hand; could the Africans do such? On the left hand, I saw, was a small stump where another sixth finger had bloomed, been plucked.

"What do they call you?" I asked.

The slave looked at me without expression. I touched my chest and said my name, then gestured at him. He glared insolently and touched his own chest. "Hallam," he repeated, as if in mockery.

I touched the wood, feeling the cold death in it, noticing again how cunningly the top of the beam had been notched and fitted, using only the dead weight of the hanged man to press the pieces together; I'd have done the same.

"Is this your work then?" I asked.

He said nothing. I reached over to grab his collar: perhaps a name was written upon it. His hand shot out and grabbed my wrist and squeezed. I could feel the power in the grip, the rough sharpness of the calluses scrapping my skin, the strange weight of the extra digit clutching my wrist. I let it go on for a while, testing. There was strength here. But six-fingered or no, it didn't approach my own. I grasped his wrist and the two of us stood for a moment, face to face, squeezing each other. The black gasped.

"I asked for your name," I said.

"Lucius," he said, and I let his wrist go.

"Lucius," I said.

"Ezekiel," he said.

"Which is it, damn you?" I said, but he shuffled backwards a few steps, as if to stay out of reach. Or as if he was trying to lead me away from something. I looked down into the darkness from where he had risen, then squatted awkwardly and peered at the base of the gallows. Figures were newly carved in the wood, fresh shavings curling in the mud at its base. I felt the surface with my own horn-hard finger, looked closer. In the strong moonlight I could see the faces of negroes, a mob of slaves, their hands gripping pikes and swords; they were attacking a small circle of whites. The carving was as good as anything I had ever seen. Even in the dark, I knew what was here: this black had captured the dream of revolt that had fled into the air from the dead man's brain before it was lost forever, buzzed off in mad circles into the air.

"And they let you wander free, do they, Lucius Ezekial?" I asked softly, looking up.

He was gone.

I heard a step, a breath behind, and spun around, fearing a knife in the back. Father White emerged again from the darkness, his pale face floating, his black robes still fastened to the night. The priest knelt down next to me and for an instant, though a part of myself was disgusted at the thought, another part amused, I saw the two of us kneeling as if in prayer at the base of a cross, the dark stinking presence dangling above us.

"Clever hands," White said, touching the carvings.

Yaocomaco

1634

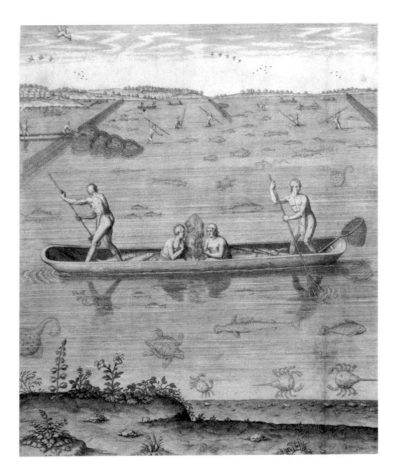

From the Narrative of Father Andrew White, S.J.

Having now arrived at the wished-for country, we alloted names according to circumstances. And indeed the Promontory, which is toward the south, we consecrated with the name of St. Gregory, now Smith Point, naming the northern one, now Point Lookout, St. Michael's, in honor of all the angels. Never have I beheld a larger or more beautiful river. The Thames seems a mere rivulet in comparison with it; it is not disfigured with any swamps, but has firm land on each side. Fine groves of trees appear, not choked with briers or bushes and undergrowth, but growing at intervals as if planted by the hand of man, so that you can drive a four-horse carriage, wherever you choose, through the midst of the trees. Just at the mouth of the river, we observed the natives in arms. That night, fires blazed through the whole country, and since they had never seen such a large ship, messengers were sent in all directions, who reported that a Canoe like an island had come with as many men as there were trees in the woods.

From the letters of George Alsop, Indentured Servant

Herds of Deer are as numerous in this Province of Mary-Land, as Cuckolds can be in London, only their horns are not so well drest and tipt with silver as theirs are.

Hallam's Song

The land pointed at me like a green knife, its blade edged in white sand and sheathed in waters; the broad bay of the Chesapeake, the wide mouth of the Potomac. The trees were taller and thicker around than any trees I had ever seen, live oaks and hickories and pines like ships' masts, a hundred and two hundred feet tall and bare-trunked up to branches like furled sails; between them were shaded faery glens, carpeted thickly with pine needles. Cypress, eighty feet tall at the least, I estimated, and mulberry and chestnut and ash and locust and cedar and trees I could not yet name.

We sailed into it. Behind me, over the stern, the helmsman let a rope slip through his palm, the line knotted every fifty feet and six inches and tied to a chip log weighted with lead. With an eye on the minute glass, he called out the number of knots that slipped through his hand in thirty seconds, a chant I had heard every day of this voyage; it stayed in my brain for years after. The Ark was doing six knots then, a fair speed. Leaning over, I could see the pinnace, the Dove. It had managed to return to an English port and weather the storm in which we had thought it lost. White had looked at me, eyes gleaming, when the ship sailed into port in the Antilles, as if to say *do you see, Hallam, the wondrous things of God*. The priest's endless whine of thanksgiving to a Providence that fed Itself on the gratitude it received from mortals who had been delivered from the Evils It brought to them. A lovely bit of theatre, that, one I had used myself on new soldiers, when as a sergeant I would alternatively be the God of Wrath and then the God of Mercy, until they would endure anything for my blessings.

The pinnace surged ahead of the bigger ship; it displaced only forty-two tons to the Ark's four hundred, a vessel for exploring the reaches of rivers, though the river was wide enough here for a fleet of Arks. I looked back then to the two Jesuits—Father John Altham was standing with White—and the governor, Calvert. Their eyes were fixed on something on the shore I at first could not see, though when I followed their gaze a flame flared into my vision, another, and another continuing up along the banks on both sides, as if the outlandish rub of the two vessels sailing up the coast was causing a conflagaration, a meeting of unstable elements. Naked men with faces painted in red and black stripes rose from the shadows of the trees, the invisible suddenly visible; their brown skin under the paint made them seem as though they had simply detached themselves from the bark of the trees, the branches suddenly a bristle of spears and arrows and bows, and I felt my empty hands itch: it was if the trees had sensed my arrival, sent forth their army, the shoreline of the country come to life as a rim of naked sprites. Richard Dunbar, one of the sailors, swung the small deck cannon around and pointed it at the silent savages, moving the barrel in small circles. *Eyes gleaming, like they're staring from a forest*, Standrop had said and I knew what vision the Africans on Barbados had opened in the ex-Virginian's brain now.

A naked man, his body and face painted with red stripes stepped forward onto the beach, notched an arrow and let it fly in the direction of the ships, in my direction. It arched into the air and fell well short, into the river. I looked at the savage, trying to hold his eye across the water, and then I nodded, making my own promise to this man who had come from the guarding trees. A drum started to beat, its boom rippling into another, and another, until the country began to pulse in my own blood. The torches and the drums and the cloud of silent painted men behind the beat continued to follow our progress along the river. I felt pierced suddenly by the same hot longing I'd felt in Barbados, when I had gone back to the inn and taken one of the black women to the beach and coupled with her among rotting, fly-buzzed coconut husks, near the foot of the gallows. As if something now was drawing my flesh to anticipate an inevitable intimacy, a mingling with secret fluids and skin.

A movement caught in the corner of my eye then and I saw that the black, Ezekiel, had come up to the rail now and was looking at the savage, smiling strangely. He raised his hand, as if in greeting. The gesture, the sight of the slave, brought me back to Barbados also, filled me with the same fury I had felt when what I had known would happen, since the night I'd visited the gallows, had concreted in the air before my eyes: Ezekiel standing in the bow of the skiff, staring straight at me as the skiff drew in its inevitable line to the Ark. Hands manacled, a bag of carpenter's tools slung round his chest. White smiling with sheep-faced stupidity. Here are two more hands for you, carpenter, he'd said, the very man who God moved to save us, and you are his reward—you will be substance and he shadow. But shadow was how I saw myself and to remember the skill I had seen in that six-fingered devil's hand, the gallow wood configured to the rebellions of its living, hating soul, to look into the slave's face, was to look at myself sold and manacled.

I stared at Ezekiel's hands now, the eleven splayed fingers, five and six, the skin the color and roughness of bark, resting on the wood of the railing as the Ark sailed up the Potomac.

WE MADE LANDFALL on an island shortly thereafter, Calvert reasoning there would be water here between ourselves and the savages. I went ashore and felled a tree and with my hands and my carpenter's tools and with the memory of gallows still tingling in my palms, I shaped a cross and stood it there. And there, with Leonard Calvert and the other Catholics, a faith I had been born to and discarded, I carried the weight of the cross on my shoulders and erected it and celebrated the Mass of Christ, while from down the river, from the Bay, the ocean, from the old world itself, a dry cold wind touched the backs of our necks like lingering memory. I heard White, as from a distance, naming the island for St. Clement, on whose day we had sailed from England: a saint who had been tied to an anchor and thrown into the sea. An odd choice of name it seemed to me. But my opinion in the matter was not asked.

From the Narrative of Father Andrew White, S.J.

Now when the Governor had understood that many princes were subject to the Emperor of Pascatawaye, he determined to visit him, in order that, after explaining the reason of our voyage, and gaining his good will, he might secure an easier access to others. Accordingly, putting with our pinnace (the Dove) another, which he had procured in Virginia, and leaving the ship (the Ark) at anchor, he sailed round and landed on the southern side of the river. And when he had learned that the Savages had fled inland, he went on to a city which takes its name from the river, being also called Potomeack. Here the young king's uncle named Archichu was his guardian, and took his place in the kingdom; a sober and discreet man. He willingly listened to father John Altham, who had been selected to accompany the Governor, (for he (the Governor) kept me still with the ship's cargo.) And when the Father explained, as far as he could through the interpreter, Henry Fleet, the errors of the heathen, he would, every little while, acknowledge his own: and when he was informed that we had come thither, not to make war, but out of good will towards them, in order to impart civilized instruction to his ignorant race, and show them the way to heaven, and at the same time with the intention of communicating to them the advantages of distant countries, he gave us to understand he was pleased at our coming. The interpreter was one of the Protestants of Virginia. And so, as the Father could not stop for further discourse at the time, he promised that he would return before very long. "That is just what I wish," said Archichu, "we will eat at the same table; my followers too shall go hunt for you, and we will have all things in common."

Kittamaquund's Song

On the opposite bank, a black bear slaps a fish out of the river. For an instant, Bear stands and stares at me, holding my gaze, the fish in his teeth, then he wheels away and crashes through the bushes, and I see Henry Fleet's Susquehannock birchbark canoe cut through the water and land on the sandy beach, near the young women gathering oysters. Fleet jumps from his canoe and pulls it up on the beach, then walks through the palisade to me, a short man, broad and solid on the earth. He is thumping his chest and grunting like the bear, and I understand now the bear was his journey spirit, come to tell me of his arrival. I smile to see him. He is a wondrously ugly man, uglier even than the other whites. Corn Nose, the Anacostans called him, as much for the shape of his nose as for the long silky hairs that grow from his nostrils and from his cheeks. Some of his ugliness the Anacostans carved themselves when he was their captive: that nose bent by a tomahawk in their gauntlet, the scars on his cheek, two of his fingers cut off by the women with oyster shells: I have heard the Anacostan women had great fun with Fleet, though he was only tortured until he learned to speak like a human being. If they hadn't meant to keep him, it would not only have been his fingers the women took.

Hunh, Piscataway, Fleet says, greeting me as is proper the first time of recognition, by the name of my people. The other English had shamelessly used my name, or called me Tayac, which is only proper once met. I thought then about the reasons Fleet might have for not telling the whites this.

Bear, I say, for Fleet has come now in that form. I think if the Anacostans had honored your flesh more with their shells, you would have remembered your human tongue more rapidly.

I am satisfied enough with the honor they paid me, Tayac, Fleet says, with his strangely twisted smile. He touches his nose.

Why have you returned?

I have a gift from Claiborne for you, Tayac.

I wait while Fleet returns to his canoe and brings back the gift, the skin of a large black bear he unrolls on the ground. I pat Bear and chant an apology that I did not recognize him earlier.

Are you Claiborne's tongue now? I ask. How is it you can fly from mouth to mouth?

I am always Claiborne's tongue, Tayac. It was Claiborne asked me to bring Calvert to you.

Yesterday the English canoe had entered the mouth of the river, a canoe made from a tree so thick it must have been old as the earth, my uncle Archichu said with his usual exaggeration: I've seen the Virginia English canoes made as this must have been, from bound and cut logs. But my uncle enjoys claiming sights no one else has seen, and he had returned with gifts of *roanoke* shells and *wampompeag* beads and axes and the whites' smooth cloth. He described the white Tayac, Calvert, to me as an arrow of a man with an arrowhead of black beard on his chin. He had spoken to Archichu through the mouth of a Blackrobe, a shaman who must be powerful with madness, for he said he had come to save me. As if I were a captive. Such humor is rare, and I enjoyed hearing Archichu's story, and asked from which of my enemies did the Blackrobe say I would be saved. The Blackrobe had told him he could help me find the fat hunting ground of the dead, for if I didn't, I would burn forever in a fire pit. So I smiled in respect, as one does with madmen, and said, ha-eeh. My people love madmen and their songs.

But thinking about his words now, a shaman's words, I try to hear the unspoken truth in the dream words under them. For was not saving my people from a fire why I had killed my brother?

Tell me what I know, I say to Fleet.

Claiborne says you know this, Tayac: do not trust the Blackrobes. They are black maggots and lice. Once they are in your hair, they will copulate and increase until they devour everything. Claiborne says: Brother Tayac, you should attack them, and you should burn them until they are gone. Otherwise they will eat your elders' forests. Claiborne says: if you do this, the Piscataway and the Virginian English can be allies as the Powhatans and the Susquehannocks and the Virginian English are allies.

Fleet uses the Susquehannock word for allies, which means *war-sharers,* and not our word: *brothers*. Perhaps he is afraid to use the word brother to me. But he remains properly silent while I think of what he has said. The idea he has given me now of different tribes of whites is new and interesting—the Blackrobes and the Virginians no more the same than Piscataway and Susquehannock. I consider more of what I know. He has told me, a gift better than a bear skin, that Claiborne and the Blackrobes are enemies. And I knew the Virginia whites have built longhouses in the territory of the Susquehannocks, on Oyster Island in the Chesapeake, near the Nacotchtank and Nanticokes. Would they raid each other?

The women wade ashore, their baskets heavy with oysters. Two men come out of the forest, laughing deeply, carrying a deer between them, the bowed hanging weight of it drawing my mind to the oysters. Fat land. I feel *orenda* opening in my heart, a weaving at the side of my vision, almost ready to reveal its design. But I am only at the edge of it now.

I must dream, I say.

Fleet nods, grips my wrists, and goes. I think: the Anacostans have done their work well with him. But I remember they also called him Shit Carrier as well as Corn Nose and this name came not only from his tasks as a captive.

As soon as he has left, Tawzin appears in front of me. He

is young and straight and beautiful. Archichu had told me that, against my orders, he had loosed arrows at the *tassantasses* when they entered the river. Still, or perhaps because of this, as if he is what remains of my brother, my heart feels full to see him.

How is your balance, Piscataway? he asks.

Bent.

So is the world.

I have noticed this is so. Tell me what I know.

Balance is a stick on a rock, each end built over a fire, Tayac. If the shape of the stick is changed, one end or the other might tilt into the fire. Or if weight is added.

He has echoed my fears. I look at him, though with no real surprise. Some were shocked when I made him a *wisoe*, and gave him a name, since he had died and it was not proper to name someone once he was dead. But in spite of his time with the whites, Tawzin often acts and speaks as does a shaman who sees the true world of dreams under their reverse reflection in the water, which is our waking world.

Are the other whites who will come now weight?

I see them rather as termites.

Claiborne tells me they are lice and maggots.

He knows both those tribes too well.

I grunt. He names my mistrust of Claiborne. One knows where to hide because one has hidden there, our people say.

What do you know of these people who came, *wisoe*?

These whites are English also, like the whites who took me to their country. But they are a different tribe.

So Fleet tells me. Who are stronger, these or the ones in Virginia, with Claiborne?

The Blackrobes are the English that took me and held me hostage.

Tawzin hasn't answered my question. I wonder why. But I see him gathering his words carefully, which pleases me.

The Blackrobes are English, but enemy to the other English, he says. There are more of the other kind of English.

Yet the English in their own country let some Blackrobes live among them, since the Blackrobes have many allies in other tribes.

It is intelligent to keep hostages.

But they fear having too many among them and so forbid many customs and ceremonies of the Blackrobes.

And this is why the English Blackrobes have come here?

Yes, Tayac. Though that is not the only reason.

Do they wish to perform our ceremonies?

You're teasing me.

Yes. Come, *wisoe*.

I call back to the house, to Arawak, my youngest wife, and my sister Mattapacque. They are sitting near the fire, grinding corn, looking at us and joking softly, Mattapacque looking more often at Tawzin, tossing her head back, and wiping the sweat between her breasts. Tawzin doesn't glance back at her and again I think how he is unhealthily attached to Nanjemoy, even to where he never goes to the woods with the hunting women. His marriage to Mattapacque would have brought him to my longhouse. But I fear the whites have narrowed his heart so it has space for only one woman. Nanjemoy had also been twelve summers when she had come to the Piscataway, as Tawzin had gone to the English. In this way their stories called each other. But Tawzin's selfishness has angered some of the women, who shun Nanjemoy or insult her by calling her Nameless since she bears only the name of the place where she had been born into us. Archihu had told me that Calvert wished us to perform a *tassantass* ceremony of alliance by drawing with him on a soft bark, and one of the drawings, my uncle warned, signed the return of all white captives. The ceremony seemed bizarre, but English captives had been returned before, even children torn screaming from their weeping Piscataway mothers, and to give Nanjemoy back would please many women. But I already have too many enemies because I killed my brother and I will not add Tawzin to them.

Something draws my eyes up now and I see He-Whose-Face-Bulges-in-the-Smokehole, through the opening in the loft platform of the House, his face configuring out of the weaved rim of reeds near the smoke hole. I see him and then, even before we enter the sweatlodge, a vision comes to me of the *tassantass* Calvert and the Blackrobe and their strange hunger for my spirit and their not strange hunger for land and trade, and their weapons, and how powerful the threat of those weapons have made the Susquehannocks. And I think of my enemies. I see my brother's eyes, staring into mine, the moment before I brought the tomahawk down. He-Whose-Face-Bulges-in-the-Smokehole stares, his eyes black holes. I chant a greeting back and his face dissolves into the smoke and leaves sparkling dust motes in the air.

Arawak and Mattapacque are looking at me expectantly. I tell them to prepare the sweatlodge.

I walk to the river with Tawzin and watch as they light a fire, heat stones and tong them, one by one, into the fire basket, which like the sweatlodge itself has its woven twigs covered tight with clay. The mud of the river bank is cold and thick with water under our feet. Tawzin's silence and stillness is pleasing to me. When he first came back to us, telling us with his child's language that he could no longer live among the whites, he did not remember how to speak like a man. He had become like the whites I have met, asking question after question without allowing a human being time to answer fully. He did not yet remember that half of a word is silence. He would speak quickly, his body dancing, his hands imitating the eloquence of dance, but without pattern, so that at first the Piscataway thought he must be a mad or evil shaman, until they understood that his spirit was so eager to remember it was shaking his body and soul, pushing it here and there until it would find its way.

I see Arawak pick up the otter-shaped rock near the bend in the stream and I laugh in embarrassment, loud enough so that she can hear me. She looks down quickly, and draws in her breath when she sees the rock is *manitou*. She replaces it carefully into its bed.

The women put the fire basket into the bath and fasten the entrance mat, and the stones fill the inside with their heat. Mattapacque touches the clay, pushing her palm against it flat, and nods to me, and Tawzin and I unwrap our deerskins and hand them to the women. The way Mattapacque stares at Tawzin, his uneasy glance away, makes me think again something would have to be done soon.

I sit and Tawzin sits next to me, our sweat flowing and mixing. I give my wind-scattered thoughts to the smoke. They rush and tangle against the low ceiling. I hold my hands out, palms up, tobacco in one palm, and sing my sweat lodge chant.

I greet you, my elders.

I greet you, grandfather.

Sky-Holder, I offer tobacco. The blessings you gave my father, the life you gave him, four times these blessings you have given to me.

Thunderbirds, You who live in the West, accept this tobacco.

Great Black Hawk, blessed by my grandfather, accept this tobacco.

You who live in the East and walk in darkness, smoke this tobacco.

You who live in the South, disease-giver, smoke this tobacco.

Grandmother Moon, smoke this tobacco.

Grandmother Earth, I pour tobacco on you.

Eagles, smoke this tobacco.

All you spirits to whom my ancestors prayed, to you I offer tobacco. I sprinkle the tobacco on the earth, on the hot stones, where it flares and its smoke, free, dances with the Invisibles.

My mind clear now, I look at Tawzin. I can see a question pushing behind his mouth. I need this man, to tell me how the whites think; no other Piscataway had lived so long with them, had gone to their land, which had to be traveled to as if to the spirit world, across the water. Yet because of this in many ways Tawzin was still a child, one who did not know that in the sweat lodge one sings only songs of gratitude and leaves troubles on the other side of the opening. The *tassantasses* had taken him when he was twelve summers and what he had seen among them had pushed his proper dreams from his mind or did not allow them to grow into their proper places.

Ask, I say to him now, as I would to a child.

That stone Arawak took. Was it *manitou*?

Good. You're learning to see.

But I'm not, Tayac. To my sight, it was merely a stone.

I'm sorry, I say, feeling deep pity for this man who wanted to see so strongly that it blinded him.

How can stones be alive, Tayac?

I say nothing. The question is meaningless.

Tawzin closed his eyes. You'd say the question is meaningless, he says.

I wouldn't say it because it is.

Tayac, are all stones alive?

Some are.

How do you know which?

How do I know you are alive? I see you doing what live creatures do.

But how does the stone do what live creatures do?

Wisoe, look at it. It is Otter Stone.

You believe it is alive because it looks like an otter? Is there any other way the stone does what live creatures like you or I do?

It stops.

For some reason, Tawzin laughs.

But does it think? Does it know?

It doesn't know what you know. You don't know what it knows.

Tayac, do you worship the stone? Because it has *manitou?*

Everything does. You do. But I don't worship you, *Wisoe.*

But my spirit now is disturbing the sweat lodge. I rise, and we go outside. We dress ourselves and walk along the river.

Wisoe, my brother became Enemy and I had to stain myself with him, I say.

A line of egrets stand against the reeds, fishing in the river. Next to them are two blue herons. I look at the reeds behind them, bending in the wind and the motionlessness of the fishing birds moves into the reeds, stiffening them. I stare until their edges blur and I see my brother's face. It comes roaring at me over the water, its human features twisted into the beaks and feathers of the egrets and herons.

Kill them now, my brother whispers off the water.

Your madness crossed over into death with you, I tell him.

My brother's eyes glow, a wave in the river weaving his face.

Yes, Tayac, I know, Tawzin says.

Wisoe, then I will tell you what you know: I had to kill my brother because he wished to kill the whites as they arrived. Even as you shot your arrows at their ships. But I knew we couldn't stand their power. Some hate me for this act.

Tawzin says nothing. But he is not Piscataway enough that I can't read his face.

My enemy lives inside my spirit now as well, *wisoe.* He tears my spirit. My own face snarls at me in my dreams like an enemy. Tell me what I know, I say to him.

Tayac, you know this. Your vision told you how you must protect your people. But Trickster caws in your dreams. He asks: have you killed your brother to protect your people from his madness or to become Tayac? He asks: then how will you protect them Tayac?

Tawzin stays very still now. He has told me what I know, as I asked. But he is waiting to see if I will kill him now. I will not. He has spoken as a *wisoe*.

Yes, *wisoe,* I say. It is what I know. And it is the question I ask. But I know this also. Claiborne has come into the Chesapeake at Oyster Island, that he calls Kent, and is trading with the Susquehannocks, and even with the Iroquois. And Claiborne is stronger than Fleet and he gives his strength to the Susquehannocks. And he has enough *wampompeag* and trucke to trade for their beaver and he gives them warriors and weapons as well. And the Susquehannocks are attacking our towns. And our alliances are breaking. The Patuxents have begun raiding us again also. The Nanticokes and the Senecas are keeping us from the beaver trade which would allow us to trade with Claiborne and the Virginians. The Susquehannocks are growing rich and powerful because they have white allies. And we have none.

Tayac, Tawzin says, Claiborne makes the Susquehannocks hungry for what they did not have before, and then he feeds it to them. Now he is both that hunger and its soothing.

I close my eyes. For the first time I feel afraid. For he has named my fear. He has told me what I know.

Wisoe, I say, two days ago the Susquehannocks raided Yaocomaco again.

I know, he says. Yaocomaco is the place where he was first born Piscataway.

And now the Blackrobes have come to me asking for a place to live.

He looks at me. Tayac, I must tell you this.

The way he has begun is dangerous. But I must hear him. Speak.

Tayac, I tell you what you know. You think now Calvert can be your ally against the Susquehannocks. You think to use the power of the new whites to silence those who speak against you for killing your brother. But I tell you the *tasantasses* are too strong. Claiborne or Calvert, it does not matter. They will destroy Piscataway. They will destroy you with your own hunger. They will destroy you with their guns or with their God. With their hate or with their love.

He has told me what I know.

The breeze is playing back and forth on the skin of the river. It has changed, I am certain, though I can't exactly see the manner of it. The breeze is not playful but hysterical, full of words it wishes to whisper but that I can't understand. I have to learn to listen. In the last flowering time, on a hunt near Portopac, I urinated into the river, and my fingers found a small hardness, almost imperceptible, under the skin on the left side of my penis. It came and disappeared, under my touch, so that one moment I was sure it was there, the next I wasn't. A trickster demon. One of the hunters; they were from the Patabanos group, called out a joke about masturbation and I stared at the man, who cast his eyes down and moved away. I have not been Tayac long, and the way I became Tayac has caused some to provoke me, but they only do so once. That night I had my youngest wife stroke me until I hardened, then touch my skin with her fingers and tongue. There is nothing, she said, and I didn't need stories of demons if I wished her caress.

But the next night, I felt it again, a hardening at the cord, a tiny knot, and that night I tilted to the left, as if a finger were pressing the base of my shaft. By the following week the hard place and the tilt were certain and my youngest wife found both hilarious, though I was not as amused. I spoke to the shaman, Maquacomen, who told me what I knew: Kittamaquund, the knot is the spirit of your brother Uwanno. I grunted. Perhaps this was the shaman's way of telling me he agreed with those who say I killed my brother to become Tayac. But I think he spoke truly. It was what I would expect of my brother; he was a malicious jokester, and a tilted man, and if he had remained Tayac he would have unbalanced and tilted the entire people.

Uwanno is attempting to divert your seed now, the

shaman said, attempting to pour his own bent seed into your wives. There was nothing to do about the tilt, he said, but there was a chant that would bring the seed back in the right direction and foil the ghost.

I had performed the chant, but now I feel the river itself has changed in the same way, or is beginning to change, as if my brother's ghost and his bending ways are growing more powerful.

I touch the hard little bead under my flesh now and see my brother's grinning, demon's face.

The young women have waded back into the river, are plucking oysters again from the sandy bottom, filling their baskets. Their breasts sway gracefully with the motion. A picture of the very peace my brother's madness would have shattered. But there was something tense and waiting under it. I look away from the river, and my eyes sweep over Piscataway, the curved backs of the houses, the sunlight gleaming off the covering brown bark. Like breasts. Like skin stretched over bones. The exhalations of smoke pouring from hundreds of smoke holes. This is Piscataway, the mother town of the Piscataway, and the stakes in its surrounding palisade are tall and numerous as a forest, and a thousand warriors and their clans live here—all this that we sing in our songs. But in my vision it suddenly seems hollowed, the tree posts of the palisade, the *witchotts*, longhouses, all standing in their form and seeming strength but their insides softened to dust by termites. Held together in a breath that will blow out. My eyes drift back; it is as if I am trying to gather my world to me with them, hold it a little longer. The surface of the river riffles in the wind, one way, then the other, madly, without pattern.

Tayac, Tawzin whispers, the *tasantasses,* how do we know they are alive?

I stare at him.

They don't stop, he says.

Ezekiel came into my dreams that night, and not for the last time. His hand scuttling six-fingered and quick across the ground to me. A shadow darting rock to rock, hunkering down in ruts, until its final charge. Flesh woven from night itself. I lay helpless and paralyzed watching, my blood thickened to sap, as the padded fingers patted and pinched the skin of my face, searching my features, touching here and there as light as breezes, but stinking of carrion. Pushing into my nostrils, one fingertip and then the other, as if to pack in their thick stinging stink. Running long nails over the top of my scalp and then the fingers working at the skin there, scratching and gashing, opening the egg of the skull, pushing and wiggling inside, and as if I were above myself, I could see the wet gray of my brain writhing and shrinking under that black touch, the crevices seething, opening visions that dropped out onto the ground as fat white worms.

I looked down at my wrists and his black hands were there and they were mine now with no stump of a digit on the one but each six-fingered and flesh melted to my wrists and the fingers undulating like the tentacles of a sea anemone. They worked the wood in a blur of speed, shaping gallows and crosses, a forest of them, a forest of crucifixes, we were covering the island with them, we were covering the land, tearing apart the Ark and rebuilding it to those lines. My black hands jerked me after them to the edge of the sea, and the Beast, the Carbunca, rose, encrusted with seaweed and barnacles, and St. Clement, his face the white round face of a Spanish priest rising dripping with him, fastened tight to the Carbunca's scaled back with the chains of the anchor, his mouth gaping like a fish, my black fingers patting over Father Black's torn, martyred body, my nails slitting his skin, my hands pushing him under the waves, his eyes searching mine frantically. When he was gone the hands told me what to do and I began gathering the crosses and tearing down the gallows, and in the center of the scorched island were Meg and my boys, their flesh blossomed with running sores, and around them my black hands shaped and fashioned a coffin and the wood of it was white and bleached and my demon fingers clawed its surface until it bled and flamed and I saw their faces screaming, bursting into roses in the center of the flames, and I never in my dreams saw them again. And I looked at my hands and saw their color was staining up into my wrists, my forearms, their blackness running up the flesh of my arms, as swiftly and inexorably as the coming of night.

Clever hands, White said.

BUT THE NEXT MORNING the light was strong and all about me was sure and solid and I reclined in the shade under a locust tree, the tip of the shadow that sheltered me just touching the shadow of the cross. I was on a slight slope, so that my head was lower than my splayed feet. I looked through their frame at the beach and the expanse of river, its surface rippled by a breeze, and at the far bank, the leaves of the trees there brushed by the same exhalation. When I sat up, several deer mincing warily along the shore flipped up their faces at me. Beyond them, a school of fish churned the surface of the river, flashing, silver-bladed knives swarming to an assassination.

A group of women were washing garments, their skirts gathered up at their waists so their lower legs were bare in the water. I watched Father White walk over to them, a bundle of soiled linens in his hand. Agnes Stotsberry, a stout, red-faced harridan from Wessex, waved a stained shift at him and yelled, "Come on, father, gie it 'ere." Next to her, pale Jane Carston, a bruise staining her cheek, straightened up and shouted, grinning, "Nay, t'me, father; she's never done a man's things afore." Some of the sailors, lounging around the beached skiff, jeered at White, who shrugged in exaggerated helplessness and threw the bundle out towards the river. Something in the awkwardness of that toss drew the contempt I felt for the man to a peak. I could barely look at him. The two women both lunged, slipped and fell into the water, cursing.

"Don't you wenches know how to wash? You stays on the dry, you puts the garments in the wet," a sailor yelled, then jumped in, joined by other hooting sailors, except for one who strutted after White, imitating the priest's frantic, worried scurry along the bank, his wildly gesticulating arms. I watched the women hauled out, watched Father White's under-linens swirling away, swallowed by the New World.

I looked for the slave, Ezekiel, but I didn't see him. Though I felt him, a dark shadow on my morning.

At that moment White turned towards me and smiled helplessly, as if some secret connected us. The smile of a hanged man, moving with flies. Suddenly supplanted by Leonard Calvert, standing between myself and White, casting his shadow over me. Complimenting me on the cross I had erected. A tall comely man with black curls tumbling about his shoulders, his lips pink and womanish. I envisaged them, the lips, gone. I started to rise.

"Nay, sit good carpenter. I'll join you."

This his manner. Congenial with all, gentle-born, free or indentured. He would joke softly with the women, bawdily with the men, reversing that manner where he saw necessary. Their fawning response to him sickened me. He was your true gentleman, not like some so tight-arsed they couldn't give a wink or a friendly smile, the colonists would say, and I wondered if I had not been given special eyes to see the world, a witch sight that saw not what they did, but rather the slight sneer hooked onto the ends of his smile, the specious expression of interest he fit to his face like a mask when he would ask a man where he came from, who his relatives were, what he sought in the New World. Seducing them. It was Calvert's kingdom we were going to carve out of this wilderness now and the little king needed subjects and soldiers and their adoration.

"I've built many such to the glory of God," I said to him, putting a hand on the cross.

Calvert nodded gravely. "I like to look at it. It is simple and sturdy and from the wood of this land. What trees are these, carpenter?"

"Chestnut, hickory and oak, for the most part; some pine, some locust, some sycamore, your lordship."

"Sycamore," Calvert said, as if proud to place the word between his teeth. "I watched you. In England I don't think I would have ever stood for hours and watched someone like you working, carpenter. Let me tell you a story—about Avalon. My father, Lord Baltimore, was an extraordinary man. While others talked of America as a forsaken, cursed wilderness where we might send our criminals and scum, he saw a *tabula rasa*. A blank page. Do you understand? You do, I see that you do. But what he didn't see was what he never needed to see. The structure built underneath. The exact tool necessary, let us say, to push the bark from wood and leave it clean and smooth as skin. The tool you used, whose name I will know."

"Adze."

"Adze. Indeed. Do you know what the old Avalon was, carpenter?"

"It was a magical kingdom, your lordship."

Calvert looked at me sharply. "You sometimes speak, James Hallam, with a degree of learning that doesn't fit the frame of a carpenter."

"I was fifteen years a soldier."

"Of that I know also, but it explains nothing. Wasn't there a Hallam family in Kent? A Silas Hallam?"

"Before I went for a soldier, when I was a child, the Jesuits taught me, a poor boy in their charge, to read, and gave me what to read as well," I said, the half-truth I had learned to reel out without thinking. The mention of my father's name made me nervous. I wondered if Calvert was goading me from the strength of knowledge I didn't know he had. "That much I will tell you, your lordship. Yet I recall that once, in England, I heard your lordship say that we would be born fresh on the other side of the water."

Calvert laughed. "So I did. And nothing more need be said of any man's past—unless there is need otherwise, for the saftey or prosperity of the colony." He smiled, remaining silent for a time, as if to print that smile and his stare like a promise. Or an invitation to say more.

He sighed. "Well, it's as you say, then, Hallam—Avalon was a magical kingdom. In a magical kingdom, winter does not lock the land from October to May, and fruits and crops and shelters to dwell within spring into existence at one's magical bidding, in the way that wine and fine coaches and hunting hounds and servants always appeared for one in England, as if by magic."

"Aye, if one is used to such matters, your lordship."

"Yes, such is my point, Hallam." He put his hand on the cross. "Lovely wood," he said. "Of course there's nothing like this in England anymore, nothing like these forests we've seen. Nor this hard sun and the harder rain that will fall this afternoon and the cold winter months coming. As they came to Avalon."

He waved at the rim of trees around the clearing. I could see the naked savages now, their eyes gleaming from the shadows of the trees behind us. Yesterday, when they had come closer, begun mingling with our sentinels, Calvert had ordered the ship's cannon shot off, to impress them. They had disappeared immediately, but were starting to draw towards us, around us again, like a child whose finger has been burnt but who still remains fascinated by the flame.

"Unlike my father, I don't believe in magical kingdoms," Calvert said. "We need shelter. Strong and simple and sturdy and from the wood of this land. We need to learn from the natives." He pointed suddenly at them. I saw a man raise his bow. I started to rise; there were no sentinels nearby. Another Indian put his hand on the arrow shaft and the first lowered the bow. And vanished into the trees, and the others as well, as if they had never been there. "Does that sound foolish to you, good Hallam?"

"Nay, and why should it, your lordship?"

"It does to some." Then he said, "Kittamaquund," rolling the outlandish word out with the same satisfaction he had said "sycamore." "The Tayac Kittamaquund," he said, to my look, as if the addition of more nonsensical syllables would answer my silent question. "The Piscataway emperor Kittamaquund, James. Ruler of the Anacostan, the Matta-woman, the Nanjemoy, the Portopac, the Choptico, and the Yaocomaco," he said proudly, the newly discovered names of tools he meant to wield. "I mean to treat with that red gentleman, my good Hallam. You see, when the Virginia colonists came, they made the mistake of thinking the savages were as inconsequential as the weather in Avalon, and had nothing to teach them. It is not a mistake I will repeat."

I bowed my head, feigning respect at this patent wisdom. He was staring at the river, at the far bank, and when he spoke it was to himself and I was only to be there, like the savages, as silent audience, an idiot mask of interest fastened to my face. Nod and beam.

"Arrogance, Hallam, that is the word," he said gravely. "At first the Powhatans gave the Virginia colonists corn and fish and game, and even attempted to teach them to hunt."

Two of the savages—different men—suddenly reappeared, behind Calvert, not ten feet away. One was tall and so thin as to almost be skeletal. Like the other, he had a long lock of hair over his left ear; the right side of his head was shaven, his face daubed with red paint, like the paw prints of an animal. The second Indian, shorter, squatter, wearing a necklace of shark teeth, was sitting at the first's feet, staring up at him gape-mouthed. Neither had bow or arrows. The tall Indian waved his hands wildly and contorted his face. It took me a few seconds before I realized he was aping Calvert: the grandiose gestures, the upturned nose delicately sniffing the air. I kept my face blank. Calvert was speaking of the Virginians, telling me what I already knew: how they had wasted their time and provisions searching for gold and precious jewels and then repaid the Indians by hanging them when they would not reveal where these were to be found. How the Powhatans had withdrawn from them then, hadn't come anymore with corn and game, and neither did the rain, though the winter did and the Virginians starved and ate bark, and the gentlemen adventurers ate their horses. And then the Powhatans. Hunted them as if they were rabbits, boiled their bones for soup, until Opechancanough rose against them. Calvert telling me this as if I would be surprised to hear of gentlemen eating those that fed them.

He looked off to the river, as if contemplating the Virginians' folly. Presenting his noble profile to me. The tall savage followed suit, poked his forefinger into the air, then brought it around and poked it up into his bum, crossing his eyes. I bit back my laughter. But a dark thought crossed my mind. Such humor was a kind of seeing intelligently, and not a gift I wished the wood I'd cut to have. I met the Indian's eyes. He stared at me for a moment, then shuddered and slowly squatted, his eyes still fixed to mine, widening under the black circles he had painted around them.

"Aye, your lordship, Oliver Standrop was one of the Virginia colonists; he's mentioned as much t'me," I said. Then, as a goad, said: "Standrop tells us that William Claiborne was different than the others though. More clever, he says."

Calvert reddened; I could see him bringing himself into control. "That gentleman," he said finally, "sits on land given by the king as part of Lord Baltimore's charter. He has taken three islands in the Chesapeake and has set up a trade monopoly with the Susquehannocks for the northern beaver fur. They control the trade with the Iroquois nations and will only deal with him. Oh, Standrop is right—Claiborne is no fool and I will not let my dislike of the man blind me to the cleverness of his enterprise. He understood that we need alliances with the savages if we are to remain in this country. He is no fool, but he is a devil, Hallam, a man whose only God is Profit. He cares nothing for the souls of the Indians."

"Aye, a pity," I said smoothly, "that such a man so prospers."

The two savages, I saw, had disappeared. As if they had been Creatures of my mind.

"He has a consortium of Puritan merchants in London financing him and pushing his case in Court. They would be quite happy to see my Catholic colony fail."

"I understand, your lordship."

"You're a Roman, is that right?"

"Yes, my lordship."

Calvert pushed a lock of hair from in front of his eyes. "Then lordship or carpenter, we're brothers in Christ. My father vowed to establish a Catholic kingdom in America. And so we are here, good Roman Hallam. Yet do you know how many Catholics there are on the Ark?"

I wondered, not for the first time, if there had been but a slight bend or twist of History, if, in a word, my father, who was no less adamant in his Catholicism than Calvert's, had put his nose up the king's arse as Calvert's had and we would have kept our estate—if so-planted I would have grown as pompous as this fool. A fate from which I'd been rescued. It had been years since I thought of my father: I had exiled him from mind and memory as his stubbornness had exiled his family from hearth and land, and it was only now, in front of this fop mocked by the savages he would woo, that I found myself grateful to the way my father's foolhardiness had forced me into a tempering life that had heated and forged my heart.

"Not many," I said.

Calvert laughed. "Aye, exactly that amount. Of one hundred and seventy-two souls, thirty-four are Catholic. My brother thought many more would come: but it seems that their faith isn't strong enough—they would rather be persecuted in England than start anew here."

"Mirabilia Dei," I said.

"James Hallam, you impress me, when you aren't worrying me. I speak too much. I must be cautious, you see, and not have our Catholics pray in public or consecrate the host or in any other way offend Anglican sensibilities." He stared brightly at me. "But this I promise you: I will have a church, even if I have to hide it in these woods."

"As I told Father White, sirrah, in this matter I will serve you as best I can."

"I have no doubt you will, my good man."

"Shall we be building here then, your lordship? On St. Clement's Island?"

He peered around him, his eyes bright. "Something in me hates islands, James Hallam." He smiled. "Though perhaps those are words an Englishman should not utter."

"Nay, your lordship. They sound the very definition of an Englishman t'me."

"S'truth, Hallam, and well said. I want no islands. I hunger for the continent itself. No, we shan't build our colony cut off from the body of the New World, or from its red inhabitants, as if we were visitors in a vestibule. That is what Smith did in Virginia, at first. As I said, I hope to come to an agreement with the red emperor. The Tayac," he said, rolling the word in his mouth again, as if he could taste it. "For a foothold on the banks of the river. Soon, it is my hope, you will have the place where you may begin your true work."

"As you wish, my lord."

Calvert threw back his head and laughed. "As I wish. Dour Hallam. Something about you opens the flow of my tongue, but you're like a tree, holding your secrets—from everyone but the chopper."

I bowed again slightly, to the question, to the threat in the question.

"Well, your wit is in your hands, not your tongue and your hands are what I need," Calvert said, as if persuading himself. "I have enough men with clever tongues."

Father White came out of the trees at the edge of the clearing. The black walked behind him, his hands folded before him as if he were still manacled. His eyes, however, were not downcast. They stared across the space of the clearing to me, to the cross I stood under. I put my hand on it, as I had seen Ezekiel put his hand on the gallows. As I had put my own on the hanged man's legs. And the African drew back his lips into the hanged priest's smile. As if this were the silent language between us.

"And what of him?" I asked Calvert.

Something in my voice made the governor raise his eyebrows.

"Him? Father White? What mean you, man?"

"I mean the slave."

"Good carpenter, that is why we bought him on Barbados—to help you. He is a man who has built churches."

"And gallows," I said, as if speaking of my own heart.

"I am sure we will need both in this enterprise. This new world is not that new. He will help you. He will be another pair of hands for you to do your work."

I took a breath. "And to whom will those hands belong?"

Calvert looked at me steadily. "Why to the one who purchased him, to me. Though, in truth, I've given him to White for now. But he is my man, as you are."

"For five years," I said, then stopped, silently cursing my fugitive tongue.

"Hallam, don't permit the freeness of my discourse with

you to allow yourself to take me for a weakling. I understand, sirrah, that you are my man for five years. And he shall be as well."

"I don't understand."

"What have you to understand? The agreement of indenture is something you signed willingly enough."

"Yet is he not a slave, my lord?"

"Only as much as you." Calvert shrugged. "I don't believe in African slavery, Hallam. I don't want it to be a foundation we build upon here. I saw its instrumentalities in the islands: the planters enslave themselves to slavery and make brutes of themselves. It is an unChristian institution to my mind."

I looked away, struggling to keep my disgust at this hypocrisy out of my face and voice. "Some say it is a natural state for the Africans, their only salvation as they have not the capacity nor the desire to turn to God."

Calvert stared. "One day I would know thee, James Hallam, the brain behind those hands. Yes, those who gain most from the trade often have that sentiment, Hallam. We have a free black with us—Mathias DaSousa. Do you find DaSousa's human capacities or facilities of lower state than those of any white man on board?"

In fact I respected DaSousa; the man was the best gambler I'd ever met, sharp. But I wasn't interested in the subject of African inferiority. I was only interested in Ezekiel.

"Your lordship, it would be a blessing and an honor to build your church," I said.

"So you've told me, more than once. But it is our church, James Hallam. And finish your agreement—I hear the tail of an 'however' growing from it now."

"There's no such, Lordship. Only a carpenter's price."

Calvert looked me up and down slowly, his face suddenly thoughtful, as if I were a tool whose name he had yet to learn.

"As you said, your hands and labor belongs to me for the next five years," he said sharply.

"Aye, your lordship. But it is my notion that the king and parliament and your brother also have forbidden the building of any Roman house of worship. Such work as you'd have me do would be contrary to law and authority."

"You are a Catholic, Hallam. You know whose law we obey."

"Indeed, but we must give unto Caesar, m'lord."

Calvert's face went red. "Don't be impertinent, carpenter."

"Begging your pardon, but I take a goodly risk in such building, sirrah. A risk I will take, for you and my faith, as your lordship says. But I would have just recompense for it."

"Speak what you would have." Calvert stared. His good fellowship had disappeared. I felt like laughing, or spitting, or both.

"A pair of hands for me, you have said. So be it. But I want those hands, milord. I want them during the years of my indenture, and after, and forever. I wish him given to me, your lordship, as part of my Order of the Country." I recited what was owed at the end of the indentured period from the agreement of indenture, each word grooved into my skull, the beginning of what I would take back from the world: "One good cloth suit, a shift of white linen, a pair of stockings or shoes, two hoes, one axe, three barrels of corn, fifty acres of land. All that, lordship, that's what comes to me, all that and one pair of black hands. Another pair of hands to do my work. Not as indentured servant, and not as yours, but as my own. I will build your church and your town also, your lordship. But I will have those hands for myself. That is my price."

I saw the ring of savages in the tree line again. When I looked again the Indians seemed to be closer. The wind moved through the tops of the trees, shivering the branches, flipping the leaves into a dance of silver coins.

From the Narrative of Father Andrew White, S.J.

The Governor had taken with him as a companion, on his voyage to the Emperor, Henry Fleet, *a Captain from the Virginia colony, a man especially acceptable to the Savages, well versed in their language, and acquainted with the country. The man was, at first, very intimate with us, afterwards being mislead by the evil counsels of one* Clayborne, *he became very hostile to us, and excited the natives to anger against us, by all the means in his power. In the meantime, however, while he was still on friendly terms with us, he pointed out to the Governor, a spot so charming in its situation, that Europe itself can scarcely show one to surpass it.*

Going about nine leagues (that is about 27 miles) from St. Clements, we sailed into the mouth of a river, on the north side of the Potamack, which we named after St. George. This river, (or rather arm of the sea,) like the Thames, runs from south to north about twenty miles before you come to fresh water. At its mouth are two harbors, capable of containing three hundred ships of the largest size. We consecrated one of these to St. George: the other, which is more inland, to the Blessed Virgin Mary.

The left side of the river was the abode of King Yaocomico. *We landed on the right-hand side, and going in about a mile from the shore, we laid out the plan of a city, naming it after St. Mary. And, in order to avoid every appearance of injustice, and afford no opportunity for hostility, we bought from the King thirty miles of that land, delivering in exchange, axes, hatchets, rakes, and several yards of cloth. This district is already named* Augusta Carolina. *The* Susquehanoes, *a tribe inured to war, the bitterest enemies of King* Yacomico, *making repeated inroads, ravage his whole territory, and have driven the inhabitants, from their apprehension of danger, to seek homes elsewhere. This is the reason why we so easily secured a part of his kingdom: God by this means opening a way for His own Everlasting Law and Light. They move away every day, first one party and then another, and leave us their houses, lands and cultivated fields. Surely this is like a miracle, that barbarous men, a few days before arrayed in arms against us, should so willingly surrender themselves to us like lambs, and deliver up to us themselves and their property. The finger of God is in this, and He purposes some great benefit to the nation. Some few, however, are allowed to dwell among us until next year. But then the land is to be left entirely to us.*

Tawzin's Song

From the top of the bluff, I stood and looked at the two rivers, as my two halves, Piscataway and *tassantass*, gathered themselves in the meadow behind me. It had been from this place I had been taken, snatched from the water, as my friends and I would pluck oysters and catch crabs in basket traps, or simply scoop them up from the bottom. Scooped and shucked of name and memory. Myself, not the oysters. Although those too for all I know. Now those that had taken me had come here after me and this place, Yaocomaco itself, would be peeled of its name and its memories, as I had been. As the river below me, as Mattapani, already had been. Though the Potomac was still too big for the whites to swallow. On the side of the bluff lapped by that river, the shore was black, jagged rocks crusted with ancient shells, and the water choppy and frothed, but as soon as a canoe glided into the smaller river, as mine had that morning, the water became smooth as skin, opening into a wide calm bay formed from a bow bend in the river. Opening into the waters of my childhood. Below me now. If I turned I would see the longhouses of Yaocomaco town, where I had been born, the forest cleared to about a mile east of the river, with stands of hickories and elms and oaks left for shade around the neat patchwork of longhouses and cornfields in the center of the town. Everything as I remembered, or as I remembered remembering. The dream vivid in the moment just before awakening, when it would vanish.

This was the first time I had come back here. An Englishman had stolen me from these rivers, and a Jew had brought me back to them. But not to here. Something in my spirit had been reluctant to see this place again. I had learned that memory is the purest and the only owning and I hadn't wanted to mar that memory. When I returned to my people, Jacob and I had traveled north along the *Catawba*, the Great Trail, from Jamestown where we had landed, and I had not turned on the fork that would have taken me back to Yaocomaco, but instead had come to Piscataway town, where Kittamaquund had remembered me, or saw an advantage in my knowledge of the whites, and took me into his own longhouse. Kittamaquund had killed me in the *huskanau*, the initiation I had never been given because the whites had taken me before its time, and Kittamaquund had drawn me from the sweatlodge into my rebirth, and named me *tawzin*, a chief's son, to honor my mother. Kittamaquund had sung me the song of my father and mother and their long deaths at the Seneca's torture stakes. Kittamaquund had given me my manhood back. Now Kittamaquund would give my childhood away to that which had taken my childhood. Another *huskanau*.

I stood now as the crowd of English and Piscataway, my two halves, my two childhoods, gathered behind me here near the confluence of the two rivers, and I waited for the *werowance* Yaocomaco of the Yaocomacos to give away the place whose name he bore, at the urging of Kittamaquund, the Tayac of the Piscataway. The emperor, I had heard Calvert call him, a word no more fitting than the names they called the rivers or the name they had called me. Give yourself, the Tayac had told Yaocomaco, so that you may save yourself. It was the same counsel he must have given to himself. For Yaocomaco was a part of the Piscataway nation and Piscataway was the Tayac's name also.

And perhaps his counsel was true. So I told myself. Yaocomaco had abandoned half of the town already anyway and would soon lose it all to the Susquehannocks if his people remained. Earlier I had gone with Jacob to see the remains of the two longhouses burned on the last Susquehannock raid. The blackened, splintered saplings of their frameworks stuck from the earth like curved ribs; in their mud-churned inner cavities were burnt flesh and bones, as if the houses were gutted animals. I had found blood trails still wet in the forest from captives who had been taken alive, to be tortured on the other side of the Potomac, from where the raiding party had come. The Susquehannocks would keep them alive for days—they might still be alive at this moment—flaying and burning them slowly, cutting them from themselves, as the Senecas had done to my parents, as I had seen the English drawing and quartering a prisoner at the London Tower, as the *auto de fe* Jacob had told me about in Salamanca. As the whites cut me from myself. Near the river, I had found a small, new mound of dirt, in one of the burial grounds. When Jacob and I dug into it, we had uncovered four more bodies: a man, two women and a child. From their faces and otherwise intact bodies, I could see they had been buried alive, something the Susquehannocks did with people they considered cursed or unlucky. It was that custom which had spurred our mad digging, in the hope some might have survived. Instead we were cursed by their spirits. As they would still be buried or burning in the *werowance* Yaocomaco's inner vision, his *odinnonk*. For he bore his people's name. Here, he was saying now to the whites, I give all this to you: those screams, that fire and murder. Take it from me. So I told myself. Here, Kittamaquund, who was called Piscataway, who was called Tayac, was saying to Calvert, place your flesh here, between my flesh and its murder. I understood him. I understood the Tayac's wisdom. So I told myself.

But how much of yourself can you give to save yourself? I had said to him. How much of us can you give away in order to save us?

Go to them, Kittamaquund had said. Answer that question for me. Be my eyes and ears. But not my tongue.

The noise of the crowd increased behind me. I turned. I saw Andrew White walking towards me, as if out of my memory. He had aged greatly, his face thinned and dried,

tight on the bones of his skull. I had gone and I had returned
here and now Andrew White was passing near me, walking
next to Calvert, and John Altham, the young priest who had
come to Piscataway. The sight of him, of White, sent a cold,
heavy shock through me. I had not seen him since we were
together in the monastery in Spain where he'd brought me to
share his exile. Though I knew he would be here. He turned
suddenly and swept the crowd with his eyes, and our eyes
met briefly. As if I had drawn him to me. The blood burned
under the skin of my cheeks. But there was no spark of
recognition in his eyes. I wasn't surprised. Men saw only
what they expected to see and their eyes fled from everything
else. I moved closer. He was waving his arms in the air, as if
to pull it all to him. Like a thief. Pull this place to him. A
gesture I remembered also, proprietary, beckoning. I heard
him compare the forest near us to the clear lanes and ordered
rows of trees in a British park. As if this place had been
created for him and the other whites, had waited through time
for their arrival and claim.

"A man could drive a carriage through the trees," I heard
him say to Calvert, who nodded enthusiastically, and I wanted
to tell my old teacher, old captor, old tempter, how carefully
the Yaocomacos burnt out the brush and saplings to have
firing lanes for their arrows. Wanted to reveal White's
blindness about the nature of the world to him, as he had
once insisted on my own. But it would be useless. This
ground was being given now to people who would measure
it always against that cold wet island I was remembering more
and more as a dream, a nightmare that clawed itself into my
brain. My people, I had learned, or (I tried to convince
myself) remembered, called dreams and nightmares the true
world, and they were right for that nightmare was here and
was claiming my life again and planting its banners on me.

I turned away from him, from priests and governors and
Englishmen, and looked again over the edge of the bluff
above the confluence of the two rivers. One silence flowing

into another. It was nearly Spring now, the weather mild, and on the opposite bank the trees had just begun to burst into leaf, a green mist through which I could still see the memory of winter's bare branches. Under the honeysuckle matted bluffs were narrow sand or rock beaches, with stands of cypress and willow overhanging the banks in places, dappling them in cool shadow, the water pellucid or rippling with dazzles of reflected light, and at night, I remembered, the deep black of the river glowed with streaks and stars of phosphorescence, as if it were the reverse sky of the world of dreams.

"What beauty our eyes are to be blessed with," I heard White say to Calvert. They had come up behind me. I could not be quit of them.

Beauty, the Jesuits would say, only exists in counterpoint to ugliness, as Evil is needed to test and shape Good. Did my people understand beauty? It was a question I had asked myself before: would I understand beauty if I had not been taken from my people who live in such beauty that it is the air and light of their common vision? Yet my people had put the town of Yaocomaco in this place vulnerable to enemies, not only because of the abundance of game and fish here—but because it also fed a hunger they did not know was there until they saw this place that would fill it. I knew that because I had found it in my own heart now. Because it would be taken away now. At the urging of the Tayac, in his wisdom. Get thee from me, Kittamaquund had said to me, when I disagreed with his decision. Get thee hence and live amongst these strangers in our midst, and spy out the land, the Tayac had told me, or would have, if his words had perhaps been in the Hebrew I had heard from Jacob's lips, a language I had studied with Latin in the seminary where the Jesuits had tried to clear and replant my savage brain until it was as neat and fathomable to them as a British park.

And I turned again, because who could turn his back on what would eat him? And here was my people, the

Yaocomacos of the Piscataway nation, gathered on the open ground above the river, under the spread canopy of a large mulberry tree, and I tried to see them through the white eyes White had tried to give me, but when I looked I saw them as if this was their last gathering and they stood in the twilight of that day, a smell of woodsmoke and tidal water emanating from them, the men tall, their bodies sculpted, smoothly and heavily muscled, naked except for kneelength deerskin loincloths hanging down in front; the women, their brown nipples painted red, full breasted and graceful in the same dress, and some of the men with their faces daubed with red paint above their eyes and blue above their noses, or dotted from lips to ears, and some with their harsh black hair hanging long on both sides, and others, bowmen, with it roached on one side, and some with long locks of hair tied only at the left ear with a string of *roanoke*, and some tied at both, and the bowmen's faces and bodies black-striped, and totem animals painted on the chest and faces of the *werowance* and his *wisoes*, and on the war chiefs, the *cockorouses*, and the children naked of both paint and clothing, as once I had been.

And now with my Piscataway eyes I looked at the English. The gentry had put on their finery: wigs, their coils soiled and discolored; plumed hats, the feathers dropping; swords and sashes, and the men were sweating in velvet waistcoats with puffs of foam at their wrists, and the women in heavy, embroidered dresses, the clothing fuzzed with green mold from the voyage, and the indentured servants in armor for the occasion: metal and leather breastplates and crested helmets, long pikes, halyards, and heavy muskets that had to be supported on tripods. And the stink of them in the wind, with their matted and lousy hair falling out in patches under their wigs and helmets, teeth loose in rotting gums bleeding with scurvy so that rivulets of blood ran from the corners of some mouths, passing over open canker sores and swelling boils, their bodies cased with filth from the months of being held in their own sweat and waste on the ships. A sharp rank stench that brought all of unwashed Europe back from memory to my nostrils wafted off them like a heavy invisible garment. And I saw my people, my river-bathing people who revered and reveled in their sweatlodges, valiantly trying to remain polite and impassive. And I knew which of these two groups I stood in back of now, I would call my own, even though the whites had had me for seventeen years.

Yet, looking at the English, their pale skin and hair, their priests, the substantiation of everything that I had come to hate, I saw in that moment also an unwanted connection to them, for I was marked now by that place from which they came, as they had been marked: by the fever to leave it and the knowledge, in its very island nature, its tightening constricture, that they could; by the hunger for possibility that drove them, motley refugees, indentured servants and ragged heretics, like wind in their sails. I could see that restlessness in the barely contained tension of their limbs, in their stare at the green rim of land beyond. And in that unsettled need, still, as much as I didn't want it, I knew I was brother yet to all this ragged, bleeding, stinking, hopeful, dreamy, arrogant group of adventurers, as I was brother and son to the Piscataway, brother and son of both and so belonging to neither. And I knew the answer to my question to Kittamaquund. I knew everything would be given and nothing would be saved. I knew the song that would come, because I knew my own song. How I had given a little and a little and a little. How I refused even their food or water when they put the chains on me. How I would bite, snap my teeth at them like a captured wolf, when they came close. Until finally, after a week, I let my Piscataway spirit rest for a moment and allowed myself only a small taste of water, a bit of food. Only a little, and then a little more. Only a vision and only another vision, and a word, and a thought, and then their God. Only a little and a little until I was swallowed.

I saw that Yaocomaco was smiling at the gifts—axes,

hoes, cloth and *wampompeag* beads and *roanoke*—that the priest was presenting to him. Not seeing the power of the trap in them, as I had not seen when, a boy, I had laughed and taken a sailor's hand and climbed up on the deck to look more closely at what the whites wanted me to have. As Kittamaquund couldn't see their true power. My Tayac, who enjoyed his own wiliness, who thought he was using the whites to protect his people. Whose spirit was tormented by his brother's spirit. Who would save himself and us by giving himself and us.

I turned away again. I was spinning. Two other ships, large and small, had come to me. They gently bobbed, the pennants of St. George and St. Andrew snapping from their mastheads. A cannon from the Ark boomed and a ring of smoke spread and dissipated, a mutter spreading through the Yaocomacos with it, a quiver passing from one body to the other, rippling through their skins, as if they were one body. The *werowance* flinched, then waved his hand expansively over the village, over the lands and longhouses and fields he was leaving for the *tassantasses*.

Now both groups mingled together uneasily and began walking in a self-conscious procession towards the edge of the bluff. Towards me. It was a moment similar to all other moments in the world, marked by the same light and air and colors, but as I looked at this stinking, bleeding, arse-scratching, lice-bitten little crowd of English and my stoic, painted and beaded, Piscataway standing on a bluff over a river at the edge of America, it seemed to me that the air itself shifted, and I was conscious in it, and I was sure they were also, that from this point where the river turned a corner, from this moment there would be a difference in the direction and flow of time and the world.

Saint Marie's City

1638

This indenture made the <u>tenth</u> day of <u>May</u> in the yeere <u>1633</u> of our Soveraigne Lord King Charles, etc. betweene <u>James Hallam</u> of the one party, and the <u>Hon. Leonard Calvert</u> on the other party, Witnesseth, that the said <u>James Hallam</u> doth hereby covenant, promise, and grant to and with the said <u>Leonard Calvert</u>, his Executors and Assignes, to serve him from the day of the date hereof, untill his first and next arrivall in Maryland; and after for and during the terme of five yeeres, in such service and imployment, as the said <u>Leonard Calvert</u> or his assignes shall there imploy him, according to the customs of the Countrey in the like kind. In consideration whereof, the said <u>Leonard Calvert</u> doth promise and grant, to and with the said <u>James Hallam</u> to pay for his passing, and to find him with Meat, Drinke, Apparell and Lodging, with other necessities during the said terme; and at the end of said terme, to give him one whole yeers provision of Corne, and fifty acres of Land, according to the order of the countrey. In witnesse whereof, the said <u>James Hallam</u> hath hereunto put his hand and seale, the day and yeere above written.

Hallam's Song

At the house the slave Ezekiel and I had built for Leonard Calvert, on the bluff overlooking the river, I received from the thin white hand of the governor himself a good broadcloth suit, a white linen shift, and a pair of shoes and stockings. I wore none of these. I had taken to wearing the soft Indian moccasins, and I owned a pair of leather breeches and a lindsey-woolsey shirt and a broad-brimmed hat. I was given two axes, one hoe, and three barrels of corn: the axes had already been in my possession, owned by my use, for two years, and I owned already also a set of carpenter's tools, a barrel of nails, a string of beaver traps, a musket, a log dugout canoe I had made myself, copying the Piscataway style, and a barken canoe Ezekiel had fashioned. I was given fifty acres of land in the tract south of the settlement called Saint Michael's Hundred, which reached from St. Inigoes Creek south about twelve miles to Point Lookout, at the confluence of the Potomac and the Chesapeake. I chose my acreage against a creek just above the narrowing of land to the Point. It was an area of marsh and heavy forest and Yaocomacos came from their new village across the river to hunt and trap beaver there, and at times, Powhatans and Susquehannocks entered the country at will from this place also, to hunt or to raid. Thus the land I had chosen was considered undesirable and dangerous. But it contained abandoned Yaocomaco longhouses near the creek, and I burned all but three of these, and these I kept for my house and one small shelter for a pen and one for a barn.

I left behind in the settlement of Saint Marie's seven houses that the black and I had erected with our hands, and more houses and structures whose construction I had supervised, including two ordinaries, a stockade fort, the governor's house, and the first Catholic church built in British America. I left a field around the church that had already been taken for a graveyard, and in it the three graves I had laid out next to one another, in a small circle, as if around a table in a hot tavern in Barbados: Standrop, Barnes, and Hervey—the first dead of malaria, the second of typhus, the third of a Susquehannock arrow—as if they were monuments to the trinity of ill Humors that had killed more of us than they spared these last five years. I left them in the ground, with three out of five of those who had first landed in this place. I left behind a town called St. Marie's; the Indian town of Yaocomaco nearly erased now, and as I walked away from Calvert's house, a free man, I could see it forgetting itself, its history and its name, as I was trying to do.

And I left behind the mask of solicitous subservience I had worn over my face for all my years as a soldier and all my years as an indentured servant. I felt it slough off me as I stepped into the dugout and glided into a hazy hot summer day on the river and I felt both free and naked, vulnerable to the world and with the same need the town had of finding a new way to call myself.

And I was given, as a gift for my work on the church, and beyond the order of the country entitled to me under the articles of indenture, enough capital to pay the surveyor's fee and buy seeds for tobacco and corn, and enough for the clerk of deeds fee, and I was given also one iron pot, and one feather bed, three sows and one eleven-fingered African slave.

Ezekiel's Song

At times, when I was so tired that my dreams and the hard light of day bled into each other, I wondered if two men, alone in the strange forest of a strange land, would not have to find each other, no matter that one was master, one slave. Then you're still a fool, I heard my name-giver tell me. Hallam worked me like a beast of burden, spoke to me less than he would a mule. We cleared trees, planted, repaired the abandoned Yaocomaco longhouses he wanted to use as living quarters and outbuildings. The main longhouse was small for a Piscataway dwelling, only perhaps twenty feet by five feet: the larger ones I had seen would embrace generations of Indians. My first sight of one of those gatherings, old and young flesh packed together, knitted by smoke and laughter, had threaded a memory back to Dahomey, though perhaps it was only my own emptiness that pulled the shimmer and shadow of those African houses into my mind.

The longhouse Hallam had taken was tight-built, its frame of ashwood arches softened in the river, bent around a form of pegs set just in the water; a trap door smoke hole in the ceiling, a latticed overhead platform, all neat and airy, and none of that truly of concern to me, for from our first night Hallam had me crawl into the small pen next to the longhouse and I had been shackled to the centerpole, and shackled every night afterwards, and whenever Hallam went off to hunt.

For the first time in my years as a slave what had made me valuable and kept me alive and even sometimes privi-leged—the skill of my hands—was now my enemy, hated by my master, as if their power leached off the power of his own, Hallam's, hands. I cleared stumps and planted two acres of tobacco, and no corn, though it was Calvert's law to plant one acre of that crop for each of the other. Hallam hunted and fished and trapped beaver instead and kept me on the edge of hunger. I worked the tobacco when it came up until my hands were stripped of flesh, pulling the tough skin-cutting weeds from around the plants, pulling off the green horned worms one by one from the leaves, hauling fresh water from the spring, hundreds of cupped green hands demanding to be filled. My hands were stripped and bent and I feared for the loss of their cunning. Once, stooped over a row of tobacco plants I saw Hallam looking at them. It was one of the few times I saw a smile on the man's face.

I REMEMBER another time. Another smile. In Dahomey, we had ceremonies to mark the changes of season in the world, and in a human life. Planting, reaping, feasting. Birth, menses and pubic hair, marriage, death. For a slave though, all seasons in existence tremble on the expressions on his master's face, the earthquakes or tornadoes of flesh and spirit that will determine the pain or lack of pain given to the day. On that day Hallam and I had finished the temple to White's God, to the White God, to the only diety I believed in and shared with Hallam, which was the building itself. I'd worked behind Hallam, correcting the imperfections, the small tacks and perversities of his labor: off center lines, slopes, angles that his hands would work into the wood—not mistakes; I could tell he was too skilled for that, and yet not deliberate either. It was as if his hands twisted to some twisting of his heart. In Dahomey, in the village whose name would no longer come to my mind, even when called and called, Hallam would have never been allowed near wood; what was broken in him came out broken in the world. So I had worked. Without words. Next to Hallam, behind him, before his unblinking eyes, always silently. The adze stroking, the shavings loosening from the surface in long curls and revealing the bright muscular whiteness of the wood underneath, under the skin of bark. Hands on adze, on axe, on plane, six-fingered brown and five-fingered white side by side. If I spoke words, Hallam would collect them in the secret purse he kept inside his body until he had all of me. Until he had soul as well as body. I would try to keep my soul. Though I knew then my body would be Hallam's. Hallam had told me so every day. And those last days, as we finished the church, he would also add the word: soon. Soon now, Ezekiel. Soon your bones will rise to my hands. Soon. The Susquehannocks, I had heard, had a method of torture wherein they would wrap soaked deerhide strips tightly around a prisoner's forehead and neck and privates and when the sun dried these, they would tighten and slowly strangle the flesh. The man who had given me his name had told me that freedom was only the right of a white skin. But in all the days of my slaving on Barbados I had never felt my skin tighten like a strangling hide on my body as it did then.

And near the end of that day's work done together on a thing built out of the tug of hatred between us, I had separated myself from Hallam and went into the interior of the temple, its ceiling high, the room for the worshippers cool and full of shadows. I touched the altar, trying to remember prayers to Gods whose names also no longer could be called. I touched what I had carved to White's dream-vision, the whites' dream-vision, the pain they worshipped: the naked man hanging from the cross, the women clustered at his feet. But I had given the man on the cross the soul of the man whose name I had taken, and the white man's face that hung on it now was like a mask over the true face my hands had touched into the wood. When the priest had come to look, he had frowned, seeing what was there but not seeing it as he was used to seeing things: his heart understood whose form this was, but his eyes saw a white man. I had laughed, to myself, secretly. And Hallam had smiled, smiled once and terribly, seeing immediately what my hands, the hands of Ezekiel, had done.

ONE NIGHT I WOKE in my pen to the sound of a soft
scraping outside. A wind, I thought, but there was something
more rhythmic about it. A painted face appeared, a stiff roach
of hair from forehead to nape on a shaved head. Another face.
I sat up, jerking my right arm up instinctively as I did, to the
length of the shackle chain. Both faces smiled. An instant
later they disappeared, and I heard a soft grunt, a thud, a
moan, and by the time I got to the entrance the two were on
the ground, the blood flowing from their cracked skulls black
in the moonlight, and Hallam was kneeling over them,
holding the top of one man's roach with one hand, cutting
back the flap of his scalp with a knife held in the other. I had
seen fights, had had them in the cane fields of Barbados,
flurries of crazed machete slashings, born of pressed rage
and heat and the brief, ecstatic freedom of inflicting instead
of receiving pain and death, but I had never seen a man kill
so quickly. Mohawk, Hallam grunted, not looking up. Be a
good gift for the Susquehannock. Mayhaps they'll come to
love me, heh nigger? And it was another time I saw Hallam
smile.

More Indians came after that, but they came with Hallam,
and often he went with them, sometimes for days, and at first
he left me shackled, some food and water next to me when
he remembered. They were Susquehannocks, not the
Yaocomaco Piscataway I had come to know in the town, and
they would only be here for raids, and I didn't know why
Hallam was with them. They treated him with solemn respect.
Perhaps they had seen him kill.

ON THE DAY the shackles were taken off, I was working in
the tobacco when I heard Hallam yell to me from the creek at
the bottom of the hill to bring the Indian spears—sharpened
stakes—we used for fishing. I went into the longhouse and

gathered them, then ran down to Hallam, who was cursing at me to hurry. The narrowed end of the creek where it broke into a fan of cord grass that ran back into the forest was boiling: the usually mirror-calm water seemed to be whipping itself into an acre of agitated, seething foam. Closer, I saw it was alive with fish: huge blues that had driven a school of alewives into the shallows to feed on them. Hallam was standing nearly waist deep in the midst of the swirl, catching the blues in his hands and throwing them up on the bank. A flopping pile was there already, some of the fish two and three feet in length, writhing like muscles stripped out of a body but still alive. Muscles with teeth; I could see the blood in the water around Hallam's knees where the blues had torn into him in their feeding frenzy and a second later I was in the water with the spears, the two of us back to back, killing the fish that were killing the fish, standing together in a growing pool of blood. We had constructed a log and net gate to draw across the head of the creek as a fish trap, but there was no time or need to draw it now, the blues were oblivious to anything but the kill and soon so were the two of us. I heard Hallam laugh and turned and for the third time I saw him smile and it was a smile of satisfaction at the killing we had stepped into, at the stupid greed of the blues that let their hunger be the instrument of their death, as if it said to him what he wished to hear: that the worst thing about us was the truest, and I could read this in Hallam's smile as I read my own heart and my own smile, and then I was aware of the blooded spear in my hand and the closeness of the white flesh next to me. And I saw him catch my gaze and read this in my face and laugh again. I turned from him and thrust the spear back into the mass of writhing fish.

On the bank, Hallam stripped off his wet torn clothes, and so did I. My legs were torn and bleeding. He faced me.

"Pick up the spear."

I stood still.

"Pick it up. I'll not touch mine."

I didn't move.

"Pick it up," Hallam said. "Kill me, y'six-fingered freak."

I picked it up. Hallam's body massive: the great shoulders sloped and bearish, the muscles of chest and belly slabbed under a fur of red hair, covered with a lattice of old scars, the penis under the mat of hair thick as a root. I screamed and thrust the spear at Hallam's crotch with both hands and in an instant was weaponless and flying though the air and hitting the ground with a thud and he was upon me. I twisted around and slammed a fist into his forehead. But he had one hand on my throat and was squeezing, holding me as effortlessly as if I were a strengthless child and I saw red spots swim in front of my eyes and the world began turning black and my heart broke me not because I would die but because I was broken. And again, I saw Hallam smile, and as he did, he let me go, and I felt the air rush cool into my throat.

That evening, he didn't put the shackles on me.

IN THE LATE SUMMER of that year we were attacked by clouds of mosquitoes. The insects were a nuisance all the hot months, but on that day it was as though the particles of the air itself turned into buzzing, stinging whirling madness. I saw them come at the sunrise, a black cloud rising out of the marsh as if on a signal and then they covered the two of us, their buzzing maddening in my ears, the sickening crawl of them into ear holes and nostrils and mouth; I felt them crawling under my clothing, the itch of them at my anus. Hallam was roaring and flailing the air madly, as if searching for an opponent large enough to grapple. We ran to the water and threw ourselves in, but the mosquitoes followed, and when we stuck our heads out to breathe, our mouths and nostrils filled. Finally, we lay twitching like fish on the bank, too swollen and pained to even move, my mind coming unmoored, it must be, for I saw a face appearing through the black cloud, another, felt hands rubbing something cooling on my skin. I snorted air and mosquitoes from my clogged nostrils and a rancid odor assailed me. I breathed it in eagerly, for as I was stripped and covered with the ointment, I felt the mosquitoes lifting from me. They were still there, still close around me, their maddening whine in my ears, but they had stopped alighting on my skin. I smiled weakly at the bearded face and passed into a buzzing blackness.

When I opened my eyes I saw a huge thunderhead forming in the sky, tongues of lightening licking at the earth below. The rain began falling in hard pelts, then sheets, washing my swollen, itching skin like a blessing. A man nodded to me. I recognized Jacob Lombroso from the few times I had seen him with the Yaocomaco, and once when Lombroso had tried to stop a settler from bleeding his ill child and had been cursed away for being a heathen Jew. I wasn't certain what that was, but it hadn't been enough to keep Calvert from allowing the physician to take a freehold in St. Michael's Hundred, at Kittamaquund's request. Though I hadn't seen Lombroso since Hallam and I had come here. He was with one of the Yaocomaco Piscataway. Tawzin, I thought, remembering this man's name as well.

"The rain is a blessing," Lombroso said. "It will carry the last of them away. By the way, you stink."

I raised up on one elbow. "So do you."

Lombroso said something in Piscataway to Tawzin. The man laughed.

"But do you itch?" he asked me.

"No. It's a miracle."

"Only bear grease and walnut oil. I'll leave you a supply. We could see the cloud descend on you. The miracle is something you didn't see; the flocks of birds that descended on us while you slept. I think there were as many as there were mosquitoes. It was a feast day for them." He put his face up into the deluge, grinning, water running down his nose. "Another miracle—this will wash away the bird shit.

It's a miraculous land, isn't it, Ezekiel? The land of wonders, beyond the river Sambatyon."

I sat up and looked around. "Where's Hallam?"

"When we put the grease on him, he looked at us, grunted, and went off into the forest. I don't think he likes my friend." He put a hand on Tawzin's shoulder.

"I think he has other friends now," Tawzin said.

From the Narrative of Father Andrew White, S.J.

They cherish generous feelings towards all, and make a return for whatever kindness you may have shown them. They resolve upon nothing rashly, or while influenced by a sudden influence of the mind, but they act deliberately, therefore when anything of importance is proposed at any time, they think it over for a while in silence; then they speak briefly for or against it; they are very tenacious of their purpose. Surely these men, if they are once imbued with Christian precepts, (and there seems to be nothing to oppose this, except our ignorance of the language spoken in these parts,) will become eminent observers of virtue and humanity. They are possessed with a wonderful longing for civilized intercourse with us, and for European garments. And they would long ago have worn clothing, if they had not been prevented by the avarice of the merchants, who do not exchange their cloth for anything but beavers. But every one cannot get a beaver by hunting. God forbid that we should imitate the avarice of these men.

On account of our ignorance of their language, it does not yet appear what ideas they have besides about Religion. We do not put much confidence in the Protestant interpreters: we have (only) hastily learned these few things. They acknowledge one God of Heaven, yet they pay him no outward worship. But they try in every way to appease a certain imaginary spirit, which they call Ochre, *that he may not hurt them. They worship corn and fire, as I hear, as Gods that are very bountiful to the human race. Some of our party report that they saw the following ceremony in the temple at (of?)* Barchuxem. *On an appointed day, all the men and women of every age, from several districts, gathered together round by a large fire; the younger ones stood nearest the fire, behind these stood those who were older. Then they threw deer's fat on the fire, and lifting their hands to heaven, and raising*

85

their voices, they cried out Yaho! Yaho! *Then making room, some one brings forward quite a large bag: in the bag is a pipe and a powder which they call* Potu. *The pipe is such a one as is used among us for smoking tobacco, but much larger; then the bag is carried round the fire, and the boys and girls follow it, singing alternatively with tolerably pleasant voices,* Yaho, yaho. *Having completed the circuit, the pipe is taken out of the bag, and the powder called* Potu *is distributed to each one, as they stand near; this is lighted in the pipe, and each one, drawing smoke from the pipe, blows it over the several members of his body, and consecrates them. They were not allowed to learn anything more, except that they seem to have some knowledge of the Flood, by which the world was destroyed, on account of the wickedness of mankind.*

Ezekiel's Song

Hallam was away often with his new friends now, giving me the freedom of a dog on a long rope. Tied to my own fear. A mocking freedom, the freedom to walk alone from one place to another, as if it were a dare. But it was time I could fill with my own thoughts and wanderings. I drifted, hulled around the name I had taken from a hanged man, into the forest behind the deep gully and creek that ran through it to the reeds and the river, under the laced leaves of the great trees, as if chasing the ebbing memory, the brush of another life, fading from the mind of the child in the womb. Hallam had told me the English names for the different trees. The whites claimed everything quickly, quickly, but these were trees that never had African names for me to forget and I showed them to the first Ezekiel, feeling his betrayed eyes behind my own. *Look where your ship has brought us.* The great sycamores and oaks and ash, ironwood, beech and birch and hickories, the holly and sassafras trees along the trail quivered and preened and whispered as I passed small and quiet under them, my legs brushing through maidenhair and the bowed heads of cinnamon fern, the trees taking me into sanctuary, even though I knew Hallam had hissed their English names into my ears as if building them into a cage in my mind.

From the top of a dead, hollow sycamore, its trunk white as diseased flesh, an eagle stared down unblinking at me, its eyes hooded. I clucked at it and it shimmered its feathers, the shiver rippling outward as his wings unfolded straight and it stepped off and hung in the air and under its shadow my footfalls crunched softly through the thick bracken and ferns and released a clean, rich smell. I saw owls and woodpeckers.

A fox standing still, staring at me with bright, fearless eyes. The forest opened to the river and I followed along the oyster shell strewn beach. It would be easy to take what I wanted from this place, run, lose myself in the continent. Run with the Red Ghosts. *Nestor said the Red Ghosts have villages like ours in Dahomey. Have eyes that see like our eyes.* The Yaocomacos who had at first lived here with the English had for the most part faded away silently to their new village across the river. I had felt a tug from my heart to theirs, but how could I know if this was a vision they would share with me or if it were just a comfort fashioned by my own desires? How would I know if they would not burn me alive, or skin me with shells, or slave me themselves, all things I had heard of them, all things commonly done to strangers? And the Indians, with their faces and bodies painted in fierce swirls and circles, with their spiked clubs and bows and arrows, seemed part of Hallam now also, and what if they had eyes that saw like Hallam's?

I walked along the narrow beach. Would I keep walking? If Hallam came back now, he would smile to see me gone, then give chase, with his Susquehannocks, run me down, chain me. Perhaps chop my hands and feet, hang me from a gallows. But it was only as though my feet were trying the idea of running. An osprey dived into the river like a living arrow shot into my heart. Fish rising, impaled and arching against its pain, water streaming off its silver scales. Where could I run? I was shelled around a corpse or a curse. I had taken a dead man's name, pulled it from his tortured body like a fish from water, it lay like a howl still in my head. Like eyes behind my eyes.

The sand here was churned up. I could make out raccoon tracks, wild pony tracks, deer, bear and human foot prints. I stopped and looked closely. Moccasins. The Susquehannocks had come to St. Marie's two nights before—I had been working in the town and heard the news—a swift lick in from the river to kill a mother and child alone near the river in the

Yaocomaco village, then to this bank and the white settlement to torch a longhouse before Cornwaylis' militia had found them, fired a few volleys and they'd disappeared into the darkness like smoke. Perhaps these were marks from the same raiding party. I could see the drag marks of two canoes, no more. Four or five young men, come for a quick raid to earn glory. To tease the lion, I had heard Cornwaylis say. Broken spars of marsh grass. On some of the spars what seemed to be dried brown droplets. Blood?

I began to follow the blood trail, if that was what it was, looking for signs; to see if I could, I told myself, but more because I wanted to see the world their eyes had seen, these men who had come out of the forest. Lombroso and Tawzin, who had taken to visiting sometimes when Hallam had left, had taught me some of the tricks of how to trace a man or beast in the forest. As if they were showing me a path I could take myself. But the trail was easy now; they had followed the natural twists of the land, into the marshes the whites feared, believing the evil humors emanating from them were the cause of their diseases, the dysentery, typhoid and malaria that had already taken a third of them. Orange marsh blossoms stood arranged against the green spiky grass and brown reeds, the seeds under them that Tawzin called "don't touches." I grasped some of the hard little berries between my fingers and squeezed, smiled as they exploded like small cannon. A spider tribe had covered the top of the grass here with a flimsy roof of web, the delicate weave only visible to me as it came next to me, its tight but fragile filaments sprinkled with tiny water droplets, glowing only as my eye fell upon their design, so the web seemed to be spinning and shaking out of my mind and the forward motion of my walk. It went forever, torn in places by birds. I didn't know how far it would lay invisible over the grass ahead of me, unawakened by my grazing sight. Perhaps to the end of the continent.

The shrouding web had not been torn by humans though. Had I lost the trail? There was a heavy rustle in front of me, and I froze. Seconds later a snapping turtle lumbered out from under a pine tree fallen in vertebrae segments across his path. The huge beast, mossy with age—a walking boulder —looked at me with lidded, wise eyes. I shrugged and followed it. Why refuse such a guide?

It went to water, a narrow, brown-silted, swift running brook. Plopped in heavily. I hesitated. My pointless journey. Then I plunged in. Cold forms under the water brushed my legs, minnows nibbled at my ankles. A tangle of water snakes fell heavily into the water upstream, as if they had suddenly come to a common decision. I grasped a ladder of mossy slick roots on the other side and pulled myself out, the silt bottom sucking at my feet. On a blueberry bush near by I saw more brown droplets. The bush had been stripped of berries. There were moccasin prints in the black loamy dirt. A small rock had been moved out of its socket. I stared at the screen of trees in front of me. Through them I could see a dazzle of light, hear the sound of wind and water. I had come in a semi-circle and was back near the top of the bluff along the river. Pin oaks, each so large it would take five men to circle their outstretched arms around it, towered over me, their roots puddled beneath them; a giant guarding picket. Their trunks twisted into suggestions of faces, eyes, mouths; my wounded hands ached to carve them out into the world. Between them the hard shiny leaves of hollies looked spiked and menacing. Jays scolded from the branches. At the end of their chattering I heard what sounded like a muffled human moan, from the heart of the grove itself.

The words Hallam had poured into my head for trees disappeared like smoke. I searched in vain for older words to describe whatever lived in this grove, my mind clutching for them like a blind man's hand gripping at space. In the center of the trampled area was a small mound of dead leaves. As I approached it, a section rustled dryly and crackled and a snake eased out from between the parting leaves, a copperhead. I drew closer. Or the mound drew me closer. I could see the stripped earth on its sides; the leaves had been scrapped up only very recently. I heard the moan more clearly now, wavering but steady.

I took up a stick, in case other snakes were here, and pushed back the leaves. In the smooth red ground underneath I saw a small hole. The snake's door? The moan rose from it, as if from the heart of the earth. I forced myself forward, then down, as if I had to lay a hand on my own shoulders, push against the backs of my own knees. Remembering the muscular flow of the rattlesnake, I shuddered, but put my ear to the hole anyway, pressed down. The moan filled my head. The breath of the earth blew into me. I rose, terrified and shaking, moaning myself now, echoing the sound of the wounded spirit in the earth. Ezekiel come to join Ezekiel. This thought seized me. I began digging into the soft earth, with the stick, with my clawing hands, grasping into the ground and pulling back flaps of it. My fingers touched something warm and moving and I cried out and drew back. And touched again, shaping the mud now as I would wood I was carving, seeing just beyond my vision, just beyond the breathing touch of my fingers, the form that awaits in the wood, in the mud here: the forehead, the cheekbones, the lips. At first a blank face, only suggesting human features, and then as my hands carved the mud away, the shape that had only been in my brain emerged, something born equally out of me and out of the world and time, out of our swirl together.

I gently cleaned the mud from the eyes, feeling the lids, the living sphere moving under them. They opened. They stared through me. I brushed the mud from the nostrils, the lips: they opened and the moan grew louder, wavering. I found the rest of her shape now, carved it from the mud, watched her form from my hands, finally pulled her from her grave, from her womb, from my womb.

I picked her up and carried her awkwardly through the trees to the bluff and down its face to the river, following the natural wash the Susquehannocks had used. In the shallow I bathed her, formed the rest of her under my hands. Her face was blank and newborn, but woke to some pained and very old wisdom as I washed the mud from her breasts, the swell of her hips, the lick of black hair between her legs. My blood quickened and I felt the air thickening and heating around us. I saw her eyes take in my stare, and a kind of passive dullness filled them like heavy water, and she spread her bruised thighs, a gesture so resigned and suggestive of weary repetition it tweaked my heart. I shook my head, pushed her legs together, said no, in Piscataway Algonquin, one of the few words I had learned. I knew most of the Yaocomaco, at least by face if not name, but I didn't recognize her. A captive, a slave, picked up by the Susquehannocks on one raid or another, but why carry her here to bury her? I sensed, wanted to sense, some unbreaking stubborness in her, a quality of the namesake I had betrayed and broken in Barbados, come again in this form.

She turned her face sideways, into the lap of water against the beach, and before I could stop her started to drink. No, I said again, but didn't need to, she spewed what she had taken, her throat and stomach convulsing, rejecting the salted water. She heaved, bringing up nothing but a transparent bile that dripped down her chin.

From how far away had she been taken in the bellies of boats, a stubborn slave who didn't know the Maryland rivers were estuarine, bitter with salt? I waded a little ways out, bent and plucked up three oysters from the sandy bottom, as if to show her what compensating blessings were in this water. On the shore, I put one on a flat rock, the form of some ancient brother oyster frozen into it, and smashed the shell with another rock. I pulled the meat out with my fingers, took it to her lips. She sucked it in greedily; I smashed another, then the third. I thought of wading in again, but then worried it might sicken her. I sealed a finger across her lips, to tell her no more. She looked at me passively, through me, into some past slipping from her like a dream.

I started to pick her up again, to carry her to the grove, but when I squatted and started to slide my hands under her shoulders and knees, she put a hand against my chest, puffed air out of her nostrils. No, I thought. She rose shakily to her feet, leaned against me and tried to walk, collapsed again at the base of the bluff, and I took her, over my shoulders this time, and brought her to the place she had emerged from the earth. I made a bed of pine needles and leaves and laid her on it, went to the brook, let it fill my cupped hands, and brought the water back to her lips. Her tongue licked at me, her lips sucked greedily against my palm, and I felt my sex stir again and I groaned. She stopped and looked at me, her eyes dulling, her legs twitching to their automatic part. I had been without a woman since Barbados, and this afternoon, this early evening now, I thought with a pang of fear—remembering Hallam, wondering if the man had come home yet—had the substance of some feverish wish-dream: the naked, acquiescent woman given to my hands as a gift from the forest. But I knew, under my excitement and anticipation, the certainty of the curse I would call on myself, as if this violation would be a continuance of the violation of my namesake's flesh, as if this woman were a daughter somehow birthed by one Ezekiel, given to the other. I groaned again, a different sound now, linked up from the depths of my strange union to this found woman, this transported captive. She started at the sound, turned and looked at me, and closed her eyes.

Character of the Province of Maryland, by George Alsop, Indet.Svt: A Relation of the Customs, Manners, Absurdities, and Religion of the Susquehanock Indians in and near Mary-Land

.....*Those Indians that I have convers'd withall here in this province of Mary-land, and have had any occular experimental view of their Customs, Manners, Religions, and Absurdities, are called by the name of Susquehanocks, being a people looked upon by the Christian inhabitants, as the most Noble and Heroick Nation of Indians that dwell upon the confines of America; also are so allowed and lookt upon by the rest of the Indians, by a submissive and tributary acknowledgement; being a people cast into the mould of a most large and War-like deportment, the men being for the most part seven foot high in latitude, and in magnitude and bulk suitable to so high a pitch; their voyce large and hollow, as ascending out of a Cave, their gate and behavior strait, stately and majestic, treading on the Earth with as much pride, contempt, and disdain to so sordid a Center, as can be imagined from a creature derived from the same mould and Earth.*

Their bodies are cloth'd with no other Armour to defend them from the nipping frosts of a benumbing Winter, or the penetrating and scorching influence of Sun in a hot Summer, then what Nature gave them when they parted with the dark receptacle of their mothers womb. They go, Men, Women and Children, all naked, only where shame leads them by a natural instinct to be reservedly modest, there they become cover'd.

....*These Susquehanock Indians are for the most part great Warriours, and seldon sleep one Summer in the quiet armes of a peaceable Rest, but keep the several Nations of Indians round about them, in a forceable obedience and subjection....*

The Warlike Equipage they put themselves in when they prepare for Belona's March, is with their faces, armes and breasts confusedly painted, their hair greazed with Bears oyl, and stuck thick with Swans Feathers, with a wreath or Diadem of black and white Beads upon their heads, a small Hatchet, instead of a Cymetre, stuck in their girts behind them, and either with Guns, or Bows and Arrows. In this posture and dress they march out from their Fort, or dwelling, to the number of Forty in a Troop, singing (or rather howling out) the Decades or Warlike exploits of their Ancestors, ranging the wide Woods untill their fury has met with an Enemy worthy of their Revenge. What prisoners fall into their hands by the destiny of War, they treat them very civilly while they remain with them abroad, but when they once return homewards, they then begin to dress them in the habit for death, putting on their heads and armes wreaths of Beads, greazing their hair with fat, some going before, and the rest behind, at equal distance from their Prisoners, bellowing in a strange and confused manner, which is a true presage and fore-runner of destruction to their then conquered Enemy.

Nameless Song

At my birth the flesh of earth that presses hot on my eyelids and cheeks, on all the skin of my body, heaves and tightens and my skin and bones shudder with it as if I am of that flesh of the earth until torn from it and the shudder in me is still the tic of the earth in my body. The small weights of its touch still press my eyelids like fingers until I feel them lift and the air on my skin. When I open my eyes I see a man with a face black as the face of Raven looking down at me, behind him the shapes of trees from a world I think I remember. But I look at his face again and know I have been born into the true world of dreams and spirits. Somewhere cored in my mind, pushed as if buried, is a memory inside a memory inside a memory, yolks floating in the shell of my mind not separate but flowing into one another: a tan plain and harsh sun-splashed mountains, horses, lodges of hide shaped like the points of arrows, a thick forest, a man with a ribbon of hair bissecting the red moon of his head pounding at my loins, women beating me with sticks in the red dust. A white man in a long black shirt murmuring into my ear. The stretched hide of a deer. The lap of water against the side of a birchbark canoe. The word *canoe*. Other words, in other tongues, loosening like crusts from the inside of my skull. Floating. An eagle circling far above me, trying to stitch the edges of time torn apart in my spirit. The smoke from the top of a lodge drifting away. Nameless lives before the womb, before the coming of this spirit or demon—I don't care which— with its black face and gentle six-fingered hand.

He bathes me and teaches me to remember the name of water and the word gentle and feeds me and the word *father* forms like a bubble in my mind, and another word that means father, and the face of a white man in the long black shirt again. The face, the eyes change and all the words for father disappear and I am for the first time aware of my nakedness and of the word *naked* in three tongues and I recognize something in the face now and my body remembers and some muscle I haven't been aware of until this moment, no more than my nakedness, clenches tight under my heart and I spread my legs to fit the memory of my flesh. And Raven's face softens and becomes all the words for father again.

If he is father I am infant and new born, so all I can do is lay still and stare at the weave of branches and leaves over my head, the sparkle of sun moving broken through it, and then the dark that forms behind the branches and thickens them until their shapes dissolve into it and become part of its lace. The things that move in the darkness, when father isn't there, that sniff and lick and slide over me. I am newly born so I lie in my own mess and stink, watching the sun move behind the screen of branches until father Raven comes and cleans and feeds me, though sometimes the light comes and goes more than once before he returns. And once he brings a white man with caterpillars of black hair on his chin and over his lips and I think it is one of my fathers from the other life, the black shirt father, but his eyes are different, and he wraps me in deerskin, and rubs oil that I somehow know comes from boiled acorns on my joints, and makes me chew sassafras and swallow elderberries, and I remember the words for these when they are in my stomach and their spirits released, and as my body clenches and voids and cleanses, I remember the word for *shame*.

Ezekiel's Song

I lay staring at the close ceiling of the pen, my racing mind more awake than my body, which was so heavy with exhaustion I felt I couldn't rise, felt as I imagined the woman (I refused to name her even in my mind until she would find her name, bring it to me) would have with the earth on top of her. I was naked, my sweat gluing me to the rough itch of the straw rick. I thought of bathing her in the river and moaned. I raised my hands and looked at them. My fingers were cracked, their tips split, bleeding. The day before yesterday, when I had finally gotten back to her, she had cried out when she saw them, taken them one by one to her mouth, her soft tongue. I tried to remember the sensation on my skin now. I missed her sharply. Hallam had taken to going off himself more and more to trap beaver or trade for pelts or hunt, disappearing for days and coming back with his clothing stiff with dried blood. His canvas breeches and linsey-woolsey shirt had disappeared, replaced with buckskin and each time he returned he was more Indian. Though when any of the few remaining Yaocomaco on this side of the river saw which *roanoke* he'd put in the braid of his hair, the design of the tomahawk he held under his belt, they would mutter darkly. I did not care to which Indians he went, as long as he was gone: his absences were times I could go to the grove. But he wasn't gone enough (*enough* would be if he disappeared forever into the country of the Susquehannocks, or into Hell) and he was often hiring me out for carpentry work in the settlement, and it was late summer and I had been left with hundreds of plants to tend, to water and weed and pluck the worms off and squeeze them, while my mind stayed buried in a grove of trees near the river with the woman.

Something soft and furred fell on my chest; I smelled

the blood before I felt its wet on my skin. I stroked the dead rabbit as if it were alive. The wall of the pen shook; Hallam's voice filled the space, telling me to raise my laggard's bones and prepare supper. I sat up, my head hitting the low ceiling, groaned, pulled my clothing on awkwardly, my fingers feeling numbed, as if they were encased in bark.

I had made a small cooking pit in front of the longhouse and I skinned and gutted the rabbit and buried it in a small cavity at the edge of the pit, then covered its raw-stripped body with earth and branches. There was nothing I could do that did not bring my mind back to the woman. I lit the fire. I placed some cattail roots and tuckahoe, Piscataway foods Lombroso had shown me how to prepare, in the black iron pot I had hung above the fire, and boiled them there, then put half into a clay, shell-tempered eating pot. The other half I wrapped in a soft deerskin pouch and pushed under a bush, to bring to her later. I thought of the food I could pilfer for her tomorrow. I'd been stealing small amounts of pone, concealing them in a small pit I'd dug under my rick. If Hallam left again, I could take the axe, build a proper shelter in the grove.

The wood over the rabbit had turned to glowing coals. I pushed them aside with a green stick, unearthed the steaming flesh, again seeing in the instant I exposed the small corpse, her body in the earth, and I shuddered and put it on top of the greens and brought it into the longhouse.

The space inside was cool and caveish and heavy with Hallam's scent: a rankness of old blood, the sweetish-sharp smell of new blood, wet fur, fetid sweat. His leather, broad-brimmed hat, frayed coat, cutlass and flintlock musket hung from the posts inside, though most of the space was taken by piles of stiffening beaver pelts. Something den-like about the place, a cave where the predator dragged back his kill and feasted on it. I imagined Hallam gone, imagined cleansing this place of him, living in it with the woman.

He was sitting at the rough-hewn bench and table, his

shoulders hunched, his face blank with preoccupation. I dished the meat and greens into a wooden trencher, put it in front of him. The man sat still, then slowly, as the smell reached his nostrils, seemed to awaken, stare at the food. He scooped out the roots and threw them onto the floor, began tearing the rabbit to pieces, stuffing it into his mouth. I stood.

"What are you staring at?" Hallam asked me.

I didn't reply.

Hallam ate silently for a moment, then tore off a haunch, threw it to me. I reached for it, but my hand, swollen and painful, closed too slowly and it dropped to the floor. I squatted down and picked up the haunch and ate it.

Hallam grunted. "Take the barken canoe in the morning and get yourself up to St. Marie's City. The Brent woman wants you to supervise the finishing work on her house."

For a moment, excitement thickened my throat. My namesake's old dream tumbled behind my eyes. I would take her, we would disappear, run to the secret sanctuaries of the Red Ghosts.

"Be back by nightfall," Hallam said, without looking at me, and his words closed around me like shackles. *No, she is still too weak to travel,* I told that constant ghost in my mind, *and your Red Ghosts only placed her, still breathing, into her own grave, and how can we go to them?*

I LEFT AT first light, paddling upriver to St. Marie's in the barken canoe. Tawzin had taught me to make this craft, and we had completed it in less than a day, as the Indians did, Tawzin told me, when they traveled the Great Trails and needed or wanted to make part of their journey by water. Last spring, when the sap was up and bark easier to cut, Tawzin and I had found a large ash tree and cut all around it, from the base above the splay of roots and up to twenty feet. We slit and peeled the bark, then cut a triangle out of each end, the point in the middle, and folded the bark up into a V-shaped hull, and sewed up the ends with deer sinew, while holding the middle apart with spaced sticks. We had water-proofed it with deer fat and though it had leaked at first, now the canoe was steady though not swift.

It was my canoe, and I brought it to the shore and ran to her, and left the food and put her behind my eyes to push out the vision of Hallam smiling in the full confidence of what vessel was his to own. I could not stay with her long. By the time I got out on the river again, thunderheads were moving in the sky to the north, silent forks of lightening spearing the water miles ahead. The sunrise and the breeze cut blood-tinted wrinkles on the gray water and it was veined with blue currents, running all around me. A gigantic shadow swam with the canoe for a mile, just under the surface, coming close enough at times so I could see the devil's head shape of a ray, its grin, the heart-aching, smooth freedom of its glide.

The two Brent sisters, Margaret and Mary, had brought nine indentured servants with them, and so had been granted nearly a thousand acres of land, according to Calvert's charter—one hundred acres for each indentured servant transported. The other colonists had assumed that the sisters would live with their bachelor brothers Giles and Fulke. But Margaret Brent had insisted they would have their own house and they had also taken five acres in the township, a freehold between their brother Giles house and the governor's mansion, and it was there we had built for them. I had, before finding the woman, been lingering out the job as long as I could. The house was nearly complete now: I had only to supervise some of the Brent's servants in framing and hanging the front door, with Margaret Brent watching. I had carved the panels to her instructions: scenes from a warrior's song called the *Iliad*—the tale of the slave Breisis, she had told me.

Do you know the story? she had asked, running her fingers over the figures. She was thirty-seven years old, a tall, handsome woman who looked at me with gray eyes that somehow reminded me of the river, always on the verge of darkening with sadness or brightening with amusement or anger. When I had first begun work on her house, she had stopped me at midday to feed me. I had sat under the live oak shading the front of the building, and my hands and knife had found the face of a god whose name I had forgotten, in the stump of one of the hickories we had taken down. Staring at that face, amused somehow to see it emerge here in this Maryland light, I'd jumped when a shadow fell over it— Hallam had whipped me for finding such faces before—(*I own your hands, nigger—they will cut only where I place them and only for my design*)—and I had looked up to see Margaret Brent staring and smiling and nodding. I had brought other faces and forms to the light for her since then; Hallam did not like it, but couldn't contradict her and he was well paid for what my fingers found and freed. Brent had taken upon herself then to teach my tongue, as she said, the same grace as my hands. Until she took on this task, English words and names had filled the space of my mouth like the diffenbachia overseers stuffed into slaves' mouths in Barbados. They had driven out all other words and names, but they tasted of chains and rot. She had read to me from her books, and for an hour each day taught me also how to shape letters on paper and read as well, and though my eyes resisted understanding, taking on the task my ears had owned until now, my fingers found letters easy to form.

No, mistress, I had answered her when she asked if I knew the story of another slave.

Ah, well, Breisis was taken by the warrior Achilles as a prize of war. A slave with whom he fell in love. Then his commander, Agammemnon, took her from him and Achilles withdrew from the war he was fighting as Agammenom's ally, in anger. Later, when Agammenom offered to return her for Achilles' services, he refused, and when Agammemnon told him he had not yet violated the girl, Achilles told him to use her as he would. Do you see, Ezekiel, how his sense of ownership had already been violated? He loved her, yet he loved the design of his own pride and rage more. Do you think you can carve that into his face, Ezekiel? That arrogant pout.

Yes, I had said. Yes, I can carve that.

She had turned to me then and smiled, as if we shared a secret language. Yes. I can see you understand the story well, she'd said, and I had felt a cold anger against her: what did she understand of my understanding; what did she think we shared?

She touched the face of Achilles now. "Thank you, Ezekiel. This is done so cunningly I don't know if I can stand having him. Come inside a moment, then."

She led me to the parlor. The pinewood bookcases I had fashioned into the walls were lined with leather-bound volumes. In the oil painting over the mantle, an old man in a white wig and a wine-colored waistcoat stared down at me, as in surprise at my presence. The way he always stared. Brent took a clay jug from the small table—Flemish earthenware. She had named objects for me here, as Hallam had named trees in the forest. She poured amber wine into two Dutch roemers. I looked at her uneasily.

"Why do you hesitate? I wish to thank you for this house," Margaret Brent said. "I wish to thank you for this room, Ezekiel. It is my room, my sanctuary. I have dreamed of such a place all my life, a fair place where one can think anything, say anything. I would like you to feel that way also, whenever you enter this room."

I picked up the roemer, ran my finger over the designs on its surface.

She raised her eyebrows. "Have you nothing to say, then?"

"I'm a slave, mistress. The place you describe is just that which is missing from me."

"You have just disproved that sentiment with those very words, Ezekiel. As does the way you fashioned this room itself. Your tongue may lie for you. It may say: I am a slave. But your art will never lie for you. In here, neither has to. Will you not raise a glass with me?"

I felt another flare of anger, at this woman, at the danger and uselessness of this conversation, its consequences that I was certain I would end up paying.

"All of me is slave," I said. "My hands fashion and carve for the interest of my owner."

She smiled. "I think your hands subvert whatever they touch." Then she looked down at my hands and cried out. I made a half-hearted attempt to hide them behind my back, then let them dangle at my side. She bit her lower lip, her face angry.

"Nay, mistress," I said softly, "There are no such rooms for me."

Yet a sheltering grove, the glint of light slanting through the leaves, the whisper of the river, came to my mind then.

"Surely you understand that subversion is what I crave?" Margaret Brent said.

She put her roemer goblet down. A book lay on the pine desk. Margaret Brent placed her hand on it.

"This is Thomas More's book *Utopia*, Ezekiel. It is one of my favorite books, and one of Leonard's also. It demonstrates how men and women can live together harmoniously."

I remembered then a word she had taught me. "Is it a fiction?"

She laughed grimly. "Until now. Until here. At least that is our hope. I'm sorry to laugh, but your question surprised me."

"Was it not the question of a slave?"

"It was not the question of a man who can not read."

"Nevertheless, mistress, I can not, in spite of your effort. And that is the truth in this room of truth."

"You simply need more time. I will still teach you."

"Why?"

She smiled. "All of my life people have asked me such questions whose answers I find self-evident."

"I don't understand."

"Yes, so you deign to have me believe. Do you understand this—that my sister and I are here as gentlemen-adventurers. Do you know what such things as those are?"

"Aye, mistress; there were seventeen such on the Ark, I'm told by my master. I think only four of those here now. The rest dead or gone back to England. I think Hallam doesn't like them."

"There are not many men who Master Hallam does like, dead or alive. But in this instance I understand him. There is a foppish quality even to the words. And to many of the men so described. They are often minor gentry, with no inheritance but their names. They dream America into a cudgel of power and property they can wield over first born brothers. Into nothing more than that. When my brothers wished to come here, my sister and I told Cecilius we would come also, but only if we could hold property in our own name, even if we never married. Do you understand?"

Second or fourth son of this earl or that baron, comes here thinking Maryland is going to be his tit the way England no longer can, I remembered Hallam muttering into his cup one evening. "He believes you can control your brother Giles," I said. Another dreg from my master's cups.

She looked at me a moment, nodded shortly. "I don't know if he was right. Do you know what my brother's plan is now? To marry the child Mary Kittamaquund when she is of age—twelve years he thinks will be the right time. To marry that child. I look on her as a daughter. He sees her as a Piscataway princess; marrying her will be as if he married a baron's daughter in England: he will come into possession of all Kittamaquund's lands. When I told this to Kittamaquund, I could see he was puzzled. But how would he possess? he asked me. He seemed to get the idea Giles would literally marry the land and asked me with great frankness how the act of consummation would take place. My brother Giles. But I lost my path; I'm afraid. I was explaining how it was that Mary and I were given this house, next to Giles, by the governor."

"Why don't you and the governor marry?" I asked.

Her eyes flared, then brightened with amusement. I held her stare.

"I thank you," she said.

"Mistress?"

"For accepting that I meant what I said about this room."

"I was seeing if you did," I admitted. "But why don't you marry?" The stories of her and Calvert were the stuff of bawdy tales in the ordinaries.

"I almost married once," she said. She smiled briefly. "In a way I'm still married to that man. Do you understand?"

"Is he dead?"

"Yes."

"Then I understand."

"He was also a Catholic and I was nineteen and he was the only man who I met who reckoned my mind, with whom I would speak of what I could only hold in its close privacy. Perhaps that is love, or perhaps it is what I have fashioned of love, but for me it was enough, for I blossomed in the soil of him, Ezekiel. Perhaps love is simply a room where one is able to speak the truth, truth of mind and truth of body. To be a woman in English society can not measure to the suffering you have endured in your life, but it is a vise gripped around tongue and body nevertheless, a rigid chaining to formulae of conversation and behavior, to a shallowness that exists to threaten no man, but that one drowns oneself in. I felt that, Ezekiel, I felt I was drowning in a shallow, before I met him. He was of my class and background, and I have no idea how he escaped the rigidity of either, but I loved him for it, and that love has not changed, even with his death. He was arrested at a mass and placed in the Tower of London. I was allowed to see him there once. He had become gray. Not merely his hair—that was too caked with filth to even see its color. But all of him. He had become a gray man, hunched over himself, his skin like thin gray parchment hung on his bones. Of course they had tortured him, his fingers had been pulled loose from their sockets and had withered in their uselessness into claws," she glanced involuntarily at my hands, then averted her eyes, "and a blow had crushed his voice box so he could only croak at me, words it took me a few moments to hear. 'Go away. Go away.' He died after ten years there. The crown received his property. I loved him deeply and that has never changed and if he came to me now, in that state, I would take him into my embrace all the remaining days of my life."

"What was his name?"

"Ah, nay, I will not say it. Do you understand?"

"Yes," I said, though what I didn't fathom was her hunger that I should understand.

She looked back at me, took up her goblet, drank. "Aye," she said. "That I see."

"But it is good you have Calvert, I think. If I may say that, in this room."

"Yes," she said. "I think so. He is the closest I had found to...the man I love. We are both dreamers, Leonard and I, and we both love the dream. And we are free here, at least more so than in England. And what about you, Ezekiel?"

"As you know, mistress."

"I know nothing. I see a crime against God being fashioned before my eyes, when I see your hands. I don't believe one man should own another. Will you ask me why?"

"No."

"Good."

"But not because the answer is...clear. Only because the belief is impossible."

She waved around at the room, in the house that had risen under my hands, on the ground next to the river.

"So is all this," she said.

Author uncertain

Not long after the coming of Father White to his palace, Tayac was in danger from a severe disease; and when forty conjurers had in vain tried every remedy, the father, by permission of the sick man, administered medicine, to wit: a certain powder of known efficacy mixed with holy water, and took care, the day after, by the assistance of the boy, whom he had with him, to open one of his veins for blood letting. After this, the sick man began daily to grow better, and not long after became altogether well. Restored from the disease entirely, of himself he resolved as soon as possible to be initiated in the christian rites; nor himself only, but his wife also and two daughters: for as yet he has no male offspring. Father White is now diligently engaged in their instruction; nor do they slothfully receive the heavenly doctrine, for by the light of heaven poured upon them, they have long found out the errors of their former life. The king has exchanged the skins, with which he was heretofor clothed, for a garment made in our fashion; he makes also a little endeavor to learn our language.

Having put his concubines from him, he lives content with one wife, that he may the more freely (as he says) have leisure to pray to God. He abstains from meat on those days, in which it is forbidden by the christian laws; and men that are heretics who do otherwise, or are of that name, he thinks ought to be called bad christians. He is greatly delighted with spiritual conversation, and indeed seems to esteem earthly wealth as nothing, in comparison with heavenly, as he told the Governor, when explaining to him what great aqdvantages from the English could be enjoyed by a mutual exchange of wares—"Verily, I consider these trifling when compared with this one advantage—that through these, as authors, I have arrived at the true knowledge of the one God; than which there is nothing greater to me among you, or which ought to be greater." So, not long since, when he held a convention of the empire, in a crowded assembly of the chiefs and a circle of the common people, Father White and some of the English being present, he publically attested it was his advice, together with that of his wife and children, that the superstition of the country being abjured, to give their names to Christ; for that no other true deity is any where else had, other than among the christians, nor otherwise can the immortal soul of man be saved from death—but that stones and herbs, to which through blindness of mind, he and they had hitherto given divine honors, are the humblest things created by the Almighty God for the use and relief of human life. Which being spoken, he cast from him a stone which he held in his hand and spurned it with his foot.

Hawksong

The locust trees that the Piscataway women felled and made into dugout canoes by burning out their centers and scrapping them clean with oyster shells received their name, called so by both English and Piscataway, from the way their roots spread quickly and shallowly and everywhere under the ground as locusts did over it, each tree hubbing out into a raveled net of tough, sinewy roots just beneath the surface and every few yards a tendril poking up through the crust to find the light, and another and another and another, a line of sprigs pushing out of the grass and in a few years full grown trees scattered everywhere, discrete, but invisibly moored together in one conjoined organism, spreading its roots, encompassing, dominating.

Yet to the hawk flying over it now, the settlement of St. Marie's seemed analogous to neither locusts nor locust trees, but rather a slower absorption, a harsh and inescapable metamorphosis: the soft ovals of the Piscataway longhouses gradually being consumed and digested into piles of shit and shell and bone by the strange sharp angularities of the English huts; the knit of longhouse, field, forest unraveling into a haphazard, vaguely contentious strew, a motley of corn and tobacco patches, the sense below him of something hungry, feeding, growing to an unthinkable vastness, a cumbered dread in the hawk's heart. Its shadow passes over a sweat-lodge and the hawk dips down into Tawzin's dreams, and in an attempt to unburden itself, it passes into the man's heart an ache of loss, the knowledge that what has been given shelter and peace below has rooted itself and will spread like locust tree roots or locusts or a devouring Beast or whatever simultudes that shared ache would connect to under the man's vision.

Now the hawk, circling back into its own dreams, sees another man walking down the path that goes through the middle of the town, striding quickly and with economic purpose as if he sees some prey at his level that the hawk cannot. He walks next to one of the horizontal, zig-zag lines, one of the reconfigurations the hawk has noticed. The man, Hallam, though the hawk does not know this, calls the line a worm fence, and in fact it was Hallam who had conceived of these fences and fashioned many with his own hand, chopping down and wedging and splitting hundreds of young trees into crude rails, their ends stacked one over the other, the rails angled right then left, and so held together by nothing but their own weight—their squirm across the land gave him the name (though the hawk decided to name them Deadtree Scars). They were New World fences, in Hallam's mind, fashioned from a land of endless wood and without need for notching or nails, improvised, invented and he liked how many trees had to be cut down for their making. If he could, he'd cut down every tree in this country; he would clear the land, clean it, erase everything but possibility, a clear parchment for him to write his name large upon.

The hawk soars higher, suddenly panicking, trying to break itself from the insistence of that preternatural hunger he has just glimpsed in the man, yet feeling it intrude and devour a corner of his soul. He spirals higher, leaping from updraft to updraft and letting each push under the spread of his wings until the village becomes only a small anomaly on the face of the world. The river meanders below him, silver crinkling in roving patches of sunlight, gripping itself with the forked claws of its creeks to the deep green country. Below, a mountain lion slips furtively into a cave on a hummock in a cypress swamp, and a bear scratches its back against a tree, an action repeated in the hawk's eye further west and further west, into the broody forests that cover the face of the world, that until this day he has thought were the immutable face of the world. But as he watches he knows he hasn't flown high enough or fast enough and he feels the dream he's snatched from the man's eyes slip free from the clutch of his own mind, as he has let dreams and visions slip free and into men's minds, and he sees to his horror how it passes from him into the dreams of trees, so that a shiver runs through the forest, a stir and shimmer of leaves and branches as far to the horizon as his hawk's eye can see, the land shivering before the anticipation of the axe, the axe man.

Hallam's Song

I stood in front of the governor's house, watching a sudden wind rustle the leaves of the oak trees Calvert had insisted on leaving standing on the sides. I spat into the black mud. The house was an H-shaped hickorywood structure Ezekiel and I had placed near the edge of the small cliff overlooking the river. Except for the church, it was the largest and grandest building in St. Marie's City, forty feet in width by sixty-eight in length. It had leaded glass windows and a paneled entrance hall and two alcoves and five brick and mortar fireplaces, a dining room, scullery and kitchen. Everything a gentleman adventurer needed to be a gentleman adventurer. Some of the other settlers had tried to praise me when it was finished. But I answered them with silence. I had taken the design from a vague memory of my father's house. But most of the work had been done by Ezekiel anyway, and I took no pride in the translation of my hidden design by that freakish six-fingered hand.

I knocked on the double paneled door. Calvert opened it himself, blinking, his long black hair tangled and streaked with gray now, his form thinner, his face grooved. I saw no match, on this day, to the man who had stood next to me on the beach at St. Clement's Island. Nor for that matter could I recall my own face then; the time we had been here now was as vast as the water we had crossed, and we had all passed into different forms.

"Come in then, man," Calvert said.

I entered the hall. Two militiamen, in armored breast-plates and Spanish helmets stood to either side of the far door, pikes in their right hands. I grinned at them. The fly entering the web. A lusher web since I had been here last.

The cupboard shelves along the walls had been arranged with pewter, English surreyware; Dutch and Flemish earthenware, Venetian glass. A wine-colored rug on the floor. Damask curtains at the windows. The light wavery and golden through the leaded glass. The light, the room pushing against my father's study in my memory. A soft room for a soft man. A dissolving room. In the sitting room, books lined the ashwood cases and a portrait of George Calvert looked down from above the fireplace lintel, that piece carved by Ezekiel's devil hand into a representation of the meeting between Calvert and the Tayac of the Piscataway.

The Tayac himself stood in front of the fireplace and his own portrait, as if he were another geegaw displayed on Calvert's shelf. His broad face gleamed with sweat. He wore the waistcoat he had worn since his baptism. I had gone to the ceremony—Calvert had insisted all the colonists attend. The priest smiling, the wives Kittamaquund were throwing away from himself for the cold flesh of Christ staring stupidly unaware, the Tayac's face painted with black stripes, the Tayac's body in that foul velvet waistcoat, the Tayac's head in a plumed hat over a soiled white wig. The same wig he was wearing, slightly askew, now. His face uncaged of its black painted stripes and floating unmoored, it seemed, in the heat of the room. Next to him now also, as he had been at the baptism, was the priest, White. He nodded shortly to me. As he had done at the ceremony. I felt jarred in time. The people in the room (itself a model of my father's false sanctuary) standing in the frame of my own memory of them, crowding a span when I had been under their dominance.

The door opened and Margaret Brent entered, her hand resting on the shoulder of Mary Kittamaquund, the Tayac's daughter, baptized now and being raised Christian by Margaret and her sister. Another Mary of course.

Brent moved across the room as if she owned it. Calvert's whore. I understood suddenly from where the feminine touches I had seen in the house had come. A female house.

She stopped next to her brother, Giles, a reedy twist with a rabbit's chin and watery blue eyes, and Thomas Cornwayles, tall, wide and bald as an egg, which is what the Indians called him. Egg. Both men were wearing breastplates and swords. Gentlemen adventurers. Cornwayles was one of the richest men in the colony, and the head of the militia now. He had pushed me to enlist, had offered a sergeantcy, and when I had laughed, his face tightened and flushed. I remembered that expression of helpless rage now as I looked at the faces around me. This circle of power displayed for me.

"Why have you summoned me?"

"James Hallam, welcome," Calvert said. "Would you have a glass of madeira?"

"Nay."

"James is a man without ceremony," Father White said. "Isn't that so, James?"

"I don't take your meaning."

Calvert raised his eyebrows. "Well then welcome to you without ceremony," he said. "I believe you have met Mistress Margaret Brent."

I bowed slightly to the woman. She acknowledged it with a tight nod.

"Is all well at St. Michael's Hundred?" Calvert asked.

"In my corner of it. I cannot speak to the rest."

"The church was dedicated yesterday. We were sorry to see you couldn't be there. We wished to congratulate you on your labor. You and Ezekiel have created a miracle in the wilderness."

"I'm a free man now,"

"And a damned rude one," Cornwayles snapped.

I held the man's stare. There was nothing more these could do for or to me.

Calvert smiled slightly, fluttered his hand, his fingers spidering, as if to unknot the tightness in the air between us. "Well, then," he said. "It appears we have obtained that to which we had aspired, isn't it? The New Man. Are you that,

James? Are you what we had hoped for? And if we had known, would we have so hoped?"

He was speaking, I saw, to Margaret Brent.

"Hoped for or no, I'm here," I said to Calvert. "What would you have of me?"

"Come walk with us for a time, Hallam."

"To where?"

"To a hanging."

"My own?"

"Not yet," White said.

I nodded to him. Remembering Father Black.

From the corner of my eye, I fixed the positions of the militiamen, tensing and gathering myself to move quickly. Then relaxing. I didn't know how much they knew, but what was best for now would be to remain quiet until they revealed what they wished to reveal. Or to goad them into an anger that would reveal more.

"Come now," Calvert said.

"The girl and I will remain," Margaret Brent said.

"M'dear, it would be important you attend to this."

Margaret Brent looked at Calvert silently for a moment.

"Yes, I see. Then I shall. But the child will not." She stroked the girl's hair.

"Of course," Calvert said. "But let us go now."

I walked next to the governor, Kittamaquund, and Margaret Brent, following White, Giles Brent and Cornwaylis down Middle Street. Moving west through the settlement towards the Mattapani trail that cut through the forest to the Patuxent river. My hand or my shadow was everywhere. The longhouses we had first shared with the Yaocomacos were falling in on themselves; the spines of their arched backs broken, their bark skins rotting off in large flakes. Next to them, sometimes attached to them, like new flesh growing from the destruction of old, were the houses Ezekiel and I had erected, squat sixteen by twenty foot boxes built around a frame of sunken posts and sided with rough locust wood clapboard that was matched and not overlapped, chinked with clay, and each with a wattle and daub chimney and a packed dirt floor. Neat-built and quick-built but dark and foul in the daylight, freezing in winter. Alive with whining mosquitoes and biting flies drawn to the piles of offal—oyster and crab shells, animal bones and guts, turds, rotting and molding leather, broken clay pipes—each house's excretions heaped next to itself. I had given my fellows that which they wished for themselves. As was my custom.

The day was cloudless. A hawk circled overhead, drawing circles against the blue. Calvert swept his hand out as we walked, encompassing the scattered houses and ordinaries of the settlement.

"Do you remember the conversation we had on St. Clement's Island, Hallam? I think we have built into the world many of the dreams we spoke of then."

"We have all come far from then," I agreed. "Though some have gone further than others, isn't it, your lordship? One in three of us was on that island are dead men. Do you dream of those some time as well?"

Calvert stopped and turned to me. "Damn you, yes," he said. "I dream of them often enough. And half the fops who were with us have run back to England. But there was no starving time, Hallam, as there was in Virginia, and no massacre of the innocents, and Kittamaquund has become my brother. We needed a place to plant ourselves and he has given us that."

"And what have you in return, Tayac?" I asked.

"My eternal soul," Kittamaquund said.

"Ah, but tis that what you have gotten or what you have given, Tayac?"

Kittamaquund looked into my eyes. I saw a cold black river that stirred with more deeps than I had names for and that had already named all of me. I smiled at him.

"Damn you, Hallam, you'll not insult my brother the Tayac."

"Nay, I beg your pardon—tis just an observance. I was only wondering, you see, your honor, what it is you wish to have from me?"

I saw Calvert bringing himself under control. "Only your loyalty, Hallam. Do I have that?"

"I dinna take yer meaning, yer 'onor," I said, broadening my accent, slipping on the fawning mask I'd once worn, so they could watch me do it now, understand at last who it had been I had given them.

At first Calvert did not react. I had only after all given him what he expected. We began walking again, Calvert's hands laced against the small of his back, scabbard slapping his thigh.

"Don't you, Hallam? Have you heard that William Claiborne has fortified Kent Island and created a small army out of his Virginian farmers and trappers?" he asked finally. "Even our friend Governor Harvey of Virginia has backed our suit. But Claiborne refuses to relinquish his sovereignty. He has powerful friends in England, friends who hate Catholics and love the profits from the pelt trade even as the Susquehannocks love the trinkets he gives them for their beaver."

"They love him, is what I hear," I said.

We were nearly at Gallows Hill now. A mixed group of whites, blacks and a few Indians milled around its base. On its ridge a line of men in breastplates and crested helmets, armed with muskets and pikes—the militia Calvert had asked me to sergeant—stood in a ragged picket in front of the gallows I had built for the colony, two years before. On the occasion of its first hanging. I searched my mind, could not find the memory of the man's face or name. I began placing other faces at the end of the dangle, White, Calvert, Ezekiel's, my own. There was no one on it at the moment. We stopped at the bottom of the hill. White peered upwards; he seemed to be looking for something.

"Tell me, Hallam," Cornwaylis said. "Tell me what sort of man is it, do you think, who would be loved by the Susquehannock?"

"Giles, read Mr. Hallam the proclamation," Calvert said. "We passed this in council today, Hallam."

Giles Brent stepped forward. He unwound a scroll and began to read, his voice high and thin, a schoolboy presenting his lesson:

"'The following acts are to be considered acts of treason. To conspire the death of the King, Queen or son and heir, to join any foreign state a professed enemy of His Majesty, or to join any confederation of Indians...for the invasion of this province, are to be considered treasonable and are to be punished by drawing, hanging and quartering of a man; the burning of a woman. The offender's blood will be considered corrupted and the offender shall be forfeit of all lands, or by punishment upon a lord of a manor by beheading.'"

I wondered—again jogged closer to the idea by Brent's little recitation—if they had brought me to hang. Join at last the long line I had sent before myself. But I thought not. If they suspected my alliance with Claiborne, they would have simply arrested me, put me to the torture. No. They were testing that perhaps. But my freedom soured their bile, was the bottom of it. They sought to seize me to them again, grip me as they had their pet Piscataway ape here, draped with his trinkets, convinced he had a soul to lose.

"I'm the new man, me," I said to Margaret Brent.

"I do not think so, sir," she said.

"It is not quite clear to me what you are, Hallam," Calvert said. "Or perhaps more to the issue, whose."

"'Tis clear enough. I'm a free man, as of the end of my indenture, and a planter and a property holder."

"Oh, truly now, Hallam," Giles Brent said. "Being free doesn't mean being unbearable."

I looked at the line of militia on the crest, saw Cornwayles' lips tighten, as if over an oath. I began to tense again, beginning to think I'd judged wrongly how much they knew.

On the hill, a tall, skinny Indian, naked but for a loincloth, was being led in chains to the gallows, John Altham, the younger priest, next to him. I had never seen an Indian hung before.

"Pennockquod," Calvert said, as if it were a word to tag the entire prospect.

"Why are you hanging him?"

"For the crime of manslaughter," Giles Brent droned, as if still reciting from a scroll, "the offender shall die by hanging unless he can read, in which case the offender shall suffer the loss of a hand, burned on the forehead, and forfeiture of all lands."

I bared my teeth at White. "The Jesuits always told me reading were a precious skill for a man. Now I understand."

"Which Jesuits were those, James Hallam?" White asked.

"Why, those I didn't hang, father."

"Pennockquod became drunk and murdered Freeman Josiah Wheeler," Calvert said impatiently. He bowed his head to Kittamaquund. "To show our love for each other, my brother the Tayac has agreed that he should be executed by our law."

"And if an Englishman had murdered an Indian, would you love the Tayac so in return and hang the man also?" I asked. I saw Kittamaquund turn and look at Calvert, as if interested in his response.

Cornwaylis had turned red. "Such a comparison is absurd."

"I see you're determined to be offensive, Hallam," Calvert said.

"Did you bring me here for a lesson then?"

"One that isn't quite finished yet,"

"The Tayac understands the justice of civilized Christians can not be compared to the customs of men who serve up their slain enemies to be feasted upon," White interjected, looking nervously at Kittamaquund, as if he'd seen the Indian's response to my question. "The Tayac understands that this man's soul may be thus saved from eternal hellfire."

"Which tribe is it does that?" I asked Kittamaquund. The discussion didn't interest me: let them hang who they would. But if those plans included me, better to set them against each other. I remembered something else Calvert had said, in that long ago conversation on St.Clement's Island, at the edge of the New World. "I thought it was only the Virginia English who ate the dead of their enemies," I said. "Do you eat your dead enemies as they do, Tayac?"

"Which tribe is yours, Hallam?" Kittamaquund asked, with great and true curiosity.

"And yours, Tayac?" I asked, feigning equal interest. White hissed in his breath. But Kittamaquund just walked away from us, from the whites, up to the prisoner. His face remained expressionless. In front of Father Altham, he crossed himself and drew Pennockquod aside. The priest hesitated, as if thinking to interfere, then stepped back. Kittamaquund spoke quietly and gravely to the prisoner. After a few minutes, Pennockquod grunted and tapped his bound hands against his breast.

"He accepts conversion," Kittamaquund said.

"Blessed be the Name of the Lord," White said. He stepped forward, took the prisoner to the side, and began the baptismal rite. The kneeling Indian took the host into his mouth and began chewing before White could stop him. Kittamaquund stood next to him. His hand had trembled slightly and jerked towards his waist, towards a knife or tomahawk no longer there, when I had baited him before. I looked at him now, feeling suddenly drawn to this Indian, to the man who had killed his brother to take a power he would not otherwise have; who danced his fool's dance before Calvert's gentry, who let this man hang, who ate his rage, so he could keep it. The New Man.

White finished and led the Indian back to the gallows.

A squat strong-looking man I hadn't seen before, brother executioner, started to put a hood over the man's head. Pennockquod shook it off. He began to chant his death song. One of the Indians in the crowd—I recognized my "neighbor" Tawzin—turned his back and walked away. The condemned man stepped up on the small stool. White pushed the cross into his face, as if to block the wail of the death chant. The man kissed it. "I be go to see Josiah," he yelled, suddenly grinning widely, and the squat man kicked the stool away.

"He goes to see Jesus," White yelled triumphantly. "Did you hear? Tis a miracle we witness."

"He dances for you," I said to Calvert, to Kittamaquund.

Calvert stared. "And who do you dance for, Hallam?"

"Neither man nor God."

"You damn your own soul," White said.

"Aye, I've felt that fire already, father. Even set a bit of it myself."

"I tell you this, Hallam," Cornawayles said, "you are still under the laws of this colony."

"I've broken none of them."

"You just have, blasphemer."

"Ah, then charge me as such. And if not and if the entertainment has finished, well then, I'll be on my way."

I saw Margaret Brent staring at Calvert expectantly, and felt a stir of warning in my gut.

"Why should you hurry so, Hallam?"

I turned on Calvert with a snarl. "I'll not strut more in your drama. If you wish to accuse me of something and have the evidence, then bring it out. If not, I'll be going back to my freehold."

Calvert nodded. "Of course. But there is one other matter, Freeman Hallam. One other small legal nicety, before you go. Margaret has informed me, and Father White has concurred, that our agreement giving you ownership of Ezekiel is not binding, as he was not ours to give, but a ward of the church, purchased by Father White, and thus the property of the Church, and more specifically of the Society of Jesus. Therefore I hereby nullify the false pact made between us regarding this man, and affirm his freedom, as a paid out indenture."

For a moment, I stood confused, Calvert's words an addling buzz in my mind, settling slowly into their meaning. Then I met Calvert's eyes. "He is mine," I said. I raised my hands. "As much as these are mine. He was a promise to me."

"As you once promised loyalty to me. He will be delivered to us a free man, sirrah, or I will have those hands and everything they have touched in this place."

Giles Brent, armor hanging loosely from his scarecrow frame, drew closer to me. He put a hand to his pommel, as if he were going to draw his sword.

I bowed to Brent, then Calvert.

"Right it is, then."

Calvert stepped back. "What are you saying, man?"

"It will be as you wish. If Ezekiel is not mine under law, I give him to you."

"S'blood, of course you will, or I'll stretch your damned neck on these gallows," Cornwayles said.

I bowed again. "By your leave, your lordship."

"Leonard," Margaret Brent said, "don't let him go. He will not..."

"I beg pardon, lady; have I been charged with some crime? I go to do your bidding and free my slave."

"You provoke us, Hallam," Calvert said.

"Has that become a crime, then, in your free colony? Then I beg your excellency's pardon. Perhaps I have been alone too long on my land, to have proper manners. I'd go now to dwell upon my sinful behavior."

"James Hallam," Margaret Brent said. "Understand me. What you have done to that man's, that artist's hands, is a crime equal to your disloyalty, and you will not escape the workings of justice for either."

I saw the governer start, and Margaret Brent's eyes widened, as if she was surprised herself at the words her mouth had uttered. But Calvert said nothing.

"Well, then that will be as that will be, lady," I said softly to this woman who spoke for what passed as a man. Kittamaquund was regarding me thoughtfully. I grinned at him. What the Indians love is a story.

"Watch me," I said.

"Hold this man," Cornwayles said to Giles Brent. Brent drew his sword and put the tip against my chest. I smiled at him, stepped to the side, grasped his shoulders and butted my head into his face. Spun behind Brent as he fell back, his nose fountaining, and then I had one hand around the nape of his neck, the other with my dirk in it at his throat. I picked Brent up by the neck with my free hand, dangling his feet just above the ground. Brent moaned.

"Do you still want me for a soldier? Do you want to see a soldier's work close then? I'll slit him like a rabbit," I said to Calvert. The militia had their muskets and pikes leveled at me. Mary Brent grasped Calvert's arm.

"Lower your weapons," Calvert said.

"Do you think to again take from me what is mine?" I said to Calvert, to Margaret Brent, to all of them. I spat on the ground. "You gentlemen adventurers."

I walked Brent toward the river, keeping the pressure on his neck, the knife at his throat, so the man gasped. The colonists and Yaocomacos following in a muttering cloud. One of the Indians, Tawzin again, notched an arrow and as casually as I had headbutted Brent, shot it into my leg below the knee. I grunted and pushed the point of the knife into Brent's throat, enough to let a trickle of blood. Someone knocked up Tawzin's bow. I smiled at the Piscataway and kept walking. Not allowing myself to limp. My moccasin filling with blood. I was sloshing in it as I reached the river. My canoe, the dugout, was moored at the pier.

"He comes with me," I said to Calvert. "If you follow, I'll cut his throat."

"He'll do it anyway," Margaret Brent said. "Don't let him go."

"He's your brother, woman," Cornwayles said.

I untied the canoe as she spoke. I pushed Brent in, on the deck under my feet and told one of the men standing on shore to push me off. I kept the knife to Brent's neck as the dugout shot out into the river, then put it down, grabbed the paddle, keeping my foot on the man's throat. As I dipped the paddle into the water, I heard a whine, like a great mosquito, passing close by my ear, and felt a burn in my chest. I grunted again. "Tawzin," I called back, like a promise. The arrow had penetrated into the slab muscle at my breast. Not deeply enough that I couldn't pull it out, hold it up, break it in one hand and throw it into the river. On the shore, someone was struggling with Tawzin.

The river was calm and I moved swiftly on it into the silence of the country and it wasn't until I was a mile downstream that I allowed myself to throw back my head and howl. As I did, I felt the dugout bob from side to side and heard a splash and then Brent was gone, slipped over the side. I hoped the slithering little bastard would drown.

The white square of a sail was behind me now. They were using the Dove, bringing the whole damnable settlement with them to chase me down. The idea pleased me. When I looked behind, the sails were closer and I could see dinghies in the water, two under sail. I paddled harder, feeling my muscles pull against the burn of pain in my chest, relishing it. The river widened and grew choppy. I moved closer to the eastern bank, skirting the edges of water lily colonies, the canoe gliding under branches canopied out over the water. A blue heron flapped off from the reeds, opening its wing spread in the disjointed manner such birds have, moving into its grace in the air. It almost took me off with it, into a gliding dream. I spotted the mouth of the small creek, just after a jut of land fringed with cordgrass, and slipped into it. From the river, if you didn't know where to look, the creek mouth was invisible until it was passed, and then you would have to look back to see it. I followed that twisting thread of water into thick marsh. The grass higher than my head on both sides. Moving into my freedom and grace. Dragonflies hovered next to my face like guides. After a mile I saw the dead tree, bleached to bone and fingered like a crooked hand. I paddled to it, beached the canoe, got out and pulled it up onto the muddy shore. A nation of fiddler crabs stared at me, signaled to each other, jumped into their wet holes. I pulled the canoe over to a clump of bushes. A bark Susquehannock portage canoe was concealed among them.

A voice called out my name. A short thick white man dressed in a buckskin shirt and leggings, his face painted, his neck hung with *roanoke*, stood in the shadows. Henry Fleet, under the paint.

"Hallam," Fleet said, as discovering the answer to a question. Behind him, painted also, two Susquehannocks stepped forward. Big men, big as I, their faces tigerish under stripes of black and red paint, their eyes yellow as panthers' eyes. Each with a tomahawk. One a waist high club with stone fit into socket at its end, the other a small steel axe fitted to a short handle. Bows and quivers of arrows also. Fleet had both tomahawk and musket. He pointed at my chest. I became aware of the warm trickle of blood. I touched it, licked my finger.

"A scratch."

"This is Dark Moon and Caws-Like-Crow," Fleet said, using the English renderings of their names, as had become the custom among the whites, who found the Indian names impossible to pronounce. Though Fleet, as far as I knew, did not have that problem, and neither did I. Was Fleet doing it deliberately, to set me among the other whites? The two men each nodded briefly and solemnly. Dark Moon said something I didn't get.

"He says they look forward to the day you can have a name they can greet you with," Fleet explained.

The four of us moved back off the beach and squatted near some blueberry bushes. The Indians picked and ate as Fleet spoke.

"What have you heard?"

"That I'm the new man. Baptized in blood and fire."

Fleet laughed, handed me a gourd. "Good. Welcome. This will make you a newer man."

I drank deeply.

"Well, man, what?"

"They'll probably move against Kent Island."

"When?"

"I don't know. Soon, I think. Cornwayles and that popinjay scut Giles Brent has been charged with forming the militia. His sister is more of a man."

"Claiborne says that she has a man's part between her legs."

"Nay, worse, she has a man's brain and has given it to Calvert."

"We've heard she gives him her cunny too."

I shrugged. "Does it matter to our enterprise?"

"Not a wit. I was only ruminating on who would do what to whom and with what. If such a condition existed. Men like to ruminate on the unnatural. Have you noticed that, Hallam? Something draws them to it. Would I? they ask. Could I? Men like to think, I think, that the order of things can be disarranged."

"The order of the country."

"Yes."

"Can it be?"

"Hallam, I lived twenty years as an Englishman and twenty years with my friends here. There is no order, save what our minds and hearts and balls bend to their needs."

"I've thought that for many years, but not put it into words."

"That makes us brothers."

"No," I said. "I have no brothers nor sisters nor parents nor wives nor children nor country nor colony nor tribe nor god. I have but things that are mine and that I will keep, and things that will be mine."

"*That* makes us brothers, brother."

I ignored this. "I'll be coming with you, then."

"You're more useful to us here."

"Not any more. It's over. They knew. They're chasing me now."

"As you wish, brother. We can use you at Kent, head and hands."

I stared at him.

"What is it?" Fleet said.

"We have to go to my plantation first."

"You say Calvert is hunting you, man."

"We have time for this."

We walked through the marsh on a raised path the Indians showed me, and came through the woods and walked up through the stumps to the longhouse. Past the pig sty and Ezekiel's pen. Even before I looked in, I could tell, something in the quality of the silence, that the house and pen were empty.

Kill those, I said, in Susquehannock Algonquin. We can take some of the meat. But leave nothing.

"You're remembering the tongue quickly," Fleet grunted in approval.

"He's gone," I said.

"Who?"

There were coals still glowing in the firepit. I watched the two Indians kill the squealing pigs with their tomahawks. I turned away. I had again watched a man kick to his death at the end of a rope today, felt nothing. But now the man-like squeal and the smell of pig blood churned to some heavy grief in my stomach. I wondered if it were for this place. I shrugged. It meant nothing. I still had more rage and need than grief.

I lowered my trousers and pulled off my shirt. My skin was streaked with blood from the wounds. I picked up the end of a stick whose point was glowing in the fire. Held the glowing end against and into each of the wounds. I heard my flesh sizzle as if from a distance. My forehead burst with sweat. But I kept the scream locked inside my throat and skull. The Susquehannocks looking at me.

"Why do they say it like that? That I'm remembering," I asked Fleet, my voice shaking only a little.

For a moment Fleet stared at me blankly. As if his mind was in the Indian order of the world and the question was meaningless. I watched his face brighten to understanding.

"They believe words are something given before birth, whispered into the ear of the nesting child. All begin the same, all words are Algonquin, Algonquin of the Susquehannock. But other peoples have forgotten the words and only make strange sounds to recall them. Some people, like the Piscataway remember the true words more closely, though not exactly. But the English have forgotten everything and so speak a childish gibberish. They believe the same of the western tribes."

"I'd like to forget English." I was coring around the pain. Wanted to curl up on the ground around myself.

Fleet grunted, pointed at my chest. "Maybe you're trying to burn it from your heart. We're brothers in that too, Hallam. What else do you need here?"

I walked over to the house. I knew what I needed here, more than the deaths of pigs. I thought of Margaret Brent's tight-lined mouth, telling me to give up what I had been owed. I asked Dark Moon and Caws-Like-Crow to show me how well they tracked.

Ezekiel's Song

I had freed faces from the trunks of the trees in our grove, a tribe to keep her company when I was gone. I thought of what Margaret Brent had told me, but it was only white people's talk and I couldn't build hope on it. But the woman was getting stronger. Jacob Lombroso had come a number of times and given her more of his berries and boiled roots; what she needed now, he told me, was meat and fish. I had nothing to hunt game with, but I set out a trotline fashioned of a vine and hung with rock-weighted pieces of fish line and barbed bonehooks I had gotten from the Yaocomaco. Each day I pulled in catfish and shad, sturgeon and croakers. I made a crab trap, a woven funnel-mouthed basket, and put a dead alewife in it; the crabs came in to feed on its flesh and couldn't leave. I brought trenchers from the house. I gathered oysters from the sandy river bed, plucked them like fruit. Her skin was becoming smoother as she gained weight. She smiled when she saw me arrive. She was strong enough now to go off into the woods to ease herself and I was relieved I no longer had to clean her with leaves, but also missed the intimacy of the act, that she had stopped feeling shame with me, as if her body was my body. But if she was strong enough to do that, I thought, she was getting strong enough for us to run.

It was turning fall now. On this day Hallam was gone to St. Marie's and when I came to her, carrying the axe to build a better shelter, she was gone also. My heart dropped. I heard a splash and went down to the river. She had made a V-shaped fish weir out of driftwood, the kind I had seen the Yaocomaco make and use and, with the edge of an oyster shell, had carved a point on the end of a stick and she had waded out thigh deep and was spearing the fish she had herded into the corrall. I watched her body smooth and wet in the sun, centered around the black wet lick of hair and I wanted the world to stop at this moment, wanted to hold the picture of her tight in my mind, as if I could pack it into a box I would open near the end of my days and know the world I would pass out from, young or old, was not all pain.

By the time she came up from the beach, I had started a small fire in the small pit I had dug. She had wrapped the Piscataway deerskin skirt around herself, but her breasts were bare, a film of sweat on them from the climb up from the beach. She brought two rockfish and laid them on a bed of clean pineneedles. Their bodies lay stiff, still wet and silver, the diamond pattern of their scales iridescent against the green. She gutted them and scraped them with an oyster shell and covered them with the meat of acorns she had ground against a small stone. They sizzled on the flat clay shard I had brought and fixed with a hickory wood handle. At first I hadn't wanted to build a fire or cook here, but Hallam's absences were more and more prolonged, and I felt there was something blessed about the grove where I had found her, a small protected pocket of the world, folded out of time and the consideration of men. A cold wind blew off the river like the first breath of winter, and the turning leaves rasped against each other in the trees, their dry smell mingling with the smell of woodsmoke in the clean sharp air. We ate the fish and the boiled cattail stems I had brought and we lay on our backs and looked at the leaves in the woven canopies above our heads, mostly still green, but pale yellows and golds and scarlet splashes and the sunlight spangling through the net of them. We looked at the faces I had carved or brought out to the surface in the trunks of the trees around them, like the gods of the grove, though I had carved them, I thought, to give her company, to put her in the middle of a tribe my hands could make in the world, and the faces that had come unthinking from under my hands and knife I saw now were a mix of my features and hers, and sometimes

Lombroso's and Tawzin's and sometimes my namesake's, young and grown and old faces, children growing into their lives. She was looking where I was looking, not following my gaze but there with me. "Who are dey?" she asked me, of the faces I had freed from the wood. In English. We could speak a little now: the English that was slowly coming back to her memory from her time with the Blackrobes, some Piscataway Algonquin that I had learned, though her true language, the words of her childhood and birth, as the words of mine, were still held under her tongue. Tawzin had spoken to her at great length, but all he could tell me was that she had come at first from some treeless land far to the West or the South, he wasn't sure, taken young to the Blackrobes when her people were wiped out, taken still young from the Blackrobes in another raid, sold or captured from one tribe to another, kept as a hunting woman, those captives or unmarried women taken along on hunting parties to service the braves. The Susquehannock who she had finally ended up with, Tawzin said, had decided she was bad luck and needed to be buried to be cured of it.

"Who are dey?" she asked again, and the words that came to my lips in answer were in Barbados talk, couched from my memory by her pronunciation, or perhaps as if my namesake were putting them into my lips. "We sort a people," I answered her.

"We sort?" she said, and touched her breasts. And I knew that she had just found her name.

"Yes," I said, and touched her breast, and put her hand on my chest. "We sort."

She took my callused, scarred hand from her breast and brought its palm to her lips and kissed it, hard, flattening her lips against it, and brought it back to her breast and I felt her nipple hardening against it and then between my fingers. At that moment, my shackles, still hung from a pole in the longhouse, came unbidden and hung heavy in my brain. I saw them and when I looked at her, I began to weep. I looked at her face, the undeserved luck of her. It was the first water my eyes had shed since I was a boy in a dusty village in a country whose name I was forgetting, and I wondered then, the shackles coming to me at such a moment, if I was born to be a man who betrayed mine own; I had betrayed Ezekiel, betrayed myself, and through that betrayal I knew I had betrayed her and there weren't enough tears in me to drown my shame. But she came to me and she touched the stream of my shame, her eyes wide, and I kissed her. I kissed her without thinking of what I was doing, in the middle of tears, and her eyes widened more with surprise at this act, but then she smiled, as if taking in a new idea and considering it and deciding to like it. She took my lower lip between hers and sucked on it, and I felt the blood swell in me, but stopped and left her also, my shame deepening and tempered with joy so that I had together in one moment the first tears and the first joy of my manhood. I had neither wept nor felt the weight of shame leave my heart since I had betrayed Ezekiel and it was only in its lifting from me now that I understood how it had been there all my days. We rolled into each others arms now and kissed each other, our lips moving over each other's faces. She pulled off her skirt and with a smile and a practicality that for a second of pain reminded me of how she must have been used, or taken her pleasure as she could, and then I did not care because there was only us now, in our grove, we sort of people, and she helped me pull off my breeches, smiling and laughing when I sprang free, holding me and kissing the tip of me so my whole body and soul was pulled to that cusp against her lips and I pulled her to me and kissed her closed eyes and the sides of her nose and held her lower lip between mine and moved down her neck, her breasts, wanting to take her into my body to live there, wanting the skin between us to vanish, and I moved down to her and kissed and licked her, she smelled of woodsmoke and once in Barbados I had touched a bolt of silk, held in a dockside warehouse for a planter and she felt like warm liquid silk against my lips and tongue. She moaned and pulled me up to her and took me in her hand and rubbed me in circles against the smoothness of her thigh and she opened and parted liquid and smooth against my finger and I saw one of the faces I had carved, a child's face, smiling at me and I saw Hallam's face smiling next to it.

I didn't need the tracking skills of the two Susquehannocks. I smelled the smoke from a mile away, then saw its black twist against the sky. When I drew closer to the place, I could smell the fish frying, and I began to see the faces, carved all around, staring at me from the trees. I drew my knife and slashed at them, opening white scars, though the two Indians looked at me in disapproval. Then I heard the moaning. It puzzled me—was Ezekiel dreaming?—but when I saw him with the woman, I smiled. I motioned for Fleet and the Indians to be quiet, and I waited and watched, the surging of blood in my cock an edge or measure for my rage now, and the moment I saw the slave would enter her, I stepped forward and let Ezekiel see my face. I smiled at him.

Ezekiel rolled off with a cry, dripping. I slammed the butt of my musket into his jaw. The girl leapt at me, clawing and kicking, but I stepped aside, pulled her up by her hair as I had Giles Brent, and punched her in the face. She fell near the fire, her hair going into the pit, and I let it burn for a few seconds before I stepped on it and rolled her away.

I told Dark Moon and Caws-Like-Crow to hold Ezekiel. Fleet had faded back into the trees, looking nervously behind them for signs of my pursuers. I took the axe and chopped off a small branch, and cut it into four pegs and pounded them into the ground with the blunt of the axe. Then I took a strip of rawhide from Dark Moon and cut it into four pieces and tied her spreadeagled to the stakes. I had the Susquehannocks lash Ezekiel to a sycamore tree, standing, rawhide around his chest and waist. Dark Moon pointed to the black's hand and muttered to Caws-Like-Crow and Caws-Like-Crow drew in a sharp breath and grunted when he saw the fingers and then both Indians said nothing. Ezekiel was conscious, his eyes rolling in his head as if they were trying to escape what they saw. I seized his jaw between my forefinger and thumb and swivelled him to look at the woman.

"Who is she?"

Ezekiel closed his eyes.

"Open your eyes." I squeezed again. Ezekiel opened his eyes.

"Who is she?"

I heard the Indians breathing heavily behind him. Ezekiel's eyes rolled backwards and he slumped.

"Stop talking so much," Fleet stepped up across from me, behind Ezekiel's head. "Do what you have to do, and let's move. Calvert's militia will be here soon. We can take the girl."

"Shut up," I said. "If you don't wish to be here, then go listen for them. Set up an ambush. You know how to do that, don't you?"

Fleet stared. "You'll not speak to me that way."

"Do as I say now." I let go of Ezekiel's face, turned to Fleet. The man was standing back near a tulip poplar, as if Ezekiel and I and the woman were behind a boundary he didn't wish to cross. It made me more furious. The two Indians looked at me and muttered something.

"They have a name for the state you're in," Fleet said. "I can't translate it. But you're lucky there is one. They respect it."

I seized Ezekiel's face again. The eyes opened. As they did I felt the wound in my chest open and bleed. Ezekiel's eyes were instantly aware and utterly devoid of hope.

"Who is she?"

Ezekiel's free hand shot up, grasped my wrist, as he had once done in Barbados.

"My wife."

I released his face, pried his hand off as if it had no strength.

"You're wrong," I said. "You have no *my*. Only I do.

Because you're mine. You're mine and now so is she and so is anything that issues from her, from now until your last breaths on earth. Do you understand? No? Let me show you."

I took Ezekiel's hand again, brushed its back against the tenting of my pants. "Do you understand me, Lucius Ezekiel?"

I lowered my pants and dropped to my knees between the woman's legs. Her eyes were open but flat, as if they weren't registering anything. I felt the same. As if I were bled from myself. As if that man I had been, that Sergeant in the dust in front of a monastery in Spain, was seeing from my eyes, moving my lips into a smile, the way Ezekiel's hand shaped faces from wood. I touched between her legs, then wet my fingers from the wound in my chest and wet her with my blood and pushed inside. There was complete silence in the grove. The faces on the trees stared at me and when I felt myself release, I stared back into their eyes and I spit. There was no feeling in any of my discharges. They were equal in contempt. If not in consequence.

I rose and pulled on my pants. I went back to Ezekiel.

"Now she's my wife," I said. "Married blood and seed." The faces still stared at me from the trees. A hanged man. The burning eyes of a burning priest. Meg raising her skirt, her crotch a mass of corruption and sores. "Clever hands," I muttered. The axe Ezekiel had stolen from me, as he had tried to steal himself, was on the ground near my feet. I picked it up in one hand. I seized Ezekiel's right wrist with my other, Ezekiel's six devil's fingers writhing and scratching and carving in my brain, and I held it against the trunk of the carved oak next to the sycamore and I raised the axe and took what Margaret Brent and Leonard Calvert and the whole world would steal from me.

Ezekiel had begun to moan and then howl during the rape and now as the axe buried into the wood, his howl burgeoned impossibly and coiled with the howl of the woman staked by the fire, her thighs wet with my leavings. As if both howls burst from the same throat. The noise shook birds from the trees and they exploded into the air as if something had been pulled from beneath them. It brought Fleet and the two Susquehannocks running back to the grove.

"I can hear them coming," Fleet said. He looked at Ezekiel, his wrist gushing, and grunted. "Come on. This one is already dead. Come on. Take the girl and let's go."

I cut her bonds. She sat up, dull-eyed, wiping at her thighs. Dark Moon reached down and she seized his hand and sank her teeth into the palm and when he jerked up to hit her, she twisted away, brown and slippery as an eel, and ran into the trees. The Indian started after her.

"Leave her," Fleet growled. I could hear it now too: the sound of men moving through the forest. She was running in that direction.

"Let her go," I nodded. "She carries me with her now. I'll find her."

I picked up what had been owed to me and picked up the woman's deerskin and used it to wrap that, so I could carry it without leaving a blood trail.

"They'll have a name for you now," Fleet said.

Wesort

The Year One

From: *The Journal of a Voyage to North-America* by
Fr. Pierre de Charlevoix, S.J.

...It is not so much with a view of perpetuating names that they renew them, as with a view to incite the person on whom they are bestowed, either to imitate the great actions of the persons that bore them, or to revenge them in case they have been either killed or burned; or lastly to comfort their families: thus a woman who has lost her husband or som, and finds herself thus void of all support makes all the haste in her power, to give the name of the person she mourns for, to someone who may stand her in his stead; lastly, they likewise change their names on several other occasions....In order to do this there wants only a dream or the prescription of some physician, or some other reason equally frivolous.

Ezekiel's Song

The old man squats in the yellow dust before the fire, his naked haunches covered with the dry powder. His body striped with ochre. He holds up his hand. He holds its wrist with his other hand, turns it this way and that in the hard sunlight. His face is skullish. Dank hair frames it like a lion's mane.

Six finger call de eye a de hand, he says.

Eye see underside. Underside de woodskin. Underside de rock wrinkle. Underside de whisper a de wind.

Six finger see the weave a de world.

See up de rivah a tomorrow.

We cut off Six Finger to save de hand.

But den de hand not de hand anymo, no ha six finger.

Dat white man din cut off you hand. You already gone to pieces, fore that white man come.

Already gone.

You cut gone Ezekiel hand jus as I cut you hand. You give Ezekiel same I give two a you, to save the people. A child is give. But not pure. When you give Ezekiel you take Ezekiel. Put him inside you. Breathe him in every wind that tickle your nose. Breathe he dreams into you heart, you bones, so Ezekiel say.

Lucius, who gave you my name? Ezekiel says.

Six finger mus be give, the old man says. We give six finger. A child must be give, the old man says. We give a child. A hand must be give, the old man says. A name must be give, the old man says. We give a name. Now we gone.

Why you talk Barbados talk, old man? I ask. Are you not from Dahomey?

Why you call you Ezekiel? Ezekiel asks.

He is next to the fire, smiling, hands gone, feet gone, propped up with a plank. He leans over and sticks his right stump into the flame. It sizzles. The smell of burning meat drifts to me.

A child must be given, Ezekiel says to me. *His eyes are burning coals.*

The old man growls and seizes my right wrist. I can't move. Not just my arm, but all my body, as if the old man has released a paralytic into my veins or his grip in some way extends over all my flesh. The old man pinches my sixth finger on my right hand between his own thumb and forefinger and begins to pull it. The old man's sixth finger curves around under my palm like the tail of a scorpion and begins to saw with its black, serrated nail at the base of my sixth finger. My Gift. I see its skin stretch, split, the nail sawing at taut tendrils then white bones until the old man pulls it off. I scream.

Six finger ladle into the rivah a tomorrow. Stir clear what not clear.

A child must be given, my namegiver, my chain, my curse, he says. *He is standing on his stumps in the fire now. I hear the sizzle of meat. A mad Barbadan moon spins overhead.*

My namegiver pushes aside the old man and seizes my wrist between his teeth, then drops to the ground, pulling me with him. He worms towards the fire, pulling me, crawls into the flames, dragging my hand into the fire with his teeth. Twisted onto my back, my arm pulled straight, I watch his grin melt around its teeth's clamp on my wrist, watch his face peel back like layers of paper. I watch my own betraying hand blacken, the blood boil, the bone turn white hot and then sear through my nerves and bones to my throat, to my howl. Sees clouds of birds explode from the trees.

My eyes opened. I saw a woman's face, inches from my own, her breath on my skin. Her eyes opened wider and then closed and then opened again, as if she were registering my consciousness. She whimpered and leaned forward and pressed her lips against my skin. I remembered her name. My lips worked.

"Wesort," I said. The word pulled me back into blackness.

My hand throbs like a heart in the fire. I hear her voice whispering and feel the whisper stirring through my mind like a sixth finger.

I was born from the womb of the earth and you are my father and mother and you are my husband and he gave me words to call you to me, and do you hear them? Do you hear me calling you back from the blackness of the earth as you called me back from the blackness of the earth?

Why did I hear her? Where did she find words? Each word loosening a face or form from the clench of my memory. From a pen in which it was shackled and cowering. I saw Jacob Lombroso's face wavering through waves of pain, felt his grip on my handless wrist, the pull, the searing agony of the fire.

I howled myself back into the blackness.

When I awoke next, I could feel the hand that I could no longer see as if it were on fire. The woman was standing with her back to me, framed in a doorway. Wesort. She turned and smiled at me. I tried to sit, but felt a wave of weakness and nausea and fell back. She rushed over, her face worried.

"Lie," she said. "You lie."

I looked around. I was on a bed of pine needles on the dirt floor of a large longhouse. Only a few feet from the fire. Covered with a thick deerskin hide. My carver's eye registered measurements. Perhaps twenty feet by fifty feet, perhaps twelve feet high. The numbers, the known dimensions anchored me back into the world. Through the bright circles of the two smokeholes I could see swirls of snow in the updraft of smoke, melting. The heavy winter smell of wet wood, dry pine needles, drying animal hides, sweat. English axes and hoes, bows and arrows, dried corn and spars of tobacco, a wet deerskin tunic, hung from a loft made of crisscrossed locust wood boughs. A roof of woven mats.

Smells of woodsmoke and bear grease and sweat. Warm as a nest. I sat up slightly. Across the room, I could see people were sleeping under hides. An Indian; Tawzin—his name coming to me after his face—sat up and yawned, scratched his bare chest. He had his hand on a sleeping form next to him, still covered by the skin.

Wesort had brought a gourd and put her hand behind my head. Most of the water dribbled over my lips, ice cold snow melt, but some slid down my throat; it constricted painfully. She patted my chest nervously. My hand ached. I drew my right arm from under the bearskin. The end of my forearm was wrapped in white lindsey, its weave bloodstained. I could feel the ache of the hand, feel each finger outlined in its burn, but there was nothing there. I felt the sixth finger itch terribly. I had known it, a part of my mind always plunging me back into unconsciousness when I was at the verge of realization. But I was wide awake now. Twenty by fifty by twelve. An arm ending in a stump. The new dimensions of existence. Wesort looked at my face and brought my arm to her lips and kissed the bandage. She touched her chest, then mine and shrugged. As if to say what was a hand between us. Perhaps. Loss welled in my chest and throat. I pulled the arm back.

"You've had your turn now, woman, at pulling me from the grave," I said.

"You for me. Now I you," she nodded.

"Who taught you?" I asked, drawing my left hand out (its wholeness, less the sixth finger, breaking and filling my heart all at once) and touching her lips.

"Tawzin. Ja-cob Lom-bro-so. Dey he'p me remember dis tongue."

I remembered, thought I remembered, a dream: Lombroso gripping my fountaining arm.

"What happened?"

"I run, from Hallam. Lom-bro-so and Tawzin are coming. Dey run, see you, Lom-bro-so takes your hand into the fire, closes it. Lom-bro-so brings you here."

She waved around the longhouse.

Tawzin had risen and walked over to me. He touched his forehead in greeting, nodded.

"You have been in the true world of dreams since Hallam stole your hand. All Fall. Here, with us, to eat and shit, but your spirit has been gone. Until you are born to us now. Sometimes you would speak, though not to us. Have you brought a vision for us?"

"I can't remember."

Tawzin nodded. "No matter. Perhaps soon you will."

A woman's head emerged from the hide cover on his sleeping mat. Her hair was dirty blond, a white woman. She smiled at me. The mat door at one end of the longhouse opened and Jacob Lombroso came in, two rabbits dangling from a rawhide string in his right hand, a bow in his left. He peered, blinking, at me, a thick man with a lined face and a short gray beard and gray eyes with deep crinkles cut around them. As if I were seeing him for the first time. *Until you were born to us now.* The white woman rose from the hides, crossed the floor and took the rabbits from him. She was wearing a Piscataway deerhide breech-clout. I burst into laughter. We sort of people. The laughter shook me and pulsed in my wrist and I began to cry.

"Good," Lombroso said. "That's what one should do when one is born. You have been given a new life."

I held up my wrist, speechless.

"Yes," Lombroso said. "So weep for the hand and be thankful for the life. And good morning."

"Lombroso. Thank you for the life. And the morning."

"Thank Tawzin—he was trying with his usual patience to teach me to hunt when we found you. What I did was only a little elemental surgery and a little elemental shamanism. A poultice of acorn oil, hellebore and corn flour. Your woman put her mouth on your navel and sucked, she said she had to remove a ghost Hallam had put into you. She may have been right. You must thank God, and her."

He patted the woman's shoulder. "She wouldn't tell us her name."

"Wesort," I said. I pointed to myself and to her. "For we sort of people. She named herself."

Lombroso digested it for a moment and then laughed. Wesort smiled at him.

"Lombroso, how long? Tawzin says I've been here all Fall. Is that possible?"

"It's winter now, my friend. You have come back and been gone to delirium. You would speak to us, and then to others and then sleep. Have you no memory of this time?"

"None."

"A blessing. As the skin grows over a wound, at times the mind grows a blank smoothness over memory."

He put the back of his hand against my forehead. "You still have a little fever. When you're a little stronger, you can go into the sweat lodge, purge the evil humors from you. By the way, Tawzin also says your carvings protected you. They are very beautiful."

"They are *mesingw*," Tawzin said. "You must thank them."

I pulled out my stump and looked at it again. I thought of the carvings.

"It will be all right," Lombroso said gently, to what he saw in my face. "Your left hand will take on the cunning of your right. I have seen it before."

Wesort was caressing the bandage.

"She is a remarkable woman," Lombroso said. "She has cared for you as if you were a baby."

She smiled. "He my father. Now I his mother."

I looked at her as Lombroso spoke, ran my left hand over her face, down her neck, her body, as if to see I had left the land of dreams that Tawzin called the true world. But the true world was the warmth of this skin next to me.

"I dreamt of you," I said.

My hand reached her belly, stopped at the hard swell of

it under my palm. I drew my hand back, as if I had reached into the earth and a snake had bitten it. I closed my eyes. Wesort uttered a short cry.

"Yes," Lombroso said. "The baby will be born in the Spring."

My ghost hand burned. Its Gift, my missing finger, gone with it and my enemy, crooked and beckoned to me, clawed at my heart. I turned my head into the pine needles. If I could put my lips to her navel, draw out what my enemy had left with my teeth, I would do it. I kept my eyes closed, willed myself to fall back into the black pit where all dimensions dissolved into the hope of chaos.

I AWOKE to voices. There was bright sunlight streaming into the two smoke holes. I heard Jacob Lombroso's voice singing an odd wavering chant, in Algonquin-Piscataway, and in another gutteral tongue, and finally in English: *"And the direction of the doors will be towards the rising sun and towards the setting sun. Three posts will be used and the logs joined end to end three times. One post is at one door, as tall as the roof. One post is at the other door, as tall as the roof. In the middle is the main lodgepost as tall as the roof. All shall be notched at the top and at the sides where the logs join shall stand opposite each other as stud posts and they shall be joined together at the top with cross ties. At the top of the posts rafter poles shall run across, and the ridge pole should be in two pieces that join in the center, and a hands breadth over the height of the tallest person the roof shall begin and bark shall be used to cover it. And the firebanks will be set on opposite sides of the center pole and directly above each the roof shall have an uncovered hole where the smoke shall go out. And on every post at a person's height shall be carved the* mesingw *of that person, each person in the longhouse, and half the face shall be painted red and the other black."*

Lombroso peered down at me and smiled. "And the height of the ark shall be fifty cubits," he said. "In Europe, I read the book of Antonio de Montezinos, who had traveled in the Americas. His revelations that the Lost Tribes of Israel had wandered across Asia and into America, his observations on the similarities of physique and custom between the Hebrews and the Indians struck a spark in me." Lombroso rubbed the hawk's arc of his nose, his cheeks, laughed, delighted as a child who had just discovered something new about the world. "Do you see? Did you hear the chant? This too is something my people seem to have in common with the Piscataway: our prayers tell us the numbers and weights and measurements of what can save us. As a carpenter, you should appreciate that. This is the Cabala's understanding, my friend, that we are here acting out patterns in the Universe whose purpose we may not understand, but whose design will become clear as we learn to imitate its dimensions. The World is Words. Of course, my people would never allow for *mesingw*—the sacred carved faces of human beings. Thou shalt not. Thou shalt not. Thou shalt not. Yet thou hast, Ezekiel. And beautifully, in the grove where we found you. So the Piscataway are singing. They say you found the faces of the restless spirits in that place and brought them out of the wood. As you heal, you will do the same for us, in this place." He patted the center pole. "On these," he said.

I drew my stump from under the blanket and showed it to Lombroso.

"No matter," Lombroso said. "You have a second." He bent down and slid an arm under my shoulders. "As I told you, it will take on the cunning of the other. Unless you forget Jerusalem."

"What do you mean?"

He grinned. "A good shaman, like a good cabalist, like a good physician, my friend Ezekiel, never explains everything." He helped me to my feet. "Come."

The bright sunlight outside pierced my eyes and I cried

out. I stepped onto a crust of snow smooth and brittle as an egg shell, the world to which I had returned danced with sparkles of sunlight that shifted as my eyes swept around me. I was barefoot, wrapped in my rank deerskin blanket. The longhouse was wrapped around by the forest, so one, I thought, would almost be upon it before it issued from the trees.

"Is this your longhouse or Tawzin's?

"Your question is more interesting philosophically than you know, my Ezekiel. Who is whose guest in this country? For me, such a condition, to be a guest, is the text of my life. For the English, at least, I'm a temporary sojourner here; welcome as long as I am of use to my hosts. It's a state I am quite used to. Calvert has given me this corner of St. Michael's in return for my services as a physician and a translator, and a donation to the coffers of the enterprise. In his mind, this is mine. In my own, and in Tawzin's, the term 'mine' has quite a different meaning."

I stared at him. I had thought my question a simple one.

Lombroso let me go, and I began stepping gingerly, my legs shakey as a newborn fawn. The burning cold on my bare feet made me aware of each step, so that I couldn't move thoughtlessly. I wondered if this was part of Lomobroso's design.

"Thus, in turn," Lobroso continued—I had thought him finished, though apparently he had just left me somewhere on the twisted path of his reply—"I gave this corner of my corner to Tawzin, and hence the philosophic dilemma—how could I give what is more his by right? I prefer, my friend, to see each other as guests of each other, though I'm not sure Tawzin would agree."

Opposite the longhouse, also among the trees, was a low sweatlodge, the snow around it melted and wisps of smoke leaking between the logs. A small platform had been erected by the entrance; it was piled with clothing. Lombroso drew off his blanket, and grunted happily in the cold, then slapped

his chest and stood grizzled and naked and grinning, his mat
of body hair black and speckled with silver, but his figure
robust and muscular. He slapped my shoulder and pulled off
my deerskin. I shivered uncontrollably, felt my muscles
contract, my scrotum shriveling up to my body. Lombroso
was a mad man. "You're a mad man," I said aloud. My
invisible hand ached. The physician's grin widened and he
held open the door and drew me inside.

The contrasting heat immediately caused my skin to
erupt with sweat. The air was thick and hazed, tendrils of
smoke twining into a silky, caressing web. The wet heat filled
my lungs. Lombroso grabbed me, and held me upright and
an instant later, as if the man had anticipated it, my head
swam with dizziness and I would have fallen over if not for
the arm around my shoulders, the hand under my armpit. A
pit filled with red hot stones was in the center of the room. I
saw Wesort, rising, her sweat-polished body making
something constrict in my chest; the swell of her belly, more
obvious now in her nakedness, turned to an ache of grief.
She picked up a clay pot and splashed water on the stones.
The heat and smoke thickened. Through it I saw Tawzin and
the white woman lying next to each other like two fish
cooking on a plank. "This is Tawzin," Lombroso said,
formally, in his odd singsong, "whose name means only the
son of a *werowance*, for the English called him John
Christman and his true name was stripped from him and
forgotten when he was taken in his twelfth summer across
the water and the Tayac so called him when he was born back
to his people, to honor his father. And he is my brother and a
cockorouse and *wisoe* of the Yaocomaco Piscataway. And this
is his woman, Nanjemoy, whose name in the English tongue
was Sally Picard of Virginia, taken in her twelfth summer
also by the Powhatans until she was found by her people the
Piscataway and called only by the place where she was
found."

Nanjemoy's narrow face was full of a humorous intelligence that made it feel both strange and fitting and easy for me to be introduced to her by name and face and real body, cross-legged and open; naked was the way to be proclaimed to people, I decided, this is what I am, this I trust to you it said, and I was peeled and handless myself in this place, vulnerable to my naked heart. Looking at Nanjemoy now, I thought I could see that she was also with child, and at the thought Hallam came, thick-cocked and turgid as I'd seen him when we fought: Hallam who would see this flesh as food.

Next to Nanjemoy was Wesort.

"Whose name has been found and given, by you and by her," Lombroso said, "and who has not another name, and this is her true name, and it is the name we will take as our own, for it seems you and she have called us as well."

"Now you come born to us," Tawzin said, rising and speaking for the first time to me, as if we had never known each other before, "and must find your name, so that we may call you to us."

"My true name," I said, "is Ezekiel, who was Lucius of Barracoon Seven in Barbados, who was a boy who had lost his name and who came from a nation that has lost its name and from a village that has lost its name. My true name is Ezekiel, a name given to me by a dead man I betrayed and who gave me his dreams and my life. My true name is Ezekiel, and if it is not your custom to keep the name a man comes to you with, then damn you and thank you and I'll be on my way."

Nanjemoy laughed deeply and slapped her knee.

"Your name, I think," Tawzin said, "must be Ezekiel. Come, sit with us, Ezekiel."

But when I took my place, I ignored the space next to Wesort and sat on the opposite side from her, as far as I could from the nameless thing growing in her belly.

IN THE MORNING, as I opened my eyes I forced my mind to keep its grip on the dream, letting it catch and be held in the crisscross of branches over my head, continuing its flux in the sinuous flume of smoke from the fire. I had seen what was growing inside her, and gone in and visited it, as if into a sweatlodge, and it squatted naked and red and stubby and sweating droplets of blood and its eyes red and glowing, its sharp-toothed grin, this Thing my Enemy had left in my life. It disappeared now, in the smoke, dispersed through the branches, and next to me I saw Wesort, her face looking out from under the sleeping skin, and I saw her see it in my eyes. She turned from me with a groan, then rose and gathered the deerskin and moved to the other side of the longhouse.

Nanjemoy squatted down next to me, her face angry. She said something shrilly to me in Piscataway, then slapped my shoulder hard and gestured at Wesort. She looked at me. I watched her anger change. She put the back of her cool hand on my forehead.

I slipped back into the fever over the next days, in and out of lucidity. Something chewed and gnawed at my wrist, and I saw the Thing squatting next to him, its contorted face grinning through a veil of steam. Hallam compacted short and wide, his malevolence concentrated. The pain seized my stump, my invisible hand, in its mouth; I felt its teeth grinding against the shards of my bones. I was aware, dimly, of other shapes around me, the circle of the sweatlodge expanding and contracting, hot flesh pressed to my hot flesh, but the forms shadowy, their edges dissolving into smoke. I saw Lombroso's lined face with its bright concerned eyes, its hawk nose, its pointed black and silver beard trailing to mist, reforming from mist again. Lombroso's mouth opened and closed, slowly as a fish underwater; words came to me in a glide of liquid heat and luminosity through my head, then one word I didn't understand: *Dybbuk*, and a chant, the circle of misty sweatlodge faces chanting around me, and I felt something lift from me and suddenly I was weightless and incandescent as smoke and reformed to myself again, to a wholeness that only knew what had been missing from itself by its return.

When I came back my mind was clear and I still felt weak and light, but the lightness had a scoured quality to it, as if I had been purged, and when I looked across at Wesort and saw her face, eyes closed, a slight smile on her full lips, my heart that had been hollow filled and strengthened. I leaned over and caressed her face with my left hand, and I kissed her eyelids and down the sides of her nose and her lips, retracing a path, rediscovering her, rediscovering my hunger for her, and she tightened her mouth against me, then groaned and picked up her deerskin cover and picked up mine and rolled into my arms, with the still hot smooth feel of her skin pushed into the length of my body, and her lips kissing my neck, and the hard swell of her womb against my stomach. I moved my right arm, its deformity stabbing me when I saw, remembered, under her back, hiding it as if in her flesh, and with the fingers of my left hand, with its missing digit that ached now as if for its missing counterpart, I found her and awkwardly caressed her and she found me and traced me and encircled me with her hand and made the noise she had before, of delight at this design, at this utility of flesh. She pulled and pushed at me, her arms around me, bringing me on top of her, and then looking down intently, her belly awkward between us, and pulled aside her nether lips and placed me against her. I pushed and entered her and I felt that hard curve of her belly pushing down at my belly, and what was inside her was pressed between us and I knew as I began to pulse within her matching, sheathing pulse on me, that child was now and forever bound to my flesh and heart as inseparably as she, was now fused and melted, in flame and pain and love, to me.

Extract from a Letter of Captain Thomas Young to Sir Toby Matthew

As soon as we were now come to anchor we decried a small barke coming out from Point Comfort, which bare with us, and about half an hower after she came to an Anchor cloase aboard o' vice admirall. We though she had been some vessell bound from Virginia to New England, whither the Inhabitants of Virginia drive a great trade for Indian Corne. I sent my Lieutenant aboard her to enquire whence she was and whither she was bound, and withall to leearne what he could concerning the State of Virgina and Maryland, which is my Lord of Baltimores Collony, as likewise on what tearmes those two Collonyes were, and what correspondence they had one wth another and with the Indians also. When he came aboard he found this Barke to be a vessell of Virginia belonging to one Captayne Cleyborne, who liveth upon an Island within my Lord of Baltimores Territory called the Ile of Kent.

Hallam's Song

The room we were in was close and seemed made of fur, as if we were in the stomach of some Animal yanked outside in. Stacks of hides, mostly beaver but also bear, deer, otter and wildcat, were piled from floor to ceiling and layered inwards, so that the center of the room was a hollow surrounded by dead skin and fur, all shades of brown and black sheening in the beams of sunlight from the one window, the hair bristling, a tallowy dead smell heavy and mucousy in my throat and nostrils. Claiborne seemed part of it, as if the ghost or Idea of what had been stripped and left behind had been translated from the wall of hair: sleek and pink, his cheeks, under a black stubble of beard, puffed; his eyes narrow and gleaming, his nose reddened, his yellowed front teeth slightly protuberant, his body swollen at hips and belly, but emanating a trim power, an impression that he would drive and gnaw whatever he seized. Though perhaps this was only a conceit of my vision, a seeing of the true world under the mist of shapes, as the Indians would have it. He had been the emblem of my dreams, but I had awakened now, and I no longer needed dreams. Seeing him, an Idea fleshed (or skinned), I felt only a chill, a kind of bubble of cold stillness moving into my mind and heart.

"James Hallam," Claiborne said. "At last we see each others' faces. How do you like my Kent Island, James Hallam?"

Until now, I had been forbidden to journey to the island, for fear my ties to him would be discovered. I had expected a rude camp. Instead there was a palisaded fort, two mills, storehouses, cabins, an Anglican church, and even a small shipyard, all neatly built and well laid out. I had seen enough traders and rangers to man four barques for trading voyages, more than enough farmers and coopers and millwrights and carpenters and hogs and whores and ministers to keep the beaver traders fat, thoughtless and happy. In truth, what I had seen he had built here, Claiborne's kingdom encysted like an abscess within the heart of Calvert's kingdom, struck me more than I would reveal to its creator.

Claiborne was stroking the thick beaver pelt on top of one pile. Waiting for me to reply. To reveal my admiration. I worked my hand between the rawhide laces in front of my own shirt, grasped the nail of Ezekiel's sixth finger and pushed it into my breastbone. The Indians wore medicine pouches around their necks; this was mine. I'd kept this. The rest of the hand gone as a gift, to the Brents. During the day, and sometimes at night when I slept, my hand would find Ezekiel's finger, caress its stiff brittle weight on my chest, press its jagged nail against my skin. As I was doing now.

"Something in me," I said, stealing Calvert's words, "doesn't like an island."

Claiborne snorted. "Nor I, nor I. But I hold it dear as long as that papist popinjay Calvert wishes to take it from me. Come, I want you to see something."

He led me through a corridor thick with bristling fur itself, the smell acrid and stinging in my nostrils, into the next room. Into more fur. It pushed in on every inch of my skin, as if seeking to root in me.

"Eight thousand pelts in this storage, Hallam," he said. "D'you think Calvert, with his damnable King's charter, could bring anything like this to London?"

Yes, if not for you, I thought. But I understood the question to be meaningless. Claiborne's fury now was but a mime, a way of introducing himself. It surprised me that he thought he needed to, but it did not disquiet me that he did. I wanted to be disappointed of him. I wanted to be emptied of all my dreams, and he was the last.

"Tell you something, James Hallam," he said tightly, his

voice trembling a little. "I sailed north up the arse of this Bay while that besotted toff's father still thought of New Foundland as a tropical isle. Tell you what they say in London: only reason Calvert got his Charter, king squinted at him and saw a Spanish twat. Me, Hallam, I put my own damned money into the *Africa*, came up here when Englishmen beshat themselves at talk of the Susquehannock. Come because I saw what the beaver trade would do. D'you know before Fleet found those diseased Piscataways, the Yaocomacos that Calvert has tied his venture to, they were burning their bloody beaver pelts? Eating the meat and burning the bloody pelts. Didn't even know what they were good for, not until Fleet told them."

His face had gone bright red and he was breathing heavily. I watched him until I saw what I had been looking for, though passing in an instant and gone: a slight twitch of his lips into a gleeful grin he couldn't quite keep back. It made everything that came before a lie. It made me smile. I did not mind if he saw it. He glanced at me, then nodded and smiled openly, as if it was the true conversation between us two.

"Come," he said.

Another room. The piles here were of *roanoke* and *peake*, thousands of blue beads. Claiborne picked up a strand, measured it to his arm's length.

"I'm having them fashioned at the Jamestown glass works by a crew of Italian glass blowers now," he explained. "Become the common currency of the Chesapeake, English and Indian alike, these have. Money from noxious weed and rodent fur and good for anything a man might want to buy. Whore to home." He laughed wildly, gestured expansively around the room.

"Takes sight, Hallam." He tapped the beads against his brow, "Eyes that see what people want. What you can make valuable to them, English or Indian. That's the true vision, Hallam. Fleet had it. Came with me from England, d'you know that? But took him five years captive to get his eyes opened. Me, I saw it soon as we landed in Jamestown. A man can see, Hallam, truly see, with American eyes, he can arrive in the Chesapeake poor as any soldier, earn more in one year than he could by piracy in seven. D'you see that? D'you understand me, man?"

He threw back his head and laughed. It trailed off when he saw I wasn't joining him, not smile nor laugh nor word. His eyes narrowed and brightened.

"Sure and I'm the new man," I said. "American eyes and all."

"James Hallam," he said, rolling my name in his mouth as if tasting it.

"William Claiborne," I said. "I hear tell the savages love you, Claiborne. Why do they love you?" I asked him. This man I had dreamt of selling myself to.

He laughed. "Why, man, are y'saying, having seen me, tis beyond understanding?"

"Why do they love you?" I insisted.

"Oh, you understand already, man. Tell me what I know, that's what the *werowances* say to their councilors, d'you know that? Tell me, they're saying, the truth I have seen but have not yet named. You know the answer. The Indians love me because I let them be Indians. That is why I will win this battle with Calvert. I let the Indians be Indians while he and White want to make them into little red Englishmen. Little papists. Don't need any more Englishmen, James Hallam, papist or protestant. Had enough damned Englishmen. Don't know an ear of maize from their pizzles, don't know a beaver pelt from a London wig. Me, I don't see this country through the eyes of London. See it through its own eyes. Saw the Susquehannock needed allies against the Iroquois and the Piscataway, and wanted trading partners and power, and had access to the best northern fur. Simple, see? Been fair with them, James Hallam. Gave them fair trucke and helped them destroy their enemies. What more can a man want? They love me because I let them be Indians. Or more true, because I let them be men."

"I love not," I said, "and care not who loves me. I care only who will bend to my desire."

Claiborne's nose wrinkled slightly, as if testing the air. His upper lip drew back from the yellowed, protuberant teeth.

"And why, you're asking me, are they different then than you, the fierce Susquehannock? Is that it?" He laughed. "Aye, that's what you have, James Hallam. American eyes. Tell you what you know. The Indians love me because they need to be loved by me. Because they fear me, my power, the power they see standing behind me. Because they would rather hate or love than fear. Because I'm a trader, Hallam. Give them muskets and cannon to fear, and trucke and guns and my true admiration of them to love and I give them Calvert and the Piscataway to hate; that path has already been there for them—the Piscataway are old enemies. I pull them this way and that. You understand that's what love is, don't you, Hallam? A rein we can pull this way and that. Until the horse fathoms reins and ridden."

He tightened the string of beads between his fingers, pulling it one way, then the other.

"I have answered your question, James Hallam," he said. "I've gven you William Claiborne in fair trade. Now tell me more of James Hallam."

"I have already. I'm a man who loves not and fears not and needs nothing you can give me."

Claiborne laughed, then furrowed his brow, as if suddenly puzzled. "Did you know," he said slowly, "that I named this island after Kent, where I come from in England. Seems to me I remember a landed family there, Catholics, called Hallam. Drained dry by the anti-Roman recusancy fines, lost their estate, and the baron took his own life. I remember how passing strange it had seemed: a man would cling to his faith through ruination, then violate it, put his soul in Hell, through suicide. Yes, Hallam, I believe that was the name. As I recall."

I pushed the nail of Ezekiel's finger hard against my chest, until I felt the skin open. "What sort of drama are you playing?" I asked Claiborne.

"How now mean you?"

I turned to leave.

"Wait, good Hallam. I only tease you, see which way you'll swipe. Did remember your father. Made inquiries, through my people in London. D'you think you'd stand here in this room with me otherwise? Had to know about you. D'you think I go into new territory without reports from my scouts?"

"And do you think you know me now?"

"Nay, I said know about you. Hide, not heart. I know this—you were secretly educated by the Jesuits at St. Omer's. I know the recusancy fines your father had to pay were three hundred pounds sterling per month, plus delinquency penalties. I know your older brother Edward was jailed as a hostage and died in prison. I know your sister Edwina died of the flux in a French nunnery. I know you went for a soldier, fought fifteen years in Spain and the low countries, for a king who slaughtered your family as much as any Powhatan scalp taker. I know you married and had two sons from Meg Aud, a barmaid you met in London when you were once on leave, and that all died of the plague. I know that death seems to follow you like a stink. I know you've been carved out hollow as a dugout by it. I know your hunger and your hate, James Hallam."

As he spoke, I pushed the nail harder into my chest. A warm trickle of blood went down to my waist. It took all my will to not leap across the small space between us and rip out Claiborne's throat. And then that rage made me feel like laughing, with a sudden, raging freedom.

"You know nothing," I said. "Your spies have the wrong man."

Claiborne threw my words away with a wave. "I said hide, not heart. But I have brought you here because I needed to know how you saw. I needed to know if you hated enough. I needed to know if you were intelligent enough to fashion your hatred into a weapon."

"What do you want from me, Claiborne?"

"Why I thought I had been clear upon that matter," he said. "I want only to let you be Hallam."

Tawzin's Song

That night I heard what sounded like fists beating against the roof and walls of the longhouse. I rose from Nanjmoy's warm skin and went to the sunrise entrance and pushed opened the woven cattail and marshgrass mat at the doorway. The hail and the cold slashed at my face and I couldn't see a foot in front of me. I pulled the mat back into the entrance. Nanjemoy had risen also and was feeding a few branches into the fire. It blazed up, forming and planing the faces and bodies of my wife, of Ezekiel and Wesort, into a memory or vision, even though they were truly there in front of me. The hail was not coming in through the smoke holes; its slant was too great. But the smoke was not escaping completely, and we all coughed a little. The pounding was very loud. The joists and pole beams of the roof began to shift and groan, the air inside the longhouse feeling as if it were compacting from the weight building up around and above us as the ice covered us. Then the smoke began to back up as the smokeholes lidded up, and we took fishing spears and broke through them, some of the ice falling in and onto the fires.

In the morning, I couldn't get the mat at the entrance open and I had to take my knife and cut through the seal of ice around its outline, then push it out with my shoulder. It made a cracking sound, the way ice did when it broke on the river.

Outside the sun was shining and a hard white, gleaming shell encased everything. When I stepped out, I slipped and slid and fell on my buttocks, cracking the crust, listening to Nanjemoy's's laughter behind me. Where the ice had rimed onto the bark surfaces of the longhouse and sweatlodge and sheathed the trunks and branches of the trees, its whiteness was opaque, the wood showing through, but drained and blanched, so it seemed like the corpse of wood. I walked into the forest. I was dressed in bearskins, with leggings made from moosehide that I had traded for with the Seneca, and that Nanjemoy had chewed to softness. I wished I had been able to get a pair of the snowshoes the Iroquois made of loops of supple wood, a woven web of gut string in their center. I'd seen them walking on snow or ice on those, sure-footed, as quickly as a waterbug browsing the surface of a pond. But the winters at the southern end of the Potomac were not usually this severe.

I began to move with more ease and competence, my feet either breaking the crust or sliding in a way that I could control, like gliding on the frozen river. After a while I could let my body instead of my mind think about each step. The air was cold and sharp in my nostrils and lungs. I skirted an opening in the trees, a small meadow near a spring where I had often killed deer. A mist-ghost of itself floated over it, as if the world were coming into being in front of me. In places the wind had carved strange, deeply shadowed faces and forms in sharp-rimmed banks of ice. I thought of the faces Ezekiel had fashioned in the grove where we had found him, just a nick, a groove, a twist, a curve, and the face would form in front of and behind my eyes, half there and half recognized from a dream. I glided silently into the trees, moving in a dream. Each branch and twig was fitted with a transparent glittering skin of ice. The branches drooped under their heavy load, and the tops of the trees were bent into arches in all directions, so that for a moment they seemed like the palms I had seen in Spain and in that instant my country became that country. There was a booming and cracking all around, like musket fire, as branches and trees cracked. The sunlight reflected painfully, sparkling all around me, so that I no longer knew what was up or down and I was easing through formless space. The spiked leaves of the holly trees and the needles of the pine trees were held in ice also, their green impossible and deep, as if it were the idea of green rather than the shadow I thought of as green, and it was so with the impossible white of the ice—the Platonic Ice, or the Universal Ice from Lombroso's Cabala, and what did my people have to describe this world I had pushed a cattail stem mat aside and entered? What did my people have that I could use to encase this ice which was encasing me, that I could use to push aside Plato's words and Lombroso's words injected into my poor, tattered and tested Piscataway soul? Then I understood it would be *manitou* ice, ice with the quality of life. Where the whites, my own White-stained soul, looked for that which stood to remind of something else, I should look for that which made everything One. What qualities of life did this ice have then? It stops, Kittamaquund's voice said in my mind. It freezes the heart. It lies as blank as forgetfulness. But the last time I had seen Kittamaquund he had become a white man's mountebank, one of those prancing jesters in foolscap and pointed shoes I had seen, I had been, in England and Spain and Holland: the Tayac so afraid of the promise of hellfire, or the loss of the power he had murdered to hold, or the loss of the people he had murdered to save, he had renounced all his wives save one, had become Charles and his wife had become Mary. As John Christman had become again Tawzin and Sally Picard had become Nanjemoy, and the blank ice had come to cover the world with a new skin.

And if we are going to live in this world, we sort of people, I told myself, I need to truly stop thinking like a white man and find some game. We had been eating the dried roots, bread made from acorn flour—we had a good store of acorns—and corn held in our stores; our last meat was the rabbits Jacob had killed and brought to share, a white man who had found more food than I had been able to. We were all gaunt and stringy. Under the skins at night, when I ran my hands over Nanjemoy's body, I felt the cage and jut of her bones, and both our bodies under the deerskin gurgled and bubbled and emitted the foul farts and breaths brewed by empty stomachs.

I tried to feel my direction and place in this suddenly strange world. I was in the forest south of the longhouse, on the northern edge of Lombroso's freehold. I knew his house would be empty: he had traveled to St. Marie's to treat Leonard Calvert; the governor was suffering from the grippe. I wished he were here, moving with me over this strangely reconfigured world. He had become enough of a hunter to help with game also, and although they were at first shocked when I had asked, so had Nanjemoy and Wesort. Only Ezekiel didn't hunt; he was too weak and I hadn't time to teach him the skills he needed.

Not that my own skills seemed to aid me now. The world was scoured of food as well as form. A line of wolf tracks crossed my path. A slight hump under a pin oak caught my eye. When I approached it, I saw two small melt holes, and when I put my hand over them, my palm grew slowly warm and moist. I thought about cracking the ice, digging down, killing the sleeping bear. The thought made me sleepy. It was a task we might have to do, but better done with the others, to help dig out the carcass. Looking at the holes, I remembered Ezekiel's song of finding Wesort under the earth.

On the other side of the oak tree I saw footprints.

I knelt and examined them. A criscross pattern, three times larger than a foot. I followed them near to Lombroso's house, then their loop back to the river. Three men. They left no more sign. They could have been Seneca, or Susquehannock or anyone wearing snowshoes. How had they come? The river was frozen solid, and they had left no marks upon it. They weren't far from the place where Jacob and I had once come across a Susquehannock family, two men and a woman with a baby squatting around a campfire as if they were on their home territory. I had killed one man with an arrow, while Jacob, cursing, had skewered the other with his dirk. The woman had leapt at me then, a steel bladed knife they must have gotten fom the English in her hand, and I'd caught the child by the feet and swung its skull against the tree trunk to distract her and was able to smash her skull with my tomahawk when she howled and leapt clawing for my eyes. Afterwards, Jacob had screamed at me that we could have saved the child. I'd said nothing to him. Jacob and I are knit together with time and water and strange journeys, as thickly as with blood. But at times his white man's arrogance infuriates me.

I looked at the river. Tomorrow we could come here and ice fish. I thought how we would do it. There was no use in thinking about the tracks. Perhaps they were just hunters. There was no use thinking of the child. On the bent branch of a locust tree were three starlings, their bodies frozen solid. When I took them and put them in my game bag, their feet snapped off and stayed fastened to the branch.

But there were tracks where there should not have been, leading back into the compound. I drew back my bowstring and moved forward cautiously. Nothing seemed disturbed. When I entered the longhouse, my eyes were still dazzled by the whiteness outside. As they adjusted, I saw Ezekiel asleep on his skins, Nanjemoy and Wesort sitting together, one behind the other, Nanjemoy grooming Wesort's hair. Sitting at the fire, smoking a clay pipe, was Jacob Lombroso. And next to him, rising as I came closer, was Father Andrew White. I looked at the priest's face, seeing it as one sees the face of a person one hasn't seen in years: first the changes, the lines and wrinkles carved and written by time, the sags of the flesh, but then the remembered face forming cleanly under the tidal markings of time. The way Ezekiel's faces formed. I hadn't looked at him that closely at the ceremony when Yaocomaco was given away; I'd been afraid to be recognized. But White was looking at me now as I was looking back at him.

"*Qua imperii ejus parte velemus, habiandi,*" I said.

"I am gratified to find you have not forgotten your Latin, John Christman."

"My name is Tawzin. And it is not because I haven't tried to purge it from my brain, Andrew White," I said. "But you dug down too deeply when you planted your seeds."

White gestured at my deerskins, my paint. "It seems not deeply enough."

"No, not deeply enough."

"Will he live?" White nodded at Ezekiel.

"He is healing. We have taken from him the demon that would kill him."

"Demons can only be cast out through the invocation of the name of Christ. You and Jacob have perhaps healed his body, John, with your salves and ungeants; I have found the native herbs helpful as well. But there is no healing of the soul without Christ."

I almost smiled. This was the White I remembered.

Jacob was looking at both of us, his eyes crinkled. I had never mentioned my past with White to him. Nor did White know of my ties with Jacob, as far as I knew. Two men who sat on the opposite ends of my former life. I could see Jacob trying to knit it together in his thoughts now.

"Andrew told me he thought he'd recognized you," he said to me. "How do you know each other?"

"John Christman was one of the Indians brought back by John Smith's expedition to the Chesapeake; the only Piscataway," White explained. "He was found in a dugout canoe."

"I was found without ever knowing I was lost," I said. "How strange an idea that was to me. But I was quite primitive then."

White didn't respond. "The man who adopted him, Randolph Devere, was a secret Catholic; he gave John to my care after I joined the Society, and I took him wih me when the crown was going to jail me agan and I was sent to Spain.

170

My study of Scholastic Theology and, as you know, Jacob, Hebrew, took me to both Valladolid and Seville. Do you know those places?"

"Oh yes. And I know Tawzin's history. Only not your place in it."

"How do you know Spain, Jacob?" White asked.

"My study of medicine took place in Portugal, at the University of Salamanca. Later my study of life took me with a troop of players to Spain. Before that, I tried to stay away from Spain, as much as I could. It was not a healthy place for a *marrano* to visit."

"Our friend John didn't think so either." White regarded Lombroso curiously. "One day, he was simply gone."

"Perhaps he felt a *marrano* also," Lombroso said. "A secret Indian."

"Oh, he never made a secret of it. I knew his history. Only not your place in it."

Speaking of me as if I wasn't here.

I cry, White said to me then in Piscataway. We speak your story while you are not here.

He had learned well in a short time.

"Oh, but I am here, Father. And now so are you."

"As I told you I would be."

"Yes."

"And you, John...Tawzin. How did you leave Europe? What happened after you disappeared from Seville?"

"He returned from exile," Jacob Lombroso said.

I remembered the Jew's face, the first time I had seen him, cavorting on the stage in feathers and paint in the Seville town square. For some reason, as if I were afraid the priest could still bring me back to that place, as if White were a parent wronged by an ungrateful son, I didn't want to tell him how I had run from the monastery, took the trade of exhibitionist that I had been brought to Europe to follow anyway, no different than Smith displaying me in front of the princes of the church and the court. I had convinced the actors—in truth, Jacob hadn't needed convincing—with some Piscataway chants I had remembered or made up, that I would be of some amusement to their audiences. I was. In my feathers and paint and outlandish turban, prancing like any fettered bear, I was as entertaining to the European rabble we played for as I had been when I had been displayed by Devere to the English court, by White as the saved savage to bishops and archbishops, the princes of the church. Amusing as I had been to all the whites, English and Spanish, explorers and soldiers, lords and priests and academicians, and finally one Jew, all who had looked into my face as if searching for something lost of their hearts.

"Jacob undertook my passage," I said to White.

"A gathering of the exiles?" White said to Jacob. He smiled, and poked a green stick into the fire, stirring it.

"My friend, I had already decided to go to America before I met Tawzin. Recife, in Brazil," Jacob said. "We went there first. Many of us went there, many *marranos*. The colony had been conquered by the Dutch and the secret Jews were now openly practicing their faith. But the Indians I found there were not the Indians I expected. To me, all of America was one idea, but to Tawzin it was only this Chesapeake country. Eventually we returned here. Or, properly, Tawzin returned, although I also feel I have come home."

"And thus here we sit, three of us whose lives cornered in Seville," White said to me. "The wondrous things of God. Your coming here was an act of Providence."

"My coming here was simply a return from where I was torn."

"I prayed that I would find you again, here. I remember you," White looked distant, "how your eyes burned during mass and when you received the Host. That vision, John, moved me to return to England, moved me to become the priest of this expedition. That hunger for God I saw in you reawakened my own. I came here to find you, John. But in truth, I never thought I would be blessed by seeing you again."

"In Europe I danced for people who laughed and clapped each other on the back in delight when they saw me. Now I return and find you have come after me and dressed my Tayac in outlandish costume and dance him for your pleasure, as you once did me."

My words burst out like fish escaping a weir. I had not thought my anger was so close to my tongue. I had thought I had become Piscataway enough again to hold it inside my heart, turn it cold and sharp and silent. But something about this man, this priest, drew out my rage and yet, and perhaps because it did, still drew me to him. It was not only the certainty of his belief, the sacrifices he had made for it. It was his need to vision me as the converge of that faith. A need so naked that I found myself still wanting to do my fantastic, cavorting dance for the priest, feed him as I had once fed the hunger to witness savagery and surrender gnawing at the guts and hearts of all those gawking, scratching crowds of Europeans who had come to view me.

"I am here for the enlightenment of your souls, as a soldier of Christ," White said. "But the Word of Christ needs an earthly base from which it can spread, and I do not apologize for my involvement in temporal matters. It is my gratification, John, Tawzin, that my relations with your people have been gentle and just, and that because of that many have accepted Christ. As my brother the Tayac has. The number of souls we save will be the final test of our Enterprise. You were one of us once. We took you from your savage state and showed you the Kingdoms of Christ in Europe. It is my task now, my friend, to bring you back to that state of grace."

I felt the heat rise in my face. "I came back to a state of grace when I came back to my people."

"There is no grace without Christ. He is the Light of the

world. In your soul you know that. You remember it as you remember this language."

"Ah," Jacob said. "Forgive me, Andrew, but I remember Christ's grace and light also. I saw it shine in the square at Salamanca, when I watched, hidden behind a friend's curtains. From that distance, I could only tell who they were by the differences in height. An exercise in light and the geometry of grace. My father the biggest torch, my mother the median, and my sister the smallest."

"I don't agree with the methods of the Inquisition, you know that, Jacob—there are no *autos da fe* here, nor will be. But many of the Inquisition are men of true faith, who act out of great love. You are a physician, my friend, you understand that pain is sometimes necessary to affect healing, that a limb must be removed to save the rest of the body, that a touch of fire on earth will save a soul from an eternity of hellfire."

"Would you save me in such friendly fashion as well, Andrew?"

"I have told you—I believe there are other ways. I follow them."

"But if there were no other way—would you burn me, Andrew. Roast a little Lombroso now to halt the slower roast later?"

"Because I love you, Jacob." White smiled.

Jacob threw back his head and laughed. "God save me from your love."

"God save you from your prideful blindness."

I looked at the two white men, my resentment growing. They spoke calmly, smiling to each other. Laughing. Their words bitter, but smoothed of anger, as if they had slipped into the familiar and comfortable discourse of friends long past any hope one would win the other over. The argument itself forming a bond between them. Somehow my annoyance now was more at Jacob, a man I felt as close to as if he were father or uncle, than at White.

"Jacob," I said, "do you not carve us to your design also?"

He raised his eyebrows. "How so?"

"The Susquehannocks we found. You tried to prevent me from killing the child. Why?"

"My love, it is wrong to kill a helpless child."

"If we had left him, as you wanted, he would have grown up to be an enemy, and his people would have thought we were soft, and regarded us with contempt."

"You could have kept him. Nanjemoy was kept. Wesort was kept."

I saw White glance over to Nanjemoy, and wished Jacob had kept his mouth shut. By treaty with Calvert, all captives were bound to be returned.

"But we are too weak and alone here," I said. "If we had kept him, the child, his people would continue to try to take him back."

"When you kill a child, you kill the future."

"The future can be a threat. When Calvert came here," I said, "Uwanna told him, since you have come to my country, it is fitting that you live by the customs of this land, rather than try to make us live by the customs of your land."

And then, I thought, Kittamaquund killed him. But I did not say it. The Jesuits who had taught me rhetoric had taught me not to present my opponents with arguments against myself.

"Tawzin, you are not simply Piscataway anymore."

"Yes. I have seen Europe now. How old was your sister when she was burned alive? Once, in London, I saw a twelve year old boy whose guts were drawn out before he was pulled to pieces by horses. It was as imaginative a torture as any of the Susquehannock. Jacob, I tell you what you know. You are like this priest. You bend us to fit you."

"Yet I believe we all bend to fit each other. That there is a universal goodness of the soul that is discoverable through reason because it is in harmony with the laws of the universe."

White looked amused. "Listen to him. He speaks the new

heresy of Descartes. *Cogito, ergo sum.* But, Jacob, tell me, does the belief that the American Indians are the Lost Tribes of Israel come from reason or from wish twisted into reason? Isn't it of that fantastic conviction that John, Tawzin, now speaks?"

"Yes," I said. "Jacob's hunger would shape our spirits to his. But yours would devour us, spirit and flesh and blood. You'd turn us into wafer and wine."

"I wouldn't permit blasphemy, John," White snapped.

"My name is Tawzin."

"We have been naught but gentle in our dealings with your people."

"Your gentleness is an *auto de fe* that burns them to nothing as completely as it burnt Jacob's family, as the Senecas burnt mine. Your English move into our lands. Our warriors hire themselves out as hunters, so your people are free to grow tobacco, and tobacco, which was for us a way of touching our hearts to the true world of dreams becomes no more than another kind of *wampompeag*. We fight each other to sell you beaver pelts, corn and even the bodies of our women for your trucke and beads, while the Susquehannock and the Seneca take advantage of our division to attack us more often, more boldly. The Piscataways are falling to pieces, our villages are being burned in your war, our people uprooting themselves, running to the saftey of the Zekiah swamp like hunted deer. The governor is sending no militia to their aid, as he promised, and last month there was even some Chopticos wiped out by the Marylanders."

"In error, and to our deep regret," White said.

"I'm certain that soothes their spirits."

"Many souls have been soothed with salvation, And that is the important thing. And John, when we speak of souls brought to salvation, it brings us to another matter we must address." He looked over to Nanjemoy again.

"Whom you look to isn't another matter. Nanjemoy is my wife."

"She has been taken from her people. She may even be Catholic. I have to ask: do you know her name? My child, do you know your name?" he called to her.

Nanjemoy stared at White, unsmiling, her eyes slits.

"She doesn't remember English," I said.

"John, people at St. Marie's have seen her. I did not know her connection to you; indeed I did not know your connection to yourself." He smiled slightly. I didn't return it. "I'm afraid the governor will have to do something, John."

I stared at this priest who had stolen me from myself, who would do it again, call me back to him by the name he had given me. Who would now steal my wife as well.

A movement caught my eye. Ezekiel had risen and was staring at us. As if we were three madmen.

"Hallam," he said to White. "What about Hallam? Where is he?"

"Ah, Ezekiel. It is good to see you better, my son."

"What about Hallam?" Ezekiel said again. Wesort came over and sat next to him, put her hand on his shoulder.

"We should have hung the man when we had him next to a gallows—he has joined Claiborne's rebels on Kent Island. There is this, I must tell you, Ezekiel: after he committed that barbarous act on you, he came back into St.Marie's that night like a skulking savage, and left what he had taken from you at Sisters' Freehold, even entering the house and placing it at Margaret Brent's very door. She didn't wish me to tell you this, but I don't wish to withold any truth from your ears. Hallam left a message on the door, written in blood, saying he was giving her what she had asked for. He's a devil. Your poor flesh, left there, had been mutilated even more grievously; he had taken the extra digit that marked you."

Ezekiel was still staring at him, as if waiting for the answer to his question.

"What else have you heard?" I asked.

"I have only returned to St. Marie's this week from visiting the northern villages of the Piscataway," the priest said, "but much has happened in our small beaver war—I'll give you what I have heard about the state of affairs around the Chesapeake." He looked pained. "Our haven here is in mortal danger from Claiborne and the Protestants. He has fortified Kent Island, and uses Palmer, Claiborne and Popely's Islands for his trade with the Susquehannock, all inside the heart of the Chesapeake, territory given by King's grant to Lord Baltimore and the Calverts and not to the Virginians. Their success, frankly, is puzzling. Tawzin, no matter your words, we have endeavored in all our intercourse with the Indians to avoid the mistakes the Virginians made; we have come as friends and as bearers of the word of Christ to our brothers; we treated for land and did not seize it. But the Susquehannock remain loyal to Claiborne; he has asked them to trade only with him, and they do. He has asked them not to trade with us and they do not. They will go further north than us, even to the Swedes in Delaware, but that devil has cast a spell on them; they not only refuse our trade, but have begun murdering our people with the help of that devil Hallam. There was a family murdered not eight miles from Saint Marie's City, only a week ago."

"There have been four Yaocomaco longhouses wiped out since autumn," Jacob said.

White sighed. "Our position is insecure. Claiborne was granted a royal trading license by Sir Alexander William, the Secretary of State of Scotland, and he is financed by the London Puritan merchants. They see his relationship with the Indians as the key to the trade. Calvert and Lord Baltimore had thought that our friendship with the Piscataway would allow us to break the Virginian monopoly. They were wise, yet they—we, for I was ignorant as well— looked at all the Indians as one nation, and did not understand the differences between the tribes, understand that our Piscataway are deer and not beaver Indians, and do not have access to the Iroquois trade that the Susquehannocks have monopolized. To the thick pelts from the northern country—

the beaver trapped in this region are thin-skinned and cannot be sold well in London. I hate the trade in that furred rodent. But it is that hair London wants now, and not tobacco."

"We must have disappointed you greatly," I said. "Your Piscataway."

From the Midrash of Jacob Lombroso, Wesort

Two books sit before me, pages open, two white blank
surfaces (now ravished by the black tracks of these words),
next to two surfaces thicketed with more words, the tattered
copy of Isaac Luria's commentary on the *Book of Con-
cealment* in the Zohar I've carried with me, or been carried
by to this barken house next to a river by which I sit myself
now, occasionally to weep, but rarely to remember Zion. A
stranger in an even stranger land. A bar of light shining
through the reeds conjoins the two books, allows the Hebrew
letters to fade and swell and dance a bit for me. Words and
letters, the Cabalists like Luria teach us, their physical twists
and curves and loops, even their march across this page, are
the very Material of the universe; their reconfigurations and
knittings and unravelings spin and unthread the reed weave
of the universe itself. In my way then, in my conceit, I can
look at this writing as a small *Tikkun Olam*, a knitting
together of the shattered universe—as the Piscataway songs
do, the rabbi's chants. Indeed Luria taught that the division
of earth into nations was the reflection of the Divine
Shattering—the cosmos, unable to contain the Godhead, had
shattered into *klippot*, evil husks that still held the sparks,
the *tikkun* of the divine Light, and our own dispersed people
were those sparks of trapped light, and the hope for
redemption came through our very wandering, our scattering
to the four corners of the world. A comforting thought, I
suppose, for some hunted peddler in Poland, some receipient
of Christian spit or steel: I am not simply a despised Jew; I
am a divine spark of light. A comforting thought for me as I
write this. Yet when my parents and little sister burned on the
Inquisition stakes in Salamanca, though they flared brightly
as divine sparks, in truth I didn't see any divinity in their

end, nor in their pride in refusing the quicker mercy of the garrote that conversion would have given them. A decision they made as well for my sister Claribel, whose secret Hebrew name was Rachel. But I would have let her lips speak whatever words, her head be bathed in whatever water, to spare her that fire Andrew White has told me is compassionate.

I can still see, even looking at the light of Yacomaco barred on this page, how my mother and father and Claribel twisted on their stakes as the crowd hooted and roared, the fire licking away their flesh so I was watching my family's metamorphosis before my eyes into, at first the skinned cadavers, and then the skeletons upon which we learned our profession at the University, somehow, in their agony, catching my eye, as I tried to blend with the mob. I had left Portugal that night, a seventeen year old suddenly aged with all the years of those three people, all the years of the People they refused to separate themselves from. I had continually warned my parents to give up their clinging to what I saw as the stale and rotten root of our ancestry. I was in the flush of my youth and strength and popularity then, and had no use for secret ancient rituals, for the taint of my Jewish blood—wasn't it enough of a sign of how our country regarded us to be called *marrano*, pig.

My first reaction in fact when I learned of their arrest was rage—not at the Inquisition but at them, at their stubbornness, their stiff-necked pride. I had tried to blend into that mob all of my life before I blended with them at that incendiary moment; I was a seventeen-year-old boy with my beauty and my scalpel-sharp mind, with my circles of witty and stylish friends; I was at the beginning of a fame and wealth I would accumulate through the triumphs of my own intelligence and will, and now it would all be taken from me. I had not asked to be born of that blood, and all it took to renounce its taint was the avoidance of certain rituals, the observance of certain other rituals, mumbles in Latin rather than Hebrew; daily discourse in pure Portugese, not mongrel Ladino. But the sights I saw burned away my selfishness, my illusions of freedom.

From that bright and dark moment I was a scattered shard, a wanderer who journeyed as far as I could from the memory of parents and sister used as Salamancan torches for an act of faith. And as far as I went, and wherever I went, I always found that same mob, that faith which burns what might contradict it. I found it in Italy where Jews were penned in that cage within cities the Italians were calling *getto*, in Germany and Poland where the Jewish towns were torched, massive *autos de fe*. I found it everywhere, until I came to the Source, to Palestine, to the unearthly light of Safed, Luria's city. I was five years in that Light, and then I went back to Europe, to seek solace in the weird gatherings and cults that were forming among the young men and women of my people. Fervent circles of believers in this messiah or that redeemer, in unfettered rites and rituals that would hasten the breakdown of the world and free us from it, in orgiastic joinings. Prophetic foreshadows of the naked and obstreperous Piscataway circles I would join around the flickering bonfires of the New World. We sought liberation from the insane shatter of the universe by reenacting it, with wine and bizarre vision-awakening plants, with the erasure of the differences between the sexes, with licentiousness and wild music. I saw myself in those days as the wild, dark-skinned *marrano*, the secret Jew finally revealing his secret soul, dancing in their center. Dancing finally with an Indian boy found and a troop of travelling players in a Spanish town square, far-wanderer from his own tribe; his own tribe a lost remnant of mine, so the circle would be complete, so I would end my wandering here, by this river, in this house of reeds, writing on this page. *Tikkun Olam*. Here, where I feel only as I did in one other place on earth, Holy Safed, where I had sat on the mountaintop where Isaac Luria had lived and died and saw the blazing weave between the blurred gold hills of

Palestine and the hard clear sky bowled above it, Heaven and Earth merging for an instant, as if to show the possibility of unity inherent in discord, and the word *ruah*, which means wind, which means soul, blew into my mind. The *ruah* of Safed. The *ruah* of Yaocomaco. The *manitou*.

And now, although I have not meant to do so, I have put myself on this page instead of recording the events of my new people. The first of new books of Moses, if I might humbly be so arrogant. And now, I will dam this flow of myself out into ink, into letters that twist and writhe in agony, and I will disappear from these pages, and chronicle instead the new history of my new and strange people.

For a people is what we have become since winter, since we were joined by our one-handed Ezekiel and his woman, Wesort, whose name we have taken to be our own. I spend more time now at Tawzin's longhouse than here in my own; indeed, the term "my own" has become as meaningless as my "giving" Tawzin a corner of his own people's land that was "given" to me by an English Lord. Swiftly, as a river finds its true bed, that land has run back to him, these trees, this water, the sound of the wind in the leaves are his, and I am still eternal sojourner here, guest and chronicler.

And now I have appeared, intruded on the page again. Begone, Jacob.

As I began to write here, since Ezekiel and Wesort arrived, our numbers here have increased in proportion as the raids by the Susquehannock, and occasionally the Seneca, have increased. The Yaocomaco, and the Piscataway Federation in general have been hard hit, and the Tayac, Kittamaquund, now Christian, prays for the souls of his people and does nothing for their bodies or for the probity of his nation. The Susquehannock have always regarded the Piscataway as rivals and enemies, as holders of the land of milk and honey (crabs and oysters and deer, if I might be forgiven a parallel that transgresses the dietary laws), and now they have joined to Claiborne and the Kent Island

Virginians, who see the Maryland English in the same light the Susquehannocks see the Piscataway—as blood enemy. As holders of that which they covet. As a people, I see Tawzin's Piscataway performing to the dance of Jewish history to which I had assigned them before coming to America. The tribes of the Federation: Anacostan, Piscataway, Mattapanient, Assamacomico, Mattawoman, Nanjemoy, Portopaco, Choptico, Aquintanack, Yaocomaco—are the Maccabeans who signed treaties with the Roman Empire which then ate them; they are the lost ten tribes of Israel; they are at the verge of their defeat and dispersal, the beginning of their American Diaspora.

And some of them wash up here, odd floatsum in the whirls and eddies of that new diaspora, and as if to reflect the coalescing mix of these wanderers, we have fallen into calling them by an amalgam of Indian and European names as well, with no notion, it seems, but whim to guide our naming. (No more, I should say, than Rachel becoming Claribel). Thus: Chitiquad, a Yaocomaco, and Chipmunk her sister who is now the woman of Simon Bodecker, another black man, run away from Virginia. Runs Through Rocks, a Choptico, and his woman Startled, and their two children whom they have let me name Israel and Sarah, of twelve and thirteen years of age. And John and Charity Slagel, two indentured servants of sixteen and fifteen years of age who loved (and love) each other and were beaten and separated and ran away (how passionately we debated allowing them and the black to stay! If not them, then why any of us? Tawzin had finally said, staring at Ezekiel, and I was secretly amused and pleased to hear in his argument echoes of those endless Jewish debates he had endured so silently in our circle in Europe). And Dream Singer of the Mattapanient—a widow with a broad face and intelligent eyes who stares at me with an intensity I find disturbing, more because I had thought I was past such wishful thinking, such stirring. And her daughter, Sook, for she is the female crab who scuttles here and there and is always forming a shell and softening it and growing bigger, and she has twelve years, and her sister Dreams of Raven, who has ten years and who is chubby and sleepy eyed, and keeps her face down, as if searching for a path on the earth.

And now Tawzin and Nanjemoy have begat a daughter, who, at least in my presence, they call Rachel. And its birth was easy.

Though the birth of Ezekiel and Wesort's son, merely three days ago, was not. I had to use finally (as I have to use more and more) the Indian medications I have learned from Maquacomen, the Yaocomaco shaman with whom I have met before, and who sometimes visits us, to keep, I think, a wary eye on me in case I will misuse my skills. I wished, as it were, my colleage was there that day, for Wesort suffered torments indeed. Her waters broke in the evening, and afterwards she squatted expectantly, in the fashion of the Indian women who do not lie down to give birth. The other women surrounded her, and tolerated my presence. But here were no contractions, and no dilation I could observe for the next twenty-four hours. Her pain must have been terrible; she was drenched in sweat and clenched her teeth, letting out a continual moan, echoed outside the wall of the sweatlodge (steam, from cedar chips, was thought to help speed delivery) by the moan of Ezekiel, which finally turned to a howl so disturbing that Tawzin had to come and wrestle the man away. I was giving her, again according to Maquacomen's teachings, a concoction of sumac leaves and *ocre* root, as well as polar bark, wild cherry and dogwood, also said to hasten dilation and contractions and to relieve pain. Finally, when I had despaired and thought I might have to either perform Caeser's birth or kill the child with the same knife, finally after constant manipulation of Wesort's abdomen by the women, in turn, the contractions began. To my horror, though, what was presented were the child's buttocks: a breech birth. I placed a piece of beaver fur over my hand to prevent wounding the vulva with my fingernails, and attempted to manipulate the child, though Dream Singer remonstrated with me that it would be more effective to hold her up and rock her from side to side and knead the child into position from the outside, as was the custom in her tribe. I ignored her, though she kept making snorting noises of disgust which disconcerted my spirit. Eventually though, because of or in spite of my treatment, to the accompaniment of Wesort's moans and Ezekiel's howls (he had entered the sweatlodge again), and against the resistance of the child, who seemed to be clutching and clawing his mother's womb with both hands, eventually the birth took place.

Ezekiel's howls stopped then, and his first action was to take the child's arms and hands and examine them. Wesort turned her head away; she would not look at the child. I watched as Ezekiel held the little hands in his own, counting, I could see, in his mind, the number of digits on each hand. On the right, and then on the left. One, two, three, four, five. Was there a nub, a slight swelling of flesh, that marked the root of an extra digit? Perhaps. Or perhaps it was only a baby's fat, my mind painting what my heart wished. *Echod, schtime, schalosh, arbah, hamesh.* I counted with him, silently, transposing the numbers to Hebrew as if the Holy Tongue might reconfigure the world. One, two, three, four, five. Only five. As if in reflection of Ezekiel's own amputation. Or of the absorbed seed of a demon father.

"You can not tell this way," I said to him. "The gift doesn't always go generation to generation; you told me so yourself."

Wesort turned her face to the wall. And Ezekiel ignored me and continued to count those fingers over and over, a terrible knowledge forming in his eyes.

Ezekiel's Song

On the lodge poles of the longhouse, working at first awkwardly but my hand slowly taking its missing brother's skill, I carved faces that I now had names for: the faces were *mesingw*, they were the faces of We Sort of people, and they included the face, and the hands, of my son. I was determined that Isaac would be so in my eyes. Until the moment of birth I had not known how I would feel towards the child, and at that moment what had come to me was a terrible hatred, not for the infant, but for its hands, and I could not look at them, and can not still, without a hollow caving in the walls of my stomach, without an ensnared feeling, as if they were waving a tight pen around my life, shackling me captive to Hallam the rest of my time on earth. Yet Lombroso was right—men and women of my line had been born five-fingered and all of Wesort's people, as far as I knew, and I would see Isaac—I had so named him at Lombroso's suggestion, named him alone, Wesort refusing to have anything to do with name or child—as my own, mine and hers. Had I spilled my seed before Hallam came to us? It was true, no matter how I searched I saw none of my own face reflected. But it was difficult to tell, with this Wesort baby, its copper skin, its straight black hair. I put the matter from me. Isaac was mine, come from my woman's body, come into what we were building between us now. Yet Wesort remained cold to the child. She cleaned him and nursed him when she had to, but indifferently and often grimacing; once she pulled Isaac from her breast and showed me where the child had gnawed at and torn her nipple, her blood bubbling in its mouth, running down its chin, mixed with milk and drool. Her eyes saying to me: you see. In truth I saw more than I wished to see. Isaac was a strangely silent child, large and sullen and never crying or smiling. When he grew hungry or dirty he howled or screamed his demands in a strange, unsettling shriek, his eyes dry and cold. The child senses its mother's coldness, Lombroso told me, be patient with both. But it seemed unnatural for Wesort to act this way, and several times we quarreled, or rather I would say something harshly and she would simply remain silent and would not look at me.

No matter. What I knew was that this small construct of flesh and drool and shit had been the life I had felt pressed between Wesort and myself as we had lain together, and now in my mind and heart I had built a palisade of sharpened stakes and I put the child and Wesort in its center, and just past that periphery but still held by it were the others in Tawzin's longhouse, we sort of people, and Jacob Lombroso, and the world outside of those two circles in my heart could go to hell, if it chose to exist at all.

But the child opened me raw to that world's perils also. Every week Lombroso or one of the remaining Yaocomaco brought us tidings of raids and massacres by the Susquehannocks and the Powhatan, their war parties often including whites from Claiborne's Sons of Wrath, and more often than not, when I heard the stories, I heard the name of James Hallam. Tazwin had chosen the location of our camp well: you could walk up until you were nearly touching one of our longhouses with your nose before you'd see it emerge from the forest that held it. But we would have no chance against a large force, especially one deliberately seeking us. We would have no chance against Hallam.

I sat next to the creek with Tawzin and Nanjemoy and Wesort and our children. We had gone to the V-shaped fish weir, and were waiting a while, letting it fill before wading in to spear and basket the fish. The two children were at the women's breasts; Isaac greedy, emitting loud slurping noises as Wesort held him woodenly. I watched Tawzin stroke Rachel's face, his daughter's lips around Nanjemoy's nipple. She closed her eyes and smiled, and I felt a wave of longing that threatened to become jealousy.

"I'm worried," Tawzin said, smiling.

"You don' look like worried man," Nanjemoy said. "Look like a happy man to me, you. Look like you want to suckle Rachel your own self."

"You think that could be?" He looked truly interested.

"I tink any ting can be, dese two chillen." Nanjemoy spoke the kind of Wesort English that we had begun using among ourselves, close to what we spoke in Barbados, and likely born the same way. She spoke a tongue we shared and she refused to acknowledge Wesort's hostility towards Isaac; it was too strange for her, I think, or it would have disturbed what her heart had built our lives into, our stir of blood and words and dreams.

Wesort suddenly reversed the baby, held him out over the creek. A golden arc of urine splashed into the water. For the first time, I saw her smile at the child. "Hunh," Nanjemoy grunted, and did the same for Rachel. I felt a swell of hope: two streams joining the creek, the children, the day, these lives.

"I worry also," I said. (I took care with my own English, at least when talking to Tawzin or Jacob: this the crop Margaret Brent had planted, but also from my old Barbadan master's bitter seeding. He would correct me, beat me—and my namesake—for speaking what he called slaveshit, as if out of some secret pride or amusement that his carpenters spoke better than the island's poor whites.) "I hear talk some of the Piscataway have begun to move into the Zekiah swamp. But I don't want bring these two children to a swamp. I want them here, with their *msingw's*."

"I don't disagree. But there is more we can do."

He began drawing in the dirt, showing me.

We began work on the tunnel the next morning. I oversaw the cutting of trees for support beams, the removal of dirt—we used it to build up an inner berm—in baskets. We put the entrance under a false fire pit in the sweatlodge.

From *The Description and Natural History of the Coasts of North America*, by Nicolas Denys

There was formerly a much larger number of Indians than at present. They lived without care, and never ate either salt or spice. They drank only good soup, very fat. It was this that made them live long and multiply much. They would have multiplied still more were it not that the women, as soon as they are delivered, wash the infant, no matter how cold it may be. Then they swaddle them in the skins of Marten or Beaver upon a cradleboard, to which they bind them. If it is a boy, they pass his penis through a hole, from which issues the urine; if a girl, they place a little gutter of bark between the legs, which carries the urine outside. Under their backsides they place dry rotten wood reduced to powder, to receive the other excrements, so that they only unswathe them each twenty-four hours. But since they leave in the air during freezing weather the most sensitive part of the body, this part freezes, which causes much mortality among them, principally among the boys, who are more exposed to the air in that part than the girls.

Tawzin's Song

That year we planted tobacco and corn and began trading
both and game and some beaver hides in Saint Marie's City,
not for *roanoke* but for pipes and tools and cattle. The beaver
we brought caused a stir of excitement among the traders in
St. Marie's City: I had some hundred pelts I received as a gift
from the Herekeenes, a tribe that lived a week's journey past
the Great Falls of the Potomac. I had led a trading party to
that area for Kittamaquund a year before the English had
come. Henry Fleet, in his cups, had pulled the fur, bent down
and licked it, then looked strangely at me.

Another child, a son, Ashanti, was born to Simon Bodecker
and Chipmunk, and both Nanjemoy and Wesort were pregnant
again. Jacob had begun to sleep with us in the longhouse rather
than going back to his own, which was falling into neglect, its
fields overgrown with weeds, so that finally I told him it was
time to leave that place and stay with us. To sleep with us, but
it was to Dream Singer's sleepskins he found his way. Though
even this didn't silence him, for to Dream Singer's disgust,
when Maquacomen came to visit, the two healers would sit
near the fire, their heads together, muttering, exchanging
concoctions and medicines. It amused me; I had seen Jacob
engaged in raucous all night debates and battles of wit with
his fellow seekers, our strange circle of Cabalists, free
thinkers, gypsies, actors, drunkards, whores and poets, in
Europe—a circle I saw now dissolve into another strange
circle, we sort of people, sitting in longhouse or sweatlodge,
discussing events or stategies or disputes, like any tribe.
Maquacomen, Jacob said to me as the three of us sat by the
fire one evening, reminded him of a rabbi.

Maquacomen said nothing.

"Except when he says nothing," Jacob said. I looked at

the shaman, compact and lynx-eyed, an old man with wiry strength in his forearms and gnarled hands, a wisp of black beard, looked back from him to Lombroso. Jacob's black hair, streaked with gray, was cut long on one side and short on the other, with a lock tied at the left ear with a string of *roanoke*, like any other Piscataway, and his skin was the same copper color; he could truly have been Maquacomen's brother, his vision that his people shared my people's ancestors true. Though I knew also how one could pull oneself to the shape of a vision, if it were strong enough.

"Shar-lom," Maquacomen said, a word he gave back as a gift to please and humor Jacob. They were speaking mostly in Algonquin-Piscataway; the other Wesorts, if not fluent in either, had taken to conversing in a mix of tongues, Indian, English, African. Maquocomen now was interested not so much in Jacob's strange theory, I knew, as his madness. He couldn't understand the difference between Jews and other whites.

My tribe are outcasts among the whites, Jacob said.

It was an artless answer, I thought, an admission of weakness that might offend Maquacomen. In so many ways Jacob still didn't understand us.But the shaman just smiled, though I could see he was puzzled.

This seems to make you proud of your tribe.

Perhaps it does. Being outcast is something that allows us to see very clearly, as a hunter can see the shape of a lion when he is further away from it.

But not always the color or sleekness of the fur, the number of teeth, the depth of the hunger.

Outcasts develop sharp eyes or die.

And what else gives you pride in your people, Ya-cob? Maquacomen asked.

This. My tribe is a tribe that lost its hunting grounds and has to live in the territories of others. They hate us. So we must have each other.

Then I saw something stir through the others in the

longhouse, listening quietly to the conversation, these words singing their own song, the Wesort song, at the edge of fire. What did you do to deserve hatred? Dream Singer asked, joining them.

We were not them.

Maquocomen nodded, as if this were a crime he understood.

When I was a child, Jacob said, I watched enemy whites burn my family to ashes. In Europe I've seen them hunt our people, burn down all our lodges, kill everyone, even to the weakest woman, the smallest baby.

Simon Bodecker and Wesort joined them. Simon nodded at Jacob's words. "We all tell such story, Jacob Lombroso. Not just Jew story."

"Were Enemy, you say? Dose wha' burnt?" Runs Through Rocks asked.

"Yes."

"Den wha' you spect Enemy to do? I do no different, mah enemy."

"Yes," Jacob said. "I know. But you kill...innocently."

"I doan understand dat word."

"That's what it means."

"What do you want to say?" I said. I was certain the remark had been meant for me—Jacob thought I had seen too much, knew too much, to kill innocently. The child I had brained stayed behind his eyes. Not that it had left mine. Not since Rachel was born. "Speak straight." I said. "Sweatlodge rules. We speak what we already know here."

"I think if we kill as our enemies kill, then we become our enemies. If the Tayac makes the Piscataway white men, to save the Piscataway, what has he saved? If we kill as our enemies kill, we are no longer Jews, or Wesorts. We do not live anymore."

"No," Wesort said suddenly, and we all looked at her, surprised. She had hung Isaac on a peg on the center pole. He watched us silently, Ezekiel's carved faces staring over his head. "If we live, we live. If we kill sum man, sum woman, sum chil', sum demon, so we live, we live. Not die. Bettah."

"But there is a question of what we sort of people are," Jacob said gently.

"No," Dream Singer said, and put her hand in alliance on Wesort's shoulder. "Dere only we sort of people. Other ting just shit. Wesort gone, dere no chance dere noting like us, dis eart'."

"Ah," Jacob said.

Maquacomen grunted and closed his eyes. The brown-spotted skin on his face tightened back, somehow making his aquiline nose jut out beakishly. I could see he was becoming a hawk. Once Jacob had told him of the Cabalist Isaac Luria who could speak the language of all the birds and animals, and Maquacomen had said, as if Jacob were a naive child, that of course Luria could, if he were a shaman.

"Why are you becoming a hawk, my friend?" Jacob asked him solemnly.

Maquacomen's eyes widened in surprise. He said something. Jacob looked puzzled.

"I didn't understand him."

"He said because it is enjoyable to be a hawk," I said.

So I remember now the first time I saw Jacob. Became a hawk myself, casting my memory in its own wider and wider swoops through the ether. Passing as I had when I was plucked from the Chesapeake, from one dark room to another, a chain of rooms, one ship to another, one country to another, and finally behind thick stone walls, the Savage, the Stranger, displayed before men who pinched and prodded me, or looked into my black eyes for some well of wisdom they apparently despaired of finding in their own. Or, later, in the monastery, flogged me until my eyes opened to their wisdom. I was a fervent believer by my thirteenth year: Christ had come into my darkness, a blurred but intense light, like the lemon colored light of Spain I would glimpse occasionally through slits in the thick and moldy stone walls, through the dead flesh smell of the thick wax candles. A light that stroked my pain and shared it. The Stranger come among the people, to bear the agony of their deaths but only after sharing the agonies and joys of their lives. Only Christ, torn from his own kith and kin, could know my loneliness, know my most secret thoughts, know the tongue I was forgetting, know who I was even in the middle of these pale stern chanting men in black robes who every day scraped a little more of me away and burnt me up in their incense.

It was for Christ then that I rose before dawn and stood naked and poured freezing water over my trembling, imperfect flesh, and flagellated myself with a bull pizzle whip until I bled, until my pain took me into Christ's pain. It was Christ who looked at me in reproach on the mornings I woke and found my member stiff and aching or my thighs wet and sticky with the filth of my body, Christ's face, censuring but gentle, forming in the swirl of dirt and discolored brick on the ceiling of my cell, elongating and transforming, softening to forgiveness. It was Christ's hand that stroked my forehead, kneaded away my dreams of sunlight on water, canoes dug out of tulip poplars and locust trees, soft round houses made of woven reeds, great flocks of geese blackening the sky, carrying me away into that blackness. It was for Christ, to share Christ's pain, that I fasted for days, touched neither food nor drink until I was a husk ready to be filled with Light. It was Christ that came to me in those states and drove away the other voices, the strange chants in a devil's tongue that would also come to me then. It was Christ's body and blood dissolving into my own as I knelt trembling in all my flesh to receive communion, as I had at my baptism, my transformation to John Christman, the name the kidnapper Devere had given me when he brought me to England:

Jesus Deus, amor meus
Cordis aestum imprime
Urat ignis urat amor.

Devere had named me, brought me to be displayed in my feathers and paint and skins at the British court, to feed the whites hunger for savages. But it was Andrew White who had taken me to the monastery in Seville. White, fleeing his English martyrdom, as many of the priests who came there had. White who became the gentle suffering Christ transmuted to earthly flesh for me, magic accomplished only by a few mild words, a few looks of interest and questions about who I was, the land and people from which I came. Andrew White who took the reamed and burned out dugout my mind and heart had become and filled it with the disciplined Christ, with words and thoughts that came into John Christman like a great expanding mass, pushing out, expelling the remnants of those memories, of that sunlight dancing on water, of naked sinners dancing around a fire.

I had remained like that, a fervent husk, until one day I had stopped when passing an arrow slit in the monastery wall, set directly next to a crucifix, and, with a guilty glance at the hanging god, put my eye to the slit and the light that assailed me was a light that was so bright and full of dancing colors that it diminished the light of Christ in my mind, so that when I looked away, at the crucifix, the thin bearded face drained of its life before my eyes and became inert, a twist of wood nailed to a wall, its crude smile mocking, if anything. I gave a cry, my heart emptying, and looked back out of the window. Men in gleaming armor, scarlet and gold pennants snapping from their lances, were riding by in a procession. My eye followed them as they drew a border along a crowd of people dressed in ragged garments of every color; they seemed to be rioting around stands filled with oranges and melons and red and green peppers, bright as jewels in the sun, and piles of multicolored cloths and hats and feathers and flowers and pots and pans. No, not rioting, I saw, but laughing, shouting, holding up foods or goods, slapping each other, drinking from skins, kissing, pissing against the wall, scratching themselves. I understood at that moment when I saw the light of the world again what had been done to me, the darkness the church had plunged me into and that square in Seville burst, as if from ashes, into a fire flickering tall before a wall of impossible trees, around it naked people dancing and chanting, their bodies stripped with red and blue and black paint.

Then that vision itself shifted back in my mind and dissolved into a line of white men and women in multi-colored tunics and tights, laughing and singing and calling to each other as they pranced before painted trees on a stage in the middle of the square. I had watched, enthralled, as a hawk-faced man in a feather headdress, his face and body striped in paint, pranced around a fire made of colored paper and howled at the crowd, which howled back at him. The hawk-faced man turned his back to them, lifted the flap of his breech-clout, bent over and saluted them with a noisy burst of gas. As the crowd laughed and howled more, the man turned and seemed to be staring straight at me, straight at the slit where I stood, so his painted face seemed framed by the two walls and somehow brought close, right next to my own and I saw it was He Whose Face Bulges in the Smoke Hole, there in that Spanish square, saying: you have forgotten me, but come now and dwell in smoke with me. Come now. Be smoke. Or I will disperse and be gone and your spirit will not be able to call me back.

That night I stirred through the halls of the monastery like smoke, darkness moving through darkness. Everything I had forgotten: my mother's deep laugh, the feel of a bow's tension in my hands, the eyes of a deer pouring into my own at the moment of its death, the endless forest, suddenly burst into my consciousness like the riotous crowd I had seen outside the monastery, its jumbled and brilliant motley whirling to call attention to itself. I only hesitated at the scarred wooden door of White's cell. I pressed my eye against the spy hole. White was at his prayers, kneeling, his eyes closed. I felt pulled to the man, to his faith, so strongly that I considered opening the door and killing him. I went on instead, fading into a shadowed niche as Diego the watchman shuffled by, looking at the man's back, my eyes flat and merciless. I took a tapir from the chapel. Going down the stairs to the basement vaults of the building was descending into a cold and clammy netherworld; the streaked and moldy walls pressed toward me, threatened to close and trap me forever in the thick wet darkness of this place. I found the wooden chests Devere had given to the monks in a storage room piled with books.

I opened one, and in the flicker of the candle light, saw Smoke had brought me to a picture of his own land: a map of the Chesapeake's water held between the crab claws of the land, a drawing of a Piscataway in the upper right hand corner, or rather what seemed to me a drawing of a white man costumed as a Piscataway: the draped tunic and soft spread of hips and belly, the languid pose of another costumed mountebank, like the actors I had seen through the slit playing at being what I truly was, as if my peeled life was only a hide to paint their dreams upon.

When I appeared at the inn where those actors were staying, I had tied my hair to one side with the *roanoke* beads I had found in the chest, painted mud stripes on my face, and instead of my old breech-clout, which no longer fit me, wore my monk's habit draped not so much as I would have worn a real breech-clout, but to the European idea of an Indian drawn on the map. In my hands though, I carried the tomahawk that Devere had carefully packed into the chest, and around my neck I wore my otterskin medicine bag.

The inn fell into a dead silence as I entered.

"What kind of painted monkey has this evening brought us?" the innkeeper had said squinting at me. A soldier, wearing a padded cotton under-armor tunic, his sword buckled to his waist, guffawed. Rodrigo, he called, do we have to drink in here with savages and lunatics?

Jacob Lombroso had stood unsteadily and walked to the man, walked into my life.

"What of actors, my friend?" he said. "Does it tweak you to drink with actors?"

The soldier smirked. "Actors fit under the first two types. Savages or lunatics. Take your pick. As low as that. Like snakeshit fits under snake. Fit under painted monkeys, for that matter, you hook-beaked swine."

"Ah," Jacob had said. "Monkeys, birds, snakes. You mix your menagerie, my friend. And what of *marranos*? Do you cage those into your circus also?"

"Jews?" the soldier said. "Jews I put here. He drew his sword. "Do you get my point?" He laughed.

I saw the small knife flash from Jacob's hand, didn't see the knife strike. The soldier fell back, holding his face, blood welling between his fingers. The innkeeper cursed and came around the table, a rusty cavalry saber in his hand. I crossed in front of him with my liberated tomahawk drawn and when the man slashed down, I caught the blade, spun it out, and smashed him in the forehead. The innkeeper fell as if he was a puppet whose strings had been cut.

And then Jacob, his pointed beard still black then, had looked at me with drunken, heavy-lidded eyes and began to applaud, and the other actors, we sort of people all, joined him.

Welcome, Jacob Lombroso had said. I've been waiting for you.

Hallam's Song

I was up to my neck in water. Up to my ankles in the bottom mud. Fifty Susquehannocks waited behind me in the reeds and cattails. They were naked, glopped thick with bear grease. As I was. A patch of waterlilies spread around us. Another seventy men, reinforcements from the Susquehannock fort and trading post about twenty miles northwest, over the Potomac, lay in the woods on the north side of the Piscataway town. The palisade on that side was high and sturdy. But when I had scouted this place yesterday, I saw that the palisade on this, the creek side, was carelessly maintained, the cattail reed mats used to block the spaces between the posts falling away or gone already and not replaced. The Piscataway must have felt secure that no enemy would approach this way. Probably because none ever had. To gain or keep their access to the creek open they had removed many of the staked posts, and some of those remaining were termite eaten and soft. They could be pulled down with looped ropes or, if sturdy, simply slipped between, with our greased bodies. I had had the raiding party leave their dugouts downcreek; the Piscataways and their English allies—Cornwaylis' militia—had sunk sharpened stakes in the bottom of the creek, and the water was full of V-shaped fish weirs set deliberately just under the surface, making passage, except through channels the Piscataway would know, nearly impossible for canoes or larger boats. On foot, in the waist and neck deep water, none of this was a real obstacle. We had been able to slit the throats of the two Listeners we had found in the marsh before either could make a sound. They had both been half-asleep anyway; I was certain the Piscataway didn't expect a raid this far north, nearly to Accoceek. Until now, we had kept most of our raids around the area of Saint Marie's. But I had received information from his scouts that Cornwalys had a small contingent in this village, to help advise the Piscataway (they were from the Accoceek tribe) about their defenses and to simply be there, to demonstrate their concern for their allies. That was why Claiborne had chosen this place for a raid. A harsh visit. Make an example of the town, he had said. It was close to Kittamaquund, he said, and its destruction might cant the Tayac away from his alliance with Calvert, serve warning that Piscataway itself, the main town of the Piscataway Federation, could be razed. Be Hallam, he had said to me.

My men had placed waterlily leaves and cattails in their headbands, and they waited so motionlessly now that from ten yards away they were invisible. They carried their weapons, bows and arrows, tomahawks, knives, sheathed in greased fur wrappings, held under the water also. I left the muskets with his force in the forest. Now the Susquehannocks waited in the water and ignored the cold and discomfort. I did the same. I could slip my mind into their time now. Let time and weather and water slide off my skin. But the watersnakes were a different matter. When we had come up the creek, clumps of snakes had been knotted and draped on overhanging branches along the shore, sunning themselves on cypress roots. Except for the cottonmouths I had seen swimming sinuously and quickly through the brown water, their heads held stiffly above the surface, their bodies flowing loose and boneless below, most of the snakes were nonpoisonous. But they were nervous and irritable and when the canoes had come too close, several times the snakes had launched themselves into them from overlying branches and bitten the Susquehannocks, who laughed, delighted at their aggressiveness. A brown snake had even twined on my arm, and its bites, when I slowly and silently unwrapped and strangled it, like unwrapping my own convulsing, liberated muscle, had ripped my skin. I knew there was no poison. But I'd seen white men in this country die within days of festering abcesses that grew from small cuts. The snake's mouth and teeth looked filthy. My men believed these creatures to be the ghosts of Piscataway enemies tortured to death in the town to provide guardian spirits. Several men had cut the heads off the snakes, held them up and let their blood pulse into their mouths, down their throats, to swallow their swiftness and anger. I did the same with the snake I had strangled. Took its cold, muscular neck in my teeth and bit through, then held it above my open mouth, filled my throat with its bitter coldness. Because I hated snakes and the thought of drinking their blood repulsed me. Because I swallowed what I hated.

Sometimes I swallowed what I loved. Once I stalked a mountain lion and stole its spirit. The cat had killed a Susquehannock boy of twelve who had walked under an overhang of cliff. He was part of a raiding party I had taken against the Patuxents; they had been threatening to shift their alliance to Calvert and Kittamaquund. We had chased the animal off before it could drag the boy's corpse off, but the kill had been swift. A blurred leap and slash, one motion, severing the carotid, the fangs in the back of the neck, a swift bone snapping shake. I caught a glimpse of the lion on the cliff just at the moment before it leapt. Patience tensed around rage, the very instrument I was shaping myself towards. A thing carved of its own hunger and fury. I needed to see it again. I had left my men and followed its trail. Claiborne and Susquehannocks didn't see me again for weeks. They were unconcerned. They understood it was my vision animal.

I had little belief in visions, but in the course of the stalk I came to feel that the mountain lion knew me. I had seen it once, ahead of me on a small ridge, looking back, its eyes depthed with a history of murder. I had felt an answering tug, a hot feral surge in my blood. I learned to identify the circle of the cat's hunt by the remains of its kills, its scat, the marking splashes of its urine on tree trunks. I pissed and shat the same way, in the same places. The more I followed and learned it and its country, the more desperate it seemed the lion was becoming, as if I were drawing off its traits of speed and patience into myself. I was. Finally, the lion had tried to disappear into the Great Cypress Swamp which covered hundreds of acres near the Patuxent's town of Quomocac. For the most part the Indians stayed out of this area, believing it inhabited by spirits. Perhaps it was. The huge, ancient cypresses, their wide bases growing from the black water of the swamp, towered hundreds of feet high and shut off the sun under a weaved canopy of needles, trapping a weird green light, a whisper-broken silence under their spread. I knew the animal's hunting patterns by then, and I had, as last night in this place, waited stock-still, squatting neck deep in the black water, my head between clusters of dwarfish cypress knees, my musket laying across their tops. Finally I saw the lion. It was crouched on a hummock rising in a gradual slope in front of me. It appeared and then disappeared again and when I saw it in the next second it emerged as if the elements of the earth and the swamp and the silence and the lap of water against the cypress trunks and the light and the buzzing cloud of insects in the shafts of sunlight, all seemingly disparate and unrelated elements, had suddenly swirled into its shape, into its leap, the directed force of that place. At the same moment its eyes, yellow and bottomless, looked straight into mine and I felt it leap into me, an instant before its physical spring, and I fired, and then it was gone. There was no sign of its passing. I didn't even hear a splash in the water, though the roar of my musket might have hid that sound. But I didn't try to find the lion after that. I didn't need to.

It was that lion's motion now that I saw or perhaps put into my Susquehanocks as the sun began its rise and we unsheathed our weapons and rose from the creek and began moving towards the palisade. One of the watchers turned his face and as he opened his mouth, Sleek Otter put an arrow through it, and Dark Moon immediately killed the other sentry. As he fell back inside the fence, the Susquehannocks wailed out their war cry. It was high and inhuman and chilled even my blood and then heated it, and I let it burst from my own throat, howling with them as we swarmed into the village over and through the wide spaced fence on the creek side. Running through the milky morning mist so we would have seemed legless floating apparitions, tall men, their feathered roach manes making them seem even taller, their bodies and faces striped and spotted, substantiating out of the dawn light itself like the nightmares of the town's uneasy sleep brought to life and terror. So I saw them. So I saw myself. Figures began spilling out of the longhouses, most of them still not dressed, still rubbing the sleep from their eyes and the Susquehannocks hatcheted them as they emerged and sights and sounds came to me clearly, but in fragments, outside the red tunnel of killing I was inside. The steady cracking of musket fire echoed from the other side of the village. A white boy, perhaps fourteen, dressed only in breeches, ran by me screaming, his eyes terrified, the Susquehannocks parting into a makeshift and mocking gauntlet, smashing at his head and legs until he fell, still screaming, and one brave cleaving his skull, kneeling and taking his scalp, proof for Claiborne, who had priced both Piscataway and white scalps at the same amount of *roanoke* that a winter thick beaver pelt of good quality brought. The bloody patch on the boy's head smoked in the still cool air. The Susquehanocks broke into small killing groups, surrounding clusters of the Accoceek Piscataway and flailing and stabbing at them; I could see the lack of resistance was increasing their fury. Only a few Piscataway men and women had had time to grab weapons. Fighting swirled here and there in the compound. But no overall battle. The longhouses were burning. I felt the heat slapping my face. The mist was gone. A flock of geese suddenly flew overhead, their necks and beaks strained forward towards some point on the horizon as if they belonged to a different universe. On the ground, in my world, several male prisoners, trussed and hamstrung, some of them crippled by arrows, were being dragged to the center of the square. A group of women and children had cut a hole in the side of a burning longhouse and run out into the ditch inside the stockade fence, most of them still naked from their sleeping pallets. My men stood on the edge, shooting arrows into them, testing their skills against each other. A child, motherless, crawled away from the ditch and Caws-Like-Crow picked it up by the heel, threw it into the air, notched an arrow and skewered it before it hit the ground. Usually the Susquehannocks would take children, women for slaves. But they wouldn't want to breed with this group.

A party of ten braves began running other Piscataway to the ditch, herding them the way we would drive panicked deer into the river and a semi-circle of waiting hunters. One of the English, the first I had seen besides the boy, had climbed onto a pile of wood. The Susquehannock formed around him, keeping few paces back, laughing and advancing, falling to their knees, jumping back, imitating their vision animals. They hoped the man—he was as big as a Susquehannock, dressed in full body armor, a twelve foot pike in his hands, a saber at his belt—would give them a fight they could sing about from this place. So far there were no prisoners even worth being tortured. One brave, Swift Squirrel, a sixteen year old I was taking on his first raid, danced in front of the Englishman, dodging the thrusts of the heavy pike, laughing. Rivulets of sweat ran over the man's face from under the crested helmet. He flung the pike, underhand, catching Swift Squirrel in the throat. The boy fell back, blood bubbling from his mouth, and the Englishman yelled "Saint Marie's," drew his saber, slashed another Indian across the chest and stomach, opening him so his guts spilled out, gray and steaming and he looked at them, as in surprise, and laughed ruefully and fell. The Englishman had meanwhile whirled around and stuck Croaker, one of my inner guard, in the stomach so forcefully the point of the saber came out of his spine. The Susquehannocks, grunting in the way I knew meant they were deeply satisfied, moved in on the man, shooting arrows into his knees, prolonging the fight out of respect and gratitude. Caws-Like-Crow imitated the man's war cry, "San Mak-ee." The man swept his saber at him, and Sleek Otter moved inside the arc and smashed his hatchet up into the man's nose, under the crested helmet. He grasped his face, blood running into his yellow beard, and Sleek Otter severed his spine at the neck with another blow.

At that moment, I saw the priest appear at the doorway of a longhouse. Out of my memory. But there. He knelt almost immediately by a woman lying in her own blood on the ground, raised her head, and began giving her the last rites. It moved me to fury. Take him, I signed to the braves who had stopped to look. Except for a few shrieks and low moans, the crackle of the fire, the village was almost silent now. I pushed the dried finger hanging on my chest against my skin. Wounding my wound. *Discite justitiam moniti et non contemnere divos.* The wonderous justice of God. I was here now and I was there, as if it were all one village, white stone of Spain to pine logs of America laced by fire and screams. World without end, amen. My men tied the priest to a stockade post. The Piscataway prisoners were being hung on others. Some upside down over kindling that would be lit under their heads. One of the men—Swift Squirrel's older brother—had begun to flay a captive, cutting deep around his brow, then clawing into the flap and yanking the skin down off his face. Other braves were heaping wood at the priest's feet. I walked over to him. A young narrow mournful face. A white oval of a face, thick black commas of eyebrows. Thin lips silently praying. He looked at me. Something changed in his eyes. "Hallam," he said.

"You know me, priest?"

"You're Hallam. The devil who took Ezekiel's hand."

I stared at him, his words turning in my mind until I understood why they had hooked me. I felt my blood freeze. It was not something one would say of a dead man. I seized the priest by the throat, raising him to his toes, slamming the back of his head into the wood. "Where is he, priest?" I growled.

The priest's eyes rolled back and a string of spittle rolled down from the corner of his mouth. He was choking to death. I released him. He rubbed his throat.

"Where?" I repeated. "Where is he now?" *Tell me what I know.* My reason had told me Ezekiel would be long dead, drained into the ground where I had left him. But my blood told me otherwise and at night I'd wake to feel Ezekiel's finger digging into my chest and now I understood.

"I'll say nothing more to you, devil."

I brought my face up close to his, feeling the snake I'd drunk move in me now, coiled and cold. "You know who I am," I whispered. "You named me, priest. I've seen you before. I've killed you before. You know me. I'm the devil what took Ezekiel's hand. I'll have all your parts too, priest, eat them in front of you. You'll yelp for Jesus then, Father Black, I'll tell you that."

I stepped back, slid out my knife and brought the point to his throat. "You know what these Indians going to do to you? Do you see what's happening over there. They'll scalp you alive, priest, then undress you from your flesh. Keep you alive until they dismember you. Put red hot embers on your flayed scalp. Pull your guts out like ropes, burn them in front of you. You've seen it. You've blessed your Indians when they did it to Protestants, didn't you? You talk to me now, man, and I'll ease you out of your life. Do that for me, father. Give me your confession."

"Get thee from me," the priest said.

"Talk to me, priest."

He turned his head. "I say only this. The man you tried to chop to pieces is alive and his child and his generations are alive. As will I be, devil, for I will live in you. All of us will. Now and at the hour of your death." He turned back to me and smiled. I had seen his smile before. I groaned and sliced his carotid. He was dead before his chin slumped to his chest.

Behind me, I could sense the silent disapproval of the Susquehannocks at this easy death I had allowed an enemy and a brave man, and I knew the priest's curse was already starting to come true.

The Northern Source

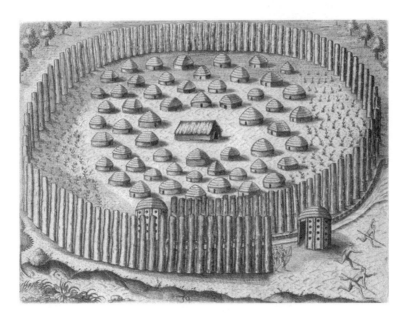

Author uncertain

In this mission are three priests and three temporal co-adjutors. This year we have learned a remarkable thing, which, though it happened many years ago, and very likely may have been recorded in our annals of former times, notwithstanding, since it has been copied by us this very year, confirmed also by the authentic testimony of an eye witness and public notary, it has seemed proper to touch upon the matter here, at least, in a brief manner. It is, however, necessary for me to premise this one thing, that it has been established by custom and usage of the catholics who live in Maryland, during the whole night of the 31st of July following the festival of St. Ignatius, to honor with a salute of cannon their tutelar guardian and patron saint.

Therefore, in [that year], mindful of the solemn custom, the anniversary of the holy father being ended, they wished the night also consecrated to the honor of the same, by the continual discharge of artillery. At the time, there were in the neighborhood certain soldiers, unjust plunderers, Englishmen indeed by birth of the heterodox faith, who, coming the year before with a fleet, had invaded with arms almost the entire colony, had plundered, burnt, and finally, having abducted the priests and driven the Governor himself into exile, had reduced it to a miserable servitude. These had protection in a certain fortified citadel, built for their own defence, situated about five miles from the others; but now, aroused by the nocturnal report of the cannon, the day after, that is, on the first of August, rush upon us with arms, break into the houses of the catholics, and plunder whatever there is of arms or powder.

After a while, when at length they had made an end of plundering and had arranged their departure, one of them, a fellow of a beastly disposition, and a scoffer, both con-

temptible and blasphemous, even dared to assail St. Ignatius himself with filthy scurrility and a more filthy act. "Away to the wicked cross with you, papists!" says he, "who take delight in saluting your poor saint by the firing of cannon. I have a cannon too, and I will give him a salute more suitable and appropriate to so miserable a saint." This being said (let me not offend the delicacy of your ears,) he resounded with a loud report, and departed, while his companions deride with their insolent laughter.

But his impious and wicked scurrility cost the wretch dear; for, scarcely had he proceeded two hundred paces from the place, when he felt a commotion of the bowels within, and that he was solicited to privacy; and when he had gone about the same distance on his way, he had to withdraw privately again, complaining of an unusual pain in his bowels, the like of which he had never felt in his life before. The remaining part of his journey, to wit: four miles, was accomplished in a boat; in which space the severe torture of his bowels and the looseness of his belly frequently compelled him to land. Having arrived at the fort, scarcely in possession of his mind, through so great pain, he rolls himself at one time on the ground, at another casts himself on a bench, again on a bed, crying out all the time with a loud voice "I am burning up! I am burning up! There is a fire in my belly! There is a fire in my bowels!" The officers, having pitied the deplorable fate of their comrade, carry him at length, placed in a boat, to a certain Thomas Hebden, a skillful surgeon; but the malady had proceeded farther that could be cured or alleviated by his art. In the meantime you could hear nothing else coming from his lips, but that well-known and mournful cry "I am burning up! I am burning up! Fire! Fire!" The day after, which was the second of August, his intolerable suffering growing worse every hour, his bowels began to be voided, piecemeal. But on the 3d of August, furious and raging, he passed larger portions of the intestines, some of which were a foot, some a foot and a half, others two feet long. At length, the fourth day drained the whole pump, so that it left nothing remaining but the abdomen, empty and void. Still surviving, he saw the dawning of the fifth day, when the unhappy wretch ceased to see and live, an example to posterity of divine vengeance warning mankind: "Discite justitiam moniti et non contemnere dios."

Innumerable persons, still living, saw the intestines of the dead man for many months hung upon the fence posts, among whom he who has added his testimony to these things, and with his eyes saw, and with his hands handled the bowels, blackened and as if crisped up by fire, of this modern judas, who, when being hung, broke in the midst, and all his bowels gushed out.

Ezekiel's Song

The other patrons fell silent when we came inside Smith's Ordinary, staring at my stump. A low mutter had broken out. I was a story for them now and the real flesh of it disturbed them. My carved stump a demonstration of the living truth of James Hallam, the monster they called up to frighten their children. I had helped build this place. With that same Hallam. We had stuck together two of the usual post and clapboard houses, one behind the other. One room a store and kitchen, the other a dirt-floored public room, crowded with seven long plank tables and benches. When visitors came to St. Marie's for trade or court cases, they could sleep on the rough locustwood planks of the tables for the price of a bundle of tobacco or a beaver pelt. Simon Bledsoe, the proprietor, had fastened crude shelves on the wall next to his barrels of ale; they were lined with pewter and clay flagons. The air was snakey with twists of smoke from the clay pipes all the men inside were smoking. It curled in the bluing beams of sunlight coming through the gaps of the boards. Bundles of tobacco hung from the ceiling joists, absorbing the smoke as if taking back their own spent spirit.

We weren't paying for anything. You're my guests, Lewis Fremond had said, smiling. His face was smeared with beaver grease. I had never seen him without it and had come to think of it as an emission from his own pores. The grease made his smile seem oiled and too easy. He was a tall gaunt man with a sharp adam's apple, a sailor on the Ark who had decided at landfall to indenture himself over to Henry Fleet. I had seen him once, when I was still a slave, beating the Yaocomaco woman he had taken, breaking her nose; he had met my eyes and sneered when he saw me looking at her and I knew it was only his fear of Hallam then had kept him from striking

216

me as well. But he had a cow and other livestock to trade, and we had more children to feed now.

"Bring ale for me friends here, Bledsoe, y' bag a' guts," Fremond called. The tavern keeper put down four clay flagons, his face expressionless, his gaze brushing my arm, flitting away when I looked back at him. I drank down the dark sour ale. It was thick with some gritty residue. I ran my tongue over the front of my teeth, feeling the grit ridge up at the tip of my tongue. The other patrons were still staring at me.

"Fookers never seen a missing flipper afore?" Fremond growled at the tavern at large.

"Damn yer temper, Billy Fremond," one of the drinkers, Josiah Broadhead, called out, scowling. "And yer foul tongue. You know why we stare."

His words, something in the silence, made me uneasy. It seemed directed to something other than my story and my stump.

"And damn your mother's crooked arsecrack," Fremond said vaguely. He raised his flagon, pushed it at our faces. "Here's to trade, gents."

"What do you have for us, Fremond," Tawzin said. His face was stiff. I saw Lombroso staring intently at Fremond, as if seeing him for the first time.

"I can spare you one cow, a good milker, and four laying hens, but no cock. Can get your cock elsewhere." He looked belligerently around the room. "Any one got a cock, trade to Hallam's Revenge here?"

I felt my blood freeze. Lombroso reached over and ran his fingertips gently and with interest over Fremond's cheek. "You'll not call us that again, will you now?" He suddenly seized Fremond's lower lip between his thumb and forefinger, pinched it, released it.

Fremond rubbed his mouth and shivered. I saw the lip had turned black. He stared at Lombroso. "Bless you, me tongue'll fall out first, yer 'onor," he said sincerely.

"Quite probably," Lombroso said.

I saw Fremond glance over at the door, then quickly back.

"Well, I 'ope no offense war taken, yer 'onor. A man 'ears certain things, as it war, in the air, his tongue curls around them."

"Do you wish to trade or not, Fremond," Tawzin said. His eyes had a half-lidded lazy look about them that I knew meant he felt the same coil of tension in the room, in Fremond, that I had.

"What d'ye 'ave for me then?" Fremond asked. "You people. You sort a people. I 'ear that's what yer calling yourselves, out there. What's that mean, loves? That mean I'm not you sort? Old sailor man like me?

"Corn," Tawzin said. "Also *roanoke*, a dozen arm lengths of Jamestown blue beads. And sassafras for medicine."

"And beaver?" Fremond said. "That northern pelt? You-sort get me a two score a those 'ides, I can gets yer 'nother cow." He glanced at the door again, smiled, slapped Tawzin on the shoulder. "More milk, free them white titties for you, 'ey lad?"

Tawzin looked at him. "Do you speak of my wife?" His hand had gone down to the skinning knife he kept at his waist.

Fremond laughed. "Damme, you tickle me, Indian. The way y'can wrap yer tongue around the King's English's, just like a white man. No, no offense, your 'onor. Just old Lewis' rough sailor's ways. No offense meant. Just, ye might say, me sort a way. Thinking 'a those brown lips at that pink little tittie."

The door opened and I heard footsteps, the creak of leather, metal hitting metal. I turned. Three militia men in breast plates and helmets, swords at their waists, walked in and stood at the wall opposite us. Neither ordered a drink.

"Let's get out of here," I said.

"Nay, be patient my lads," Fremond said. "We were speakin' a beaver. Northern beaver. We sort speaking a northern beaver and white titty."

I registered the knife in Tawzin's hand afterwards, but the draw and cut had been too quick, a move my vision had to catch up to. Fremond fell backwards over the bench, squealing. His forehead was bleeding. "Get 'im. Get the bloody fookin' savage; ya seen 'im attack me," he screamed. A militia man stepped forward, started to speak. I clubbed my stump into his face and the man staggered back. Lombroso grabbed my arm.

"Stand still," he ordered. "they have us."

Two more militia had come inside, their muskets leveled at us. Fremond was on his feet, groaning and holding together the lips of the wound on his forehead. The cut didn't look deep but there was a dramatic gush of blood.

"John Christman," one of the militia men said. "We arrest you under the laws of the Maryland Charter and its treaty with the emperor of the Piscataway, for the kidnapping and forced captivity of the white Christian woman Sally Picard."

Lombroso was still gripping my arm.

"Now, calmly," he said. He began to move towards the door.

"Take 'em," Fremond said to the militia men. "These two also, dinna let 'em go. These sort."

The militia man hesitated, then stepped in front of Lombroso.

"Do you have orders to hold us as well?" Lombroso questioned the man. "Is that you, Christian Slagel? I hardly recognized you in that helmet. How are those boils on your behind doing?"

"They're doin' ripe well, thank ye, sir."

"A pox on yer ham boils," Fremond said. "Damn you, Fleet wants 'em all 'eld. Dinna you see 'em attack me?"

"Shut your mouth, Fremond," Slagel said. "We don't serve Henry Fleet."

"Does that truth shine as bright and clear as it should, friend Christian?" Lombroso asked.

"Tis not my concern, doctor. Our orders are to arrest John

Christman." He waved his hand at the other militia men. "Let these two go."

"Damn you, Slagel," Fremond said.

"Get your skinny arse out of my sight, Fremond, afore I arrest you for interferin' with our duties."

The militia men surrounded Tawzin. He looked at them without expression, his eyes still half-lidded. "Don't," Lombroso said. Tawzin nodded shortly. He said something to Lombroso that I didn't understand. Lombroso nodded. When the militia men began to move, one behind Tawzin, one at the side, he moved with them, looking straight ahead.

"Where will you take him?" I asked.

"We got a gaol house up nae, just beyond the guv'ner's house," Slagel said, with a certain amount of pride.

"Gaol house and gallows, you want for naught then," Lombroso said. He tugged at my arm. We walked to the door.

"What did Tawzin say to you?" I asked.

"'*Lech mahair m'can v'sim otah tahat ha'adomah,*'" he said. "Hebrew. It means 'go quickly from here and put her under the earth.'"

Tawzin's Song

The room was narrow enough that I could touch both walls with the flattened palms of my hands, pushing against them, Lombroso might say, as if I were Samson pushing against the Philistine pillars. But I had been neither shorn nor blinded nor betrayed by my own. Nor was I strong enough to collapse the temple no matter I pressed until I could feel the veins standing out from my forehead. I'm sorry, Jacob, but it was another Hebrew analog that would not do for me. Nor was there a Piscataway story to live with me in the darkness either. My people could imagine and visit every torture conceivable on flesh but confinement.

I felt around the walls and roof for the hundredth time. If there were clay I could claw through it, but the gaol had been built of logs, not clapboard, heavy poplars lying tight on each other. The cell was even floored. I squatted and closed my eyes. The figure that came to me then was not Samson nor *manitou*, but the tortured Christ, his agony frozen on the crucifix above my plank bed in a narrow and cold Spanish room, the inexpressible pain of the heart expressed and visible, the god that shared loneliness, need, and temptation and so could forgive. I had watched Kittamaquund's baptism with contempt and hatred, but suddenly, now in the darkness and solitude, I understood with the understanding of a lonely child again; it was not the arrogant Christ of sword and fire had come to the Tayac, but the Christ who was there in the darkness, for who else could forgive the murder of a brother, the betrayal of a people?

A crack of light fell over me. The door opened and Andrew White came in, holding a candle. I laughed.

"Are you real or a manifestation?"

"It gladdens my heart to see you can stil laugh at me."

"I had thought Christ was sending me a sign."

White seemed moved. "It is in the darkness that Christ comes to us."

I felt a chill. "So you taught me. And this place is not different than my cell in Spain, and it is natural that your words, printed in my mind there, come to me here."

"There are many paths to Christ, John Christman."

"My name is still Tawzin. It is true, you have given me Christ; I saw that just now. I was thinking of Christ, Andrew, though perhaps these were only such thoughts that a man has in the dark. You see, that is the way of it. You place me in the dark, you take everything away from me, and in the dark and terrible emptiness in which you leave me, you put in Christ. That is our history, you and I."

"Sometimes a man must be made to see the Darkness before he can see the Light."

I laughed shortly. "When the gaoler who put me in this cell came with food and drink and light tonight, I was not such a fool as to think he was the food and the drink and the light. Or to be grateful towards him who keeps me here. I have Christ, Andrew. But your Christ and mine are not the same. Your Christ grows from darkness, mine from light. The Christ I seek sees through all eyes. He is the God who comes to men in cells to say they are not alone."

"We seek the same Man."

"No. I saw your Church. I saw Christians. I see them here. He is not the same."

"John...Tawzin, even this troubled speech shows our Lord is still not dead in your heart. You still seek him."

I laughed again. "Is that why I've been put in this cell? So I could find him again? It's true, as I said, the dimensions of this place call up my cell in the monastery."

"Let me sit down. I was a younger man in Spain and was able to argue theology on my feet. I no longer can."

"You'll have to sit in piss. They don't allow me outside to relieve myself."

"I've smelled yur stink before." White sat down, his back against the wall, the candle, in its dish, on his knees. I sat against the opposite wall, our legs touching in the tight space. "I think you know why you are here," he said. "But it will not last." He stared at the candle. "Forgive me, Tawzin. I told you I hated the beaver trade. Yet I spoke not against it; in my arrogance, I had thought it could yet be a blessing for our enterprise, God's kingdom on earth."

"Fleet apparently felt the same. Though I doubt it's God's kingdom he seeks."

"Nevertheless, here we find ourselves. Why is it against your heart to help him find the Northern source? It may enrich Fleet, but it could still frustrate Claiborne's designs for us."

"Yes. It could. And then what weight would Kittamaquund and the Piscataway have in Calvert's Maryland colony, if Calvert finds new Indians to use?"

"Our Piscataway are enfolded in the True Church and would be protected."

"As Lombroso would say, then God help them."

White laughed. I looked at him.

"Sometimes you surprise me."

"I heard Jacob Lombroso's voice in your words. Yes, he would say that. But you are mistaken. John...Tawzin." White drew in a breath. "And you're mistaken if you believe I had anything to do with this arrest."

It wasn't a question. I answered it anyway. "At first I did. But then...no. I don't. You destroy with love not greed. In the end that is why I will bring no more Indians to white men. Neither the northern tribes nor Nanjemoy."

White sighed. "I have asked to question you at your trial tomorrow. There is opposition because I'm a priest; there are people here who think the Jesuits already have too much say in the colony. But it is through the church that I can save you."

"You have already saved me one more time than I desired."

White bowed his head. "The charge of the abduction of Sally Picard," he said, "is a pretext; it is understood she is with you of her will, and she has no living relatives presenting a claim. More, Fleet stirs resentment against your group because you've permitted run away slaves and indentureds to live among you—all of the Piscataway tribes have signed treaties agreeing to return such fugitives to their rightful masters."

"We're not a Piscataway tribe."

"You and I understand that you have been given an unspoken choice, John: cooperate with Fleet or you will lose the woman and child and possibly your life. Calvert, I'm convinced, would not have permitted this, but he is in England, arranging more trade goods for the colony, seeking the court's intervention against Claiborne. That's why Fleet acted now. But still, Fleet must follow the law. Thomas Girard will judge your trial, and he is an honest man. John, you must take two actions. Firstly, although I have been to Lombroso's freehold and your longhouse, Sally Picard is nowhere to be found, and neither are the runaway slaves and servants who must be returned. Your friends will tell me nothing. She must come in, and she must testify that she is with you of her own will. And she must marry you, baptize and marry you according to the laws of the Church. The council could not rule to dissolve such a union."

We sat pressed to each other in the narrow cell.

"And so you have what you wished," I said.

"I did not not wish to have it this way, John."

"My name is Tawzin. Nanjemoy is already my wife. She was born to us when she died from her old life. She was asked if she would take me as husband and she agreed and we passed together through the door of the longhouse according to the laws of our people."

The candle flickered and almost went out. I fought the scramble of panic in my chest. I thought again of Wesort, in the darkness under the earth, sealed.

WHEN THEY BROUGHT me blinking into the light, I wasn't sure how many days had gone by. They marched me to the wooden council chamber on the northern corner of Governor's field, the hundred acres above the river bluff that held Calvert's house and the fort, and the gaol as well. On the ground I had stood when I watched Yaocomaco give away his people. Inside, it was not much bigger than Smith's Ordinary and was permeated with the same warm smell of wood, urine, sweat, rum and tobacco. In fact the building was used as an ordinary when court or council was not in session, and I saw that many of the spectators were drinking as if it were in that use today. I recognized some of the men who had been at Smith's, Fleet's men. The chamber room was fronted by a large U-shaped clay and wattle fireplace. On the wall above the fireplace was fastened the coat of arms of the King and the new Maryland seal, which contained the figures of the goddesses representing both Avalon and St. Marie's. It was as Andrew White had described it to me, the night before.

Two militia men and a baliff stood sweating in front of the judges' long oak table. The baliff rang a bell for silence. The presiding judges, Thomas Girard and Abell Snow, wore powdered wigs, the curls rolled above the napes of their necks in deference to the heat. Under his pale, damp neck, Girard wore a corded purple silk waistcoat embroidered with a pattern of ivy vines that emphasized the florid and unhealthy flush of his skin; he was a large, comfortably paunched man. Snow, to his right, was sallow-faced and leathery; as had happened to most of the colonists, he must have lost much of the clothing brought from England to moth, mildew and fire. But he still wore a heavy linen waistcoat, ruffles at his sleeves. Beads of oily sweat ran down his neck and into his collar.

I had discarded the linsey-woolsey shirt and trousers I had been given in the gaol and wore nothing but my Piscataway breech-clout. That garment, my ochre and blue clay, my beads and medicine bag, were brought to me by Lombroso, who had finally been allowed to visit. He had assured me that Nanjemoy and Rachel were well hidden in the tunnel. I had painted red stripes above my eyes and blue beneath them, as if on a war party. My appearance, when I entered between two militia men, caused a mutter of hilarity to run through the court room.

"Baliff, that man may not appear before this court dressed in an indecent and outlandish manner." Gerard said. "You, he said, leaning forward and addressing me, making his voice louder, "You, where are the clothes we gave you?"

I didn't reply.

"Damn it, who will speak for this man?"

"I will, your honor." Andrew White rose.

"I'm sorry, father. But according to the covenants of the colony, you are not permitted to speak as advocate or officer before this court."

"Your honor..."

"Be seated, Father." Girard said gently.

"Sit down, priest!" a raucous voice yelled from the room.

"Baliff, keep your order." Girard banged his gavel against the table. "In the name of his majesty the king, and of Cecilius Calvert, Lord Baltimore, and holder of the King's Charter for this colony, and in the name of its governor, Leonard Calvert, I declare these proceedings open. John Christman, if you don't cooperate I will have you forcibly clothed; this is a civilized court."

"Y'tell the bleedin' savage, yer 'onor," someone yelled.

Abell Snow rose, his eyes blazing. "Shut your scut face, Hiram Green; I see you hiding behind your tankard."

I sat on the bench. I said nothing.

"If it please the court," Andrew White said, "I might press on John privately to cover himself decently."

"He'll cover or be covered, sir."

Margaret Brent, who had been sitting in the rear of the room, stood up.

"I beg your pardon, your honor, but what is there to find indecent about this man?"

"He's bare-arsed as a monkey, y'blind slut," a man yelled from the right side of the room.

"Sergeant at Arms, eject that foul-mouthed villain," Girard said. "Mistress Brent, you know well you cannot speak before this court."

Margaret Brent stared at him. "This court should not have been convened at all. As it has, I have a right to be heard before the Assembly as a landowner; my status in this colony is as gentleman-adventurer, not wife. And you know as well, that the governor has given me power to act for him in his absence."

"Miss, as I understand this attorney is given to look after the affairs of his estate, not public affairs."

"Sir, my interpretation is that he has asked me to care for his affairs in all matters. I am here to speak for the governor. Do you wish to exclude him from these proceedings?"

"That is not my intent. But, mistress, he is not here, and the decencies call us to protect your sex from such indelicacies as the very first issue of this hearing."

"Tawzin wears the garments of his people. We have all seen them dressed so, your honor, without unduly offending our decencies. And since this hearing will examine the customs of the Piscataway, the clothing he wears is of import; that, I am certain, is why he has made this choice of dress."

"Miss, we are not here today to examine the customs of the savages; we're here to rescue a woman ill-used by them. Tis the clothing he doesn't wear concerns us, miss, and should properly shame you."

"I am not shamed by anything of God's creation."

I rose. "May I speak for myself."

"Sit down, man," Girard said.

"May I not speak for myself?"

"Let the man speak," Snow said impatiently. "Let's be on with this."

Girard nodded. "What do you have to say, then?"

I stood in silence for a moment, then raised my head and looked at the two judges, turned and looked to Margaret Brent, who lowered her eyes, and then settled my gaze on Father White. "When I first came to you I was naked, as a child is naked at birth. Then men in clothes stole everything from me, and they even stole the voice at the center of my heart who told me who I was. When they had so stripped me of what I had had, in its place they gave me...clothes. And now you would take everything again, you would strip me of wife and child, and you would give me your garments in their place. But I want nothing of you. I want you to leave me what is mine and I want nothing of what is yours."

"We have had this talk before, John," White said gently. "Remember that we gave you God also."

I closed my eyes, opened them. It was as if we were continuing the conversation we'd begun in the gaol. "Yes. You gave me a cell that was like my emptied heart and to fill it I had only the God you gave me fastened on the wall, for I had forgotten mine."

Abell Snow leaned forward, clenching his fists spasmodically, his mouth twitching as if the words were crowding his lips in too clamorous a mob to fit through those narrow gates.

"Thomas, what are you allowing here? The woman, the priest, this blasphemous savage, these drunken swine." There were hoots from the spectators.

"Sputter it out, scarecrow; y'got straw in yer gob?" someone called out.

"This is not trial, but farce," Snow said, glaring at the people in the chamber.

Girard compressed his lips. Sunlight, coming through the distorting mizen glass of the window, painted a spot of red on his right cheek. His face seemed to form around it in my gaze.

"Father White, retire yourself or you will be detained. Mistress Brent, you may sit or leave. The subject of this court is the kidnapping and forced servitude of Sally Picard, an orphan, by the accused John Christman, known also as Tawzin. John Christman will you accept garments and step forward and take the oath?"

I stood still.

"Baliff, and Sergeant at Arms, you will drape the accused and place him in chains."

As the weight of coarse blanket and chain settled on my chest and shoulders, I felt the cold grip of imprisonment on my flesh, as if the cell that had confined me had closed in on my body.

"Call Sally Picard," Girard said.

A small cry burst from my lips. I couldn't help it. I pushed against the chains. But there was no response to Girard's summons. I made myself note the formality of the man's tone. The summons had been perfunctory, a tack of the court.

"The witness remains unlocated, yer honor," the baliff said formally.

Girard nodded."Call Henry Fleet," he said.

Fleet stood up in the rear of the chamber. He carefully placed his beaverskin hat on the bench where he had been sitting and stepped up to the table. His waiscoat was made of buckskin softened in the Indian style. I remembered how he had appeared in bearskins and beads when he'd come to Piscataway.

Fleet stood impassively while the baliff swore him in.

"Master Fleet, tell the court what had come into your possession regarding the matter of Sally Picard, orphan."

"I will tell you what you know," Fleet growled. I stared

at him. Part of the clay of him forever kneaded by us. He had authored this play, but those words, the words of a *wisoe* to his *Tayac*, his disdainful glance at the audience he had gathered, somehow made him seem a reluctant player now. Perhaps he was. Fleet had merely wanted to use the threat of this trial as a club over my head, so I would bring him to the Northern tribes. But with Nanjemoy and Rachel out of his reach, all he would have now was a hollow vengeance and no beaver.

"You will tell us what we have to know, sir." Girard said.

Fleet slowly looked around the council chamber. Silence followed his gaze, the snickers, whispers and laughter dying.

"You know me," he said, his deep, rumbling voice almost a growl, and I understood then that if all Fleet was going to have was vengeance, he was going to take a full measure of it. "You know I was taken by the Indians. They wrote their name on my hide with their torture," He raised his hand and caressed the scars on his face, "They took my tongue, ripped my language out by the roots of it, so when I came back to England, five years later, I couldn't speak a civilized Christian word. They took out my heart and in its hollow tried to put their own. They took what I was just as this one," he pointed to me, "told you he was taken by whites, stolen from himself."

"Sir," Abell Snow said, "it is an impertinent comparison."

Fleet stared at him and Snow flushed. "They took me as Tawzin says we took him," he continued, as if Snow hadn't spoken. "And they tried to take my God, the Lord Jesus Christ all of us here, papist or true church, hold in our hearts. That is the difference, sir. That is why it is impertinent indeed for this savage to make such a comparison. It is as the priest has said. It was the Lord Jesus Christ we brought to him, and Who he spurns from his heart."

Margaret Brent stood up and left the chamber.

"Aye, some might flee the truth. But He stayed in my heart," Fleet called out after her, "and He allowed me to rise as Joseph rose in Potiphar's court and He led me home, and he guides my enterprise to bring a Christian kingdom to this land, and so, aye, Abell Snow, it roils my soul now," he looked again at Snow, "to hear Tawzin, to hear John Christman, make such a foul comparison, when he is holding his own captive heart. I will tell you what you know. I will tell you how the Indians came to us in Virginia. How they crept up on innocent sleeping Christian families who felt encradled in the homes they had built with their own hands in this hard land, surrounded by the fields they had planted with God's help and the sweat of their labor. You know how that savors, gentlemen, when you crawl safe, into the warm nest of home and hearth after a heart-breaking, back-breaking day and look around you and your heart is full. Now limn that nest torn to pieces. Violated. The ungodly howls outside your wooden walls, the thud of arrows into your roof, the flame bursting through like hell itself, and then the devils themselves with their cruel painted faces—look at his cold-eyed furious face, gentlefolk," he pointed at me. A woman sobbed and moaned from the back of the chamber, "the devils themselves smash into that sanctuary, split your husband or wife's skull with the tomahawk, or howling like bare-arsed devils indecently violate your daughter before your eyes, skewer your infant like a squirming fish..."

Girard and Snow were watching spellbound. The moan had spread through the spectators, rising high here, growling low there, unifying into a mutter, and I sat in paint and chains in front of them, the nightmare always crouched in the forest shadows of their joys and fears. Fleet telling them what they knew. Only I could see the glint of amusement in his eyes.

"Now fancy yourselves watching as they carry that daughter off, throw her over their naked shoulders, her all screaming and bleeding in her shame, and as you die in agony and in fire, your pain is increased tenfold because you know that hers is just beginning, and will go on all the days of her life. That is what you know. That is what happened to Sally

Picard. That is what you must see when you think about the white woman this savage has captive in his lair. I have been among them. I have seen their degradations with mine own eyes..."

"'Ang the red bastard," a voice screamed. "Tear 'is 'eart out."

Girard banged his gavel. He was sweating profusely.

"John Christman," he said. "Do you have anything to say to this court?"

I remained silent.

"His silence measures his guilt," Fleet said. "You've all heard Father White and the Jew Lombroso say that white woman is the willing mate of this savage." There were hoots from the room. "If that is true, why don't we hear it from him? Why doesn't he let us see her, hear it from her own lips, if she is indeed not murdered by him already for convenience? I'll tell you why. Lies don't come easy to the Indians; they are a simple people and in that way perhaps even more virtuous than the civilized races."

"Tis not true," someone shouted, and there was a sudden wild cackling laugh from the other corner of the room.

Fleet held up his bear's paw of a hand. "No, we must admit here what is true to sift it fine from the lies, in this court," he said. "The lie wouldn't come to this savage tongue. So he sits, silent as a tombstone."

The laugh rang out again; it sounded insane. People looked around nervously.

The door opened, sending a sudden breeze into the room. "On the other hand, Henry Fleet, I understand I've been accused of an unbecoming garrulity," Margaret Brent called out. She walked into the chamber. Behind her walked Nanjemoy, holding Rachel in her arms. Nanjemoy's eyes searched the room desperately, fell on me, in my chains. I refused to meet them. She gave a cry and rushed to me and fell on her knees in front of me, pushing the baby to my lap and, embracing my knees as fiercely as the chains embraced my arms and chest.

I groaned and turned my face from her. I glared at Margaret Brent. Her eyes were alight with wild triumph.

In the midst of the uproar, Andrew White stood. "If it please the court," he began,

"Why is this priest speaking?" Fleet said. His face had gone rigid with anger. Looking at him still, trying to ignore Nanjemoy and Rachel, who had begun crying, I saw a mirror of my own face.

Girard reddened again; he was Catholic and Fleet's tone seemed to irk him.

"The father can speak as witness, not as officer," he said. "Stand down, Mr. Fleet. You've said enough."

"If it please the court," Father White said again. "We have just seen demonstrated the true nature of this union. Moreover, Sally Picard has told me she bears no memory of her true Christian parents, and that it was John Christman who rescued her from a life of cruel usage amongst other tribes; John Christman to whom she feels bound in love."

"But surely father," Abell Snow said gently, "neither state nor church can sanction such a heathen union."

"Of course not, sir. But that is the other news Mistress Brent and I bring, after a long discourse with Sally Picard. She has agreed to the baptism of herself and the child, to be followed by a Christian wedding to John Christman, just as our son, the Tayac Kittamaquund has received the heavenly doctrine and put aside his concubines, and he and his queen are now joined in holy wedlock."

Girard looked moved. He wiped his forehead. "This is a day which snatches at my gut and pulls at it like a dog worrying a bone." He smiled at me. "Well, what say you, lad? This will clear the goblet, what?"

I rose. The room became silent. I looked at Fleet, then at White.

"I will tell you what you know," I said. "I want nothing from you. You smile gently at me now, and you're a gentle man, Andrew, but you bring my memory to the moment when I stood in my dugout and first saw those Englishmen smiling at me and gesturing at me to come, to come up into the belly of their monstrous canoe, to come see their wonders. When I saw them smiling, I thought: these are not enemy. How can enemy smile? So I went up to them and they stole me. Now listen. I will make my life in the gaol you placed me in. I will stay in darkness and chains the rest of my time on earth. But I will not, not for Fleet's threats nor for your gentle smile, bring my wife and child over the rail of that ship, to be torn from their own hearts by white men, as I was torn from mine. I will not give you the souls of my wife and child as I gave you mine. Not for Fleet's threats nor your gentleness. Not for your garments nor for your goods nor for your God."

My own words stirred me. I had poured all the bitter waters of my heart into them. But in my mind, like a mocking counterpoint, I heard Fremond's words again: *Damme, you tickle me, Indian. The way y'can wrap yer tongue around the King's English. Just like a white man.*

Lionsong

The lion let the deep shadow under the lip of rock move into his muscles so when he moved out of the dry place now, it was with the same silent flow of the shadow over dead leaves and rock. He had been sleeping, but a whiff of blood scent had come into his nostrils, waking him from a dream of being inexorably pursued through a world of endless grass by an alligator that moved more quickly than a rattlesnake, staying behind him no matter how fast he ran and leapt, no matter where he hid, until finally it clamped its jaws on his leg, rolled over and dragged him under the green water. When he had been a cub in fact he had seen his sister taken in that manner, though it was a memory that only existed now in such uneasy dreams. He had growled in his sleep, and it was the growl and the nightmare as much as the scent that had awakened him. At first the scent was part of the dream and he was for a moment the alligator himself but in another instant sharp and awake and moving. For an area of perhaps a thousand yards around the dry place, the air and earth had become an layer of his skin, and he experienced every scent or press on earth and wood like a touch on his hide, a brush across a field of tense awareness.

He skirted carefully around a clump of rocks where he knew a timber rattlesnake was coiled, its dry scent bringing back for an instant the alligator in his dream. He stopped suddenly, froze, then went down on his belly and began to inch forward. He came up on the stag from behind. It was leaning against a red oak, breathing heavily, its flank twitching. An arrow was embedded in its haunch. It had been one of a herd driven into the river by a Patuxent hunting party a week before. One of the men waiting in the line of bowmen in the river had hit it, but it had charged straight at him, horns lowered and run over him, then swam almost to the center of the river, becoming a Patuxent song by that night. Herdless now, exhausted, it had wandered erratically, urinating copious amounts as if to frantically create a new territory for itself.

The lion bared it fangs and claws and very slowly drew his hind legs under his body and tensed his muscles and filled his lungs with air.

The lion was eight feet in length and stood twenty-eight inches high at the shoulder. He weighed close to two hundred pounds, and he was cinnamon colored, though the fur inside his ears, under his nostrils and on his chest and belly was a silver gray. He could sprint up to thirty-five miles an hour from ambush, and though he had great stamina, he could only maintain that speed for short periods. From his crouch, he could jump fifteen to twenty feet into the air and forty feet on a level. It was perhaps a little less than that distance now from the wounded white tail, and when he saw the deer's eyes, clouded with pain, register his presence, he immediately made his leap, the tension he had held releasing him like an arrow shot from the bow made of itself, his front legs and paws stretching forward. As he landed on the deer's back, he sunk his teeth into the neck, crushing the spinal cord, while he slashed deep rips into the flanks with his claws.

Deeply satisfied, he dragged the deer by the neck to drier ground and fed on it, growling away some turkey buzzards. When he was sated, he groomed himself with his tongue, and went back to his shadow for a nap.

Once the lion had been what human beings would call a panther; he had lived in the great flooded grasslands and cypress swamps of the far south. He was also called, variously, cougar, or puma, an Incan word that means powerful animal. Others called him Mountain Lion, Silver Lion, Brown Tiger. Some called him Swamp Screamer and Grass Creeper or, some, Felidae Mammalia of the order Carnivora. None of the names mattered to him. When he thought of himself, the closest words in human terms for his name would be Hunger-Alone. He and his kind had been both feared and regarded as sacred, *manitou* by the Indians in that area, and so an understanding grew between the cat and the Seminoles and Miccuskees; he didn't stalk them; they left him his hunting grounds. But his size—he had been observed killing an alligator—had excited a group of Spanish explorers and their strange appearance and odor had roused his curiosity also: he had wondered if these were edible. Unused to muskets, he had allowed himself to get too close, observing with great curiosity as one Spaniard set up a strange, stork-legged instrument, stalking closer, then hearing a roar like a thunder clap and falling into darkness. He awoke caged. The terrified man who had shot at him had thought—inasmuch as he thought at all at that moment of terror—to kill the baleful-eyed creature baring its fangs at him, but muskets were notoriously inaccurate and the musket ball had just creased his forehead (though for the rest of the voyage, the man claimed a deliberate shot and so became known as a braggart and a liar). Rather than finish off the lion when he was unconscious and take his skin, the Spanish had decided to take him, along with a group of captured Florida Indians, as trophies to the court in Spain.

Their caravelles swung north first, intending to stop at the Spanish colony located at the head of the Chesapeake in Delaware. Caged in the hold, the lion remained sick and confused in the darkness. As they skirted the outer banks of North Carolina, a storm had battered the ships, wrecking three of them, including the caravelle which held him. Hungry and dazed, he had eaten his first man, one of the surviving, shipwrecked Spanish sailors, though not, as would have been more poetic, the man who had wounded him and who had drowned in the storm. Although very hungry, he hadn't like the taste of the man—too salty, too much debris to get in the teeth—but the meat gave him the necessary strength to go on. He had hunted in a wider and wider circle, north, until he encountered another group of the humans with thunder sticks. By now he had learned not to go too close, but to come up from behind: without the sticks pointing towards him the men were slow and easy to kill and he was starting to like the meat. When he killed them though, he noticed other humans seemed to increase their efforts to eat him and although he didn't understand the concept of vengeance, he took this fact into his hunting and surviving lore, and after a kill he would change his hunting territory, always north. It was at this time in his life that the panther became a lion, first called so by a British surveyor who saw him. He found, in his travels, other cypress swamps, and these became his refuges as he gradually wandered further and further north.

Hatred was alien to him. The lion had a complex intelligence. He knew himself, yet didn't feel a sense of separation from his surroundings. He hungered. He thirsted. He hunted. When he killed he felt fury, as if the life of the creature was a barrier between himself and his own survival, and when he ate, he felt a kind of satisfaction that was more than belly-fullness. For example, when he had killed and eaten the half-dead Spanish sailor, even though there was much meat, he hadn't felt as full as when he stalked and killed the alligator, or the Virginian planter who had stalked him. He felt only curiosity. He had mated for a time, in a cypress swamp in North Carolina, and when his mate had been killed, he felt despair as well as loneliness. He felt loneliness now. But he had never felt hatred. Not until the human had stalked him for such a long, sustained, unrelenting period. Not until he had looked into that human's eyes. Something of that creature had passed into the lion then. From then on he slept poorly, even when his belly was full. Dreams troubled him. He growled irritably at nothing at all. He felt as though a thorn had lodged in his heart and guts and was driven in further every day. The thorn was the hatred. The thorn was the man. The hatred was the man who had chased him so long he had now become a part of the lion.

Ezekiel's Song

I dipped my paddle into the roiled water. I had fitted my stump with a wood bracelet that socketed the top of the cherrywood shaft; my left hand gripped the middle in the usual manner. The bracelet was my own design. The last construct of my argument to convince Tawzin to let me come on the expedition. I'd practiced for a week in the creek and on the river. I couldn't switch grips, but I could cross my left arm over my chest and paddle one handed for longer and longer periods, and the strength in my left hand was increasing. Tawzin had laughed when I had shown him my skill with the bracelet. It will be worth bringing you simply to see the look on the faces of the Indians we meet, he had said. But I knew he could read the other need driving me. His laughter had not been mocking; it was the deep Piscataway cough that spoke a sudden seeing. I needed to go with him. I needed to go. I had taught myself to shoot and to plough and to carve one-handed, but I craved distance and water and a going into the world again from the womb of the longhouse, the compound, even from Wesort, who had been since my wounding as much mother as wife. I needed to go from her so that I could come back to her.

P'haps we need de same, man, you an' me, she'd said to me, when I told her this, and though she smiled I could see my words had pushed something between us.

We go den same, we two, she had said, and when I had reminded her of the child, and that Tawzin and Jacob Lombroso were not taking their women, her eyes had gone cold, though she must have known the truth of my words. I understood then that in opening this path I had shown her a way that one day she might take also. It was the first time since I had been born this sixth time in my life that I felt we weren't living in the same skin, we two. It filled me with fear. But I thought, so let it be, for I would bind no one's soul to my soul's dreams, nor would I be so bound. *Not for your garments nor your goods nor your God.* Tawzin's words had spoken the Wesorts onto the earth for me.

Fine words. Though in the end they had to live on earth with the rest of us, and here we were, and Tawzin was with us. Lombroso and Fleet and I had met in his cell the night after the trial, and he agreed to bring Fleet to his Northern Source, if Nanjemoy and Rachel were allowed to go unmolested and unbaptized back to the Wesorts. If Fleet would arrange for the protection of the compound by the St. Marie's militia. If no attempt were made to resell Simon Bodecker or take any other Wesort, runaway slave or indentured, into custody.

It was a surrender I had hated. We can run, I had told Tawzin, when Fleet had left to consider the offer. You don't have to give anything to that man. We can take everyone and disappear.

Where? Lombroso asked sadly.

The Zekiah.

Half the Piscataway nation is trying to disappear into the Zekiah, Lombroso had said.

It's a big swamp, I had replied. The Piscataway are all gathering in the stockade they've built at the center. We can go there, or there are other places to hide.

To hide until when? Tawzin asked. And we are neither Choptico nor Mattawoman, nor Accoceek nor Yaocomaco. We would not be welcomed.

We have people now from all the tribes.

It was true; as the invasion continued, both lone men and women and families had been making their way to the Wesort compound. We had grown to four longhouses now, some twenty-three men, women and children.

We are all, Lombroso had said, therefore we are nothing. Except to ourselves.

Tawzin had remained silent for a long while. We need time, he had said finally. We need time to become a people. If we run now, we will be like a herd of deer fleeing into a thick forest, breaking up around the trees, losing each other.

Why, Tawzin? I had asked. Why must we become a people? Why not only those of us who started, in the first house. We didn't ask the others to come to us.

We didn't ask you either. But we have found each other, Wesort. We need each other in the world. I will bring Fleet to his dream. Let it be. Perhaps it will turn to mist in his hand. And there's more. Explain it to him, Jacob. You understand me.

There is this, Ezekiel, Lombroso had said gently. We three need to be scouts unto the land. We need to go unto it and find a place where we can dwell.

I watched my paddle part the water now, the swirl, the dip, the swirl. Tawzin's sweated brown back in the bow, Lombroso in the center of the canoe. Point Lookout on our left, the hickories and loblollies standing behind the white thread of beach. Something dark and sad about them, sentries guarding a keep already empty, a heart already stolen or fled. The Yaocomaco I had seen following the Ark like spirits when we had first come here were gone, their time on this land marked only by the columns of smoke from their burning towns, rising and fading like the memory of a dream.

When we had started north up the Potomac, we had seen those pillars of smoke tying earth to air in at least a dozen places. These were the funeral pyres of the Piscataway nation. Whole tribes were being chased from their towns by the Susquehannocks and the Senecas, Claiborne's allies, and the Maryland militia had stopped coming to the Piscataways' aid now, even though White's Jesuits objected. They are our allies and who we must save, body and soul, White said. Let the Indians kill each other, the settlers said. The Piscataway were little use to them anymore. They didn't have enough warriors to help against the Susquehannocks and Claiborne. In truth many of the colonists saw them as the cause of the raids. Fleet and the Saint Marie's beaver traders couldn't get good prices for the pelts taken by the Piscataway: the Maryland beaver were too thin-furred. There were more whites now and they had learned to feed themselves. There were more whites now, and they needed more land. The dreams of the two peoples disturbed each other now.

And we were a dream of neither and our journey up the river was a slippage between them as was our life on earth. Twice on the Potomac we had been pursued by Susquehannock canoes, only escaping when we made landfall and hid overnight in the marshes, not far from where we had started. We were to meet Fleet in Piscataway, where he had gone with a pinnace loaded with trucke: five hundred yards of cloth, three gross of wooden combs, brass kettles, axes, Sheffield knives, hoes, and hundreds of arms-length of *roanoke* and *peake*. Fleet had been able to journey upriver unmolested because he had gone in an English pinnace: Claiborne had discouraged his allies from attacking the St. Marie's English, outside of priests or militia, reasoning, as I said, that if only Indians were killed, the colonists would not risk themselves against him. But we were a different matter, and finally Tawzin had decided we should turn around, go back down to Point Lookout, then come up the Patuxent and go overland to Piscataway. The Patuxents were not always enemies, Tawzin explained, but now some of them and the Nanticokes from the Eastern Shore had been taking advantage of the Susquehannock attacks to raid the Piscataway also. But, Tawzin had reasoned, the Patuxents respected the neutral buffers of the Zekiah and the Great Cypress Swamp, and it would be easier to slip by their territory through that area.

We paddled around the Point and into the moist heat of a summer day, the haze rising white off the dark water, thickening until it felt we were moving into a substance neither air nor water but their hot melt into each other. We stayed close to the western shoreline, at first on the Bay and then around Point No Point and into the narrowing of the river, the banks pressing close around us after the open water of the Chesapeake, like a lesson of limitation. We glided through a panicked school of alewives chased by blues and I was pulled with their panicky white churn back into the slaughter I had committed with Hallam on a creek on the other side of this peninsula. On our left the marshes stretched back to the country we had left, cattails and sawgrass limp and heavy in the heat, the marsh flowers flicks of white fire almost painful to the eye and it was as if the sight itself of that hot moist growth dusted us with weight and dulled our brains. We passed groves of sycamores and hickories and oaks now, the woods thickening so we could paddle under thick overhangs, the water so still it reflected each leaf and tree perfectly and it was as if the bow were breaking through a painting of the country. At midday we paddled up a crooked sliver of water through a red cypress grove and wedging the canoe between some cypress knees, drank water from the gourds we had brought and ate pone and jerky and then slept for a while, waiting for dark. From this point, the Patuxents had towns on both sides of the river and we would have to stay in midchannel and move at night.

It was a moonless night. The oily heat didn't break with the sun going down, only changed into something heavier that prickled our skins, as if the darkness was the heat made visible. We paddled into it. Lightning forked in the sky, its flashes causing the suddenly visible trees on the bank to leap at us, the quick snap of a jaw that just brushed our skins. Between the flashes the river was utterly dark and I steered with the stern paddle to Tawzin's whispers with no idea how the man knew where to go; water and air and heat, dark and flowing darkness had melded into each other and I was without up or down. We had gone perhaps five miles further up the river, when we saw fires floating in the blackness, looming closer and larger towards us as we advanced, so for an instance I perceived our float was up rather than level and we were moving among stars. I didn't wait for Tawzin's whisper—I knew he'd have to remain quiet—but twisted the paddle to the right and we glided past, holding our breaths just outside the outer halos that the fires shimmered on the black of the river. I could see the Patuxent fishing party on the long dugouts, firepits in their centers, naked men and women standing, half-illuminated by the flickers of the fire, casting nets or spears and the strange light reflecting off black water and charged air, the tall naked forms, hove me into a country of dimly remembered songs and stories, bordered by the faint sound of drums.

I turned the paddle slightly again, trying to ease our canoe further into the darkness. A face turned towards me, eyes gleaming in deeply shadowed sockets. Mouth opening, another pit, its edge framed by three stripes of red paint. The howl across the water pierced me between my eyes.

Tawzin and Lombroso began paddling swiftly and I angled the blade of my paddle, swinging the bow towards the nearer, eastern shore of the river. We could outrun the heavier locust wood dugouts for awhile in mid-river, but with so many paddlers it would only be a matter of time before we were caught. An arrow whizzed close by my ear and dropped with a splash near the starboard bow of the canoe.

The shore was only a thicker darkness. I could smell and hear it before I could see it. The hot skin odor of parched soil, the thick fleshy warmth of the foliage and, closer, a sharp tang of smoke, the packed human odors of people sleeping next to each other in tight, bark-roofed spaces, invisible clouds of sweat and exhalations threading into the heated moisture of the late summer air. We must be coming hard into the village, I thought, and saw Lombroso's right hand gesturing frantically, echoing Tawzin's signal to me to veer away. As I turned the canoe, heat lightning forked the sky and flashed the picture of a village yards away from my eyes, the size of its palisade along the shore taking my breath. And then gone. I'd thought I'd seen a face looking at us on a watch nest above the palisade, but if an alarm was raised, its cry was lost in the crack of thunder. A second later, the rain whipped down on us like a punishment for violating something. It blew horizontally into our faces, stinging my eyes, and I lowered my head and dipped my paddle into the pull of the churning river, following Lombroso's and Tawzin's example. Within seconds we were soaked to the skin. I had no idea where we were heading, but Tawzin seemed to; he kept calling back with steering directions through Lombroso. To pretend that direction existed in this storm seemed childish as a wish. Blinded, paddling without direction, I came to understand that such a force of pure mindless strength and hunger could only have come from Hallam. He was in the village, I thought; he was following us. The notion seized my mind. Now he had come for me, in the storm, come to take my other hand, that which belonged to him. Take it then, and damn you, I thought, and damn the tricks of my mind, and dipped the paddle down again. As I did, a hand seized my right wrist. I screamed. The grip was vise-painful, and the Indian, a Patuxent, I would reason later, who had slipped over the side of one of the dugouts following us, yanked me towards the dark water. His grip slipped as I pulled back against it, but he inched up until he touched and tried to hold the wooden socket at the top of my wrist. I felt a momentary slackening, as if his hand, unsure what it held, had drawn back, and I swung the heavy cherrywood paddle down with my left hand, felt it vibrate as the blow connected, the grip release completely, the man gone into the soup of storm and river as if he had never existed.

"Right, turn us right," Lombroso was yelling at me, and I caught my breath and steered, to their yelled directions. Within a few minutes, I felt and smelled, rather than saw, the trees pressing around us close, and my paddle hit the bottom. The rain slackened, or was broken by the forest. Tawzin had somehow led us into a narrow creek that wound back into the trees.

As we continued up it, the rain stopped. Mosquitoes whined in my ears. The whirr of the cicadas around us rose and fell, at times to a frantic, panicky peak, as if the forest had become suddenly aware of the strangers who had entered it. Whenever the noise declined, thousands of frogs added a full throated chorus; their croaks full of good humor directed at themselves. The water held a phosphorescence that streaked off our paddles and trailed in our wake. We slipped around a bend and the sun began to rise, bringing the overhanging foliage to dark gray to pale green to lush, a slow gathering of color and solidity, as if the world were reforming to its idea of itself after its dispersal into darkness and dreams.

We entered another waterway, and then passed among guarding giants into a bald cypress swamp. We floated among the trees along a skein of shallow black water, avoiding the red cypress knees that stuck out of the water like small congregations of dwarves. The cypresses towered hundreds of feet above us and they were old and had dreams we couldn't imagine. Their tendoned and muscular bases, swollen wider than their trunks for purchase in the black, silted water, couldn't be circled by two men embracing them with outstretched arms, and some would not be held by three or four. The canopy of feathery pine needles knit above our heads and we floated in a cool semi-darkness. Furry black poison ivy vines caterpillered up the trunks, and the blackness of the water backdropped bright red scatters of cardinal flowers, snouts of pink turtlehead, drooped white clusters of lizard tail. The cypress were interspersed with equally tall and thick poplars and red maples and smaller arrowroots and whenever a beam or patch of sunlight broke through the canopy the shadows of the leaves lay on the suddenly lighter water like dark coins. Silence was held like a breath in whatever center the canoe glided through and every place the canoe was seemed a center and I understood why the Indians called this place *manitou*, and didn't come here. The silence seemed not a real silence but one held in a kind of tension inside my brain and I had the sense suddenly that this held silence was somehow an emblem of the cypress swamp itself: its ancientness and isolation suddenly not protective or dwarfing but fragile, held in an instant of consciousness, the moment before a terrible bright awakening. I could hear the lap of water against the canoe, our small wake swelling against the tree trunks, the tap-tap of a woodpecker, the splash as a painted turtle came off a cypress knee and into the water. But all the sounds seemed held away from us, outside an invisible circle.

A hummock swelled out of the water in front of the canoe. Its lower slope was covered with a carpet of bright green ferns, rippling here and there as if rooted in a twitch of life. Above the ferns was a thickly matted carpet of dead brown leaves.

We pulled the canoe onto the slope, into the fern carpet which concealed most of it. We covered what showed of the craft with saplings and moved cautiously up the hill. At the top was a small grove of red maple and poplar, but when we went through the trees, we saw they were really pickets on the edge of a small hollow. Tawzin stopped and sniffed, then pointed to a line of blueberry bushes going down the slope and I saw it marked a fresh water spring flowing shallowly over flat rocks. We went to it, looking at each other, grins breaking our faces, and I got down on my knees and splashed my face and drank deeply of the cold water that tasted faintly of silt and dead leaves. Dragonflies made lazy patterns just over its surface. Jacob Lombroso gathered a handful of blueberries and sat against the trunk of a tree, sighing.

Tawzin finished drinking and stood. He peered at the ridge line of the small hollow.

"We need go sit up there."

I nodded. We were blind in the hollow.

We gathered more berries and some paw-paws and went to the top, where we had a view down the slope. We lay on our bellies on the ridge.

"They wouldn't come to this place," Tawzin said. "But we must be cautious. When there are customs, there are those who break customs. We may speak, but quietly."

"I would rather sleep than speak," Lombroso said.

Tawzin smiled. "Then you must truly be tired."

Lombroso grunted, lay his head on his arms. In a moment, I heard him snoring.

"I think he must be your father," I said, looking at him.

Tawzin chuckled. "The Piscataway take the boys away when they begin to have hair on their parts, and paint them white—the boys, not just their parts—and put them in their own longhouse, under the teaching of a famous *cockarouse*. We come to love him, for his skills. But also because he is not our father."

"Do you remember your father and mother?"

Tawzin said nothing for a long time. It was a habit of all the Indians, I had seen, to listen to words carefully and then reply thoughtfully, so that conversations with them were a patching of silence and words, each patch of equal length. But Tawzin often spoke more quickly than other Piscataway, and I wondered now if I should have asked the question.

"I remember very little," he said finally, "except as a man with a deep laugh who lifted me so his laughter seemed to have been what had entered my body and raised me into the air. My mother, I remember, was a very serious woman. She was a *werowance*; she ruled in Yaocomaco."

"I didn't know a woman could be a *werowance*."

"Sometimes. The rule is passed through the mothers, as the blood is passed through the mothers, but if there is a male child, he will take it. My mother had a brother, but he drowned when he was young. In our custom, the son of a *werowance* is called *tawzin*: this is the name Kittamaquund found for me when I came back, so people would understand the place he wanted me to have in their eyes. And also, I think, to tie me to him and to make Yaocomaco uneasy."

I saw then, at the base of the hummock, a blue heron standing motionless in the water as if listening to our talk. Touched by my stare, it rose and flapped away.

"Can a woman become Tayac also?"

"None has."

I drew a circle in the dirt with my forefinger, the stump of my sixth finger suddenly tingling, aching. "Calvert calls the Tayac an emperor."

"Yes, I know, but it is to give him a name so the English understand the place Calvert wanted him to have in their eyes. It is not truly the same. If there was no Tayac, the tribes might war with each other, but they do not always give their loyalty to the Tayac, to the whole nation, before their their own tribes—Yaocomaco to Yaocomaco, Chaptico to Chaptico..."

"Dan to Dan and Zebulon to Zebulon and Judah to Judah," Lombroso said, sitting up and yawning. "So it was with the tribes of Israel when Saul and David became kings and tried to unify them."

"Jacob would have us all lost Jews," Tawzin said to me. "He would find his lost tribes, just as Fleet would find his. Did you ever fancy, Jacob, that perhaps the Children of Israel were lost tribes of the Piscataway instead?"

Lombroso threw back his head and laughed.

A strange noise, a deep cough, then a roar, echoed deeply in the swamp. I looked nervously at Tawzin, but he was just smiling at Lombroso.

"There is a thing I don't understand," I said to him. "I had heard that Fleet learned of the tribes who were the Northern Source years ago, when he was trading among the Anacostans. I heard a story that he had even met a factor from that tribe, who helped him prepare a map, as to where his people could be found."

Tawzin grunted. "Yes, it's true. It was the year before the English came to St. Marie's. Fleet was on that trading expedition when Calvert and the Ark and Dove met him, when he convinced them to negotiate with Kittamaquund. When Kittamaquund gave us away," he added.

"Why then does Fleet need you, if he knows where the Northern Source is?"

"For safe passage. The Anacostans bcame very angry and chased him away when they learned he had met the factor from the northern tribes. They understood that if Fleet had direct access to the Herekeenes, they, the Anacostans, would no longer be needed as factors themselves."

"Then what part do you play?"

"Oh, he knows I came to Yaocomaco, to St. Maries, as the Tayac's eyes and ears. The Anacostans are allied with the Piscataway now, against the Susquehannock. They would honor the Tayac's wish to let him proceed up river, and Fleet is convinced the Tayac will do that upon my advice, for me."

He is convinced. Tawzin's words seemed strange, but I decided not to question him. Perhaps it was an Indian way of speaking also. I stretched out. Something swelled full in my chest. The soft straight talk, the hummock, with its breezes moving in the branches of the trees, made me feel held to the breast of this moment.

"I have heard that Kittamaquund killed his brother."

"It is true."

"To become Tayac?"

"Kittamaquund was the *werowance* of Portopaco; this rule was given to him by his older brother, Uwanna. The Tayacs will do this if they can, to satisfy their brothers and sisters hunger for rule, and to strengthen the alliance of all the Piscataways. I think Kittamaquund could never forgive his brother's generosity."

I squinted up at him, feeling a warmth towards this man who had no doubt I would share his understanding. And then angry, for mine was a slave's response.

"But it was not only for this reason," Tawzin said.

"Uwanna wanted to kill the whites when they landed,"

Lombroso nodded. "He knew already what had happened in Virginia, and was against allowing them settlement land. Kittamaquund wished to be Tayac, but he wished more, I think, to protect his people. He also knew what had happened in Virginia in the end; he thought the whites too powerful and he thought an alliance with other whites, enemies of Claiborne, would make the Piscataway strong enough to resist the Susquehannock."

Tawzin peered straight ahead.

"He thought to give his people some time and perhaps the world would change in that time," he said finally. "He didn't understand that his spirit would be devoured in that time." Tawzin smiled. "I tried to tell him what he knew, but I was not a very good *wisoe*. I tired to tell him because it had happened to me. My captors spread Europe before me like the kingdoms of the earth and when I saw it, even its worst— its disease and misery as well as its cathedrals and art—my spirit shifted in me. I could see what I could never see before, for before I had nothing to see next to it. I studied Grammar at the monastery, but what changed in me was a Grammar of the soul and of the eyes. I came to see not what is, but what could be. Before I only knew what is. But once the grammar of 'could be' had nested into me, I could never be the same. I could never see with the same eyes. I had been brought to a mountain and then I knew there were mountains and also that there were valleys. I had been brought to a mountain and told if I sacrificed what I was, all this would be mine. But it didn't matter. Just the seeing of it had already devoured what I was."

"What do you have that they want so much?" I whispered. It seemed to me the most important question I could ever ask this *wisoe*.

"Oh, I think you know what they want. You just wish me to say it. To say what you know."

"Tell me what I know then. What do they want?"

Tawzin closed his eyes and took a deep breath, then

opened them. "They want your hands. They want us to dance for them like mountebanks. They want us to eat the flesh and blood of their god."

I squinted at his features in the twilight. The trunks of the cypress were glowing gold-red in the pine needle broken light and the light had spread like something molten on his skin, a motley of shadow and luminescence, so he seemed on the point of a fiery dissolution. "Yet aren't all men as you say?" I asked him. "My people were once a conquering people also. A slave-taking people. A hungry people. As were our Gods."

"Yes. And my people. We are wolves to each other. And the whites are wolves to other whites."

I held my right wrist in my left hand; the stump had started to ache and was bleeding a little. Lombroso saw it and make a ticking sound with his tongue against the roof of his mouth. He rose stiffly, groaning a little, and gathered some leaves; sassafras, I saw, and went down the slope and came back with the leaves mudded together; this bundle he placed on the stump.

"Thank you," I said. I touched the wet mass. Its coolness seemed to leak down into my wrist. I looked at Lombroso, smiling down at me, and felt suddenly as if a hand had lightly stroked my heart.

"There is this also," Lombroso said to Tawzin, "Don't forget this also. We have found each other on this small island in the midst of a dark swamp."

"I wish that to be so," Tawzin said. "I wish it so much that my heart is afraid."

We were silent for a time. I remembered Margaret Brent's room then, and a different silence in it, my refusal to shed that dullish shell which is a slave's shield, for the sanctity of that place was held by her wish, and not by my history. But now Lombroso had spoken what I had felt, in this place. He stroked Tawzin's shoulder, a gesture that to my surprise tweaked a small pang of jealousy in my breast.

"I had a friend," I said to them, needing suddenly to speak what had not been spoken. "We were children together in Africa and slaves together in Barbados. He dreamed of escaping and finding your people, as if you were a reflection of our village waiting on the other side of the clouds. But also as if you were a reflection of the dream he had but never dared speak into the world. Now I find I am living in his dream."

"Such patterns exist and repeat," Lombroso nodded. "Tawzin spoke of Kittamaquund's alliance with the British. Listen. When the Hasmonean warriors, led by Judah and his brother Simon, fought against the Syrian Greeks who had invaded Israel, they allied themselves with the Romans, a hungry nation that helped them rid themselves of the Syrians' yoke...and then ate them. Why do I tell you this? The Cabala tells us that human beings merely repeat endlessly and helplessly the patterns of the universe, of conflicts on the heavenly level, beyond our human domain."

Although my stump had stopped hurting, my left hand, the stub of my sixth finger began tingling strongly now, as if it were growing, as if the amputated digit was struggling to break through my skin. I pushed it down onto the ground, pressed my weight on it. "Then our actions are only dreams of freedom?" I said.

"We are sparks, each one of us, exploded from the dissolution of the Divine Light, moving back towards the *Tikkun* which is the rejoining of us to ourselves and to the Universe. Which is the perfect justice we yearn for and move our lives towards. Yet without us and our words," Jacob Lombroso said, "the universe would not be conscious of itself." He looked at me. "You're bleeding again," he said. I looked at my right arm in surprise, saw it was so. Lombroso got up, stretched, sighed, and went down the hill.

I watched him then, for the last time, and it is this picture that remains: Jacob squatting by the spring, soaking sassafras leaves, saw his face turn towards me, the flash of his smile, framed by his gray and white beard.

Then time and memory were torn to pieces. Leapt out from a shape I had held clenched in my mind and it formed into that shape and as it did its name composed with its forming, its name in my mother's language, a scream from her lips bursting from my own, and then she was gone and its name in her language was gone but it was there, solid and tawny in the filtered golden sunlight of a cypress swamp in America, springing through the veils of memory and dreams. A pattern repeated in the universe. The instant froze in my brain: Lombroso's smile, the flash of the fangs echoing it as if in mockery, the fangs sinking into the back of the fragile neck, the fierce, snapping shake, the swift staccato punches of the claws. Tawzin rising, howling. Picking up and throwing a rock. The lion raising its huge head, its jaws drooling blood, and Tawzin and I roaring with it and running down the hill.

It looked up at us, jaws blood-flecked, and then, almost lazily, leapt sideways and was gone.

Tawzin held Lombroso cradled against his chest, stroking his hair. Lombroso's chest rose and fell laboriously, blood bubbling at the corners of his mouth, and from the wounds on his chest. His eyes stared, bright with wonder; he was looking at us, but we weren't what he was seeing. He reached up and seized Tawzin's head between his hands as if he was going to pull him down for a kiss.

A broad smile spread over his face. "The Lion of Judah," he rasped, his face close to Tawzin's. "Did you see him?"

Nanjemoy's Song

As I walked back towards the longhouses, I could see strings of black smoke curling against the red sky, and I pressed Rachel to me. But the warm weight of the child knifed a fear into my heart rather than soothed me. The smoke was from our own longhouse fires, but it pulled my mind to the burnings of the past month. Not a day when the sky to the north wasn't stained with black smoke. In those rising twists I had begun to see the paths of my people written on the air, running north to the Zekiah, or curling up to the spirit world. I brushed my lips against the crown of Rachel's head. These days I felt the ghost of my white mother's lips against the skin of my forehead. These days I had begun to see her face again: green eyes bulging with fear, the door behind her splintering as blades smashed through the wood. As hands reached in for us. This vision had not come to me since my time with Tawzin. It came now with his absence.

Run, Sally, run and run and don't stop, my white mother whispered in my ear.

I pushed Rachel's weight against my breasts to show her what held me to this ground. Rachel woke, nuzzled against me and I let myself think of Tawzin, his lips ringing my nipple, drawing it into his mouth, running his tongue under it. A spike of lust and loss pierced my loins. I passed the grove of oaks, almost back at the compound, my steps quickening until I could see the bark laid over their roofs, the curved backs of our longhouses among the trees. Their sudden standing out. Tawzin had said we should neither clear a central space nor build a palisade. He said, my husband, that we were too small to protect ourselves that way and instead our longhouses must be woven into the forest, so they would only appear when the eyes had taken time to learn to

255

unravel them. So my husband said. But now I saw them. And he had left us here, not invisible enough and marked by pointing fingers of smoke.

I would have mumbled the few words to please the Blackrobe, let the water splash my forehead and my child's, to keep him here. What mattered was not the water but the child.

One of the militia assigned by Fleet to protect us, Billy Hewitt, was standing next to a tree, pissing an arc into the stream. My anger turned towards him. We had told the soldiers that it was rude to piss upstream from the compound. He touched his broadbrimmed hat—the militia had stopped wearing the armor they had strutted about in like lusting roosters their first days here. "Beggin' your pardon, Dame Christman" he said to me, twisting each word as it left his mouth, so it became a lie. I didn't answer. I felt his stare touch my back as I walked from him. But the words "Indian's whore" came into my ear as if his lips were next to it.

The militiamen slept in a row of pointed tents on the other side of our longhouses. Most of the time they didn't speak to us or come among us, though one had been put in the stocks by Giles Brent for trying to rape Chipmunk. I had to speak long and hard to Simon Bodecker, Chipmunk's husband, to keep him from killing the man. We had asked for these white soldiers to come here to protect us and we knew they despised us for needing them as we hated them because of that same need. For this too, I felt a hot knot of anger against my husband and as each day went by, it grew bigger and tighter. I saw now the smoke was from their fire. I went over to it, and doused it with water from a clay pot next to one of the tents, and kicked dirt over it, Rachel wailing. The militia inside the tent was snoring loudly. Even my curses didn't wake him.

I looked to the right of the first longhouse, to the open door of the longhouse we used as a barn, vented with wider openings between its weave of branches. Rows of browning tobacco leaves hung from the cross struts. This was our trading trucke. Half the plants had been cut and were hanging to air dry. But in the small field next to it too many plants, each on its small mound of dirt and crowned by its yellow flower, remained uncut, crawling with worms. There should have been people working in the field.

As soon as I entered the longhouse, Simon Bodecker stood and looked at me uneasily, scowling under the net of face scars that were the mark of his tribe. The others sat around the firepit. We were twenty adults now, and two longhouses; most of the newcomers Yaocomaco and Choptico, but also Dream Singer, who was Mattapanient, and the woman of Jacob Lombroso, and a black woman, Mary Fairfield, now the woman of Falls on Bear, and another white man, John Evans, a trapper who had lived for years with the Massawomek, and who had no woman for himself, for a wildcat had clawed his genitals. All were in the longhouse.

"Nanjemoy, com' sid palaver wid us," Bodecker said. "We palaver too much, is worrisome. Com' spik wid us as Tawzin tongue, you."

I looked at him. "Simon, I com' spik as Nanjemoy, a free Wesort me. Nah Tawzin." If they wished me to palaver, it was my words they would hear, not my husband's.

"Ah you wish," Simon Bodecker said and smiled, as if to say whatever I could call myself, the others would still take what I said for Tawzin's words.

"What bring we this worry palaver?" I asked.

Wesort caught my eye and patted the ground next to her. She had Isaac at her breast, as I had Rachel, and we two women smiled at each other, as if sharing a secret. I went over and sat next to her, but I knew as I did I was accepting the name-power Simon was giving me. We had no *werowance* here. Even though Jacob Lombroso had said we should, and I had agreed, both Tawzin and Ezekiel said they did not want to weigh and name what place each of us held among the Wesorts. When we had to decide what path to take, we would have a palaver, a word Simon gave us, though Ezekiel said he knew it also. The words of each adult in a palaver would weigh the same, Tawzin said. Just as our words and our names came from the mix of all our tongues. But I knew it wasn't true. The others saw him and Jacob Lombroso and Ezekiel, saw me and Wesort, and now Dream Singer, as fathers and mothers of the people and looked to us to speak first. Though it is true they did not always listen to what we said.

So I sat now thigh to thigh with Wesort, Rachel sleeping in my arms, Isaac in Wesort's. Everyone in the circle remained silent.

"Com' heahr palaver, nah silent," I said. "What troubles you Wesorts?"

"Trouble us dat soljer-man try hardfuck Chipmunk," Mary Fairfield said, and Blind Owl, a Choptico, made a joke in Piscataway and received a reprimand fom Charity Slagel: "We spik palaver, us."

"Dat's it. Spik Wesort, be Wesort," Conochaquoc, a Portopac said. "Troubles us hab de white soljers heah. Dey sort."

"Troubles all Wesort hab dem soljers," Wesort said, "but wors' trouble Susquehannock man come."

"We know dat," Simon Bodecker said. "But tings get wors' and wors' dem sort. Dey taken food, ask nobody. Dey talkin' Wesort low. Need Jacob Lombroso, need yo' mans come back, be heah wid dere own people, Nanjemoy, Wesort."

"I need ol' mon Jacob come back my way," said Dream Singer, and rubbed the curve of her belly.

"Need my man com' back be dere in my own sleep skin," I added and the Wesorts laughed. But it was a laugh to loosen the stiff skin growing between us. Too much pushing inside us to say and not yet enough words we shared.

"Listen, me," I said. "We mus' be patien'. Dey comin' back by an' by."

"By an' by happen too long time," Blind Owl said slowly.

"Not jus' we be angry militia man. Tink, deese militia man no hep us. Susquehannock man see clos' and more clos'. See dere smoke, heah cries my dreams now. Alla time. Englishmon try hardfuck Chipmonk. Englishmon look wid shit eyes us. No good, I tell you dat, what you know. Need move de people, go to de swamp land, de Zekiah."

"You tink we go widout Tawzin, Jacob, Ezekiel?"

"Dey know to find Wesort dere. Cotch us up."

And I thought then he was telling me what I knew. What we knew. The militia hated us and we could all see, in our dreams and out, how the Susquehannocks were coming to us. But when I dreamed Tawzin coming back here to empty longhouse, my heart pained.

"Blind Owl, I say we hab de tunnal heah, hide us I tink bettah dan de Zekiah."

"Mebbe dis true," he said. "Mebbe no."

"Wesort all free peeple heah. Some dey can go, some dey can stay, do dat way."

"No," Wesort spoke up. "No do dat. Stay Wesort one peeple. Odderwise all dead us. Who be us? What be us, dat time?"

Our circle was silent then, even the children playing on its rim. I started to speak again, but Jacob's woman, Dream Singer, rose suddenly to her feet and was staring at the longhouse entrance. All our eyes turned to follow her vision. Suddenly she screamed and clutched her belly. Dream Singer's eyes rolled upwards and she collapsed onto the floor. I couldn't see what she saw. But behind her I saw the ghost of my white mother, screaming at a splintering door.

WE WRAPPED Dream Singer in her sleeping skins, for she was shivering though the day was warm. She held the skin to her nostrils, and sniffed in deeply, and I knew it was Jacob's scent she was trying to hold to her and then I shivered also. But she would say nothing. When she finally slept, I took

Rachel back to the forest. I would go to the creek, take the crabs from the traps. I needed to be in my own place, where I could speak to Tawzin in my spirit. I let Rachel's lips take his place at my nipple again, the suck pulling at a root deep inside me. I walked down by the spring, its water flowing brightly over steps of mossy rocks, between swaying cattails. A salamander lay still on a flat rock in the middle of the water. The pull at my breast, the stir of the water moved in my spirit now, and I gave a sharp cry that made Rachel pause and I had to stop and let her begin her suckling again. Visions were pushing at me like hands pushing at a locked door. I pushed back at them. I had buried them in my life with Tawzin. Heaped them under rocks. Under the scent of his flesh. But Tawzin was gone. I sat down by the creek and let my hand dangle in it, feeling the cold muscle of its flow against my palm, letting it push the fan of my hand back, drag it forward. I couldn't remember the faces of my white parents nor even the place we lived. But a shatter still waited in me. A vision called to me by the push and chill of water, by the suck of Rachel at my breast. The bear grease and blood stink of the flesh pressed into me. The hard hand sealing my mouth. My white mother's screams as she turned into burning daylight. A boy dressed only in a soiled white lindsey-woolsey singlet sobbing and holding his bleeding leg and trying to walk as the painted men clubbed him. One picking up a mossy rock, its bottom wet with green fur and then matted with blood and the boy's red hair. The English words *linsey-woolsey*. The English word *Joshua*. The English word *brother*. The deerskin hide pressed into my face. The smothering weight. The flame of pain between my legs. A bear's grunt. And nothing. Nothing until I was Nanjemoy born in Nanjemoy and the women bathed my limbs with wet, cool mint leaves and took me into them and among them in the sweat lodge and the next vision I had was Tawzin's smile and his touch opening me and at the same moment weaving walls I could trust back around me. And I wanted no visions before that new birth and beyond this small life breathing against my breasts now. But still they came to me.

I pressed Rachel to me, and she raised her head and yowled until her hunger pulled her back to my nipple. Looking at her head, feeling her lips, the warmth of her body, it came to me that the visions I had forgotten had been born again to me now with this child so that I could remember now what I needed to protect this child from.

I felt a chill prickle the flesh on the back of my neck then, as if something had touched me. I turned quickly. Nothing. No sound, no stir of branches. Three or four cardinals netting a red blur around the lower branches of a tulip tree. Rachel stopped nursing and looked at them and laughed in delight. There was nothing. I kissed her. Nothing. A heavy stone of fear grew in my stomach around the sudden understanding of what I had not heard. Nothing. The steady whir of the cicadas had stopped. No birds chirping. I searched the shadows of the trees, and there was nothing, and this was my safe place among these guarding trees. A shadow between two pines in the corner of my eyes trembled and something yellow or brown flashed in that space, and the word that came to my mind and lips was from the stories my Piscataway mother whispered to make me behave. *Lion.* I turned and again saw nothing. Only my fear and my visions, forming to shadows; the world had walls I could trust now. Doors that held. I stepped forward and looked down and saw the body of Billy Hewitt lying in the shadow, his grin widened and echoed in the slash that ran across his throat from ear to ear.

Something snarled.

I turned, holding Rachel close and opened my mouth to scream. A hand clamped over it and held me tight to a hard body behind me, my mouth against the rough callus of the palm's meat so it was mashed against my teeth and tongue and I tasted something rank and acrid, and my memory-vision had come back into the world and had seized me to it. I could see another hand held lightly, just behind Rachel's head. I pressed the child to my breast again, to keep it from crying out. The strength I felt in that paw of a hand, its pad rough against my mouth, stilled me. Once I heard a hunter sing a mountain lion kill, and he brought those hearing his song with him, moment by moment, as the good singers did, and what came to me now of his song was how the fawn given as bait for the lion had seemed to shiver and surrender as soon as it felt the lion's teeth begin their clamp on the back of its neck, before they had even penetrated its hide. In this moment now, I felt that same shivering surrender, as if I were in a song that had already ended. Then I felt Rachel's mouth, strong with life, still feeding on my life, and I struggled. The hand released me and I turned.

I had only seen him once before, in Saint Marie's, but it was true his shape had shifted, become leaner. He was more lion than bear now, the red mat of fur on his bare chest sleeked, and in its center, held on a rawhide cord, what seemed a black and twisted stick. He stared at me, stroking that strange medicine bag, and then I understood what it was and tilted my head to scream. But my voice was frozen in my throat, as if his hand was still clamped on me. That same hand, broad and padded as a paw, reached towards me now, and out of my visions and towards Rachel.

"I'll have what's mine," he said, his voice growling and creaking, as if a spirit were moving his tongue behind his stiff lips.

WHEN I AWOKE I saw Wesort's face inches from my own. It was streaked with tears. I was dead in the earth. The earth was pressed around me, as it had once wombed Wesort, its darkness given form only by a dim red light that seemed to come through the walls, as if blood were pushing on the other side of them. In those walls and in that light I knew the world had reformed around me and had taken me back to my beginning. But soon, I knew, it would convulse and shit me out into harsh light, for walls are tricksters, they protect nothing, they dissolve at a breath or a scream. Wesort was moaning, and Mary Fairfield, her black skin burnished with sweat, pushed her aside and held me, and Dream Singer held me, and I saw I was in the sweatlodge and all around me, their flesh echoing my flesh, were the women of the Wesorts, enfolding me. And this time it was only the women around me, trying to keep me pressed to life, and I only knew of Tawzin by his absence. My breasts ached and were full to bursting with undrunk milk, and then the knowing of what female flesh had been torn from my life shot to my mind and brought me upright and screaming as if a claw had been thrust in through my eyes.

Ezekiel's Song

We buried Jacob Lombroso on the hummock and Tawzin said words I didn't understand except that each one meant goodbye, goodbye to a dream and goodbye to a dreamer, and I thought then that Tawzin loved Lombroso as a wise son does who forgives his father for seeing a dream in his son's fallible flesh and forming spirit. I watched Tawzin dance under the guarding tree, a man dancing as if in front of a mirror only he could see and the image it reflected to him was Jacob Lombroso, dancing silently also, each move matching his own, as he had once in a sun-splashed square in Spain.

We came out of the swamp and back to the Patuxent and we went north until the river narrowed and we left it and followed the skein of creeks to the Potomac, silver veins through a green country. We crossed the land of the Assamacomocos, staying in the cool shadows of the thick forests, off the main trails. We went west, through the narrow northern neck of the Zekiah swamp, leaving our canoe and struggling on foot through brackish, knee deep water tangled with water lilies and marsh grass and jeweled with white orchids. The jagged trunks of dead trees scratched the sky above us like the clawed fingers of skeletons. Egrets, curved and white as bones themselves, rose like spirits ahead of us. We moved from the swamp back into Piscataway territory, into a land of torn and smoking villages, trampled corn fields and flayed men, as if the lion had moved through the country ahead of us.

For a brief time we ran along one of the Piscataway trails that pushed like a tunnel through the overhanging trees, its dirt hard packed by the feet of many travelers. Tawzin told me that such trails ran like the rivers and creeks and one could travel on them to join the *Catawba*, the Great Trail that came up from the south where the leaves of the trees were like those in Barbados, and joined into other trails all the way to the far north country of the Iroquois and beyond, even to the seal eaters, and to the west, to the Mother River, Mississippi. I thought of my namegiver Ezekiel then, and of his dream, and I dreamed how it would have been if we had both known of the *Catawba* and had taken it north, to the Wesorts he had seen waiting at the end of our path.

But we were afraid to stay too long on any trail, and soon started moving through the woods and marsh again. We had just passed a corn field, the first unburnt we had seen, and had moved into a grove of sycamores and tulip poplars, when Tawzin stopped and stood very still. I followed suit. I watched the muscles on his back and neck tense, then relax, and I started to relax with him until I saw the Indians who had been standing there all along appear to my vision, motionless among the trees. I stiffened, but Tawzin put a hand on my arm and told me they were Kittamaquund's pickets.

He spoke briefly with one of them, a squat, grim-faced man with a chest broad as two shields, who kept glancing around nervously. He had black half moons painted under his eyes and a row of stiffened scalps dangling like strange privates at his waistband. When they had finished talking, Tawzin motioned for me to continue. We came back onto the trail.

"Fleet is at Piscataway," he said. "Waiting for us. But the Tayac has taken ill."

"How badly?"

Tawzin stopped and turned to me, his face lined and strained, and that was my answer. I wondered if it was for him as if he was losing another father.

"He is as ill as his country," Tawzin said.

We passed more watchers, some in trees, others nested in concealed places along the trail. The Piscataway signalled our coming with bird calls, a trail of cries unrolling before us. The forest ended then and we were in a cleared area and in front of us was Piscataway, the Tayac's town, hard against the bend of the Potomac. For a moment, the sight of it began to push the memory of a town or city I had seen in Dahomey into my vision, tall, carved pillars, a teeming marketplace, but when I tried to fasten to it, it was gone. What had brought it to me, Piscataway, was the largest Indian town I had seen, The palisade posts were thick, five to seven thumb joints around and as tall as the tall trees they had been. They were spaced about a foot apart, and I saw they had a barrier of wattlework, daubed with clay, set between them, and a deep ditch running around them. The log wall spiraled around and overlapped itself like a snail shell, and the overlap made a corridor that was the entrance to the town. For an instant I was filled with confidence, for what force could take this? But the Dahomey city that had come to me was gone, its name forgotten, dissipated like mist from my mind and I feared from the world as well, gone and the hands that had built it gone, and only the reminding trace of their pain left.

We walked into Piscataway watched by bowmen standing on a platform set above the wall. Inside, the large central square between the longhouses and the garden patches was crowded and I saw the town had become a kind of Wesort compound. People from all the Piscataway nations were there: Yaocomacos, Anacostans, Nanjemoys, Mattawomans, Portopacos—I could tell their tribes now, by face and by the designs of body paint and the way they cut their hair. They had formed separate clusters, according to their tribes, around campfires, but had otherwise not erected any shelters for themselves and there were too many for the longhouses to take in. Many sat in the dirt staring ahead, silent, some swaying slightly. They looked dazed and hungry, and even the children, who in the towns I had visited would scream and laugh all day and much of the night while the adults smiled, were dull-eyed and quiet. *He is as ill as his country.*

I passed a woman working clay into a pot. The vessel seemed oddly distorted and she was tearing it apart as soon as she smoothed it. Near her was a pile of shattered pots. A deer skin, half-scraped, fly-blown, was stretched on a frame, apparently abandoned; next to it a small boy squatted and shat, his discharge black and watery and streaked with blood. The stench that had burst from his bowels, I realized now, was everywhere, the air itself in this place was sick with a thick foulness.

"Halloo!" a voice cried, and Henry Fleet, dressed in a breech-clout, came striding towards us, his energy, in this sickly crowd, angering me. But somehow Fleet always angered me. Several of the men and women turned slowly to look at him, their faces expressionless.

"S'blood, I had despaired upon seeing you again," Fleet said.

"What news have you from Yaocomaco?" Tawzin asked.

"The river has been closed to our commerce and messages these weeks; I have heard nothing. But be easy, Tawzin; your people are well-guarded. Keep your mind on the task in front of us. Give me a few weeks now, and I will grant you and yours freedom from fear for the rest of it."

I saw Tawzin stiffen with anger. "I will go to the Tayac now," he said.

"Yes, you must do that." Fleet peered at me, then next to me, as if at a blank space, a question forming in his eyes. "I will accompany you." He nodded suddenly, as if an answer had come to him. "Where is the Jew?"

Tawzin didn't reply.

"He left us on the journey to take another path," I said. It was how the Piscataway told a death.

"Ah," Fleet said after a moment. "Tis a pity. The Tayac had wished to see Lombroso particularly."

Tawzin had already started to walk, as if he couldn't bear staying in Fleet's company. We followed him across the square. The Tayac's longhouse was near the central firepit, one entrance facing the pit, the other canted towards the river. When the mat door was pulled aside, a waft of rot and sickness struck my nostrils. It was the same stench I had smelled from the child. At first, as my eyes opened to the smokey gloom, I thought we were too late. The Tayac and Mary Kittamaquund were prone on two pallets, fully dressed in European clothing, as if they were being displayed. The Tayac wore a wig of silver coils slightly askew on his head, a claret-colored waistcoat, a yellow vest, and white lace at his throat. His wife was in a blue camlet gown, a yellow bonnet framing her round brown face. I knew these words because Fleet was murmuring them, and the price of each in fur, to me, or to himself, as if he was cursing the Tayac. Closer, I could see their faces, man and wife, were shiny with sweat. They sat up slowly, corpses coming to life. Both smiled weakly when they saw Tawzin, a mirror smile that passed as if its left corner was on one face, its right on the other.

Kittamaquund gestured weakly at us to come closer. As we did, I could see the clothing was falling apart: seams split, wig unraveling in a tangle of silver strands, a large hole in the side of Mary Kittamaquund's bonnet. Kittamaquund's breeches were split from knee to crotch on his left leg. Fleet, in his Piscataway breech-clout and paint, stood in front of the Tayac and his wife in their rotting English finery, some twist in the pattern of the world held in this longhouse, with its thick, tainted air, its alive but dead inhabitants.

"In the name of our Lord Jesus Christ, I bid you welcome, brother John Christman," Kittamaquund said in English. His voice was surprisingly strong.

My heart rests to see you, Piscataway, Tawzin said, in Piscataway-Algonquin, words I understood.

"We will speak the Lord's tongue, *wisoe*," Kittamaquund said weakly.

His wife tried to sit up, sighed, and sank back down. "Tawzin, I am happy..." she said.

"We are both happy in Christ," the Tayac said.

Tawzin's face remained impassive.

"Come," Kittamaquund said to me. I came forward hesitatingly. The Tayac reached out a tattered sleeve and touched my stump, running his forefinger around the hump of it. He laughed a little. "Hallam," he said, nodding to Tawzin, as if confirming his understanding. He looked more closely at me. "The black one. He Who Names Himself. I know of you, black one."

"Piscataway, I would speak to you of our trade upriver," Fleet said.

Kittamaquund swung his gaze to him. "Yes, Bear. You would speak of trade. I think, perhaps, the Anacostans did not scrape enough off you with their knives." He threw back his head and laughed. It came out a series of "ha's," each as if spoken rather than laughed. "Speak, Bear," he said at the end of it, unsmiling. "Speak to me alone. My *wisoes* no longer come, and the council of the *Matchacomoco*, the elders, is finished also. Now I speak only to Bear." He laughed again.

"Tayac, this venture can save the Piscataway," Fleet said. "If I can gain access to the northern beaver Indians through you, you will become as valuable to the English as the Susquehannocks."

Kittamaquund smiled joylessly at Tawzin. "Do you see, *wisoe*, how Bear would save us once again. He will guard us from Claiborne and Hallam and the Susquehannocks once again by making us of value to Calvert once again. What a blessed people we are to be so needed, yes, *wisoe*?"

He sank back, coughing. Mary Kittamaquund put a hand on his shoulder.

"We pass the black water already, *wisoe*," Kittamaquund said. "Where is the shaman Ya-kob? Bear told me he would come." He nodded at Fleet.

"That one left us to journey his own true path, Tayac."

A look of pain crossed Kittamaqund's face. "I would ask how he made his journey, *wisoe*."

"By a lion, Tayac, in the cypress swamp."

Kittamaquund's face grew thoughtful. "We have heard of this lion." He sighed and turned to Fleet. "Where is my brother White, Bear? You must bring me White, to hear my confession. You said he will come."

"I have sent for him, Tayac."

"I am Charles, Bear." He laughed, and a string of yellow spittle drew from his mouth to his chin. "I am Charles and here is Mary. So we were baptized, and our son and daughter were wet also that day. I am saved from the fire, Bear, and would have my people saved from it also. Where is my Ya-kob, Bear? You said he would come and now he is with Lion. Where is White? He lifted the sickness from me before," Kittamaquund said slyly to Tawzin. "And he has cleansed me with the water of baptism. So I will not burn, *wisoe*. He must return. He must open all the veins of my people to bleed them of themselves, and wet their skins with God's water, to guard their spirits from the fire. Don't you hear them, *wisoe*? Don't you hear them howling outside? He must come. He must end their howling or it will go on forever in my ears."

"He will come, I promise you, Tayac," Fleet said.

Kittamaquund smiled weakly. "*Wisoe*, listen. Bear promises again."

"Tayac," Fleet said. "Our venture..."

"Yes. Go, Bear. Go to your venture. I have talked to Anacostan, my brother in Christ. The Anacostans will give you passage if you travel with Tawzin. Tawzin knows the way. Now go, Bear. My eyes hurt when you are here."

THAT NIGHT THE AIR was troubled with howls and moans from the blackness around us, outside the circle of Fleet's fire. I heard in these the linger of my own wail, torn from my throat when my hand had been torn from me and that outcry itself had contained all the severances of my life. I saw Tawzin flinch and I knew my friend was hearing the wailing that had refused to burst from his lips at Jacob's grave, given a voice now by the night all around him, by his lost people.

"It was in '32," Fleet said, poking at the fire, hearing nothing but his own voice. "I heard him calling to us from the bank, words I never heard before. Something like: 'quo, quo.' Like a bloody duck couldn't quite say its quack. So I go to him and he lets me know he wants to trade. Lets me know he'd heard of me and my trucke. He said he came from the city of Usserahak and there were seven thousand Indians in that place, and he could bring me sixty canoe-loads of beaver. So he says. Thick beaver pelt, such as I had never seen, he shows me—it had come, he said, from the far north, the best on the continent. A tall man he was, taller than the Susque-hannock, and he wore a coat of thick beaver, a red fringe all around it. But I had little to trade with him then, and I lost him. But it's there, I know it. Usserahak."

Fleet scratched at a mosquito bite on his neck. How was it, I wondered, we could sit round the same fire and this man be so chained to a vision it palisaded him away from the sounds of a world cracking to pieces all around us.

"I had the *Warwick* then, eighty ton pinnace, given to me by Grffith Company, when I was their fur-buying factor," Fleet said, nodding. "But that scut Charles Harmar was there before me, cleared both sides of the river of fur, just like he'd pushed a bleeding scraper up them. Fifteen hundred pounds of fur. S'blood, but I ate that and went on, back to my Anacostans, up near the Falls at Trading Rock, and traded for a good eight hundred pounds. But I tell you that hair weren't the most valuable trucke I won on that voyage. See, we were anchored next to the Anacostans, same town where I had slaved for five years and maybe they were worrisome that I held some ill will towards them—aye, ill will and deck cannon worried them, I'll lay, and they told me about the provenience of those furs. About the four cities, a week's journey north of the Great Falls. Tonhoga, Mosticum,

Shaunetowa, and Usserahak: over thirty thousand Indians, they said. Tonhoga, Mosticum, Shaunetowa, and Ussrahak."

"The Massawomecks," Tawzin nodded. "They trade with the Iroquois. But they are not the source. The source was spoken for by the man you met. He is Herekeenes. From the Canada Indians."

Fleet squinted at him. "Aye, that makes sense. Soon as they saw me palaver with him, the Anacostans got angry, put a foot up me arse and helped me out of there. It's the source, lads, the Eldorado of beaver hair. Don't you see what that can do, we trade direct with them, Tawzin? We cut all the trading tribes. Cut out the Susquehannocks. Put ourselves right where Claiborne has put himself. The Herekeenes," he drawled the name out slowly, smiling: he had found a name for his dream. "And you know them," he said to Tawzin. "You can take me to the four cities."

I stared into the flames. Fleet was close to his dream now and he spoke about it with ease, as if he was certain we shared it. But he could not see Tawzin's cold hate nor his indifference, nor mine, no more than he could hear the cries of the destroyed people around him. He spoke what moved his own heart and could not imagine any other human heart could be stirred differently. I saw suddenly that this was a great evil and perhaps the greatest evil, the source, the Herekeenes, of evil. I saw that this was the very hand that had carved my life and severed my hand to its desire and that had flayed and gutted these Piscataway falling howling around us. I saw, a knowing that sickened my heart coming to me at a small campfire surrounded by the howls he could not hear, that in the end they, Fleet and Claiborne and Hallam, would prevail, in the way the carver who only saw the path of the cut would prevail over the carver who could see also the pain of the tree.

"Yes, I know them," Tawzin whispered.

I understood this. I, Ezekiel, the live bearer of a dead man's name, I, who had been a measure of wealth, a bit of food, sold to feed a hunger. An arm's length of beads, a sheaf of tobacco, a beaver pelt. The scraped hair of flayed Piscataway, the bounty scalps Claiborne paid for with the scraped hair of beaver. Two hundred and sixty pounds of good beaver pelt was worth seventy arms length of *roanoke*, Fleet was saying. One pound of beaver fur worth some one hundred and forty-four pounds of tobacco. Tobacco was worth fur was worth shillings was worth *roanoke* was worth tobacco. We would be wealthy, Fleet was saying, in front of the fire playing on his face, the shrieks all around us. We would eat our guts out of our own bumholes and grow them again and feed again, he was saying. He was the greedy man in the Piscataway tales who became a dog eating its own tail, then its own anus and entrails. But first he would devour us. My immersion in my woman and my child and in Tawzin and the Wesorts were all I wanted of the world now and I knew that such a limited desire would, and had, aroused a hatred unto death in the breasts of those who lived by feeding on the unfettered hungers of other men. I felt a chill of fear in my bones for the fragility of the twig house Tawzin and I were trying to preserve: the Wesorts, so weak among lions.

These things I thought at Piscataway.

And what were we doing here, with this man? It came to me that as I understood Tawzin's words, I did not understand his actions in making this voyage when we should have turned and gone back to our women and children and people after Jacob had been rent, that we should have never embarked at all.

NOW I HEARD something like a sigh move like an invisible wave through the dark, stirring through the people who had been sleeping on the ground. All around us people began to rise silently, their naked copper forms licked by the red light from the fires, so it seemed for a second that I was seeing them at the moment of their creation from the forge, half their flesh molten, half still in cool darkness, as if I was witnessing the beginnings of a legend-song just rising now to name itself. People were coming out of the longhouses now also, mothers nursing infants, the prostrate sick carried out on their branch litters. I was aware suddenly that I had risen to my feet also, as had Fleet and Tawzin, and was looking with the others to the entrance of the town.

"What in Hell's name is it?" Fleet asked.

"White," Tawzin said. He smiled briefly. "Come to once more save the Tayac."

Author uncertain

Whoever shall contemplate, in thought, the whole earth, will, perhaps, nowhere find men more abject in appearance than these Indians; who, nevertheless, have souls (if you consider the ransom paid by Christ,) no less precious than the most cultivated Europeans. They are inclined indeed to vices, though not very many, in such darkness of ignorance, such barbarism, and in so unrestrained and wandering a mode of life; nevertheless, in their disposition they are docile, nor will you perceive in them, except rarely, the passions of the mind transported in an extraordinary manner. They are most patient of troubles, and easily endure contumely and injuries, if they do not involve danger of life. Idols, either many or few, they have, to whose worship they are greatly addicted; nor are there any priests or mystae, to whom the administration of sacrifices appertains by appointment; though there are not wanting those who interpret superstitions and sell them to the people; but even these are commonly not at all numerous. They acknowledge one God of heaven; nothwithstanding, they distrust that they know in which way he is to be worshipped; in what way to be honored: from which it happens that they give willing ear to those that teach this knowledge. They rarely think of the immortality of the soul, or of the things that are to be after death. If, at any time, they meet a teacher clearly explaining these things, they show themselves to be very attentive as well as docile; and by and by are seriously turned to think of their souls; so as to be ready to obtain those things, which, they perceive, conduce to the salvation of the same. This natural disposition of the tribe, aided by the seasonable assistance of divine grace, gives us hope of the most desirable harvest hereafter, and animates us to continue our labors in this vineyard with the greatest exertion. And the same ought to be an incitement to all those who in the future, by the will of God, may come hither to us for supply or assistance.

Kittamaquund's Song

I lay on my pallet and around me was the pressing flesh of my wives, even those who I could no longer call wife and whose flesh was only mine in memory, but all of them could not warm me. My bones had turned to sticks of ice under my skin and my skin to a rime of ice over my brittle organs. The fires blazed on either side of us and the sweat of my wives and the juices of their bodies poured over me but turned to ice also and that layer thickened and pressed me in the core of its coldness. In my hand I grasped Hawkstone. I stared upwards and in the smokeholes I saw a glowing light and the hole opened as does the center of an eye and it became my eye and I could see through to the Other World. And I rushed up out of myself like smoke and twisting back I could see my stiff form under my wives and hear their wail and then something forced my face forward and I could see an endless forest and when I saw the green of the leaves on its trees I knew that my eyes had not known what green was before, nor what trees were nor rivers, for I knew that what I saw in the world of the living was but paintings of these I saw here and it was all *manitou*. And I was *manitou* and I was sweet wind and I rushed forward laughing into the Other World and in my hand I still grasped Hawkstone. Through the trees then I saw a deer taller than a man and with a man's smile on its face and I felt I had a bow in my hands and I knew this deer was for me, and once I had stalked and killed it I would hunger no more forever. And I chased the deer through the great trees and leapt over rivers and waterfalls and I did not tire. But then we were in a country stript bare of trees, with deep scars rutted everywhere into the land and everywhere the tangled tracks of great serpents that had slid here and venom that was not only behind their fangs but pooled under their scales had leaked out their scales and soaked into the land and poisoned it, and everywhere it was bare and yellow. I saw Deer look back at me softly and fall to his knees and die and rot. The sun blazed down on me now with a heat that licked me like flames and I felt the poison seeping up through the soles of my feet, burning at first, then the feeling dropping from my skin so when I was next to my deer I could no longer feel my feet nor my flesh. I cried out for Hawk, my guardian spirit, to guide me from this place, but his stone turned red hot in my hand and I dropped him and when I could no longer stand, I fell forward onto the great side of the Deer. Then I was hollow but with a great hunger and I began to gnaw at the flesh of the Deer and it burned my mouth. And its great head rose and looked down at me as I ate into its side and it smiled mockingly and its face was my brother Uwanna. Look into the hole you have eaten in me, he said, laughing. I looked and I screamed for in him was a fiery pit such as the Blackrobe had told me and in it, writhing in agony, were all I had known who had gone to the Spirit World, staked as the Susquehannocks bind us when we are captured and burning but not consumed and their eyes coals and their mouths shrieking at me and I felt my brother's hands on my back, pushing me forward. *How much of yourself can you save by bleeding yourself away?* my brother asked. I felt a prick in the vein of my arm and I looked and saw a wound open there and the blood flowing from it, glowing like fire. As it flowed from me, I became lighter and cooler and I was drawn back, pulsing with its current and borne away from that pit and into the cooling sky and back and back, as if floating on a gentle path of my own blood. And I knew I could save myself by bleeding myself away. And when I opened my eyes I saw the face of White, and his hands were on my forehead and he was pulling me back from the pit of Hell.

And I know that which I had done out of a trickster's cunning to ally myself with the white men and their weapons was but a Blessed Trick played on myself by God, to bring me to Him and to bring my people to Him, for now I have passed into His Longhouse and now I know Him.

Ezekiel's Song

At first light we walked to where Fleet's shallop and his two smaller barques were moored. I had slept as badly as the rest of the town in that night filled with groans and howls, and my head felt gummed now, but the cold air and the flame red and yellow of the leaves along the banks—the trees had started to turn now—woke my brain. As we neared it, the river separated itself from the sky into a heavy silver smoothness, so still it seemed solid. Fleet's boats, with their triangular sails, lay mirrored on themselves. The men on board—there was a crew of four on the shallop, two more on each smaller barque—milled uneasily when they saw Fleet. He had discarded his breech-clout and wore a feathered cap and a beaver-lined cloak, over a plum-colored vest and trousers. Dressed in his finery to meet his dream. During the night, Tawzin had gone to see the Tayac and White, but had told Fleet and I not to come, saying it was not proper for us to enter his longhouse during a curing ceremony; it would bring bad luck. I did not know if this were a true custom, but I understood that he could not stand to bring Fleet back to Kittamaquund. When Tawzin returned to our fire, earlier in the morning, he had said nothing except that White had eased the Tayac's pain and there was no reason now to delay the expedition, though we must stop first at the Trading Rock, and leave gifts for the Anacostans. They had told Kittamaquund they would not oppose our passage.

As we boarded, the crew remained silent until they saw me, and then began muttering. It was bad luck to have a man with missing parts on board, a sailor called out. Fleet turned and faced them.

"Henry Fleet makes his own luck," he growled.

We sailed on the tide, the three boats forming an arrowhead, with the shallop at its point. As we drew further north, the river narrowed, and the enflamed banks pressed in on us and the current pushed against our passage. I was not sure how many hours had trickled out of that day marked by the creak and groan of wood and oiled canvas, the smell of tar and raw hemp, when I began to feel the water shake under the pine planks of the hull. The roar was a low rumble in my ears at first, and my skin prickled with fear and I searched the forest for the lion. The roar grew louder, echoing between the banks and ahead of the bow now I saw gigantic coils of gray rocks plugging the river, the seething water breaking around and through the narrows between them in hundreds of foaming channels and falls. I had expected the Falls to be a single arc of water falling from a height, but what was ahead of us was a jumble of boulders that sieved and churned the river through their tangle. The current caught the shallop now and the stern swung right, around the pivot of the bow. I glanced back and saw Fleet, his face intent and sweated, handling the long curved wand of the tiller himself. The boat lurched, as if a hand had grabbed it under water, then straightened, caught in some tendril of current he must have known. He threw back his head and laughed into the wind, his face, soaked by the spray and strained with the ferocity of an intent that was pulling us all after itself through the chaotic waters.

He seemed to be edging the shallop from one current to another, in a series of lurching angles, towards a flat table rock jutting out into the river before the jagged cliffs. Tawzin came up next to him. He had dressed in his *wisoe* finery; his face painted, a shell necklace dangling to his chest. He smiled slightly into the spray.

The flat rock was shaped like the sail of the shallop and only rose a few inches past the surface of the river. There were small cairns of rocks at the point of it, next to the calm channel between one of its sides and a large gray boulder that also jutted out from the shore, overshadowing it. Trading Rock. Fleet swung the shallop into the passage and a crewman, barefoot, his canvas pants rolled to his knees, leapt out and fastened a rope to the cairn. He pulled us in closer, and the other crewmen jumped out and pulled the bow up onto the rock. They helped the two smaller boats moor up in the same fashion.

Fleet put his hat back on and adjusted it carefully, smoothing out the now wet and drooping feathers. He had had the crewmen prepare bundles for the gifts: axes, *roanoke* and cloth for the Anacostan *werowance*. "If you don't separate it," he'd told me, "the savages will be all over your trucke, fingering like it's a bloody market, snatching whatever they want." He'd worried that if he gave too much to the Anacostans, there would not be enough trucke to trade for pelts. He need only give tokens, Tawzin had assured him: the Anacostan *werowance* Wamanato had agreed with Kittamaquund to give us fair passage in exchange for a tax on whatever pelts we traded from the Herekeenes.

A bark canoe came towards us now, from the direction of the Falls. Three men dressed in deerskin cloaks and draped with beads were sitting in it. The craft drew almost parallel to Trading Rock, and then the rear paddler twisted his blade and the canoe pivoted and shot towards us, carried on a crest of white water. The men were close enough that I could see grins on their broad faces, under the masks of paint. Several of the Indians on the rock pulled the canoe up to its mooring.

Fleet smiled as well and stepped forward, then stopped and frowned. The tall heavy Indian who had been in the bow stepped out, then swayed to the side and nearly fell. The men behind him snickered loudly. The Indian looked at Fleet's face and laughed also. He looked very happy. He lurched forward and tried to embrace the white man. Fleet pushed him off and glared at Tawzin. "What in Hell's name is this? Where is Wamanato?"

"That is Banocanquoc," Tawzin said quietly to me. "The name means Drunken Bull."

I said nothing. This was his now, I understood. I would stand back and let it unfold.

Drunken Bull shouted something I didn't understand. "He bides you welcome back, Shit Carrier," Tawzin said to Fleet. "Was that your captive name? I did not know."

"Damn you, I understand that tongue too well already," Fleet said. He began to raise his musket. The other Indians in the canoe—they seemed drunk to a man—had been fingering the gifts Fleet had laid out, passing clay gourds to the men in Fleet's crew. Grinning, they surrounded Fleet, pushing up the musket, patting him, passing remarks to each other, laughing crazily. Drunken Bull came over and threw his arms around Fleet, who cursed furiously and punched him in the chest. He sat down heavily and muttered something. The other Indians laughed until tears came.

"He said you do not seem happy to see him again," Tawzin said.

One of the white crewmen laughed also. "Shut your damned gob hole," Fleet yelled. His face was mottled.

"Look," Tawzin said. "More have come, Shit Carrier, to do you honor. To welcome you back. You must have been a very useful captive."

He waved at the top of the boulder. Dozens more Anacostans, men and women, were standing on the edge, some smiling, laughing, others staring intently at the shallop. Each man held a bow, an arrow loosely notched in it. Suddenly more people began swarming from the trees along the shore, coming onto and over the rock. The Indians who had been on the overhanging boulder started jumping down or making their way quickly along the sides. There must have been at least three hundred of them. They seemed in a good mood, laughing and smiling, but there was a playful menace behind it, like a drunk who might turn on a man in an instant for not laughing with him, for some slight seen only by his own eyes. The crewmen looked at the Indians nervously. They stood in a tight circle around the bow of the shallop now. One of them, still on board, a trapper in fringed buckskins, slid over behind the small deck swivel gun. "Shoot the scum, damn you," Fleet yelled. His hat was askew on his head and Drunken Bull had risen and was trying to kiss him. The crewmen stood shifting, unsure what to do. The man behind the gun swept it back and forth. The Anacostans laughed. They were pressed so closely to the whites that a man would only have a chance to get off one shot before being over-whelmed. The Indians began thronging on board the shallop and the barques, unloading the trucke. The trapper who had been behind the gun was suddenly gone. I hadn't seen what happened to him.

"Damn you, leave that be!" Fleet yelled, and threw off Drunken Bull. He leapt forward, scattering people, striking one man in the forehead. The Anacostans laughed harder. "Damyu, damyu," several younger boys screamed shrilly, imitating him, jumping forward, waving their arms, "lee'dat bah." Other people were trooping back from the boats, laying the trucke out along the rock, as if on display. A woman, hooting in triumph, held up a handful of wooden combs. Others were holding up axes and hoes. A man unrolled a bolt of bright green cloth with a whoop. Drunken Bull draped himself in *roanoke* and perched a brass kettle on his head. He pounded it with his tomahawk and then laughed. "Damyu, damyu," people were yelling, as if Fleet had given them a war cry. They were pressing clay gourds to the crewmen. The whites stared at them, then a man shrugged, grabbed a gourd and gulped the whiskey down, his throat working. A tall thin redhaired man in canvas trousers and a leather vest threw back his head and began laughing. I saw Fleet, stripped of his weapon and his hat, sit down heavily on the rock. A small boy sat down next to him and put his head against Fleet's shoulder. Fleet's eyes had gone blank, as if something had been poured out of them.

"It is time to leave," Tawzin said quietly to me.

We went to the smaller barque, empty now, and pushed off, letting the current carry us out to center river, the whoops of the Anacostans growing dimmer behind us. Neither of us looked back.

AN HOUR LATER, I said, "I felt pity for the man. He is like a hungry child." I pulled the tiller to the right, avoiding drifting debris: some woven matting, a dead deer, its belly stretched into a smooth drum by gas.

Tawzin was looking at the banks of the river. A thick plume of smoke rose from the eastern bank. He stared at it as we drifted past. I looked up at the pennant of St. Andrew and St. George still flapping from the small mast. It was our hope any Susquehannocks watching the river would not look past the flag of this lone boat to see it crewed only by a white-souled Piscataway and a one-handed black. By Wesorts.

"There is something of the hungry child about all of them," Tawzin said. A bitter smile creased his face.

"What will happen to Fleet?"

"Oh, the Anacostans said Shit Carrier had always been useful to them. Tayac made them, made us, promise he would not be killed. They won't harm any of them. They don't want to risk the whites' revenge."

"Wouldn't they have risked that now in any event?"

"I think not. They were very intelligent about it. They made him into a joke song."

I thought of Fleet's face, the laughing Anacostans, the white sailor shrugging and taking a drink, and I laughed. But Tawzin's face remained grim. Two posts lashed together with rawhide throngs floated by, a cattail-woven mat door: from a longhouse, I thought. Then the first human debris, an infant, its body worn and melted by the water so at first it seemed a gigantic white shining worm, spinning in the current, the nubs of its arms and legs fin-like. It knocked against the boat. A cloud of minnows was hovering and darting around it.

"I thought Kittamaquund asked the Anacostans to give him passage," I said, taking my eyes from it.

But Tawzin was still staring at the child's body. "The Tayac was only waiting for his last rites, for White, before he left us on our journey to take another path."

It took a moment before I understood what he had just told me. "Then you arranged all of this beforehand," I said. I meant the Anacostans' reception of Fleet. I felt a little wounded that Tawzin had not told me of this turn, of Kittamaquund's death.

"I did not leave you out of it, my friend," Tawzin said. "Wamanato was there, when Kittamaquund left us. We spoke. I had not time nor place to speak to you, away from Fleet."

I felt a sudden chill go through my body. We had gone with Fleet for the protection of our women and children and people. What would happen to them now? "But what else has changed, besides Kittamaquund's death? What will we do now?" I asked Tawzin. We had found no place to run, had only left Jacob Lombroso dead in a swamp and seen our enemies closing in from the north and east like the jaws of an animal. "We can't stay in Calvert's colony after this."

Tawzin turned around completely now and sat facing me, our knees almost touching. His face was tight with strain. "White told me what I know," he said softly, his words threading to my fears. "Fleet has been loyal to Fleet. He has worked for both Calvert and Claiborne, one and then the other, and one against the other, as he saw it to his advantage. He brought Calvert to the Tayac to thwart Claiborne. But he also brought Hallam to Claiborne. And he brought Hallam to you, Wesort. He brought him to you that day."

For a moment, I was confused; Tawzin's words made no sense to me. I stared past him at the river's swelling strength. A breeze touched and cooled my forehead. I tried to call my memories of the day I had lost my hand, the day of Wesort's violation. They had become sharp but scattered shards cutting into my brain. Hallam's distorted face, Wesort's eyes, the bite of the bark against the back of my hand. Sometimes I saw other faces as well, no, a face, further away, behind leaves. A flitting, staring image that fled as soon as I tried to fix upon it. But I saw it clearly now, Tawzin calling it out from behind the red mist of pain: Fleet's face, squinting at me worriedly, behind Hallam's demon face. I saw now, as if I was a stranger in my own body, that I was shaking so violently it was passing into the boat. I felt as if my veins were on fire, coming together into a hot knot pulsing between my eyes. The world grayed and went out of focus. I started to swing the tiller. Tawzin grabbed my hand, swung it back.

"The reasons for not killing him remain the same for us as for the Anacostans. I swore it to the Tayac. And our people are as vulnerable to revenge. Perhaps more. Listen to me, Wesort. White will let what Fleet has done and what happened to him here be known. And then you may do as you wish. And then I will help you kill him. But we must both eat our anger now. Until we know. Until we see." Tawzin's face was rigid, and I saw now, through the mist of my own rage, the way the muscles on his jaw were twitching.

"See what?" I asked. "What in the hell do you mean?"

"This is what White told me. The Wesorts are gone. The militia who were protecting them are dead. And the priest does not know where the people are."

From the Unpublished Journal of Father Andrew White, S.J.

Once I sat in a house made of reeds next to a Piscataway mystae and listened to a Jew speak of the cabalistic belief that words, that is, the physical twistings and arrangements of letters themselves, reflected the Twistings and Arrangements of the Universe, and as one configured and reconfigured those marks, one could mend the torn weave of the Universe itself. I wish it were true, Jacob. If I could, I would reconfigure my life now on these blank pages, riffled by a cold wind coming from that river to which I once diminished the Thames in comparison, at a time when England still was edificed in my brain as the World to which I needed compare and define the rest of God's creation. As I sit in this place a whisper or devilish laugh seems to echo in my mind, and this place, its emptiness, its silence, seems alive with the power of unborn voices, their whisper and laughter a forewarning of freedom so great it threatens dissolution.

I sit here now, in the territory of the Anacostans, on their side of the Potomac, down-river some miles from the Great Falls, where my prodigal son in spirit, John Christman, must at this time have enacted his latest dramaturgy. The Anacostans, whose king, as my beloved Tayac did, has come to the true faith, for which conversion I profess in my correspondence and at times truly feel a miraculous joy. And yet today I am devoured by dark doubts. These days come to me, perhaps more so lately, and perhaps more so in this place. I have become accustomed to solitude; indeed, perhaps sinfully, at times I long to be deep in the wilderness, away from all congress with my fellow men. But it is that solitude and this place itself that bedevils me particularly and peculiarly. It is a particular and peculiar place—so the

Anacostans say—and I do feel in its earth some evil struggle written to which the obligation of my faith calls me to soothe. Yet soothe what? My own words, thoughts seem dangerous and almost mad here. It is here that the tribes from the north and the south and the west: the Iroquois Federation, the Herekeenes, all the Algonquin peoples, even to the Creeks and more, send their chiefs and emperors to gather at times for a Great Council of the red men. Yet when such council is not called, the place is given to a spirit they call *Evil Mind*, and who must doubtless be the manifestation in them of Satan himself, and it is thus avoided by all. What perversity is it that makes such unholy ground a place of council? I would ask my brother Kittamaquund if he were still with us. And I can see his puzzled look, hear him answer, as if he were: *why where else would such council be more needed, An-drew?*

Yet here I sit also, and surely it is the Temptor himself who so troubles me when I should be at peace and rejoicing in the salvation of my brother the Tayac and his blessed wife, in their lives and at the hour of their death. The same circle of forty *magi* (forgive me this word, Lord, but it comes so strongly to me when I see them) who had witnessed my cure of the Tayac had come as well to witness my failure to save his earthly form and my triumph in saving his soul. They sat so near I could feel their warm rank breath on me and smell the rancid scent of the bear oil with which they cover their skins. Whence at first such an assembly had always given me cause to hold down my fear of their savagery with an iron grip, I have changed enough over the years to find the close press of their flesh a comfort, akin to an embrace of the spirit. God forgive me, but I felt God's presence manifested in that congregation, even though my intellect rebelled at my heart's finding, knowing these were shamans, idolaters to a man. My intellect, I write, and yet should not it have been both heart and mind that rejected the notion of congruence between us?

They had remained silent, those *magi*, with that

impassivity I had once taken for a coarse inability to discern finer emotions until I came to see it was their dignity, (and so now find myself responding with an unseemly distaste at the garrulity of my fellow Englishmen). The Tayac, my brother-in-Christ, stared long into my eyes, before the exhalation of his soul. His obsidian eyes glittered deep within with that spark of savagery I have never seen diminish from the orbs of the Indians, no matter to what degree they become civilized. In his fixed gaze I saw love and yet I also saw formulated, at the end, not peace but a terrible question. In that gaze I saw his face as I had first seen it, the sensual face of a cunning savage, and I saw the doubt creep behind his eye, and the triumph, and then, on his deathbed, a question. And that stare took me to John Christman, as if my former protege's face had been fixed over the features of the Tayac.

Once, I recall it was shortly after Ezekiel had been brought wounded and delirious to John's longhouse, I had sat and spoke with John and Jacob, one of our long-night dialogues which both delighted and troubled my soul. Freedom was our subject that night, with John insisting that it was possible to have a human society without a rigid hierarchy, and that if (forgive him, Lord) there is a Heaven, it is such a Place. In other words, he said, if we can conceive heaven, we can create it. Refusing to be goaded, I bade him to merely cast his gaze around him to where Ezekiel was moaning on his pallet, delirious for so long we thought him half in the Kingdom of Heaven already, or at least in that Purgatory reserved for righteous heathens and suffering innocents. There is a Beast in human nature; did he not see it manifested in a Hallam? In such a world as he postulated, would not the Hallams quickly, piloted by ruthless Appetite, rise to the apex of human society and impose their will upon multitudes, as indeed one Hallam had imposed his on the flesh of that poor black? It is such a world that has fashioned Hallam, John replied, and not a matter of Nature. Injustice, he said, grows from tyranny and creates twisted men. A free society would create free men and hence good men. It was his not-so secret creed of course; it was what John—and Jacob—dreamt his Wesorts to become. A childish dream. I dismissed his argument as verging on madness, as first, being void of God, Who has placed men in relation to each other, King or Servant, in accordance with His Design, and as second, being doubly disproved by the very loosening of bonds which has here allowed a Hallam, a Claiborne, a Fleet: free creatures all, subject to naught but the Godless laws of Trade which I have seen destroy my red children.

Yet I felt myself, that night, swept by a doubt I would not have had, not in my darkest hours in England, persecuted by the apostate Protestants. It was a doubt which rooted in the most fetid corner of my soul, seeded there not only by John's words, but by the graceful and sweet natures of the red men, by their surety of the truth of their *cosmos*. Can that which is called Just and True by the Piscataway or the Susquehannock contain the same weight and worth as the Christian's notion of Justice and Truth? Or, to put it more directly, how come I to know that I carry out the Will of God if each man's mind and the way he hears God is shaped by the *logos* of Nation and Circumstances? Once I had seen a tree, brought back by one of the Spanish Jesuits who had been nearly martyred in Japan—a country, he informed me, devilishly arrogant about its ways and determined to not see the Light of the True Faith. It was a tree in miniature, cunningly shaped by wires and weights over the years of its natural growth, to the design of the Japanese artist. Was its true form, then, that resultant of man's conception, or was it the *logos* of God's Design, straining to liberate and reflect itself under that twisting? Of course my answer, as a believer, as a Jesuit, is the latter.

For what becomes of me if I begin to think that the *logos* I see as Heaven's Order come merely from the pushes and pulls of my own tribe's, my own Wesorts', wires and weights?

For what becomes of me then if I think of what I have

brought to the Tayac and to the Piscataway in the name of eternal salvation?

I sound to myself now like Jacob, as if his lion-gnawed ghost hand were moving my quill upon this sheet. These thoughts, these cursed doubts which leave me feeling feverish, seeded into me by this country, with its Satanish emptiness, its emptiness which men will try to fill with letters twisted forward or backwards or any way at all. This place I know now I will have to leave, if I am to save my own soul.

The Zekiah Swamp

I knew immediately that the longhouses were empty. No smoke spiring upwards. A slight collapse of the spine of the centerpole in one, the grass overgrown between the dwellings. Inside the first one we entered, flies buzzed around several dried rabbit carcasses left hanging from the supports and a beam of sunlight shone through an unrepaired, fist-sized hole in the roof. Some sleeping skins were still crumpled on the floor like shucked cocoons. I smelled dried shit, piss, blood. The village was Mattawoman and not Wesort, but as I had gone in the longhouse, it was as if I were stepping into my own dwelling and the buzzing emptiness awakened a heavy dread in my stomach.

"Why didn't they burn this place?" Ezekiel said, his eyes so sick with fear I knew we had shared the vision, and I had to turn away.

"Perhaps the people fled before the Susquehannocks arrived. If we went home, we would see only the same, Ezekiel. Our people are gone, White said. There is only one place they would go."

"Death is a place they could go."

I didn't answer immediately. We had argued on the river; Ezekiel had wanted to continue directly home, but I was certain that the Wesorts would have gone north to the Zekiah Swamp, where the remnants of the Piscataway were regrouping. We would waste days, I had said, going south only to have to come north again. Yet I understood Ezekiel. I wanted as badly as him to complete the circle, to go back to what should never have been left, as if we could gather back what had been torn from us along this voyage.

I put a hand on his shoulder. "No. It is as this place. If the people who lived here had been killed, the longhouses would have been burnt, and there would have been signs left. There are none. And White saw none in Yaocomaco. Only the dead militia." I saw Ezekiel draw in a long breath. We had both seen the signs the Susquehannocks and Hallam left behind, all through the country.

WE WALKED INLAND, through the abandoned country of the Mattawoman, until we passed into the Zekiah swamp. We were not in it and then we were, a transition I could see Ezekiel was unaware of, though I felt the crossing as a heaviness; as if I knew past this point, I was passing out of the life I had hoped to make for myself, for the others, and into Diaspora. I cursed Jacob now, as if putting that word and that history into my mind had created disaster, as if my pride hadn't brought that fate on those I loved.

We followed along Zekiah creek, at times wading through it, sinking to our ankles and then knees in the noxious mud. None of the Piscataway would usually live here: our towns and villages were all built along the rivers and large creeks, for fishing and for trade. The Zekiah formed a buffer, as well as a common hunting ground, between the different Piscataway tribes and between us and the Patuxents: high water-shed country, its ground quickly flooded in any rain, low and hot and wet and full of mosquitoes, cottonmouths, copperheads, black flies and miasmic, unhealthy vapors. A country that seemed to be struggling against itself, strangling itself in a silent, frozen battle. Strands and wide meadows of marsh grass, spotted with white orchids and pockets of dead trees, wound around and between forest thick with creeper vines and tangled jungles of underbrush. As we worked through it, we began coming across corpses, torn by crabs and buzzards, or larger beasts—we saw several corpses with their throats torn out, their flesh more worried than devoured. Turkey buzzards sat perched on branches everywhere, when they weren't crowded, in their council, around their meals. But we saw no living people.

In late afternoon, we came upon a palisade, hastily erected, the poles crudely cut and leaning haphazardly in all directions. Piscataway warriors, their faces intent and hollow-cheeked, stared at us from the watch perches. Several of them seemed half-asleep, eyes heavy-lidded, bodies swaying dangerously. One watch perch—a pole with struts lashed to it for stairs and two struts lashed near the top for a foot hold—had been erected directly next to the entrance of the palisade's overlap. The man on it peered down at us and began to chant. He had painted black tears under his eyes, a pattern I had never seen or dreamt of seeing and I felt my own answering grief to that man's face, grieving to the knowledge that the *manitou* of the people must have fled to allow a warrior to so weakly mark himself. The tear-painted man had the body of a fat man whose flesh had collapsed like a tent around the frame of his bones. He drew back his bow string and pointed an arrow at us, its tip wavering. His eyes met mine and he lowered the bow slowly.

"Do you know me, bowman?" I called up to him.

The man continued to stare at me. His eyes were filled with some memory that had nothing to do with who was standing before him.

"I know you," he said. "You are Lion. You are Death Stalker. You are He Who Walks in the Grass." He threw back his head and howled. After a moment he stopped and looked down at us again. "I can not let you enter," he whispered loudly.

I would as soon enter a mad mind. "Tell me bowman, have you seen a tribe of Piscataways and whites and blacks such as this"—I gestured at Ezekiel—"who walk in each other's footprints?"

The man peered around anxiously. "I have seen many such demons. You are one. He is another."

"I know whom you seek, *wisoe*," a man on one of the other perches called. "Tawzin, isn't it?"

"Yes, *cockarouse*." I recognized Nantochuac, a Yaocomaco with whom I had once gone on a raiding party into Powhatan territory.

"Keep north, until First Fork. They have gone past Cotton Mouth Marsh. Stay alive."

"And you, *cockarouse*."

"And all of us, *wisoe*. But I do not believe it will be so."

WE CAME ACROSS two more bands before we broke out of a mile of snarled underbrush that left our skins criss-crossed with welts and gashes and saw the marsh spread before us, sentried with dead white trees, the air above it flickering with insects. We started across, walking carefully, the thick warm mud and water sucking at our ankles. In a pool of black water near a dead tree I saw a tangle of the snakes that gave the place its name, twined like caressing, boneless fingers. Past that pool, we came upon Simon Bodecker, who rose suddenly from a strand of grass and stood, his fishing spear cocked back and ready to throw at us. When he recognized us, his face and shoulders relaxed and he lowered the spear. But he didn't smile to see us.

He led us without a word to the wall of bramble and wild rose bushes under the trees at the other side of the marsh. I saw the notch marked in the fork of the sycamore just before Bodecker stopped. It worried me. If I spotted this marker so easily, so would any Susquehannock scout. Bodecker knelt and pulled aside a section of bramble bush: its branches were raveled, I could see now, on a woven mat. Behind it was a tunnel going through the undergrowth.

I took a handful of mud and smeared it into the notch, then covered it with apiece of bark, using the mud to blend the bark's edges into the trunk while Bodecker waited without comment or expression. I let Ezekiel go first, then pulled the mat after us. We crawled on our hands and knees for perhaps two hundred paces, then emerged in a shaded grove near a stream. We followed along it through the thick, dark woods, the air wet and thick and stinking of marsh gas. I didn't see the first dwelling until we were nearly on it. This I had taught the Wesorts. But I saw then that it wasn't craft, as I hoped, but only a sign of indifference.

Instead of longhouses the Wesorts had built small huts, woven of branches and covered with leaves and marsh grass, each one only large enough for one family. They were built sloppily and strewn as if thrown across the clearing—though it was hardly open enough to be called so—and around them were piles of bones and offal. People, my Wesorts, lay in front of their huts, or wandered about as if lost. It was, in small, what I had seen in Piscataway, as if that vision had cursed us to its lines. There were several fire pits, but all were cold, and the old bones left from meals were strewn about them. A woman rose from her squat in front of a hut. It took me moments before I recognized my wife. She was dressed in a buckskin skirt and was naked from the waist up, and her breasts were heavy with milk, so heavy drops were leaking from her nipples, coursing down her skin like the weeping of her body.

Ezekiel's Song

In the closeness and heat of the sweatlodge in which we lay
together now, visionless, Tawzin told me how he had leaned
close and the Tayac had stroked his face, the gesture so
unexpected, so like something Jacob Lombroso would do,
he had felt tears spring to his eyes. Kittamaquund had turned
from him then, towards White, his eyes pleading, and White
had given him the words the he had wanted to hear, and the
Tayac had died in peace and in a lie. But Tawzin didn't want
absolution, he said. For who could absolve him? We were
rotting. The dream Tawzin and Lombroso and Nanjemoy and
Wesort and I should have blown on like a single feeble ember
until it flamed beyond our care was dimming in the wet mists
and fevers of the Zekiah, its eclipse marked and measured by
Nanjemoy's dull-eyed distraction, by Tawzin's mourning for
Rachel, my brother's child, snatched by my enemy who had
come out of the forest, like the lions I heard sung of when I
was a boy, to take one child from the village, from the
campfire. Even her pregnancy, the tight protruding drum of
her belly, seemed more threat now than promise, as the future
was more threat than promise. Even Wesort's pregnancy, he
said. Wesort. My wife, who had named herself and named
us, and that name was becoming a joke song, as we had
thought to make Fleet's name. The Wesorts had taken even to
fighting each other, over the scarce game, the roots for which
we grubbed, the berries we gathered. Worse, our quarrels
were seamed between black and white, English or African or
Piscataway. Between husband and wife, men fighting over
women and women over men, and some coming to blows
and almost to murder over game, or crabs and snails or roots
and berries, or worse still, over strings of *roanoke*.

He knew that the reasons he had given to the Wesorts

and to Nanjemoy, and to himself, for going on Fleet's quest, were all true and they were all lies, Tawzin said. We could have fled earlier. We should never have relied on the protection of the English—were we any better than Kittamaquund? He had felt love closing on him, and he had wanted a legend, and he had wanted a woman to come home to from the legend, and a people to sing it and instead, as the Tayac had done, he had brought them fire.

Ego te absolvo, I thought: the words White had taught me. But I would not speak them aloud. Not to him and not to myself. I shouldn't have even thought them. I saw Tawzin as I saw my own heart. Who was I to forgive or comfort either? I knew whom Hallam had been seeking, as I knew myself, and if he had not been alone, and if Wesort and Isaac had not been in the midst of the encampment, I knew who he would have taken. But he did not know Isaac, I thought. And then banished the thought and the reason for it from my mind. Who could absolve me now of bringing Hallam to Rachel? Of bringing Hallam to the Wesorts?

"What do you want from me?" Tawzin whispered, his voice so low it seemed a part of the smoke. "I am not the Tayac of the Wesorts. I'm not even their *werowance*. There are no Wesorts. It was only a mad idea, an accident, a point to worry with our teeth around a campfire because lost Jacob needed a lost tribe and an ideal. I have not asked anyone to share my fate. Not even you."

He sat up, the muscles in his neck and back knotting under the sheen of sweat. He had painted black tears under his eyes and they melted and ran down his face now, in the heat of the steam. Before I could reply, he leaned forward onto his hands and knees and crawled out of the sweatlodge.

Before I could reply, but what could I say to the man? We were all cursed with each other as we had all been blessed with each other. And I knew the name of the curse and I knew I had brought him into our lives.

I lay back and stared at the ceiling, my hand running

down, touching my wet body, chest, nipples, belly, sex. I pressed against the skin at the base of my scrotum. Hand tracing the paths Wesort's hands no longer took. Balls full and aching. Gut and heart and sex hollow and aching with the missing of that touch. With the missing. Stump hurting. The pain spreading in a slow fire up into the hand that was no longer there but felt as I could still feel the absent sixth finger on my left hand. I knew what I had only in the ache of its loss. My hand, my finger, my love, my child, my people. *Ego te absolvo*. I stared up at the swirls of smoke against the low press of the woven branches. I was standing next to a pile of coffins, a wall high as the palisade I had seen at Piscataway. No, higher, because when I looked up, straining my neck, I saw it stretched on and on, into the clouds. I looked back down and saw Hallam, his eyes red embers, grinning at me, walking towards me, holding a body cradled in his massive white arms, against the white slabs of his chest. The body was small but stiff as a board and Hallam put it on the earth and the two of us worked with each other as we once before had worked, nailing the coffin together. Then Hallam knelt and picked up the body and I saw it was Rachel. Her face was white, as if covered in flour. It rested against Hallam's sweated, red furred muscle, I thought I saw a smile twitch its lips. The dead do that, Hallam said to me. It means nothing. Only that they know they are dead.

But as I looked at her, the smile widened, and Rachel's eyes opened and they were blue and glowed and now her lips moved also. I leaned forward to listen to what she was trying to say.

Hallam's Song

The whole of the area inside the palisade was ash. The remaining posts were charred sticks. The longhouses were higher piles of ash. Bone poked out of it. If Ezekiel were here, could he call the bones to life, like his namesake prophet? I picked up Ezekiel's finger from my chest and pointed it at the remnants of the village. Of all the villages, world without end. All night I had heard the roaring of the lion I had stalked. Always full and yet always empty now. Too much easy food. It would make him lazy and irritable. The lion. He would miss the long stalk. His stomach would feel hollow even as he gorged on the soft man-parts that were everywhere for the taking. Meat killed just before his arrival. Laying waiting for him, sometimes torn. As if chewed by another lion. Now he would only kill the buzzards who would come first to the man-meat. Though sometimes he had to fight off the packs of wolves, and the bears that were growing bolder and half-insane with the plentitude of meat. Neither the wolves nor the bears would fight very hard. Too much man-meat for the taking. Yet the more the lion filled himself, the deeper the hollow inside his stomach would grow. Sometimes he would be tormented by dreams, and he would growl in his sleep, and awake feeling a fear in his belly and chest that slowed him and made him uneasy and testy. He would sometimes feel gorged and sometimes faintly nauseated. Yet the more he ate of the man-flesh, the more he would crave it. Wherever he went now the air was heavy with the scent of man-blood. Bristling with the energy of killing. It made him dream and remember his dreams so he no longer knew when he was awake. It had never happened to him before. It made him heavy and sluggish and full of gas and worms that he could feel eating his guts. He would taste man-

303

fat in his saliva, feel its soft rot between his teeth. But he was a lion. He killed. He fed. He shit. He fucked. He slept. He dreamt. He would wake and then move on, helplessly following the feast the world had left for him.

Ezekiel's Song

A foul strangeness touched the camp like a heavy, noxious mist rising from the swamp of our own waste and neglect. We could trust nothing, not even the next moment. We still huddled together, but what held us was not love, as it once had, but fear and, worse, simple habit. And I knew the name of the curse on us.

I resolved to slip away without telling Wesort. I knew she would try not to stop me, but to go with me. But the thought of bringing her into Hallam's reach again called a vision to me of him pumping himself into her, his eyes fastened to mine. Of our violation. I would never bring her close enough to him again to be within the grasp of his hands. That night, as if she sensed my intention or my fear, she came to me and touched me as she never had before, taking me in her hand and tasting the slit of my sex with her tongue, and pushing that opening against her nipples, as if she wished to enter me with them as a man enters a woman, and then painting her breasts and the pregnant curve of her belly with snail trails of me and I lay and let her do as she would. As we lay side by side, caressing each other, she took me not deep inside, but only between the lips of her sex and squeezed me with these and I understood and shared the hunger in her to partake not only of our bodies but of freedom itself, and a defiance of fear: with you and I, her body said, there is nothing secret and nothing forbidden and no hungers we need hide in shame; we touch each other as we touch the hungers in our own flesh, of our own hearts.

I slept deeply afterwards, and that night Jacob Lombroso and my namesake came to me also and sometimes they melted into each other and I understood what Tawzin and my own dim memories of Africa had told me, that for the

Piscataway, our lives are but shadows of the dream time. In my dreams then, we were chained together, the three of us in the slaver's ship, and Jacob turned to me with his twist of a smile. *Tis a strange life,* he said, *I come fleeing Christians and end in the belly of* Jesus. *What are you doing here? What happened to your hand?*

I lost it. It was painful.

Ah. I'd forgotten pain. I think the idea of that was to test us, no Ezekiel?

This to my namegiver. The first Ezekiel. He turned. He was crouched in the darkness of the hold, his stumps clamped off in manacles. His eyes were closed and his face wet and slick like a newborn.

Why are we being tested? he asked.

I forget, Jacob Lombroso said, furrowing his brows.

Are the two of you in hell? I asked.

Are you?

Lombroso waved at the wooden walls of the hold and they dissolved. We were in a longhouse, Jacob and my namegiver's face, one under the other, carved on the center pole. *Mesingw.*

Is that better?

What will happen to us? I asked.

Chut, Jacob said. His mouth gaped into a knot hole. *Why should I tell you what you already know?*

What will happen?

Jacob made the pole shiver.

Happen is a frightening word to us, Ezekiel, my namegiver explained. *Look at me.* He showed me his stumps, pulling them from the pole, two matches to my one; *Look at Jacob. These are things that have happened. We try not to happen anymore. Otherwise what good is being dead?*

But I must.

But you must, you must, you must, you must, they agreed.

Before first light, I rose and for a time listened to my wife's breathing. There was a rustle to my left and when I looked, I saw Isaac. He was secured in his swaddling, and staring at me silently, his eyes glittering in the hint of first light, a strange child, and my heart ached with helpless, unreasoning love for him.

Wesort and I had fallen asleep clutched together and I pulled myself out gently now and rose as quietly as I could. *I'd have what's mine,* he'd said to Nanjemoy and he'd left her alive to give me his words and had taken a hostage for that debt. Did he know whose child that hostage was? It didn't matter. He knew what he had to know. He knew that I would come to bring him the debt he was owed. He knew I would come to pay it. I took my knife and my tomahawk and the fish spear Simon Bodecker, who came from the headwaters of the Congo and who had a secret name he had never told us, had made for me. I must, I whispered. I left Wesort sleeping in our warm nest of deer skin, and I carried with me, as I went, the crusted annointments of her body on my skin.

Death Song

I could taste ashes in my mouth. A film of ash lay on my skin. Ash shelled my heart. The ash of priests coned in my ear canal. They whispered to me. *Et iter praebuit populo terae ut enarrent mirabilia Dei.* Their faces came loose in flakes that were crusted on the inside of my brain. They were growing difficult, my priests. I lashed them to poles, hung them upside down, burned and flayed them. I had taken out their eyes so they would no longer stare, their tongues so they could no longer speak. I had taken the hand of my enemy and now my enemy's finger pressed on my heart. I had taken enough parts to build a man of my own and it moved through the swamps and forests, while I sat back, a man of ash and bones. *Mirabilia Dei.* The wondrous things of God. I had found my name. I could sing my own song now. The Susque-hannocks saw the ashes and bones of my soul when they looked into my eyes. They were deserting me now, refusing to fight with me. They left me alone now, except for my woman, Silence, who of course said nothing. Not since my child of her was born into silence and stayed silent and cold, as if she had delivered my own heart, and I took that dead flesh from her breast and now brought her another, and we had built our longhouse in the Great Cypress Swamp, surrounded by silence and trees whose height and width so defied me that I wanted to live in their midst so as to live rooted in the black water of my own hate, in a forest of gallows and crucifixes, closed around me and mine like the bars of a cage. I was not there now. I was alone except for Silence and Dark Moon, who had finished his work on the last prisoner, and now was walking towards me out of the ashes, his face blood-spattered and unsmiling. He tucked the scalp into his waistband. I caressed Ezekiel's dry finger. It caressed my heart.

"I must go, Death," Dark Moon said. He smeared his hand over the net of scars on his thick chest, as if the hand had been grabbed by the motion of my hand. "Come with me."

"Where can I go that I am no longer Death?"

"You have named yourself."

"Can I unname myself."

Dark Moon said nothing.

"Then I am Death," I said. "Then I am not finished." I waved at the burned village. "There are more."

"There has been enough. If there are no more Piscataway, how will we teach the young to be Susquehannock? But Death kills because it is Death. Opechancanough told us this about you whites. But we did not believe him. Now I know you, Death. Death has been my brother. Brave Death. Mad Death. Death the Stalker. Death in the Grass. Opechancanough has spoken again, Death. And now we listen to him. Perhaps soon we must stop killing the Piscataway. Perhaps soon we must all rise together to kill Death. Perhaps that will put the world in balance again."

I thought I could do that. But perhaps it was too late.

"There is one more village I must visit, brother," I said. Death said.

Ezekiel's Song

I walked for the next two days, and when I met anyone still alive, and even when I met the dead, I had only to say Hallam's name to be directed to my next destination. He was close. I had known when I left and I knew it more with every step I took. I held my steps to a spiral shell in my mind, with the Wesort camp at its center, and I spun out towards him, as I knew he was spinning in towards me, the two of us as always caught on the axis of each other.

And so although my circle took me leagues further, I don't think then I was five miles north of the Wesorts when I came to a village of ashes. It lay heaped on a low lying island in the midst of a marsh meadow, like the gray idea of a village, forming, distorted and wavery behind a shimmer of marsh gas. I saw in that forming the shadow of the Piscataway, as if this delicate suggestion of the shapes of longhouse and sweatlodge and campfire was the last remnant left of their presence on the earth, passing now into the air and water of the Zekiah. Here and there in it, I could see the idea of men and women also; gray corpses standing upright like sentries, like memorial statues to themselves. I came low through the tall grass, my feet in the cold wet mud, and then I lay down in that mud and smeared myself from head to toe, and, holding the spear as best I could, I crawled forward, as if I were crawling across the border to the other world. My flesh had been stripped from my nerves and they tingled with the feel of him in the air.

Something rustled ahead of me and I brought the spear up quickly. There was a small grove of loblolly pine to my left and as I watched it, I saw the small thatch lean-to I hadn't seen at first grow visible among the bushes. I crawled to it, keeping behind a screen of saw grass.

A Susquehannock woman was sitting in front of the lean-to nursing a child, her back three quarters to me. It was cold now, late Fall, but she was naked from the waist up and her back covered with goosebumps. She turned slightly, sticking her nose up in the air and sniffing and as she did I saw that the child at her breast was Rachel.

The woman was staring straight at me, her face broad and peaceful with the feeding, and for a second I was certain she could see me. But she turned again and hunched her shoulders slightly. I stayed where I was, watching for Hallam, or other Susquehannocks. But the camp was empty, save for the woman and Rachel.

I should just take the child, I told myself. Step forward and kill the woman and take the child. I thought of Tawzin and Nanjemoy's faces as I would step to their longhouse with her in my arms. But Hallam was still here.

I backtracked into the marsh, and then crawled around to the edge of the village. Several scalped bodies were rotting in the cold water, man-torn, crab-torn. I began to think of what I was doing as coming to a lair, passing the kill of what was inside it. I went into the ashes, and now I was covered with their gray flakes as well as stinking mud. And I saw him.

He was arranging corpses against the charred framework, his fingers sinking into the charred flesh. What he was creating looked to me what the village had seemed from a slight distance: his hands were shaping the bodies, a man, a woman, a child, the ruin of a home, into what they had been, as if their forms could call to life. The huge square of his back was to me; he was shirtless also, wearing the long fringed skirt-like breech-clout the Susquehannocks wore in the winter. His muscle layered back, blood-splattered and ash-stained, was bare of scar tissue, though I could see three different, puckering wounds on his sides.

He was speaking to the corpses. I thought at first that his voice was ringing with that mockery I had grown to hate so much when I belonged to this man. As soon as I thought those words that I had never used before to describe my ties to Hallam, I knew also they were true. I belonged to him and I would do so until I could scour him from my heart. Something in his voice caught me then: what I had thought was mockery was instead the wavering wail of an Indian death chant, sung to bring a spirit to peace. He was singing his song.

I got up and stepped closer, and I raised the spear and let it fly.

He seemed to spin at the instant the spear reached him. The spear point ripped a red streak in his right side. He rocked back on his heels and stared at me, his right hand holding and caressing a long black amulet hung on a rawhide cord around his thick neck. A bruise had formed on his skin around the wound and blood streamed down onto his hips. He ignored it. His eyes were rimmed with ash, and were bloodshot and slightly unfocused, as if they were fixed on something only he could see.

"Your finger told me you were here," he said, and I saw what he fondled in his hand. I pulled the tomahawk from my waistband.

He sat down suddenly, on top of a small heap of what had looked to be only ash, but must have been a rock or stump. He was looking at me calmly. There had been nothing of collapse in his movement; he was at ease, and I knew that even though I would make the attempt, my weapon and my strength were nothing to him. He pointed my finger at me and made a stirring motion.

"It called you." He laughed flatly. "At times it writes on my heart. At times I think it hooked up into Silence and scratched my issue to death. I knew it would bring us together again."

I asked him then to answer the question that rose in me when I saw him.

"What do you want, Hallam?"

312

"I want what is mine," he said. But it was as a ritual chant between us and his voice was hollow and flat, as if his tongue were forming to the words without connection to anything left in his thoughts or heart.

"I am here," I said. "I am what is owed to you. Take me. But bring the child back. Kill me, if you wish. If you can. I will fight you, but you know how it will end. But bring the child back and leave the people in their lives."

He took in a deep breath and let it out, then turned and touched the head of the corpse next to him. "The Susquehannocks call me Death, did you know that?" He laughed. "Tis a passing strange thing, for a Kent boy, isn't it, Ezekiel? All of this," he waved around the village of ashes. "D'ye think then, in London, they smell what is in the fur? I believe it so. I believe it is what they love. I believe it must be what God loves." He laughed. "D'ye want me to kill you now, Ezekiel?" He rose and stepped towards me. "Man, I am gorged on death. I am Death sick unto death of death."

I held the tomahawk and waited. "I'll be your slave again then. If you'll give back the child. If you'll leave the people in peace."

He regarded me for a long time. "I am what I am, Ezekiel. I will have what is owed to me."

If I can kill him, I told myself, I will. My words to him were true; I would give myself. But if there was a chance to kill him, I would have it. "Take me, then."

He stepped towards me, and I began my swing, and his hand snaked out, both movements so fast I saw only the memory of them a second afterwards. My tomahawk fell into the ashes, raising a small cloud. His hand clutched my wrist.

"What the hell do I want with a one-handed nigger," he said. I saw his fist grow large before my eyes.

I WAS CERTAIN I was among the dead. But I was only a visitor in their country. Hallam had propped me up next to the family of corpses he had arranged, a cord around my neck holding me loosely to a charred post, my skin caked gray as theirs. Life gathered me back to itself with pain. My face hurt and my ears rang. The cord was loose; only placed to hold me into Hallam's strange carving, and I was able to free myself. My tomahawk had been left in the ash, a gesture of contempt I could not bring myself to even rage about. The spear lay near it. Why had he left me alive? *I am gorged on death*, I had heard him say, and his eyes showed the truth of it. But he was Hallam and he would have what was owed. Then I knew where he would go.

The lean-to, the woman, and Rachel were all gone. I began running.

I was no longer travelling in a searching circle, and it did not take me long to reach the Wesorts. That there were Wesorts to be reached was my concern. If I came this swiftly, Hallam would also.

But our flyblown camp lay in the autumn sun as it had been when I left. It was still early in the morning. I passed the dwelling of Tawzin and Nanjemoy, its construction— branches haphazardly heaped over a sagging framework— mimicking the sadness and indifference of my two friends. For a second I thought of stopping and telling them of Rachel, rousing them so we could prepare for Hallam, perhaps even ambush him. But I needed to see Wesort first. I needed to touch her so I could return from the village of the dead. Two boys, the Accoceek Weasel and Adam Beekman, the child of two indentured servants run away from the Trent plantation, smiled at me as they walked by with fishing spears, heading for the creek. A black woman I didn't recognize, one of the new group of escaped slaves, passed me and nodded; she was carrying a basket on her head, walking with a loose-limbed, long-necked grace which, without reason and in spite of the heavy fear sitting like a rock in my chest, allowed me a thrill of hope. Striding in front of our branch-woven homes in this American swamp, she could have been a picture of the fancy my name-giver dreamt and pushed into my dreams on a dock near the slave pens of Barbados. "Good mornin', fadder," she said to me: I was still given the respect of being one of the Founders. I was in the middle of the Wesort encampment, and seeing it now as I had seen that woman's graceful, hopeful stride into the morning, through eyes that had seen the village of ashes. Seeing it now waking into the sun, the Wesorts emerging from their entrances soft-faced, their faces sill open with the hope in the day that lays in the crack between the soft erasures of sleep and the sad flooding knowledge of wakefulness.

It was that heavy knowledge and wild hope that swung me madly between them to our hut. I knew before I entered what I would find, for Wesort was always the first to rise, and of a morning I would see her outside preparing flat cakes of maize, or nursing Isaac. But the fire in front of our dwelling was cold, a small gray pit, as if an eye that had seen what I had seen and had filled with ash.

The woman with the basket, perhaps concerned at the look on my face, had followed after me.

"Why dat surpri' you, dey gon', fadder?" she said.

I turned to her. "What do you mean, woman? Where are they. Whar dat mah woman and chil?'"

She stared at me. "Dat why I ast. Gone along behin' you, time sat you lef.' Bot a dem.'"

"When?" I said, seizing her by the shoulder, forgetting in my fear that one hand was gone and the stump, with its encasement, bumped her shoulder.

She stepped back. "Don' hurt me, fadder." The fear in her face sickened me.

"I'm sorry, chil'. Tell me what you mean."

Tell me what I know.

She still looked confused. "Mon, I tell you. Dey goan aftah you, near same time. 'Swhy I thinkin' dey com' return wid you, dis moanin.'"

I turned and began running. I groaned, deep in my chest, seeing Hallam, his dead eyes, his dead smile, his outreaching hands. I was suddenly full of ashes. Hallam, I screamed. Who had made the world into ashes. Who had made my life and what I loved into fuel. I screamed out in rage and pain, so loudly I could hear echoing shouts behind me, as the Wesorts, roused now, came out of their huts. I ran through the muck of the swamp. Clouds of insects rose around me and buzzed into my ears. A copperhead reared like an orange finger raised from the ground and struck hissing as I ran by, straightening, flowing away after it missed. A woodpecker was pounding madly on a hollow tree, its thunk-thunk-thunk drumming in my ears like my own heartbeat. I would kill him now. I would take him from the earth, he who had taken my hand and my Gift and now had come back for my heart.

I was at the edge of the wet meadow.

I saw Wesort on the other side, holding the child to her breast. My life walking towards me. I ran out to meet it. As the distance closed between us, I saw that the child she held was not Isaac but Rachel.

Wesort's Song

I had followed him until I came to Silence. He had taken me from the earth and to the light and now I would not let him descend into the darkness without me. I followed him into the pit of ash where his own spirit was buried. Isaac sucked at my breast. You must love him, child, Jacob Lombroso had said to me when I had thrust him from me, he is flesh of your flesh. But now I hardened myself against him again. He had rooted and grown inside me but was not of me. Heavy at my chest. Heavier than his size, as the dead are heavier than their size. All this I thought. But he looked at me, his eyes suckled to my eyes as lips to breast. And became light in my arms. When he suckled I felt the rock inside each breast melt and flow. Flesh of my flesh. I stopped and I would then have gone back. This child had been buried in me as I had been buried in earth. Brought to light by a gentle hand. Seeded in me by a hate as strong as love. But seeded in me again when Ezekiel had lain on me and opened me as he had opened the earth. And born to us again in light.

Once we had gone down to the river, Ezekiel, Isaac and I, on a warm and moonless night. The black sky was thick and milky with stars and the water was as dark as the sky, and cool and thick against our skins. Ezekiel had cried out, and when I turned to him I saw his body was traced in dancing points of white light against the black river, and when I looked down I saw the same light glowing on my skin, pulsating in the milk spilling from the tips of my breasts. My husband pushed his hand swiftly through the current, and the lights churned and trailed after it, and Isaac had started then to slap his own hands against the water, laughing in delight as each splash woke clouds of tiny lights. Look,

Ezekiel said again, softly this time, and I saw a white globe had nuzzled around the end of his stump as he turned it gently in the dark water. We lay on our backs then, and floated in that blackness of water and sky, Isaac on my breast and the stars above us, and the fireflies twinkling against them so we were bathing in stars, and we held then for a moment, drew together like a breath against the drowning of time. That moment Isaac's true birth to us.

Now I followed Ezekiel into ashes and to Silence.

For Silence was my sister. Sister slave. Sister captive. She was sitting by the embers of the fire, rocking, her back to me streaked with ash and sweat, with the raking of Hallam's claw marks. She turned slowly and calmly, her eyes locked to mine, letting me know she had heard me. Rachel at her breast as Isaac was at mine.

You're his woman, I said aloud. That he had one wrenched my mind so I saw around to the side of what I had been seeing.

She touched her lips in the sign for name and the sign for Silence.

I had not thought a demon could have a woman.

I am Silence, she signed again.

How can you stay alive when he rends you?

I am Silence, she signed again.

Can you kill him when he has spent?

Silence made the sign for love.

Then she made the sign for man.

I knew then Silence saw the man buried in the demon as Ezekiel had seen the form of his love buried in the earth.

What must I do? I asked. What must I say?

But she didn't answer. She saw what was in my arms and she knew I knew already what I must do.

She pointed to the other side of the village of ashes.

She made the sign for a waiting lion.

When he came, the demon was still raging in his eyes. I held Isaac out to him. I watched the fire leak from his eyes.

I gave him the words Silence told me I knew: this is what is owed you. This is yours. This is what you left in me. Give me the other. This is what is owed to you. Let my people live.

I can take it and you and them, he growled, his eyes gleaming as if with fever. But his face was tired. His skin sagged down suddenly on his cheeks as if pulled by stones. This I saw.

A child must be given, I said. I placed my heart down in the dirt at his feet. When I straightened, my arms were terrible with lightness.

She understood now, she told me, how absence filled time and touched flesh and pressed the heart more than presence. Only in loss do we at last understand what was had. She understood now the burning and invisible hand fastened to my wrist. What has he done to you? I had asked, when we had returned, when we had given Rachel to Nanjemoy and Tawzin. The light that broke on their faces had darkened when they looked into my eyes and hers. Absence fastened to Wesort's breasts in weight and pain, and they ached as my missing hand did, for it is only in absence that we understand what we had.

This will end it, she said.

"I will end it."

She had looked into Hallam's eyes and had seen a mad and powerful spirit that howled for balance. For a counterweight to death. In his balance, she said, we would have peace.

In his death we would have peace and we would have Isaac both, I said.

"I cannot tell you not to do this," Tawzin said to me, in the sweatlodge.

"Good."

"What Wesort has done for the people is already an ancestor song though. It pulls us back to each other. It makes all our separate songs one again. It is so strong that we must live to it. She knew that. If it is undone, so we will be."

"That is their song and yours. Not mine and not Isaac's."

"Only your death song awaits you."

"Lombroso remains in you," I said.

He didn't answer.

"You cannot tell me not to do this, you say. But then you do. It is as if I hear Lombroso in your mouth."

He smiled briefly and stared at the smoke flattening on the ceiling, running towards the smoke hole.

"He is my son. You have your child again. Wesort gave her back to you."

He turned his face from me. "That is why I cannot tell you not to go," he said. "And it is also why you cannot tell me not to come."

"Then who will be here for the people?"

"Both of us, when we return."

"You speak beautifully, *Wisoe*. But you speak nonsense."

"You must be *werowance*, Ezekiel. I do not have the strength for it anymore."

"Now you only speak nonsense."

"How will you know where to find him? Before he finds you."

"He is in the Great Cypress. He told Wesort this."

For a long time he only looked at me. "He told Wesort this," he said. He shook his head as if in disbelief.

"It doesn't matter. He carries me on his heart. He will know when I come."

"Twice you've gone up against him."

"More," I said. "And now again."

He had not stopped looking into my eyes. "Then come," he said.

The air outside the sweatlodge was not that different than the air inside. The Zekiah's humid haze lay like wet skin pressed to wet skin. Several Wesorts, digging furrows in the pestilent ground with hoes made from deer horn lashed to hickory wood handles, looked up at us dully as we went through the camp. I followed Tawzin. We walked to a copse of tulip poplars, their bases held in brackish water, their white blossoms open and large as a man's heart, emitting a sweetish odor that only made the stink of the marsh more unbearable in my nostrils. On the other side of the tulip poplars was the reedy marsh, its tall grass rippling back and forth in a slight breeze as if breathing. Between the trees and the grass, a seam of dry earth ridged up out of the ground. We went to it. At its top, Tawzin got down on his hands and knees and began digging near a small cairn of rocks. I joined him. Soon we had uncovered a beautifully made pine chest with rope handles on each end. I knew what would be inside. Tawzin opened it. He unwrapped the oiled cotton wrapper, revealing Henry Fleet's brace of pistols, packed butt to barrel. We had buried many such caches, throughout the area, so that if the people were surprised or dispersed, they would be able to arm themselves. But these pistols would have better served kept in his lodge, and I wondered if they were *manitou* to him, potent with a power only to be awakened for sacred moments. I thought, then, of the killing of Hallam as a sacred moment, and I smiled. Balance enough. My stump felt like it was on fire.

Tawzin carefully lifted one flintlock out and handed it to me.

"You're right," he said. "I can't go with you. But this can."

He reached for the other, but I stayed his hand.

He stared at me for a long time, the silence building between us under the whine of mosquitoes, and then he wailed: the keening Piscataway grief song.

That wail sent me into my last journey.

It was not a long one. From the northern reach of the Zekiah, it is only a two day's walk east, swamp to swamp, to the Great Cypress Swamp—and then only because of the difficult country—though it seemed to me the distance should have been much greater. We had buried Jacob Lombroso there and even though that ending was not many days ago, it seemed rooted as far back in my memory as Africa, as Barbados, for to me, to the Wesorts, it was an ancestor song now, and men are reluctant to travel too far into the dreams of their own beginnings except in song. But

I knew Hallam was there. Even if Wesort hadn't been told. I only had to follow the death.

It was a short journey and it was my longest, and often I am still on its path, travelling endlessly through the thigh-deep brackish water amid the reeds and the tangled thorn bushes, and the brushing webs, a *Catawba* skeined and tangled through all the other paths that had brought me here now, to this place and to my life in it. The beginnings, and sometimes the ends as well, of that path were tagged to the yellow dust of a village of dried reeds, to the dark stinking womb of a wooden ship, to the foot of a gallows where I had betrayed my own name and sheared it from me and hung it, only to have it fly out and fasten to my heart. It was a path back to the beginnings of all my paths and a path through villages of ash where the dead watched me with live eyes under their dusting, and all along that path, they stared at me, even as the scaly, wise faces of turkey buzzards watched me, their forms silently hunched on dead branches. Even now, in my sleep, or if I shut my eyes in the middle of the day, or if I don't, I am back running in that dark tunnel that takes me to Hallam and to Silence, to take back my own at last, and the song I sang was Enough. He had torn enough from me, that man, and if my life after Barbados was a curse out of my betrayal of my namesake, I would no longer allow Hallam to be the instrument of it. He was too terrible an instrument. The curse he carved on my deserving flesh, he carved as well on the flesh of all around me, on land and on village, on creature and on people, on those I loved, as if wherever I moved I would bring death, bring Hallam: he followed the scent of my wound and rended all those around me. He could take me now, as he had taken my hand, but he could no longer have those others, and he could not have Isaac. I was the child to be given, and my son's hands had not been branched with fingers to be gripped by my curse. It was finished, there were no more children to be given, not in my son's generation, not in this land.

I followed the creek and the sun and the death until I

came again to the cypress swamp where we had lost Jacob. I moved into the shadowed darkness under the great trees. I had thought I would need to find a log I could straddle and take through the water. But unlike the Zekiah, most of the water here had drawn down into the earth, leaving the ground a stinking bog that sucked at my feet and bore clouds of whining, biting insects. I walked through it as a man walks through a dream, pursued by enemies, and the further he walks the heavier his limbs grow. In the Zekiah we covered ourselves day to day with bear grease for protection from the mosquitoes and horseflies, but I had not so protected myself now. I was afraid Hallam would smell it. Instead I covered myself from head to foot with the black swamp mud, as I had covered myself in ashes, so that I would only stink of this place. Perhaps my finger told him I was coming. But I would not come as myself.

I was close to him. I could follow signs as well as any Piscastaway now, the break of twigs, the displacement of a small stone from its socket of earth, the depth of faint tracks, the freshness of scat. But I needed none of those skills to follow Hallam. We called to each other. The veins that ran to my stumps, the stump of my wrist and the stump of my sixth finger, burned and I could feel them filament to him, the pulse of my heart moving closer to the beat of his until they would beat together, inseperable.

It was nearly sunset when I came to a low mound of red earth growing out of the mud, crested with a roach of high grass maples and edged with a border of lighter-colored mud, a boil growing from the skin of the swamp. The mud was rutted in places with moccasin tracks.

I waited until dark, and then crawled out of the swamp and onto the mound. I moved carefully through the grass, parting the stalks with my left hand, feeling in front of me for any dried twigs that might crack or break. Something suddenly grew out of the ground in front of me. Or seemed to. A low, branch-woven shelter. I nearly bumped into it. I lay still, listening. Silence. A faint sound of breathing, then the snort of a snore. But not Hallam. I didn't feel him here. I pushed my face against the weave of the wood. The inside was dark, but striped with moonlight. Several bundles of hides were stacked along the sides. A bundle of dried tobacco also. I watched until a face formed, level with my own, eyes closed, a mask of black around the eyes and mouth. Mouth open, snoring slightly. I recognized Dark Moon from the pattern of black crescents painted on his cheeks. From the songs—I had never seen him. Or didn't remember him. Tawzin had told me he had been there that day.

I crawled around to the entrance. The shelter was a little larger than the sweatlodge Tawzin and I had built in our Zekiah camp. Almost high enough to stand upright in. I touched the knife in my belt. Hallam was not here, but would not be far from his man. Too close to risk a pistol shot. And that was for him. I wondered if he had more men here. If he were starting his own tribe, his own Wesorts. The thought filled me with rage. I took a breath and slipped inside. I would crawl a little closer and then leap.

The ground where Dark Moon had lain was empty. I heard a breath drawn in, to my side, from the ground, and at almost the same instant saw the blur of the tomahawk. Pain shot from my knee to the top of my skull. I fell sideways, and scrambled back into the shelter. Dark Moon leapt after me, springing out of his crouch on the ground. The air was thick and dry with the smell of tobacco and the sour stink from the skins, from Dark Moon's sweat. He got a grip on the back of my neck with one hand, his fingers working around, pinching the cord, pushing me forward, into the nest of tobacco leaves, slamming the flat of the tomahawk into my face. He wanted to capture me alive. I pushed back, but he turned my force and shoved my face into the brittle leaves. They raked my skin, rammed up into my open mouth. It filled with their stinging bitterness, the raspy dry weight of them in my throat and nostrils. I was drowning in them. The grip on my neck

325

slipped for a second against my struggle and Dark Moon grabbed for my left wrist and the weight slacked off instantly on the back of my head. I let my hand go in the direction he was pulling it, then clutched, felt the little slipping sacks of his balls, twisted and yanked. He squealed and the weight lifted and I bulled up and out, like a man breaking out of water, hanging on, twisting more. Dark Moon grabbed for my other wrist. His hand slipped off the stump. He grunted and swung the flat of the tomahawk again at my face as he slid to the side. My head exploded in blossoms of red. I fell, hanging on, bringing him with me. He groaned, struck at me again with the tomahawk, his force weaker. But I was dimming to a small point of light. I felt the knife, the hard knob of the hilt, beneath me and pulled it out from under my own weight, pulling myself back out of my mind in the same way, forming pointed and sharp. Dark Moon's foot came towards my eyes and I thrust the knife upwards, hard. The point sliced through his sole and I arced it back and stabbed it into his ankle. He scuttled backwards, fell on his buttocks. I got to my knees and fell forward, stabbing into his legs, flailing him with my stump. He kicked. I hauled myself up his body as if I were pulling myself from the black hole I'd been pushed into, stabbing and pulling myself higher with the purchase of the knife, so when I reached the top, my face to his, there was silence.

I gasped in deep breaths, spitting out the wads of dried leaves still in my mouth. Dark Moon turned his head and moaned. I moaned with him. I should have known. He was Hallam's man. Hallam would not let me come to him until I cut my way to him through living flesh. The moonlight drew Dark Moon's face, striped with shadow and moons and paint and blood, and I saw it suddenly hanging in the trees as Hallam moved on Wesort. Forming to my memory. I saw Dark Moon's face and then the light drew Fleet's face from my dreams where it had nested, where I had not seen it in memory until now. I grabbed Dark Moon's roach and pulled his head back, then held it with the weight and push of my stump. I put the tip of the knife on his throat. Something ticked against it. I bore down, letting my weight drive the point, feeling it push through easily, until the point stopped. Then I drew it sideways and out. Then I left that place.

I went deeper into the swamp. My heart was swollen with blood now, and it beat heavily, pounding in my ears, in my veins, a drum calling to the drum of Hallam's heart. I felt the pulse of both converging. A hummock rose before me, its lower slope thick with ferns. A grove of red maple and polar on its crest. A song finishing and beginning again.

I went behind a little picket of cypress knees and lay in the mud until dark, letting the mosquitoes feed on me. Licking salt from my lips. I was dizzy from Dark Moon's blows and my leg and head hurt badly. The air was stale and stank of rotting leaves and blood. He was very close.

I covered my wounds with black mud and waited. The moon waited with me, its light broken by the tall cypress but still bright. I waited longer. I let the night gather to itself, and then I broke myself out of the mud, like something being born. I crawled in the path of shadow onto the hummock, through the ferns. The cry of a hawk. Fireflies in mad darts of light above me. I put my left hand in front of me, brought it slowly and noiselessly to the ground. Then my stump. Then crawled forward, as slow as time's passing. No different than time's passing. Moving as a shadow spates along the ground. The heavy ridges of the wrapped pistol and the knife at my waist pushing into the ground, pushing back into my stomach.

His camp was on top of the ridge, in the same place where Tawzin, Jacob and I had camped. I was not surprised. He had built a longhouse, and in front of it in a cleared area was a sapling frame, with a deerhide stretched on it, and a dark log already indented on its top surface where he and Silence must have been digging out the wood to make a canoe. A scraper made of an oyster shell lashed to a wooden handle lay next to it. I picked it up.

I went back a little ways. I would not try to crawl inside his den as I had with Dark Moon. The Susquehannock had sensed me as soon as I crossed inside. And this was Hallam. And I had Fleet's pistol.

I stayed still for a long time, listening. Hearing nothing but a rise of the wind. A snore from the longhouse. My finger, my Gift, pressed to his chest brought the beat of Hallam's heart slow and even to my ears, my chest, almost merging now with the beat of my own.

At the edge of the small clearing, I found an oak, its roots twisting high out of the ground, poison ivy vines twining it like dark furry snakes. There was a slight hollow between a forked V of roots, and I lay next to this and began scraping away the earth. The canoe had put this into my mind: I would dig the ground out deeper, enough to get below the surface of the ground, the way we would construct hunting blinds. I would place grass in front of the ridge of roots, just enough to conceal my face. I would rest the pistol barrel on the top of a root, aim at the center of his chest as he emerged from the longhouse. Or perhaps his head. I was close. The shot would not be difficult, even for a one-handed man.

I was hard around Dark Moon's death. The wind rose and I thanked Tawzin and his *manitou* for this noise moving in the trees and masking the sound of my digging. I could make my blind deeper now. I could bury myself and rise as Wesort had risen, new-born. Cleansed with Hallam's blood as White would have cleansed my soul with the water of baptism. But it was the blooding my namesake wished us in Barbados, that baptism I sought now. A light rain started to fall. I dug down. Scraping with the oyster shell. Opening the earth more than digging into it. The trees stirred around me. The rain stopped. But the wind continued to blow hard, whistling and moaning among the cypress and the red maple and the oak. I scraped deeper and then wider and then deeper. Kneeling at the edge. The resistance against the edge of the scrapper suddenly dropped away, as Dark Moon's flesh had

softened in a kind of surrender. There was a slight draw at
the center as if the ground was sucked to an abscess
underneath. The palm of my hand was bleeding against the
wood. I let the blood drip into the little hollow. Moonlight
flowed after it. I saw a jumble of dark shapes, and then the
grin of the skull, its eye sockets packed with dirt. At first I
thought: Jacob. But we had buried him on the other side of
the hummock, unless he had moved here under the earth to
greet me with his grin. No. There was a dark hole in the skull,
where it had been smashed. How many other songs did this
earth hold? How many old curses still held us in their teeth?
And we had come here to be free, I thought. I grinned the
skull's grin back at it. I saw my joining then to the song of
this skull, released into wind, as if its boney claw had gripped
my handless wrist. For an instant I wished this were Jacob.
What would the old Jew say to me? Once he had told me
God had hidden himself to allow space for the universe to
grow, as a parent gives its child freedom. But the reflected
Light of God had been too strong for the universe to hold
and it had shattered into shards and so had left cracks where
evil could enter. What we must do, carpenter, we humans,
We Sort, is to mend the universe again, to cleave it back
together, he said. But it had shattered me also, and I was
sharded and a part of its sunder now. I had cracked open and
evil had come into the place of my breaking.

I took my place in the song. Nested myself on top of the
old bones, the ancient murder.

Daylight came weak and gray, but still heavy with wet
heat. I waited, feeling my heart beating into the earth, into
the bones it held. Then feeling a slight throb to the side of it,
growing, shifting until it pounded in tandem with the rhythm
of my heart and Hallam came out of the door.

He was as I had seen him at the river, naked, his flesh
gray, slabbed with muscle and ridged with scars. My Gift
hung round his neck, clawed towards his heart. I aimed at
that point and tightened my finger on the trigger and he

turned towards me. Our hearts beating together. The pulse of it roaring in my ears. He didn't see me. A woman came out of the entrance, and she was holding Isaac at her breast. Silence. My heart caught. She laughed and placed him on the ground, and he crawled towards Hallam, his face raised and intent. He has not yet begun crawling, I thought stupidly. The sight opened a cold anger in me. The opening of murder. The skull on which I lay pressed into my chest, kissing my breastbone, whispering its song into my heart. I saw Hallam glance at Isaac then turn suddenly, as if to follow Isaac's gaze. The roar in my ears moved outside of me and I knew what presence I had felt I was drawing to in this place.

The lion was on top of the small ridge of rock, the same place from where it had taken Jacob. The muscles in its hindquarters were ridged with tension. Its coat looked sleek, smoothed taut with fat, but its eyes dull and rheumy. A low rumbling growl spilled from its mouth. A curse that would leap again and again on my life. Let it take him, I thought. But I saw where it had fastened its attention. Isaac stared back at the beast, drew his lips back, and a cricket like whir came out, as it he were trying to imitate the lion's roar. Hallam crossed in front of him and stood, staring at the lion, his mouth open in the same fashion as Isaac's and then the roar came from all three mouths, as if they were linked, as if they were instruments played by whatever Invisible had fashioned them. And now I saw Isaac crawl to him, and he sat in the dirt at Hallam's feet, staring up at the beast, the angle of his face, the set and downward hook of his mouth, the tiny chest with its suggestion already of breadth and power heaving, a mirror of the man. The three locked to each other, lion and Hallam and his son together owning a heart beat I had only imagined I shared with them. I blinked and in it the lion leapt away and was gone, leaving only an emptiness where it had been.

In that emptiness I left them, Hallam and his son.

Wesort's Song

I GAVE BIRTH in the flowering time. The child was a boy and we called him Jacob and we cut his foreskin as Jacob had instructed, eight days after his birth, and not in his twelfth year as my husband had been cut. And on his hands were the Gifts, and these too will not be cut from his life as they were from my husband's. Nor will they be useful for anything, I told my husband, if he did not stop pressing his lips to them whenever he was with the boy.

And as had happened with us before, my sister Nanjemoy gave birth at the same time, and their daughter is Hopeful Swan, as we have kept the Wesort custom of calling our spirits by the White tongue and the Red and the Black. For we must begin new songs, Tawzin said. And so my sister Nanjemoy was named also by the people, and her true name is Opequon, and its meaning in the white tongue is Cool White Pool in a Stream, and so she has been to us, both refuge and sustenance and path.

We must begin new songs. If I was a man and *werowance* I would sing first of death and wanderings. But if the Wesorts wish a woman for *werowance* they must accept also a woman's song, and I will tell you first of these births. There were four others as well, on our Trail north, but of these children only one, Wildcat, born of Falls-On-Bear and Blind Owl, has remained with us. And of the those others gone from us in these hard days of journey I will not sing here, for one so taken was Dream Singer's son, born of Jacob Lombroso, and there has been enough death in my song.

For this is Wesort, *werowance* of the Wesorts singing now. Though I wished this thing of being *werowance* to my husband, as is proper. It's true, I held a vision, but I wished to push and pull and carve my people to it through Ezekiel, to whisper (or scream if I had to) my vision into his ears so his eyes would open. But he said no. He told me how when he had left Hallam and he whose name I will not speak, when he turned to come back to me, he had found Tawzin, waiting behind him in the swamp, holding Flint's other pistol. He had told his brother not to follow him to Hallam, as he had told me not to follow him to Hallam. "You see," he said, "I can not be *werowance*. No one heeds me anyway."

We laughed, as we do, my husband and I, easily and often at sayings and sights no one finds laughter in but us. But I knew that what Ezekiel wished in his heart was to bring us the *mesingw* his hand found in wood and stone, and in this way, and not with words, would he lead the people by showing them the paths they did not know were drawn on their hearts, before his hand brought them into the world. In this and in the bringing of Jacob to his Gifts will my husband lead us. But in my song and vision I will lead. And perhaps in my true heart to be *werowance* is what I wish, for in the real world of my dreams I see the paths we must take now.

Both Jacob and Hopeful Swan were born in this place, and most of us are here now, though some remained in the Zekiah and some went to Conoy Island, north of the Great Falls, with the other Piscataway, and too many are names we can no longer speak. Even the name Piscataway, for Conoy is what the Iroquois have begun calling the Piscataway, a word none of us knew before. I heard it came from the sound of a white man's word, the word Gone. We are Gone now also, fled to this place made of our dream-vision, as we are a people that names and makes itself. Though I have not yet dreamed the name this place calls itself.

And we know the world we left is still roiled, and though Hallam no longer troubles us, except in the songs we sing to quiet children and to make ourselves afraid, that which his unbalanced spirit tilted is still loose.

For Hallam is there again, at the point where we drifted together and snagged to each other and began. We have heard of what has happened in Yaocomaco and the other Piscataway lands; we have heard what has happened to those who were part of our song, from the Anacostans who trade with us. This is what they tell. A war began in the country of the English against the Blackrobe Tayac who was Calvert's father, and the *werowance* Calvert returned to England to see and give his allegience to his Tayac. While he was there, Giles Brent captured a man called Ing-les, who sung indecent songs against the Blackrobe English Tayac in front of all at St. Marie's. The Anacostans tell that this came to happen because Calvert's woman, Margaret Brent was left as *werowance*, in his place, by Calvert. She had told her warriors not to capture Ing-les, and to let him sing what he wished, for she knew she had not the power to hold him. But her brother Giles was jealous that a woman was *werowance* instead of him and so he captured Ing-les to defy his sister. And Ing-les could not be kept for the *ga-ol* (we have no word for this place), where Tawzin had been held, had been burnt, so he was set free, and now Ing-les vowed a great revenge. And in this time also, Claiborne, Calvert's great enemy, who had been forced to flee from the Chesapeake country, returned and stirred the Susquehannocks' fury against our people and against Calvert's whites even further, and they slaughtered those Piscataway who were left, village and town, even into the Zekiah, until they were Conoy, and it was then that we fled north, to this place. Though I fear in my secret spirit that perhaps no place in this World is safe for Wesort.

And Opechanough of the Powhatans rose again, against all the whites. And Claiborne was made war chief of the whites and destroyed him. And so Claiborne's strength increased, fed on the flesh of his enemies.

And Ing-les returned, and he was a *werowance* then of the Blackrobe Tayac's enemies, and his anger had made him a tilted man. And Hallam was with him, whispering in his ear, blowing on the fire of his anger against Calvert and the Blackrobes. They came together, Hallam and Ing-les and their warriors, and they captured Yaocomaco that the whites call St. Marie's and slaughtered many and burnt the dwellings, so that Calvert fled as we fled. And Hallam burnt the spirit house he and my husband had built, with their hands and with his hate. And the Blackrobe White, who had become brother to us, was weighed with the metal ropes the whites use to keep a man from running, and was sent back so, as once my husband was brought from *Af-ri-ca*, to the country of the English, where the *ga-ols* had not been burnt.

In this way, his breath blowing on the fire of hatred in Ing-les, Hallam was able to return to the ground he left and make it his again, and now his son hunts with him and so where he goes, I go also, and so I am stained always by him and so I soften him as well, as I know Silence softens him, for she sees the man in the demon. For Silence has lost a child and found one, as I have.

So I sing softly to myself. It is what I desire, though I fear that wish is so strong it may shape my vision falsely. And it is true he is at peace, Hallam, as my dreams told me he would be. It is true he no longer leads warriors, and we were told he kept Claiborne and the Susquehannocks from our paths when we traveled north. But my dreams did not tell me how many other lives would be devoured to bring him to his place and his peace, and so perhaps my vision was wrong also when I told my husband to let him live in balance so we might all live in balance. Perhaps he is too tilted, so that he will forever twist one way and then another, and his *ondinnonk*, his secret vision is too powerful; it is a vision that names and so awakens the secret and terrible hungers of too many other spirits.

As for us, we fled all such visions. When the Susque-hannock where almost upon us, we fashioned canoes from the bark of elm and cypress, and in these and at night we went north, and then we went onto the Trails, until we came to this place where my vision led us. For the forests are skin and the mountains bone, our songs say, and under skin are veins and these are the Rivers and the Trails. As the rivers flow to all places, so do the Trails, to the North and to the South, to the East and to the West, and to the real world of dreams. One must only know they are there. One must only shut her eyes and see them.

And when we came to this place, we built our firepit and on our first night and our sweatlodge, and we cleansed ourselves of blood and terrible visions by singing them. And that first night we sat at our fire and sang the song of our coming here, the song of Tawzin and Opequon who was Nanjemoy, the song of my husband Ezekiel and his Gifts and Jacob Lombroso and his dream, the songs of all the fragments drawn by different currents and from different fires, down the River to a dream, to one song, the song of the Wesorts. And we sang the song of Hallam, and of my son whose name I can no longer say, torn from heart and breast, and we sang how a child was given to save the people. And we sang how we would give no more children to Death.

This is our song. Wesort song. There are the bones of many songs buried and nested under the Trails, and they mark the true paths under the skin of the world, and the paths on it we see are but the traces of deeper, older paths, and the songs we sing are but echoes of the true Song.

But the old songs are lost, you say, as our Wesort song will be lost; the songs are lost and wandering the skein of Trails under the earth. They are lost, you say, for you no longer can see their trace on the earth, nor hear our words whispering in your ears, those songs. Yet listen. They are here. We are here. Buried under the mounds of dirt our enemy placed us into to kill our sprits. Waiting to be released by the curse and blessing and need of love. Our song is still here. Wesort song. Listen. It is here like the Light sleeping in the river, coming to glow and life when called by your movement through the black water and you lay floating in stars and of stars and the holding clench and weight of your flesh on your spirit disappears and you are *manitou* pouring out of yourself into the song of river and sky and land. They are still here, all the songs are still here, singing us the paths where we have been and the paths we must take to live in this new world we have all crossed into, born out of murder and ashes and hope, this place of binding and dissolution, this small clearing we hold onto tight as love in the true world of our dreams.

ACKNOWLEDGEMENTS AND AUTHOR'S NOTE

Although there is a general agreement on the meaning of the name Wesort as coming from "we sort of people," as applied to the racially mixed descendents of Native Americans, blacks and whites who form a distinct group in Southern Maryland, the origin of the term is still obscure. There are several stories that have circulated, and the one in this novel is of course one that unthreads only from my imagination, and only in service of the story I wished to tell. I made it up. But the Wesorts are still here, my neighbors, as are the Piscataway Conoy, and I hope they will forgive my presump-tiveness. Their story is, of course, our story.

The history we hear and have taught to us is also a story, as has been said before, made up by the winners, and thus it is usually about those people who were the public figures of their day. Yet the world we live in, and the world our ancestors lived in, is and was made up of the weave of all our songs, and it is the stories untold in the histories that I wished to imagine in this book, for indeed we are in the midst, at the beginning of this century, of a great movement to finally hear and listen to the voices that for so long have been left out of the American narrative, and a great debate about how to do so. In this book, I have taken the novelist's liberty of stretching or compressing or creating time and events in order to serve my story, and while the general structure of colonial Maryland history has been adhered to and told in this novel, it also has not bound me. I used real people and events. I made other people and events up. Among the real events are the voyage of the Ark and Dove, including Father White's account of seeing an "African servant" hung in Barbados, the Claiborne-Calvert rivalry, the murder of Uwanna by his brother, the settlement of St. Mary's, and the alliances between the Virginia and Maryland British settlers and the Powhatans, Susquehannocks, and Piscataway—and the costs of those alliances. Among the actual historical figures are the Calverts, Fathers Andrew White and John Altham, the Tayac Kittamaquund and his family, the shaman Maquacomen, Cornwaylis, Henry Fleet, William Claiborne, and Jacob Lombroso. Their personalities and interactions, in this novel, are of course only as I have imagined them for the needs of my narrative, though I have also tried to depict them as real human beings, with all the frailties and strengths real human beings have. The descendents of the settlers—gentlemen adventurers and indentured servants both—are as well my neighbors in St. Mary's County, and I hope they and their ancestors and their ancestor's ghosts, will also forgive my presumption.

Those narrative sections in italics in the novel are transcribed verbatim from a number of works: Clayton Colman Hall's *Narratives of Early Maryland, 1633-1684*, published in 1925; Sebastion F. Streeter's *Papers Relating to the Early History of Maryland,* published in 1876, and Father Andrew White's *Narrative of a Voyage to Maryland,* published in 1874. I am grateful for those works, and for the information and advice I received from my neighbor Tim Riordan, the archaeologist at Historic St. Mary's City who discovered the lead coffins containing remains of the Calvert family in a field about a mile from my house—an event which inspired this novel. I gratefully thank the Maryland State Arts Council for its work and contuned support. I'm also very grateful to Sandy Taylor and Judy Doyle for their very existence, to Gloria Emerson, to my brothers- and sisters-in-letters Michael Glaser, George Evans and Diasy Zamora, to Ho Anh Thai and Le Minh Khue for their love and encouragement, to Edgar Silex, who reinforced the importance both of transcending one's own voice and of doing so with respect, and finally, to Lucille Clifton, who lent me some of the story of her Dahomey ancestors, and their gifted fingers, and the gifts they have given her of seeing the true patterns under the illusions and mists of this world, and for bringing that vision to words.

Several other books and articles were particularly helpful and should be mentioned. These include *The Indian Peoples of Eastern America,* edited by James Axtell; "Present at the 'Creation': The Chesapeake World that Greeted the Maryland Colonists" by J.

Frederick Fausz, and Russell R. Menard's "Population, Economy and Society in Seventeenth Century Maryland, both in *Maryland Historical Magazine's* special 350th anniversary issue; "The Wesorts of southern Maryland: An outcasted group" by William Harlen Gilbert, Jr., from the Library of Congress; *History of St. Mary's County, Maryland, 1634-1990* by Regina Combs Hammett; "The Hidden History of Mestizo America," by Gary B. Nash, in *The Journal of American History; Powhatan Foreign Relations, 1500-1722,* edited by Helen C. Roundtree; *Native North American Spirituality of the Eastern Woodlands*, edited by Elisabeth Tooker; "The Turn of the Tide: A Study of the Piscataway and the Seventeenth Century Chesapeake" an honors thesis for St. Mary's College by Danielle Eva Troyan; and *American Indian Medicine*, by Virgil J. Vogel.

Illustrations:

pg. ii, title page: "Nova Terrae-Mariae Tabula, 1635." *Courtesy, Maryland Historical Society.*

pg. 1. "The Voyage to Maryland. Nov. 1633 - Mar. 1634." *Courtesy, Historic St. Mary's City.*

pg. 27. "How They Catch Fish". Frankfurt, 1590. From Part I of Theodore de Bry's "Grand Voyages", from sketches by John White. *Courtesy, Southern Maryland Studies Center, College of Southern Maryland. Hansen-Holdmann Collection.*

pg. 71. "Captain Samuel Argall Concludes A Treaty with the Chickahominies Who Accept James I as Their King". Frankfurt, 1618. From Part X of "America". *Courtesy, Southern Maryland Studies Center, College of Southern Maryland. Hansen-Holdmann Collection.*

pg. 141. "Their danses vvich they vse att their hyghe feastes", an untitled engraving by Theodore de Bry based on a painting by on a watercolor by John White. *Courtesy, John Carter Brown Library at Brown University.*

pg. 211. "A Fortified Indian Village". Frankfurt, 1591. From Part II of "America", Le Moune's Florida. *Courtesy, Southern Maryland Studies Center, College of Southern Maryland. Hansen-Holdmann Collection.*

pg. 293. "How They Build Boats". Frankfurt, 1590. From Part I of Theodore de Bry's "Voyages to America", Virginia, from sketches by John White. *Courtesy, Southern Maryland Studies Center, College of Southern Maryland. Hansen-Holdmann Collection.*

pg. 331. "Their manner of prainge vvith Ratels abowt te fyer," 1590. Engraving by Theodore de Bry, based on a watercolor by John White. *Courtesy, John Carter Brown Library at Brown University.*

Photo © by Roger Horn

Wayne Karlin is the author of six novels and a memoir, a co-editor (with the Vietnamese writers Le Minh Khue and Truong Vu) and contributor to the anthology *The Other Side of Heaven: Postwar Fiction by Vietnamese and American Writers,* and the editor of the Curbstone Press *Voices from Vietnam* series, which publishes translations of novels and short story collections by contemporary Vietnamese authors. He has received a fellowship from the National Endowment for the Arts, five Individual Artist Awards in fiction from the State of Maryland, a Critics' Choice Award, and the 1999 Paterson Prize in fiction for his novel *Prisoners*. He is a professor of languages and literature at the College of Southern Maryland, and directs a fiction program at St. Mary's College of Maryland. He lives in Southern Maryland with his wife, Ohnmar, and has one son, Adam.

CURBSTONE PRESS, INC.

is a non-profit publishing house dedicated to literature that reflects a commitment to social change, with an emphasis on contemporary writing from Latino, Latin American and Vietnamese cultures. Curbstone presents writers who give voice to the unheard in a language that goes beyond denunciation to celebrate, honor and teach. Curbstone builds bridges between its writers and the public – from inner-city to rural areas, colleges to community centers, children to adults. Curbstone seeks out the highest aesthetic expression of the dedication to human rights and intercultural understanding: poetry, testimonies, novels, stories, and children's books.

This mission requires more than just producing books. It requires ensuring that as many people as possible learn about these books and read them. To achieve this, a large portion of Curbstone's schedule is dedicated to arranging tours and programs for its authors, working with public school and university teachers to enrich curricula, reaching out to underserved audiences by donating books and conducting readings and community programs, and promoting discussion in the media. It is only through these combined efforts that literature can truly make a difference.

Curbstone Press, like all non-profit presses, depends on the support of individuals, foundations, and government agencies to bring you, the reader, works of literary merit and social significance which might not find a place in profit-driven publishing channels, and to bring the authors and their books into communities across the country. Our sincere thanks to the many individuals, foundations, and government agencies who support this endeavor: J. Walton Bissell Foundation, Connecticut Commission on the Arts, Connecticut Humanities Council, Daphne Seybolt Culpeper Foundation, Fisher Foundation, Greater Hartford Arts Council, Hartford Courant Foundation, J. M. Kaplan Fund, Eric Mathieu King Fund, John D. and Catherine T. MacArthur Foundation, National Endowment for the Arts, Open Society Institute, Puffin Foundation, and the Woodrow Wilson National Fellowship Foundation.

Please help to support Curbstone's efforts to present the diverse voices and views that make our culture richer. Tax-deductible donations can be made by check or credit card to:
Curbstone Press, 321 Jackson Street, Willimantic, CT 06226
phone: (860) 423-5110   fax: (860) 423-9242
www.curbstone.org

IF YOU WOULD LIKE TO BE A MAJOR SPONSOR OF A
CURBSTONE BOOK, PLEASE CONTACT US.